FULL CYCLE

A Novel

Christopher Blunt

FULL CYCLE is a work of fiction. All of the names, characters, organizations, places, and incidents portrayed in this novel are either products of the author's imagination or are used fictitiously.

PELICAN CROSSING PRESS
1574 West Fitchburg Road
Leslie, MI 49251

ISBN-10: 0-9766596-4-6
ISBN-13: 978-0-9766596-4-8
LCCN: 2016935272

Cover design by James Hrkach.
Original front cover photo © 2014 by Alan Stover, remixed by James Hrkach.
http://alstoverphotography.zenfolio.com/
Back cover photo of Jubilee Pass Road, Death Valley National Park, © 2009 by Ken Lund. Licensed under Creative Commons Attribution-Share Alike 2.0 Generic license.

Author website: ChristopherCBlunt.WordPress.com
Author email: CCBlunt@aol.com

Printed in the United States of America

Rob. In an age when there has been such a disconnect between Dads and their families, the book is inspiring, in a simple, natural way. It's a story with many little points of human insight and love that deserve to be savored."

— Michael Giesler, author of *Junia, Marcus,* and
Grain of Wheat (Scepter Publishers, New York)

"Full Cycle is a story of a father-son relationship, of the importance of working together as a team, and about encouraging our children to reach beyond their limits. It's a wonderful story about focusing on abilities, not disabilities. This would be an ideal novel for a parent and child to read together. Highly recommend."

—Ellen Gable, author of *In Name Only, A Subtle Grace,*
Stealing Jenny, and *Emily's Hope*

"I really enjoyed *Full Cycle.* As an educator, father, and fiction author, I think both young adults and their parents will get a lot out of reading it. A gifted athlete, Alex Peterson is seriously disabled during a foolish dare (and seems to have ruined his life) until he discovers his father's former athletic passion, cycling. I like the way Blunt gets into the interior lives of Alex and Rob, his father, as both struggle against their own pride and laziness to forget about themselves in order to give themselves generously to others. Blunt shows how the ordinary things in life can be made to be quite extraordinary, as Alex sets out to accomplish something 'not a lot of other people in the world have ever done'."

—Kevin Aldrich, author of *Benjamin and the Paradise Project*

To my StoKids, and to all seeking to do something "not a whole lot of other people in the world have ever done."

PROLOGUE

May 29, 2007

I T WAS EVERY NINE-YEAR-OLD BOY'S DREAM. THE LAST GAME OF the year. Bottom of the final inning. Runners at second and third. His team trailing by just one run. Alex Peterson watched from the dugout opening, leaning on his bat. He'd already pulled a helmet over his short blond hair.

Alex's best friend lined straight back to the pitcher for the second out. The other team's fans erupted in cheers.

It's all coming down to me, Alex thought, his heart already racing. He wiped his hands on his perfectly-clean jersey, picked up his bat, and stepped onto the field.

"Oh, gawd," one of Alex's teammates groaned.

"Please, please, please. Anybody but Peterson," another begged.

Alex took a quick practice swing, and pretended he hadn't heard. *I'll show them,* he thought. He began hobbling toward the dusty batter's box, the way any other kid would walk with a hunk of two-by-four strapped to his right foot.

The other team's coach stepped from the dugout, and waved toward the outfielders. "Wayne! Ike! Brent!" he called. "Farther in!" All three boys grinned and took exaggerated steps toward the infield.

The coach kept waving. "Couple more!" he hollered. The outfielders drew closer.

"We've got this one, no problem," the first baseman said, pounding his glove.

Alex waved the bat over his shoulder, dug his worn-out cleats into the dirt, and tried to ignore everything else. Still, he couldn't help noticing the way the shortstop and second baseman smiled at each other — and then made exaggerated steps of their own toward the plate.

Alex took two angry practice swings, and spotted his coach jogging toward him from the dugout. "Yeah?" he asked, turning and stepping from the batter's box.

"I just wanted to tell you that I know you can do this," Coach replied. "Pop it over their heads. Any little base hit at all. Gilson and Quinn will be running on contact."

Alex smiled at his coach's encouragement. *I'm going to do this*, he told himself, taking another practice swing. *Doesn't matter that I've only gotten six hits all year. I'm finally going to be a hero.*

The first pitch came in like a rocket. Alex swung, and whiffed so hard he almost toppled over. The catcher laughed as he tossed the ball back.

The next pitch streaked toward him just as fast. Alex froze in panic as it crossed the plate. His teammates, and many of their parents, groaned as the umpire called Strike Two.

Flushed with rage and fighting back tears, Alex swung with everything he had at the third pitch. The bat connected with the most satisfying "Ping!" he'd ever heard. Alex whooped as the ball cleared the leaping second baseman's glove. *A base hit for sure! That's what they get for playing in on me! We're going to win!* Alex began hobble-trotting down the line, and the roaring crowd came to its feet.

"Faster! Faster!" the first base coach screamed.

As swiftly as Alex tried to run, the right fielder was already closing in on the ball. He snagged it, made a perfect throw, and gunned Alex down by half a clumsy stride.

Too ashamed to face his teammates, or even his own family, Alex hobbled straight from first base to his mother's station wagon. He locked himself in, and buried his face in his hands.

ONE

May 15, 2008

FROM THE MOMENT THE OPENING TITLE FADED OUT, AND A seemingly-endless sea of bicyclists at the start line faded in, Alex couldn't tear himself away from the monitor. He'd never seen so many bikes in one place, and they were all illuminated in the soft tones of a summer sunrise. The shot zoomed closer, focusing on small groups of riders dressed in colorful jerseys. He saw every kind of bicycle imaginable: sleek racing bikes, rugged mountain bikes, tandem bikes with two riders, and even recumbent bikes pedaled by people laying on their backs. All of them were smiling and looking like they were already having the time of their lives.

As the camera continued panning, Alex noticed children among the crowd. Some were dressed in street clothes and waving good-bye to an adult who was riding. Others were dressed in their own cycling outfits and riding with their mom or dad or both. Most looked a few years older than his own almost-eleven, but Alex saw a few who were clearly younger than even his nine-year-old brother. Some had their own bikes, and others were perched on the back of tandems. Alex wanted to climb into the computer monitor and immerse himself in this pure joy and excitement.

Mr. Larry Jansson, an upper-grade math teacher he'd never met before, had given Alex the DVD after school that day. On the recommendation of Alex's organ teacher, Mrs. Janet Rossi, he'd asked if Alex would like to try improvising some music for the similar promotional video his bike club would be producing this coming August. "We'd really like to add something original this year," he'd said. "We're hoping last year's video will give you some ideas you can get started with."

Mr. Jansson had gone on to explain that the video showcased the club's biggest event, the Seattle to Portland Bicycle Classic, or STP. It drew nearly ten thousand riders each July. Most took two days to finish. Some went the whole 202 miles in a single day.

Alex had been intrigued. Two hundred miles seemed an impossibly long way to ride a bike. He'd almost even wondered aloud to Mr. Jansson why anyone would attempt it.

Now, alone in the privacy of his bedroom, watching these thousands of wheels thundering along the scenic rural roads of Western Washington, he understood. Yes, the distance was vast. Yes, it was exhausting. But that was all part of the excitement and the challenge. And there were so many other people along for the adventure!

Alex was no longer just intrigued. He was hooked.

Alex had intended to watch the entire twenty-minute video one time before improvising any music. He made it just seven minutes before he simply had to flip on his electronic keyboard and let his fingers wander. Alex yearned to be able to ride free and fast, like the cyclists he was watching. His fingers flew across the keyboard, continually finding new melodies to harmonize with the participants.

More than anything, he longed to be welcomed into this special fraternity. His heart ached to be one of them, as together they accomplished "something not a whole lot of other people in the world have ever done," as one of the one-day riders put it. STP was something not even the best athletes in his school would imagine doing. Alex pictured their astonishment as he cruised triumphantly into Portland.

Alex continued daydreaming long after the video ended. Finally, coming back to reality, he realized he was still wearing his school uniform. He'd been in such a hurry to watch the video, he'd completely forgotten to change. He hastily traded his polo shirt for a favorite Mariners t-shirt, and then pulled off his navy slacks and socks.

Alex limped to the closet, his left foot landing about two inches lower than his right with each step. He stopped at the mirror and took a long look at his pale legs. *There were lots of different bikes on STP, he thought, but no riders with misaligned kneecaps and scrawny, scarred thighs.*

Alex pulled on some comfortable jeans, sat on the bed, and rested his chin on his pulled-up knees. All he could remember now was the rest of his conversation with Mr. Jansson.

"Are you looking forward to the Fun Run next month?" the teacher had asked. The four-mile event was a prime fundraiser for St. Clement school, and Mr. Jansson was the organizer.

"I don't think I can do it," Alex had admitted, gesturing to his left foot.

Mr. Jansson had studied Alex's special elevator shoe. He'd then explained that "students with disabilities can still help, especially at the finish line. Come see me next week."

Alex's ears flushed anew as he recalled the teacher's piteous look, and the way he'd emphasized the word "disabilities." *Like I'm a broken car or something,* Alex had thought.

Still, bitter as the reminder made him, Alex had to admit it was true. *I can't even run four miles. How could I ride to Portland?*

A knock on the door interrupted Alex's mope. His mother leaned into the room. "Dinner's in five minutes," she said. "How's the video?"

"Really cool. Getting lots of ideas for music," he replied. "Be there in a minute."

He'd told his mom about Mr. Jansson's project that afternoon, as she'd driven him home from school. At the words "Seattle to Portland," her eyes had flashed. Then, before she'd been able to say anything, Alex had changed the subject to the Fun Run. "By volunteering at the finish," he'd concluded, "I'll get out of having to run."

"I know you don't like running," his mother had said, "but your father and I do think you should get more active this summer."

"It's not that I don't *like* running," Alex had replied. "Running too much makes my knees and ankles hurt."

"Maybe you could try swimming?" she'd suggested. "Swimming is easy on your joints."

"Maybe," Alex had muttered.

"I could sign you up for something at the Northshore Pool for the summer," she'd offered.

Alex had simply turned and gazed out the car window, watching as the gray suburban Seattle drizzle had grown more miserable.

At the time, Alex hadn't known what to say. Now he did. *I want to be a cyclist. Bicycling is almost as easy on my joints as swimming. Is there any possible way that cycling could be my sport?*

He knew it was too laughable even to mention. He figured a good bike cost a hundred times more than a whole summer of swim sessions. Or as much as a decade's worth of custom elevator shoes. *I hope Mom and Dad haven't figured out I need a new pair already. I've got to make these last longer.*

Alex rose and hobbled to the dining room, where his mother and Ben were already seated.

"I thought Dad was getting home tonight," he said.

"Late," his mother replied, dishing him a plate of meat loaf and mashed potatoes. "The trip's just about done. Tonight's groups are in Kirkland, but he won't get in till we've gone to bed."

Alex frowned, but was glad his father was finally almost home. The dinner table seemed empty without him.

After they'd said grace, his mother added, "And that reminds me. Make sure you tell your father about the STP video. I know he'll be interested."

Alex was puzzled. Music had never interested Dad before, and — as far as he knew — his father had never even owned a bicycle. "Why's that?" he asked.

"I'll let him explain it," she replied.

Alex wondered how his mother even knew the event was typically called "STP." He hadn't mentioned that acronym.

Just then, Ben launched into a monologue about little league practice. "Coach says we're looking good for Saturday's game," he said. "I get to start at shortstop. I'm batting third. Hopefully I'll get to stay in for all six innings."

Alex took a long look at his brother, and tried not to be jealous of his natural athletic ability. *After all,* Alex reminded himself, *Ben's not the one who did something stupid.*

Everyone said he and Ben looked like identical twins who'd been born 22 months apart. They had the same sandy-blond hair, buzz-cut by their mom in the same short style. Both had their mother's green eyes. Both had their father's short nose and elongated mouth. At the start of each school year, Ben's new teacher always said — even before learning his last name — that "You must be Alex's little brother."

"How many more games are left?" Alex asked, taking his first bite of meat loaf. He mostly wanted to know how many more weeks he'd have to listen to Ben's heroics.

"Four," Ben replied, chewing a forkful of potatoes. "And the last three are easy. If we can beat the Red Sox this Saturday, we'll be Triple-A champs for sure."

Great, Alex thought. *You can put another trophy on your shelf. Assuming there's any room left.*

Alex tried to ask if he could skip the game, so he could stay home and work on his music. Before he could say the first word, though, Ben was talking again. "I hit up Jimmy and Jacob Flynn's mom, and Coach, for pledges in the Fun Run," he announced. "That takes me to $587. Mrs. Tompkins says she's never had a third grader raise more than $500. Hopefully I'll win for my class."

"Good for you!" their mother told him.

Yeah, good for you, Alex thought, as Ben continued detailing the people he'd gotten pledges from. Collecting pledges was the biggest reason Alex hated the Fun Run. He was almost happy his leg gave him an excuse to get out of it. He'd never understood why Ben was so much of a natural extrovert, and able to start conversations or ask for pledges so easily. Alex was sure that if Ben didn't become a professional athlete, he'd end up as a salesman. Or maybe a sports agent.

"Oh! Alex, guess what?" he said. "I almost forgot. Tommy Gilson got an Easton Stealth composite bat for his birthday!"

Alex looked up in surprise. He'd heard about fancy composite bats, and seen high school kids playing with them, but he'd never actually held one. "Tim Gilson's little brother? Don't those cost, like, over $250?"

"Yeah, but the bat is totally amazing. You should've seen the way Tommy was hitting today."

"Did he let you try it out?"

"He let us hold it and swing it. But he said it had to be broken in a certain way, and used a certain way, so he didn't want anybody messing it up. And he wants to totally master it before going to baseball camp."

Ben paused and got a wistful look. He then returned to describing his team's preparations for the upcoming game, and the marvels of Tommy Gilson's bat.

The longer Ben talked, the more Alex decided he wasn't really hungry. He pushed his plate back and asked to be excused.

"Aren't you going to finish?" his mother asked, brushing an errant strand of brown hair from her eyes.

"It was delicious. Just too much for now," he said, not wanting to hurt his mother's feelings. From how tired she looked, Alex could tell she'd had a long day at work. She'd even been a little late picking him up from school. "I'll finish it tomorrow."

Alex hobbled to his room, and once more got comfortable in front of the old computer his father had handed down to him. Soon he was again watching the video and playing his keyboard, mesmerized by the bicycles and their riders. Minutes melted into hours, and the evening melted away.

Finally, at 9:30, his mother insisted he get ready for bed. Alex reluctantly shut down the computer, put everything in its place, and carefully laid out his school uniform for the next day.

As he climbed into bed, he wondered if his father would make it home before he fell asleep. And why on earth his dad might be interested in a video about STP.

In the meantime, his only wish was to stay up all night making music. Or to ride like those cyclists he kept seeing on the screen. Or both.

TWO

ROB PETERSON WISHED HIS CLIENTS A GOOD EVENING, AND tried to clear his head for the twenty-minute drive home. The week had been a grueling marathon of six focus groups, all of which were now a blur. Spokane. The Tri-Cities. Suburban Seattle. Four sessions with unmarried mothers. One with family law attorneys. One with unmarried fathers. He felt genuine sympathy for the parents he'd interviewed, and hoped his research would help improve the state's child support system for all of them.

I don't have to write this report right now, Rob told himself, and let his mind drift up the nearly-empty freeway to home. He imagined Alex and Ben, sleeping peacefully. *I'm so glad I was the moderator, and not a participant, in that group tonight*, he thought. He resolved to finish tomorrow's work by the time they got home from school. He would do nothing but hang out with them and Meg after that.

Which is what I love most about being self-employed, he thought. *As long as I get my clients what they need when they need it, no one cares what I do with the rest of my day.* For the next week, all he had to do was write the report. Then a couple of local focus groups the week after that. No real traveling for at least several weeks, when tonight's client — Frank Hurwitz — needed him in Boise and Helena.

The extra free time is nice, but this is way slower than last year. Too slow. He was glad Frank mentioned some other upcoming projects Rob might be needed for. He couldn't imagine where he'd be without such a solid "anchor client" directing overflow work his direction.

Rob exited the freeway, and wound his way through the deserted blocks of downtown Bothell. He loved driving home late at night, and being one of the only people still moving. It took just a few minutes before he reached their modest Craftsman-style rambler, in one of the town's oldest neighborhoods.

Rob pulled around to the large detached building that served as both garage and office. He parked next to Meg's Taurus wagon in the garage portion of the building, then slipped through a door into the office.

The long, narrow space occupied all of the building's back wall. His brother-in-law had helped him finish and insulate it as nicely as any house. They'd even built a lengthy set of shelves into the lower portion of the entire far wall, which Rob had jammed with books. He paused for a moment, savoring the dozens of crayon drawings Alex and Ben had pinned to the upper portion of that wall.

He set his laptop on the large, cluttered oak desk, and rifled through the mail. One check from Frank's firm, Decision Strategies. Otherwise, just bills. *When will everyone else get around to paying me?*

Rob kicked off his dress shoes, and tossed his blazer over a wooden chair. He traded his slacks and polo shirt for an old University of Washington sweat suit. Pulling on some comfortable sneakers, he made his way across the inky black driveway to the house.

He knew in theory that he should go to bed, but he was much too wound up from the focus groups — and too hungry — to sleep. This happened so often, he and Meg had worked out an arrangement: Rob could eat and stay up as late as he wanted after moderating groups, so long as he did it in his office.

Rob quietly opened a few cartons of Chinese food his clients had left untouched at the focus facility. Cold already. The microwave was broken again, so he searched the battered kitchen cabinets for a large enough saucepan. Finally, he had the leftovers warming on one of the stove's two functioning burners.

Rob wandered from the kitchen to the living room. He paused at the ancient spinet piano, and gazed at the wall of photographs Meg had assembled behind it. The images spanned generations of her family, and all the years the two of them had been together. Rob marveled at how much bigger Meg's smiles seemed when she was holding one or both of the boys, or when she was posing with her extended family, than when she was alone. Especially after they'd left California. Her complete immersion in family, and her readiness to shelve everything else for the family's sake, was still what Rob found most attractive about her.

He only wished he'd been able to get them all back to Seattle sooner. And that his income could finally let her quit her part-time paralegal job. *Without her paychecks, I don't know what we'd do.*

Back in the kitchen, Rob stirred the beef, broccoli, and rice jumble with a fork. *Definitely warm enough.* He then secured the house and slipped across the driveway to his office.

Rob fired off a quick email to his freelance transcriptionist, Emily Greer, letting her know the audio was available for download from the focus facility's website. Then, the night's work complete, Rob raided his office fridge for the first of several beers. Chinese leftovers in hand, he eased his lean, six-foot frame comfortably onto the couch, opposite the wall with the book shelves. Switching on the television, Rob reveled in having a space that was completely his own. He couldn't imagine any place he'd rather be.

THREE

May 17, 2008

A LEX WAS SO EAGER TO RETURN TO THE MUSIC PROJECT, HE set an alarm for early Saturday morning. He'd enjoyed watching baseball with his dad and brother last night, which had kept him from away from the STP music. He hoped to make a lot of progress now, before Ben's game.

Alex watched the video so many times, it continued playing whenever he closed his eyes. Over and over he saw the riders pedal. Sometimes in large groups. Sometimes struggling alone. Sometimes laughing and acting silly. Sometimes looking like they'd rather die than go on. But everywhere they went, and everything they did, Alex sensed they were *free*. Especially when they were racing at top speed, but even when the riding was difficult. They kept pressing ahead. They kept smiling. They kept encouraging each other.

Alex realized the scenes could be divided into groups: expectant or hopeful, racing free and excitedly, struggling hard in a difficult situation, emotional or 'tugging at heartstrings,' and triumphant. He figured he could come up with a basic score for each type of scene. Then he could develop variations on those.

Just as Alex was deciding on a scene type to start with, he heard something behind him. Startled, he turned to see his father standing in the doorway.

"Didn't mean to disturb you," he said, "but we've got to get going to your brother's game in a few minutes."

"Already? Can't I stay and keep working?" Alex asked.

"Mom told me you had a special music project, but she wouldn't say what it was. Is that what you're doing?"

Alex had meant to tell his dad about it the day before, but the timing had never been quite right. "Yeah. In the middle of it," he replied.

"There are things I'd rather be doing today, too. But we need to be there as a family, for your brother. This is a very big game. Mom even took Ben early, for some extra practice the team was having."

"All right," Alex sighed. "Be there in a minute."

Once they were cruising toward the elementary school where Ben's game would be played, Alex's father asked him what the music project was about.

"Mr. Jansson, one of the teachers at school, is with a big bike club," Alex explained. "They're making a video, and he wants me to try improvising some music for it."

"Which bike club?" his father asked.

"Cascade," Alex replied. "The video's about a ride called Seattle to Portland."

"STP?" his father said, as they pulled into the parking lot.

"Yeah," he replied, surprised that Dad knew the acronym. "Mom said you'd be interested in it. How come?"

"I've ridden STP," his dad said.

Dad? A cyclist? Alex thought. He knew there was a dusty Italian racing bike hanging on hooks in the basement. He'd never seen anyone actually ride it. *Was that Dad's bike? Why's he never said anything about having done something as big as riding to Portland?*

As they walked toward the baseball diamond, Alex peppered his father with questions: "Did you ride in one day or two?" "How long ago?" "How much did you have to train?"

All his dad's answers were vague: "Both, in different years;" "Before you were born;" and, "Way too much."

Alex wanted to ask more questions, but the game was starting. They found Mom, who had saved them good seats near first base. It was turning out to be a hot day, and there wasn't much shade to hide in. As he settled in and tried to get comfortable, Alex almost wished he'd worn shorts.

Once Alex was sure his parents were focused on the game, he slipped off his aching shoes and set them to the side. He tried to keep his stocking feet out of their sight as well.

The second batter hit a sharp grounder that looked like a base hit for sure. Ben sprang to intercept it, and then made a perfect throw to beat the runner at first base. Alex's family, along with the other Rangers fans, applauded wildly.

In the bottom of the inning, neither of the first two Rangers batters reached base. After that, Alex and his parents cheered as Ben managed to get a bloop single. Then, as the next batter came to the plate, a boy sitting a few rows behind the Petersons said to a friend, "Check out what my brother can do with his new bat."

Alex turned, and immediately recognized Tim Gilson and Richie Quinn. Tim was a full head taller than any other fifth grader at their school, and outweighed every classmate by fifteen or twenty pounds. Richie was Alex's height, but with a much more muscular build. Both Tim and Richie had dark brown hair that was pushing the St. Clement dress code's length limits.

Tommy Gilson took two pitches out of the strike zone, and then crushed a home run. Alex and the other Rangers fans erupted in cheers as Ben and Tommy trotted around to score. Alex noticed the fielders didn't even find the ball until Tommy was rounding third. *What I wouldn't have given for a bat like that when I was playing,* Alex thought. *Heck, I would've settled for some cleats that would've corrected my gait.*

Everyone quieted down as the next batter came to the plate. The boys behind Alex resumed their conversation. "Think Tommy'll pitch next year?" Richie asked.

"Gonna try," Tim replied. "I've been working with him."

Ben's probably already a better pitcher than Tommy ever will be, Alex thought. Even though his little brother's favorite position was shortstop, he'd been spending a lot of time practicing pitching. Alex enjoyed playing catcher for Ben in their backyard, and watching his technique improve. Ben would probably rotate to the mound in the third inning today, and he hoped to be a starting pitcher next year in Minors.

"How's your team doing this year?" Richie asked.

Alex cocked his ear a bit. "Probably going to win the championship this time," Tim said. Then, continuing in a louder voice, he added, "Helps that we lost some of our really LAME players." Tim and Richie then began laughing.

Alex's ears burned. He glanced at his parents, but they were too focused on the game to have heard the insult.

Off in the distance, Alex spotted a pair of cyclists riding by. He tried to get some music going in his head. For the next couple of innings, he imagined himself cruising freely down the road with them.

Free. That's the way the kids on Ben's team seemed, too. Even when someone blew an easy play, someone else would clap his hands and call out, "That's okay! Get him next time!" *This is what little league is supposed to be like,* Alex thought.

As Ben's team continued racking up runs, Alex's only regret was that he had to remain so close to Tim and Richie. He did his best to ignore them, and was happy his father offered to take him home right after the game.

Once they arrived, Alex went straight to his room and kicked off his aching shoes. As the computer took several minutes to reboot, he warmed up with scales and chord progressions on his keyboard.

Before Alex could choose a scene to work on, a knock at the door interrupted his concentration. "Yeah?" he called.

His father poked his head into the room. "Have the video up?" he asked. "Mind if I watch it?"

"The whole thing?" Alex asked.

"If you don't mind," his dad replied. "You could even keep playing your music if you want. Just curious to see what STP looks like these days."

Alex shrugged, and started the video at the beginning.

Alex offered the chair to his father, and then moved to his bed with the electronic keyboard. His dad settled comfortably into the chair as the opening sequences rolled.

"Husky Stadium parking lot?" his dad asked.

"Yeah," Alex replied, playing a soft melody of expectation on his keyboard. He didn't usually like having an audience. For his father, though, he figured he could overcome his shyness.

The video continued rolling. Alex played the notes and chords that filled his soul to overflowing. He glanced up a few times, but his father always had the same look of fascination on his face. Scene after scene, and musical piece after musical piece, rolled by. Dad barely blinked. Yet as focused as his father was, he also seemed strangely distant.

Only as the final credits were rolling, accompanied by Alex's triumphant score, did he break his silence. "That's really remarkable. And your music was perfect," he said.

"Thanks," Alex smiled.

"I don't mean to keep you from working," his dad said, standing to leave.

"It's okay. Can you tell me more about STP?"

"What do you want to know?" Dad asked, sitting back down uncomfortably.

Alex wasn't even sure where to start. He certainly hadn't expected the look his father was now giving him. "Was it as fun as the video makes it look?" he asked, hugging his mismatched knees to his chest.

"It was fun. Hard work, but fun." His father got a wry smile before continuing. "Why do you ask? Do you want to ride to Portland someday?"

There's nothing I'd rather do, Alex thought, but dared not say it aloud. Not yet. STP was his own secret dream, and for now he wanted to protect it deep within himself. "I just wish I could be a cyclist," he said. "It seems like such an awesome sport." That was true enough.

His father gazed at Alex's legs, not saying anything.

"How come you stopped riding?" Alex asked, trying to change the subject. "I didn't even know you had a bike. Is it the one hanging in the basement?"

"That's the bike. There were a lot of reasons I hung it up."

In a flash, Alex realized there might be a way around the problem of finding money for a bike of his own. "Could I use it?" he asked.

"Frame's way too big," his father replied.

Alex had a hundred other questions he wanted to ask about cycling and STP, but his dad was now staring into space and seemed far away. An awkward silence filled the room. Alex wondered if he'd said something wrong.

"I'll let you get back to work," his father said at last. He stood, and then slipped out the door.

I'm glad Alex has something he can be passionate about, and success-ful at, Rob thought. *Without music, he'd have nothing. He'd be about as good at cycling as he was at baseball.*

Struck by a sudden impulse, Rob made his way down to the basement. He found the light switch, traversed the boys' play area, and wandered into the long-term storage corner. The blue Colnago road bike hung upside down on hooks, just where Rob had set it the day they'd moved up from California eight years ago. Cobwebs filled all the spaces between the spokes. He ran his finger across the layer of dust on the frame, and then continued looking around. His bike tools still littered a rickety table, where he'd tossed them during the move. On the floor, a few U-Haul boxes marked "BIKE STUFF" still sat undisturbed. He supposed his helmet, jerseys, shoes, and everything else was still in them.

Back on the table, Rob spotted an old coffee can. He pried off the lid, and found a rolled-up stack of bib numbers he'd worn for each of the 200-mile "double century" events he'd ridden. He unrolled the numbers, and read "Death Valley Fall Double 1999" on the top one.

Rob spent the next several minutes sifting through the pile. When he reached the bib numbers from certain events, he paused for a moment to think and remember. The snow at the top of Idyllwild Pass, and trying to descend the other side with frozen fingers. The year it'd turned cold in the middle of the Davis Double, and he'd made an emergency stop at a garage sale to buy a sweatshirt. The Los Angeles Grand Tour, when he'd done the especially hilly "highland" route, and had momentarily fallen asleep along the closing stretch of Pacific Coast

Highway into Malibu. The Death Valley Spring Double, when the whole area had been carpeted in wildflowers.

Toward the bottom of the stack, he found what he'd been thinking about most: his Seattle to Portland bib numbers. Among them, the mud-spattered number from the year it'd rained all day. Then the one from the year it'd been so blistering hot, he'd been ready to jump in the Cowlitz River to cool off. The one from the year he'd talked his best friend, Paul Santucci, into riding with him. And his very first STP number, from 1984. *The year I turned eighteen, and didn't need Mom and Dad's permission.* The only number missing was the one he'd framed and given to Meg.

Rob took another look at the Colnago, but didn't remove it from the hooks. On his way back to the stairs, he selected an older bottle of blackberry wine from the cellar rack. He looked forward to a quiet evening with the television later.

Alex picked a new scene in the video, and let his fingers find some notes to match his feelings. He was soon immersed in a world of bicycles and bicyclists, floating on waves of music as he accompanied them on their epic journey.

Every time Alex closed his eyes, the video continued playing in his mind. Except his version was shot from a camera mounted to his own helmet, and he could feel the energy of the riders surrounding him. In his version of the video, nobody thought he was lame. *Alex, you're one of us,* their smiles told him. *We're all doing something not a whole lot of other people in the world have ever done. Here with us, everybody's a hero.*

Alex decided that someday he'd be a cyclist. This would be his fraternity. This is how he'd soar free. And maybe he could even convince his father to come along. *How could Dad not want to ride anymore?* he wondered.

Alex wasn't sure how he could set up a bike to fit his weird legs. With the dizzying variety of bikes he'd seen, he figured someone somewhere must know how to help him.

But where could he find the money? All he had was $252 that he'd saved from Christmases, birthdays, and picking blackberries for his father. With his birthday coming up in about a month, gifts from his grandparents might lift him to $350. With that, he'd been hoping to buy a more sophisticated electronic keyboard.

Even if he gave up on the keyboard, $350 wouldn't buy a bike like the ones in the video. It certainly wouldn't stretch to cover the rest of the equipment he'd need. And he swore not to ask his parents for a dime. *They've already had to spend way too much on me.* He decided his best hope was for someone to notice the STP video music, and then offer him a paying project.

Or something. Alex didn't care how long it took to scrape the pennies together. He didn't care what he had to do to set up a bike the right way. He didn't care how hard he had to work to strengthen his scrawny legs. He was going to be a cyclist. And someday even ride to Portland.

FOUR

May 19, 2008

LEX AND BEN COASTED ACROSS THE PARKING LOT THAT separated St. Clement Church from their school. Morning sunlight glinted off the sixty-year-old stained glass windows, warming the boys' faces. Alex was sure nothing could dampen his excitement about making music and becoming a cyclist.

The area was already bustling with kids getting dropped off, shooting baskets, and talking. The Peterson boys locked their bikes in the rack, and Ben ran off to join a friend. Alex adjusted his backpack, and went straight into the school.

St. Clement School was only slightly newer than the church, and the two buildings had a matching gray stone exterior. Between the church, school, parking lot and playground, the complex covered an entire residential block. The surrounding neighborhood was filled with tidy 1950s ranch houses, making the two-story church and school resemble a mother hen hovering over her brood.

Alex hustled upstairs to homeroom. Like pretty much every classroom at St. Clement, it had several rows of one-piece desks and chairs, all facing an ancient blackboard that'd faded to muddy brown. Tall windows let in lots of natural light, supplementing the softly buzzing fluorescent fixtures. He slipped off his backpack, and slid into the open desk next to his best friend, Connor Crowley. Alex lifted the desk's lid, and stashed his sack lunch inside.

A few inches taller than Alex, Connor's thin frame and long limbs gave him a "bean pole" look. He was dressed in the same white uniform polo shirt as Alex, but Connor wore navy uniform shorts. Alex looked around. It appeared he was again the only boy wearing slacks.

"Hey," Alex said. "How'd your baseball game go?"

"Won eight to three," his friend replied. "I scored a run when Tim drove me in on a grand slam. You have fun at your Grandpa's yesterday?"

"Yeah," Alex replied. He paused to slip off his aching shoes. "All my cousins were there. We played football."

Even with his shoes killing him, Alex really had enjoyed running around his grandfather's huge rural property. Fresh air had cleared his head, and given him a new perspective. When his family had returned home after Sunday dinner, he'd dashed straight to his keyboard and recorded the melodies that had been swimming through his mind all afternoon.

Alex and Connor continued chatting until the bell rang school to order at 8:15. The room quieted as Mrs. McArthur's voice crackled over the school's public address system, delivering the morning's prayer and announcements.

"Bike music's coming along great," Alex told Connor, once the announcements ended.

"Awesome," his friend replied. "Make sure you get me a copy of the final video, when they make it this summer."

They continued talking until the bell interrupted their conversation. Alex pulled his shoes back on. He and Connor then walked together to language arts.

Alex was happy to discover this was a day they'd get to read a lot in class. He kicked off his shoes, and settled in to enjoy some short stories. He usually finished long before the other kids, which gave him time to read ahead in the book.

After language arts came math. Alex was good at math, and especially enjoyed discovering mathematical patterns in classical music. Math class itself was usually pretty dull, though. Alex wondered what it'd be like having Mr. Jansson as his math teacher in the fall. He hoped that'd be more interesting.

His favorite subject was science, which was third period. Today, by that time, all he could think about were his aching feet. *Maybe I finally need to break down and ask for a new pair of shoes,* he thought. An instant later, he caught himself. *I really have to make these last till summer break.* He again loosened his laces and slipped his shoes off under the desk. That bought enough relief to concentrate on the lesson.

Alex sat toward the right side of the science classroom, several rows back. Richie Quinn sat directly to his right. Alex kept thinking about the insults that Tim and Richie had thrown his direction on Saturday.

Toward the end of the period, a textbook fell from Richie's desk. Startled, Alex jerked his head to look. Richie tried to pick the book up, and dropped several other papers in the process.

Their teacher, Mr. Connelly, paused for a moment as Richie continued retrieving his books and papers. "Let me help," Alex whispered, and then leaned over to corral a couple of Richie's papers. Richie smirked as he took his things back.

Alex heard some snickers and tittering laughter from a couple of kids on his left. By the time Alex turned his head to see what was so funny, the chuckles had stopped. He couldn't even tell who'd been laughing.

Mr. Connelly finished his presentation about electrical circuits, and Alex packed up his books. *Just social studies and then lunch,* he thought, wondering what his mother had packed today. But when Alex stretched out his foot, he could only feel one shoe. Looking under the desk, he realized his left shoe was gone.

"Anyone seen my other shoe?" Alex asked. Several kids had already left the room, and those remaining either snickered or looked at him blankly.

"Shoes are to be worn at all times throughout the school day," Richie told him. He used a mock official tone, as if quoting the St. Clement uniform policy. Richie then laughed and slipped out. Alex immediately realized Richie's dropped book was part of a prank to swipe his special elevator shoe. He felt stupid for not having seen it coming.

"Is there a problem?" Mr. Connelly asked Alex, who was now one of the last students in the room.

"No, sir," he replied, hiding his shoeless foot while he finished packing his bag.

Connor sidled over from his desk on the far side of the classroom, and stood between Alex and their teacher. "I won't let him see you're out of uniform," Connor whispered.

"Thanks, man," Alex whispered back.

He and Connor now had to hustle upstairs for social studies. With the discrepancy between his leg lengths exaggerated by the missing elevator shoe, Alex limped very badly. Nearly every student in the hallways gaped at him. Alex had never felt so self-conscious.

"Out of the way!" someone exclaimed, "Bigfoot's coming through!"

Before Alex could even turn to see who'd said it, he heard another kid call out, "Or stumbling through!"

Alex's face burned with shame. Lowering his head, he hobble-trotted faster. "Did you see what happened with my elevator shoe?" he asked Connor, who was jogging to keep up.

"Not exactly," his friend replied. "I did see a shoe getting passed around. Didn't know it was yours."

"See who ended up with it?" Alex asked.

"Not positive, but probably Tim," Connor said.

He and Connor were the last to arrive at social studies. Alex managed to take his seat without the teacher, Mrs. Davidson, noticing his missing shoe. Kids were noticing, though. As Mrs. Davidson called the roll, Alex could hear whispered comments all around him.

Mrs. Davidson began her class presentation about the growth of cities and the industrial revolution. Alex tried to pay attention and take notes, but he couldn't stop thinking about the prank. He figured at least a few other kids must have been involved. Brett Zielinski sat to his left in science, and Brett was friends with both Richie and Tim. Tim sat behind Brett. Connor was probably right about Tim ending up with the shoe.

But what do I do now? Alex wondered. *What if my shoe is gone for good?* On the one hand, it would be the perfect excuse to get a new shoe. But how would he explain it to his folks? *What kind of idiot loses a shoe at school?*

Alex's shoes had to be ordered over the internet, and usually took a week to arrive. Would he have to limp around with a standard shoe on his left foot for a week? Had his parents even kept the standard left shoe matching his right one?

By the time social studies ended, Alex had to use the bathroom really badly. Once he reached the boys' room, he was in such a hurry to get to a urinal that he didn't look carefully at the tile floor. Just as he was about to unsnap his slacks to relieve himself, his left foot came down in something wet. After he finished at the urinal, his sock made a slapping noise as he hobbled to the sink.

Alex was halfway to the sink when Brett Zielinski pushed through the door. Brett was shorter than Alex, but with a stocky build and dark brown hair. Brett stared at Alex's left foot, and snickered. "Looks like you didn't get your sock wet enough, Lame-o. The top's still dry."

Alex washed his hands and did his best to ignore Brett, hoping that would make the boys stop bullying him. That's what his mother always told him, anyway.

"Guess we can't call you 'Bigfoot' no more," Brett called out from the urinal. "Gonna have to be 'Lame-o' from now on."

Seething with anger, Alex grit his teeth and continued on to homeroom. His wet sock slapped the floor with every step.

By the time he arrived, most of the other kids were already eating their lunches. Alex slipped into his desk next to Connor's. Alex forced himself to eat, but was too upset to enjoy anything his mother had packed.

Alex could hear several kids murmuring about his shoe. *Are they also noticing how bad my sock smells?* he wondered.

"From what I've been hearing," Connor said quietly, "I'm pretty sure it's Tim and Richie and Brett who took your shoe."

"Any idea where they've put it?" Alex asked.

Connor shook his head and took another bite of sandwich.

"It was crazy expensive," Alex added. "And it's at least a week to get a replacement."

Connor leaned toward Alex and switched to an especially quiet voice. "I think we should find a way to get back at Tim. Maybe plant a can of beer in his desk or something. Or some of my mom's cigarettes." Connor's blue eyes always looked a little mischievous, and seemed especially so now.

"He'd know it was us. He'd kill us," Alex objected.

Suddenly, above the buzzing din of student conversations, Mrs. Fernandez called out, "Alexander Peterson, why are you wearing only one shoe?"

The room fell silent. Alex's face turned bright scarlet as he sensed two dozen pairs of eyes trained on his wet sock. "Um," he stammered, his heart racing, "My special elevator shoe wasn't fitting right. Had to take it off."

"Was it fitting correctly when you left the house this morning?" she asked.

"Um," Alex replied, trying to think of an answer that wasn't exactly a lie. "Sort of. But it got worse."

Mrs. Fernandez looked at him skeptically. "Shoes are to be worn at all times throughout the school day," she said. Alex cringed at the echo of Richie's words. "I'm afraid I'll have to ask you to put it back on."

Alex dropped his gaze and felt defeated. "Actually," he admitted, "I, um, lost my shoe."

"You *lost* your shoe?" Mrs. Fernandez asked.

Alex glanced at Richie, who was staring daggers through him. Then, turning back to Mrs. Fernandez, Alex explained that his shoe had disappeared sometime during science class, when he'd taken it off because it wasn't fitting.

"And you have no idea where it is now?" she asked.

Alex shook his head, his cheeks burning hotter than ever.

Mrs. Fernandez thought for a moment. Then, addressing the rest of the room, she said, "All of you were in Science with Alex. Did anyone see what happened to his shoe?"

To Alex's complete unsurprise, not a single hand went up.

"That is unfortunate," Mrs. Fernandez said, "but not believable. Someone here knows what happened to that shoe, and where it is now. By the time all of you are back here at 2:45, Alex's shoe must be found. No fifth grader will be dismissed this afternoon until it has been. Is that understood?"

The whole class murmured in surprise. Alex wished he could crawl into a hole. He knew Mrs. Fernandez meant well, but he'd a hundred times rather have lost his shoe for good than be singled out in front of everybody like that.

As a buzz of conversation again filled the room, Alex forced himself to finish his lunch. "What're you going to do for recess?" Connor asked, between bites of his own sandwich.

"Go to the library and do my homework, I guess," Alex replied. The playground was the last place he wanted to go with just one shoe. Since the other kids never picked him for games, he usually spent recess by himself anyway.

After lunch and recess, Alex managed to limp through his final two classes — literature and religion — without teachers mentioning his missing shoe. No fifth grader gave him the shoe back or told him where it'd been hidden, either.

Alex hobbled back to homeroom at 2:45. He wondered how long the whole class might get kept past the usual 3pm dismissal time. *Will I even be late to my organ lesson?* he wondered.

Alex and Connor made their way to their desks, and discovered a note on Alex's seat. "OPEN THE DESK, BIGFOOT," it read. Relief swept him as he discovered his shoe inside.

He figured most of his classmates knew who was behind the prank, and how the bullies had pulled it off. Yet no one had bothered to tell him. No one had even expressed sympathy. The more Alex thought about this, the more his relief evaporated into anger. He'd never felt so much like Connor was his only real friend.

Mrs. Fernandez nodded at Alex as he pulled his shoe on. A moment later, Mrs. McArthur began reading the afternoon announcements over the public address system. She reminded everyone that the Fun Run was now just a couple of weeks away, and that there would be prizes for the boy and girl from each grade who raised the most money.

The announcements ended a moment later, and all the kids began talking. "Riding straight home today?" Connor asked.

"I just remembered I need to talk to Mr. Jansson about the Fun Run. I'll meet you at the bike rack."

The Crowleys and the Petersons lived only a couple of blocks apart. Most days, Connor and Ben would shoot baskets or get homework done until Alex finished practicing on the church organ at 3:30. But on Mondays, when Alex had organ lessons later, all three boys would go straight home.

Once the bell rang, Alex hustled to Mr. Jansson's classroom. He arrived just as the last students were leaving.

"Alex! Good to see you! How's the music coming?" Mr. Jansson smiled. He was one of the shortest teachers at St. Clement, but husky and very muscular. From his gray hair, Alex would've guessed him to be in his fifties. From the shape of his body, Alex would've guessed him to be in his twenties.

"Really great," Alex replied. Something about Mr. Jansson's warm greeting immediately made him forget about everything else that'd happened today. "And I wanted to volunteer to help with the Fun Run. What do you need me to do?"

"Excellent. We have a meeting this Thursday after school, right here. Looks like there will be four of you. We can discuss assignments then."

"Sounds good," Alex said.

Before Alex could leave, Mr. Jansson seemed to remember something. "And I wanted to tell you — I spoke with the person at Cascade who's making this year's video. He gave me more details about what they need."

"Yeah?"

"He'd like the music in early August," Mr. Jansson continued. "You should compose different types of pieces that are about 30 seconds long, with variations on each. As many as you feel like doing. Burn them all to a disc and then drop it at school for me. He said we can trim them, fade them, whatever, to fit this year's video."

"Basically, give him a bunch of raw material to work with?"

"Exactly."

"I've already done several basic pieces," Alex replied, looking forward to more long hours alone with his keyboard. He especially liked how Mr. Jansson was treating him almost like a partner, and not like a little kid. "It'll be fun making variations."

"Good. And if you think it'll give you more inspiration, you're welcome to join us at the STP start next month and watch the riders in person. I'll be there."

"Are you riding?" Alex asked.

"Fifth year in a row. Your folks can get all the start line info from Cascade's website."

Alex's heart raced at the idea of being able to see all those amazing bikes and riders up close. "That sounds really fun."

Alex hurried outside to meet Connor. Once at the rack, Alex unlocked the bicycle he was stuck with for now. It had only one gear, and both wheels were out of true. It beat walking, especially with his shoes hurting this badly, but not by much. He wished he could press a button that would magically transform it into a real road bike.

Connor had already unlocked his bike and slung his backpack over his shoulders. "Where's Ben?" Connor asked, pulling a helmet over his reddish brown hair.

Alex yanked the bike from the rack before snapping his own helmet in place. He hated the dorky, little-kid helmet almost as much as he hated his bike. "His team has a game at West Hills, so my mom picked him up."

The two boys started pedaling up the street in front of the school. The late spring sunshine, filtering through the leafy maple trees lining the streets, bathed Alex's face and reassured him that everything would be all right. The boys turned and began coasting down the first of a dozen quiet residential blocks.

"Ever miss baseball?" Connor asked. "Coach said you could've kept playing."

Alex thought, *Yeah, if you call "playing" standing around in right field for four innings, and getting thrown out at first base on what would've been a hit for any other kid.* "I'd rather watch the Mariners on TV," he said. That was true enough.

They rode in silence for a block, before Connor spoke up again. "What's going on with the Fun Run?"

"I'm not running. Me and a few other kids are going to help Mr. Jansson with logistics."

"Dang. I was hoping we could run together," Connor said.

Alex studied the road ahead, and pedaled in silence. Back in second grade, before the accident, they'd had a great time running together. Alex had given it a try in third grade and last year. Even when he had well-fitting shoes, though, running that much made his joints hurt for days.

But he didn't want to admit he was really that lame. Not even to Connor.

The boys soon reached the intersection where Connor had to turn off. "See you tomorrow," they said to each other.

Alex glided down the remaining blocks of leafy residential streets, and tried to think of anyone who was as good a friend as Connor. Nobody came close. He liked his cousins, and enjoyed seeing them every Sunday at Grandpa's, but they didn't count.

His mind drifted ahead to that afternoon's organ lesson. *I need to make sure I thank Mrs. Rossi for telling Mr. Jansson about me. I just hope she doesn't keep bugging me to play in that recital next month. Or the Christmas concert.*

Alex stopped and collected the mail from the mailbox. There was nothing for him, but he did notice what looked like another bill from the hospital addressed to his father. They seemed to come about this time every month. He wondered how many more years they'd be coming.

Alex studied the envelope, feeling an odd joy about how uncomfortable his shoes felt. *At least there's something I can keep doing to help,* he thought. As Alex pulled into the driveway, he resolved not to say anything about shoes to his parents. He'd make them last all summer if he could. No matter how much his feet hurt.

FIVE

ROB'S FINGERS FLEW ACROSS THE LAPTOP KEYBOARD, AS HE raced to get the last of his conclusions into the focus group report before they faded from his mind. Insights were coming left and right, and he sensed he had nearly enough content for Frank Hurwitz and Decision Strategies' clients at the child support administration. At this rate, Rob would be able to deliver a draft report even earlier than promised.

Rob heard his office door opening. His fingers slowed as he looked up. Alex slipped through the door, kicked his shoes off, and stood waiting silently.

Rob hated being interrupted when he was in a zone like this, and so close to finishing a piece of writing. Struggling not to scowl, he completed the paragraph before turning his full attention to his son. Alex — unlike Ben — always tried so hard to remain quiet, it was impossible to be mad at him.

Alex was dressed in what Rob called his "after-school uniform," jeans and a Mariners t-shirt, and was munching on an apple. It struck him that Alex was remarkably slender for a boy whose only exercise was walking or riding a dozen blocks to school each day.

"Hey!" Rob greeted him. "Anything special happen at school today?"

"Not really," Alex said, handing him the mail.

Rob flipped through the envelopes. *Still no checks. All Bills.* Tearing open the first, Rob said, "Looks like I'm taking you to your organ lesson. What time do we have to leave?"

"About 4:15," Alex shrugged, putting the last piece of apple in his mouth.

Rob glanced at the clock. That gave him barely enough time to finish, if only Alex would let him get back to work. "Are you going to practice on your keyboard before we go?" He hoped Alex would take the hint.

As he waited for his son to respond, Rob opened the envelope from the hospital. He tried not to cringe at the remaining balance.

"This week's songs were so boring, I've been transposing them to B-Flat Major. But I guess I could practice some more."

"Good. Meet you at the car at 4:15."

Rob noticed Alex wincing as the boy pulled his shoes on. His son was trying not to let him see his face, but there was no missing Alex's expression — or how loosely he left the laces tied.

Now that he thought about it, Rob realized Alex hadn't been wearing shoes much lately. He'd been leaving his laces loose whenever he did. He wondered why his son hadn't said anything, or asked for new shoes.

"Outgrowing this pair?"

"I'm okay," Alex assured him.

Rob got up and knelt at Alex's feet. "Wiggle your big toes," he said, putting a hand on each shoe.

"Ouch! I can't."

"Thought so," Rob replied, and returned to his desk. "Looks like we've gotten our money's worth out of these. I'll order a bigger elevator shoe online, and we could go shopping for a sort-of-matching right shoe tonight after your lesson."

Alex stood shame-facedly in the doorway, looking at his feet. "Thanks," he murmured. "And when I saw Dr. Singh last week, he said my difference is up to 53 millimeters."

"About two inches," Rob said, pulling up the website for the elevator shoes they liked. "They have a few good choices in stock. Any particular color you'd like?"

"Doesn't matter. Just get whatever's cheapest. A couple sizes up from whatever you ordered last time." Alex then slipped out of the office.

Rob couldn't stop thinking about his son's words. *Just get whatever's cheapest.* When they'd take the boys out to eat, Alex always chose water over soda pop. "I just don't like pop anymore," he'd say. And at ball games, Alex never wanted peanuts or anything else. When his little brother begged for ice cream, Alex would insist he wasn't hungry.

Rob decided the report wasn't going to get finished this afternoon. He surfed back to the website for Alex's elevator shoes. Perhaps if he got the order placed before close of business, the new shoe could arrive a day sooner.

It turned out the company was running a clearance sale on some of the sneakers with the proper amount of lift. Rob selected ones in the sizes Alex might need before his leg length difference increased by too much. He hoped if larger shoes were already in the house, Alex wouldn't hesitate to ask for them.

Rob only wished he could've afforded to pay for overnight shipping.

Six

ALEX GROANED AS THE THIRD OPPOSING PLAYER IN A ROW tossed his bat aside and jogged to first base. He knew Ben had been nervous about making his first start as pitcher, but this meltdown was beyond anything Alex had expected. *Bases loaded and nobody out in the top of the first.*

Alex wished he could trot to the mound and put his arm around his little brother's shoulder. "Remember what you worked on, back at home?" Alex would say. "Slow down, and don't hurry your release. Breathe steady, all the way through the delivery."

Ben ran the count full for the next batter, and then lucked out when the boy chased what would've been ball four. Ben's luck evaporated when the fifth batter lined a pitch to the outfield, easily scoring two runs. Only a strong relay from Tommy Gilson managed to nail the third runner at the plate.

With the previous batter grinning at third base, Ben's next three pitches were out of the strike zone. *Come on. You can do it,* Alex silently pleaded. He knew this first start on the mound was hugely important for his little brother. Especially since it was the last game of the season, and Ben would be thinking about it for months.

From two rows behind him, Alex heard Tim Gilson's unmistakable voice snickering, "Looks like 'Lame' might be genetic." Alex struggled not to turn around or say anything.

Ben's next pitch was fat and slow, right across the heart of the plate. It would've been an easy home run if the batter hadn't been taking all the way. The boy dug in his cleats, took a couple of frustrated practice swings, and then hit the next pitch straight back at Ben. Alex, along with the rest of the Rangers fans, cheered as his little brother caught it to retire the side.

Ben's team scored a run in the bottom of the first, which seemed to settle him down. He allowed only one hit and one walk in the second, and then Ben's friend Jimmy Flynn knocked in a two-run homer to take the lead.

After again walking the first three batters in the third, and then giving up a grand slam home run, Coach moved Ben to shortstop. Jimmy took over on the mound, and struck out the next three batters.

"That's how it's done," Tim remarked. Alex grit his teeth and said nothing.

Despite his solid play at shortstop the rest of the game, Ben's team never retook the lead. His face was awash in disappointment as the final out was recorded.

The Rangers began ritually shaking hands with their opponents. Alex's mother touched his shoulder. "Why don't you ride home with me," she said. "Dad and Ben will come later. I need to get ready to go volunteering at Women's Resources. You can even go volunteering with me if you want."

Women's Resources was a crisis pregnancy center in Seattle, where his mom had been helping out as long as he could remember. She and her friends collected and organized donations of all kinds of stuff that babies and pregnant women needed. The center then made it available at no cost. Alex usually enjoyed listening to music and working by himself in the back room, while his mom and her friends talked with the women coming in for help.

Right now, Alex wasn't sure he wanted to do anything but go home and get his mind off the disappointing loss. He didn't even want to watch the Mariners play the Red Sox that afternoon, because that'd probably be a bloodbath, too. As block after block of the trip home rolled by, Alex found himself increasingly enveloped in the same broody frustration that he knew his brother was feeling. *Maybe if I'd played catcher for him again this morning, instead of playing piano, Ben would've gotten off to a better start,* he thought. *I wish there was a sport where your only opponent was yourself. Where the only way you lost was not working to do better than you had before. And nobody thought you were lame.*

Alex headed straight to his room. He flipped on his keyboard, warmed up his fingers with some scales, and then launched into the second movement of Beethoven's Seventh. Playing by ear, and working his way deeper into the dark and foreboding melody, he felt his own frustrations harmonizing with the tensions and angst of the chord progressions. Alex grew so immersed in the symphony, the whole rest of the world seemed to disappear.

As the final notes faded, a voice from behind startled him. "Beautiful," his mother said. Alex turned to see her leaning against the doorway. "Want to tell me what's bothering you?"

"Nothing," Alex muttered.

Before Alex could decide on another piece, his mother took his hand. "Come with me," she said, so firmly that Alex knew he had no choice. He flipped off the keyboard, and let his mom lead him to the living room.

Without another word, she sat him down to her right on the piano bench. She then began playing the opening notes of "Heart and Soul," the only piece she'd ever learned.

Alex smiled, and harmonized with the duet's right hands. As the two of them worked their way through the simple and happy melody, Alex sensed his whole world brightening. His only disappointment was that the song lasted just two minutes, and that his mother's repertoire was now exhausted.

"Tell me what's on your mind, Alex," she said, putting her arm around his shoulder.

Alex rested his head against her, and felt secure in everything. Nothing in the universe seemed worth worrying about. He took a deep breath and summoned all his courage. "Promise you won't laugh? Or think I'm stupid?" he asked.

"Promise," his mother said, hugging him closer.

"I want to be a cyclist. Like the ones in the video. And like Dad was. I know it probably costs too much, and I know my legs are all wrong, but there's gotta be a way to do it. I just don't know how."

"I don't think you're stupid," his mother replied. "Have you talked to Dad?"

Alex shook his head. "Tried to, when I was working on the video. He just looked at my legs. I could tell he thought it was a big joke."

His mother continued holding him for a long moment. "I will make sure Dad knows it isn't a joke," she said, kissing the top of his sandy-blond head.

Alex smiled and thanked her. Still, he knew better than to get his hopes up yet. If ever.

SEVEN

ROB SETTLED INTO THE WICKER LOVESEAT WITH A BOTTLE OF wine. The evening breeze brought with it the slightest chill. He was glad he'd worn a sweatshirt. With the exception of a few streetlights and an occasional passing car, the neighborhood was quiet and dark.

The front door creaked open, interrupting Rob's train of thought. Meg stepped onto the porch, wearing an old U of W sweatshirt and carrying a wine glass. "Boys are both finally asleep," she said, brushing back her shoulder-length brown hair.

Meg settled in next to Rob. He filled her glass with wine. She pulled her feet up, got comfortable, and took a sip. "This is really good," she said.

"Thanks. Blackberry. From two summers ago. How was Women's Resources?"

"Lots of clients. I think it's the economy. But we got them all helped. Sorry we were late getting back for dinner."

"Is the center getting enough donations?"

"So far, so good," Meg replied, taking another sip of wine. "They'd gotten in a mountain of baby clothes. Mostly unsold garage sale stuff. Needed to be sorted and folded. If Alex hadn't gone with me, it'd still be piled up."

"Like father, like son," Rob joked, topping off his wine glass and thinking back to his first date with Meg Sullivan so many years ago. She'd been by far the cutest girl in his sophomore American Government class, and he'd enjoyed their casual conversations. Still, it'd taken him nearly all of winter quarter to muster the courage to ask her out.

Washington Husky basketball had seemed like a safe bet for a first date. To his surprise, she'd readily accepted the offer — with one condition. Rob had to come volunteering at a crisis pregnancy center with her and her friends the afternoon before the game.

It was the last place he'd imagined setting foot in. He'd stammered in surprise for a moment. Then, before talking himself out of it, or even stopping to think that he might be the only male in the building, he'd agreed. It'd ended up being not nearly as uncomfortable as he'd imagined. He'd even gone back a few more times.

Only months later, after they'd been steadily dating, Meg confided that the "volunteering test" had been her screen for potential suitors. Rob was the only one who'd ever passed.

And the rest had been history.

Back in the evening chill of the front porch, Rob tried to change the subject. "Ben sure took the loss hard," he said.

Meg swished her wine glass and contemplated the purple liquid. "But as I put him to bed, he was already talking about next season," she said. "It's our other son I'm worried about."

"Alex?" Rob asked. "Since when have we had to worry about him?"

"He sits inside by himself all day, reading books or playing music," Meg replied. "Sometimes for hours. Even when he goes volunteering, all he wants to do is work alone in the back. I don't think it's good for him."

Rob couldn't disagree with that.

A breeze picked up, and Meg cuddled closer. "How do we get Alex as passionate about a sport as he is about music or books?" she continued, taking a sip of wine. "I suggested swimming, but I know he hates it."

"He does need a sport," Rob said, putting his arm around Meg's shoulder and taking a long sip of wine. "It was pretty cute the way he did so much to pump Ben up this morning."

"He's always been such a cute kid," Meg mused.

"He was cuter when he smiled more often," Rob observed. "And I haven't seen him smile like he did this morning for a long time."

Rob gave Meg's shoulder a quick squeeze as the two of them sat in silence.

"Suppose there were a sport that Alex loved," Meg continued. "With a passion. That he wanted to do pretty much every day, whether he was good at it or not. Would you help him? As much as we help Ben get to practices and games?"

Rob got the uncomfortable sense that he was being set up, and that there was only one correct answer. "Of course," he replied, putting the glass to his lips.

"Good. Because your son wants to be a cyclist."

Rob laughed, and nearly choked on his wine.

Meg pulled away and frowned. "That's exactly the reaction he thought you'd have. That's why he's kept it bottled up and been afraid to even ask."

"He told you that?" Rob asked, feeling a little guilty about being so dismissive.

"Not in so many words. But I could tell." Meg set her glass down and folded her arms before continuing. "Rob, I don't know if he'll ever be any good. But he's passionate about wanting to try."

"Fine," Rob said, refilling his glass. "Let him ride his bike more."

"You know that thing barely gets him to school and back. He wants a real road bike. Like yours."

"If he doesn't mind a used one," Rob shrugged, "I'm sure we could find something by his birthday. Then he can ride all he wants. I'll check Craigslist."

"I'd worry about him taking long rides on his own. A few blocks to school is one thing. An open road, or even the Sammamish River Trail, is something else."

"He'll be eleven in a couple of weeks. We've got to let him grow up sometime," Rob said.

"He daydreams too much. About music, and everything else. He needs someone to keep an eye on him when he rides."

Rob shifted uncomfortably on the wicker loveseat, and studied the headlights of a passing car. He knew what Meg was getting at, but he refused to say it. And he knew Meg knew that he knew. That only made it worse. Still, he resolved to play dumb.

"Rob..." Meg said at last, swishing her wine glass and studying the purple liquid.

"I'm never touching that thing again," he replied.

Meg's gaze was so piercing, Rob had to look away. "Nobody's asking you to ride to Portland. Would it kill you to get your bike tuned up and ride with your son to Woodinville a few times a week?"

Rob knew any objection would sound pig-headed, but he hated feeling goaded or shamed into doing something he didn't really want to do. "I'll think about it," he muttered.

"Maybe think of it as reconnecting with an old friend."

Rob shook his head. "When people go through a nasty divorce, they don't reconnect for dinner and a movie. Look at Pam and Larry. Or my sister and Jack."

"Even Larry and Pam manage to be civil with each other," Meg pointed out. "For their kids."

Rob knew he'd lost the argument, but wasn't ready to admit it. "It's just that I've never been a casual rider. I hate simply pedaling around, without having some goal I'm working toward. It'd drive me crazy. I'd rather not ride at all." *And I'd never admit to being lazy, but I'm very happy not riding at all.*

Meg thought for a moment. "Hold on," she said at last, putting her glass down and slipping into the house.

Alone with the music of neighborhood crickets, Rob topped off his wine glass and tried to formulate arguments against cycling. Still, his mind stubbornly returned to the same image: his own first road bike, purchased at the age of twelve, with money hoarded from delivering newspapers and recycling aluminum cans. Initially it hadn't even been a bike. Just a nice Peugeot frame he'd spotted at a police auction. He'd then spent the next several months sanding it, repainting it, and scavenging components. One piece at a time, as the rest of the family had scoffed, he'd assembled his dream machine. And he'd fallen in love. Even now, he could remember the shape and texture of the Simplex gear shifters.

Meg returned clutching a small picture frame, displaying STP bib number 1859. "The one wedding gift that I have treasured most," she said.

She sat and looked him in the eye. "Because you were wearing it when you gave me this," she continued, holding up her left hand to display the simple gold band that'd served as both her engagement and wedding ring. "Do you remember what you told me?"

Rob closed his eyes. He was again in Portland's Delta Park, under a fading evening sun. His short blond hair dripped with sweat. Every muscle in his body had been squeezed to its limit, and his back ached so badly he could barely stand. There'd been no question of trying to kneel. He'd asked her to sit next to him on a bench. He'd put his arm around her. Then he'd pulled out the ring box.

"I carried something in my pocket for you today, to wear the rest of your life," Rob said, amazed he could still recall the words after eighteen years. "Every time you look at it, I want you to remember I carried it 200 miles, under my own power, over hills and across rivers. And I will always, forever, go any distance and cross any mountain for you."

Rob opened his eyes, and Meg gazed directly into them. "Will you find your son a bicycle and ride with him to Woodinville a few days a week?"

EIGHT

ALEX GAZED AT UNFAMILIAR STREETS AS HIS FATHER DROVE Mom's station wagon deeper into the heart of Ballard. He'd had a grand time with his dad that morning at the Ballard Locks, watching boats navigating from the Ship Canal and Lake Washington to Puget Sound and back. He wasn't sure what he'd liked best: seeing the way the locks raised and lowered all the sailboats and fishing craft, or having a whole morning one-on-one with his dad.

His father turned down a side street, and glanced at a set of directions. "We're close. Look for a driveway with a Ryder moving truck."

"What is this place we're going to?" Alex asked.

"Something I need to take a look at."

A moment later, they found the right house. "I believe somebody has a birthday coming up," his father smiled.

Alex had had so much fun that morning, he'd almost forgotten about tomorrow. He jumped from the car, and hurried to follow his father.

Furniture and moving boxes filled the garage. From the looks of it, Alex assumed the owners were moving out.

"Mrs. Larsen?" Alex's dad called to an older woman who was labeling a carton. "I'm Rob Peterson. We spoke yesterday."

"Oh, yes," she smiled. "This must be the birthday boy."

Alex's curiosity was now nearly uncontainable. Still, he was too shy to do anything but nod.

Mrs. Larsen disappeared behind a wall of boxes. She emerged a moment later, pushing a small red road bike. "I hope this fits," she said. "I'd like to see another boy enjoy it as much as my Henry did."

Alex couldn't believe what he was seeing. "You're ... you're getting me a bike?" he stammered. "A real bike?"

"If it fits. Otherwise, there are a few others we can look at."

Alex was stunned. He put his hand out and grasped the handlebars, not believing it was really his. *His.*

"I'm sorry it's not in nicer shape, but that's the way Henry left it when he went off to college, and why I priced it so low," Mrs. Larsen continued.

Alex was too busy admiring the bike to hear anything else she said. Yes, the paint had lots of chips. There were cobwebs between the spokes. The chain looked rusty. One of the pedals was broken. But none of that mattered. It had nice components, and it was a Trek. Alex had seen a lot of Treks in the STP video.

His father had him straddle the bike, and his crotch cleared the frame's top tube by about an inch. "Perfect," his dad said.

"Can I ride it?" Alex asked.

His father was already retrieving Alex's helmet from a duffel bag in the car. *So* that's *what he packed. And why we took Mom's station wagon.*

His dad produced tools and a tire pump from the bag. He then inflated the tires, adjusted the seat and handlebars, and showed Alex how to operate the gear shifters. They were built into the brake levers, and one operated the rear shifter while the other operated the front shifter. "You have eight choices in the back and three choices up front," he explained, giving him a quick lesson in gear selection.

Wow! A twenty-four speed bike! Alex thought.

Alex was soon pedaling up and down the quiet residential street, trying gear after gear, with a huge smile on his face. His father and Mrs. Larsen stood in the driveway talking. They waved at Alex every time he went past.

"Is it a keeper?" his dad asked, when Alex finally pulled in.

"Oh, yeah!" Alex exclaimed, dismounting.

His dad paid Mrs. Larsen, who thanked him and wished Alex a happy birthday. Alex then helped his father slide the bike into the back of the wagon.

"Thank you!" he beamed, once he and his father were cruising out of the neighborhood. As they drove across town toward the freeway, Alex talked nonstop about his new bike and how much he'd enjoyed riding it. Even though it ran and shifted rough, he could hardly wait to show it to Connor — and then spend the whole rest of the afternoon testing it out.

Then, instead of continuing toward the freeway, his dad turned and approached Green Lake.

Green Lake was one of Alex's favorite places. The lake itself took up about 260 acres, which he'd learned on a school field trip earlier that spring. It was surrounded by a three mile bike-and-walking path, and by several acres of grassy parkland that were perfect for picnicking. When he and Ben were younger, they'd spent hours romping on the play equipment. They'd especially liked going to Green Lake after visiting the Woodland Park Zoo, which adjoined it.

They were soon driving along Green Lake Way, which ringed the edge of the park. "Where are we going?" Alex asked.

"The bike needs to be overhauled before you start riding it. There's a good shop up here. They'll make sure everything's perfect."

A few minutes later, they'd parked at Gregg's Green Lake Cycle and were rolling Alex's bike toward the service entrance. While his dad waited in line for a mechanic, Alex wandered off to explore the main part of the shop.

Alex was so overwhelmed by the array of cycling equipment, he didn't know where to start looking. There were not only dozens of new bikes, in every imaginable size and configuration. There was also display case after display case of beautiful components. Alex had no idea what some of the parts were even for, but gazing on them was like being in a jewelry shop. And then there were the racks upon racks of shorts and colorful jerseys and rain gear and touring equipment and …

Just as Alex thought his head might explode, he realized his father was talking with a mechanic. Alex hustled to join them.

"We're completely jammed with pre-STP service," the mechanic was explaining. He looked young, and had a name tag reading "Jeff" pinned to his green smock. "Is it okay if we do it on July 11th?"

"I imagine it's the same all over town," his dad said.

"Pretty much, unfortunately," Jeff replied. "But I can promise it for pickup first thing on the 12th."

Alex's face fell. He couldn't believe he'd have to wait two whole weeks to be able to ride his new bike. "Can't I just ride it for a week and bring it in?"

"There's really too much that needs to be done," Jeff explained. "It's borderline unsafe in this condition."

"At least you'll have the whole rest of the summer with a perfect bike," his dad said.

Alex frowned, but was glad his father hadn't spent a fortune on a perfect bike.

"What kind of pedals would you like us to install?" Jeff asked, gesturing to the broken one.

Alex almost blurted out, "Whatever's cheapest," but caught himself. *If I'm going be riding seriously, maybe I should start with some good pedals.* "What'll help me go fast?"

"I'll show you what we have," Jeff replied, leading Alex and his father to a display with a dozen different pedals mounted. "The next step up for you would be these," he said, touching a platform pedal with a U-shaped clip bolted to the front of it. "You'd put your foot in the toe clip, and tighten it with this strap. Makes pedaling more efficient."

Alex looked at his feet and tried to hide his discouragement. His left shoe was way too big to fit into one of those clips. The kids at school didn't call him "Bigfoot" for nothing. "What's the next step after that?"

"Clipless pedals and cleats like mine," Alex's dad said, "but I think that's going to be out of your price range."

"Show me anyway," Alex said, thinking about the money he'd been saving.

Jeff patted a slick yellow pedal with a funny hole in it, and picked up a cycling shoe. The underside of the shoe had a cleat mounted to it. Jeff snapped the whole thing onto the pedal. When he twisted the shoe, like a cyclist rotating his ankle outward, it snapped free.

Alex definitely wanted a set. The whole system looked sleek and efficient, and he loved the way a cleat could snap a shoe so perfectly into a pedal. With a set of those, Alex sensed he could truly be one with his bike. He could fly. "Cool!" he exclaimed. "Can I mount those cleats to my regular shoes?"

"You need a shoe like this, with a special sole that's pre-drilled," Jeff explained.

Alex again stared at his feet. *I can never be a real cyclist,* he thought. *My foot can't even fit in a toe clip. And no matter how much I spend, cycling shoes with cleats won't work, either. Without being able to mount cleats to my elevator shoe, the seat will be too high for my left foot or too low for my right foot.* "Just put on some plain platform pedals," he murmured.

To Alex's surprise, his father spoke up. "Our challenge," he explained to Jeff, "is a left shoe that won't fit in a toe clip. And a difference in leg lengths of more than two inches."

Alex liked the way his dad called it a "challenge" instead of a "problem." Even more, he liked that he'd said "our," instead of "his." Alex felt the faintest grin return to his face.

"I wonder if it's possible to install a left crank arm that's 55 millimeters shorter than the right?" his father continued. "Then we could use clipless pedals and cleats?"

Jeff gazed at Alex's mismatched shoes. A flash of understanding crossed his face. "I see what you're getting at, but finding a crank arm that short would be tricky. But there may be a simpler solution."

Jeff excused himself, and ducked into the back room. He soon returned, carrying a small, almost-rectangular piece of metal. It had four threaded holes and some bolts. "This is called a crank arm shortener," he explained. "It bolts on, and then you put the pedal in one of the four holes. Depending on the hole, you can shorten by 24, 41, 59, or 76 millimeters. We usually put them on the back of a tandem, so a kid stoker can spin the pedals easier. We only sell them in pairs, but there's no reason you can't use just one."

Alex was so happy, he wanted to give Jeff a high-five.

Then Alex's father turned the shortener over in his hand, revealing a $115 price sticker. "Let's think about it. I'm not sure he needs to get that serious just yet."

As deflated as Alex felt, he knew his father was right. By the time he got the shortener, and the pedals, and a set of shoes, nearly every dollar of his life's savings would be wiped out. That wasn't even counting the cost of the overhaul. He figured he'd have to pay for that, too.

Alex's father finished filling out the repair ticket, and the two of them were soon back in the car. Alex looked at his feet in silence as they drove, and regretted even thinking about special cycling shoes or pedals. As much as he wanted a set, Alex wanted the hospital bills to stop coming even more. When his dad had been out of his office the other day, Alex had peeked at the latest hospital statement. His parents still owed more than $9,600! How could he even think of spending money on something special, when his family was still in such a hole because of him?

"I feel bad about how much the overhaul is going to be," Alex said. "I'll pay for it from my savings account."

"Consider it part of your birthday present. Okay?"

"Okay," Alex replied. He just hoped his dad wouldn't go overboard and buy the crank shortener and everything else, too. Alex decided he'd feel worse about that than being stuck with plain platform pedals.

NINE

ROB SWISHED THE COFFEE CAN, WATCHING HIS COLNAGO'S old chain slosh around in fresh oil. He'd almost forgotten how much he loved the smell of solvents and lubricants. While Alex looked on, he hung the chain over a dowel and let excess oil drip into the can. "Should be ready in a few minutes," he said.

From the workbench, Meg's brother, David, looked up from a set of ball bearings he'd been examining. "Everything looks fine," he announced. "I'll repack them, and your bottom bracket will be ready to go."

David Sullivan was short and stocky, and had sported a bushy brown beard for as long as Rob had known him. David worked as a mechanic for a local trucking company, and was the extended family's unofficial handyman. Although for safety reasons Rob had wanted a real bike shop to overhaul and adjust Alex's new bike, he figured the Colnago just needed a good tune-up. He'd been grateful when his brother-in-law had encouraged Rob to bring the bike for one of their regular Sunday get-togethers at Meg's father's place. Pete Sullivan had an excellent garage, with almost every tool they needed. The job had been a snap.

"Can you show me how the gear changer works?" Alex asked, squatting at the rear wheel to examine it.

"Sure," Rob replied, relishing the way Alex regarded him as an all-knowing cycling guru. "It's actually called a derailleur, and—,"

"De-RAIL-er," Alex repeated.

"Right. And as I click the shifter lever one notch, watch the way the derailleur moves over. That would take the chain to the next cog in the gear cluster." Then, squatting next to Alex, he pivoted the pulleys a bit and added, "If the chain was on the bike, the derailleur would pivot like this to take up the slack caused from now being on a smaller cog."

Alex's eyes lit up with understanding. "That is so smart!"

Rob glanced at David, and they exchanged a quick smile.

"Did Grandpa Peterson show you this kind of stuff?" Alex asked, still exploring the ways the derailleur moved.

Rob shook his head. He was soon lost in a memory from his own eleventh birthday.

Rob slipped into the garage, and was enveloped in a masculine aroma of oil and gasoline and grease. The melodious voice of Dave Niehaus, calling balls and strikes over a crackling AM radio broadcast, echoed through the building and seemed to harmonize with the pings of wrenches and ratchets. Rob drew closer to the black Plymouth sedan, and spotted his father working under the hood.

"Watcha doing?" Rob asked.

His father froze, staring at the engine block, a cigarette smoldering in his fingers. "Changing the oil," he said at last, his face eerily illuminated by the shop light.

Rob was fascinated by the maze of wires and hoses. He longed to be initiated into the club that knew how everything fit together and what it was all for. "Can I help?" he asked.

His father slowly turned his head, narrowed his eyes, and seemed to be looking straight through him. "I'd really rather you didn't disturb me, Robbie," he said. "This is something I like to do by myself."

Silently, hoping not to irritate the old man any further, Rob crept back outside.

The bicycle chain finished dripping. Rob carefully lifted it from the dowel. He then showed Alex how to thread the chain around the cogs and through the derailleur. Finally, he held the chain's open link together with his fingers.

"If you'll bring the chain tool," he told the boy, "I'll show you how to reconnect it."

* * *

His eyes still shining from helping his dad and Uncle David tune up the Colnago, Alex scampered from the garage to find his Sullivan cousins and Aunt Cathy. Nicholas was a year older than Alex, and Patrick was Ben's age. They and their two little sisters — Frances and Rose — were at Grandpa's almost every Sunday afternoon. For him and Ben, romping with their cousins through the acres of woods and fields and streams surrounding their grandfather's old farmhouse in rural Monroe was the highlight of the week. They usually drove straight there after church, and stayed until after dinner.

Alex jogged across the driveway, savoring the spectacular sunshine and blue skies. *Summer birthdays are the best,* he thought. He found his cousins on the massive lawn behind the house, throwing a Frisbee.

Grandpa Sullivan and Aunt Cathy were watching from some lawn chairs. They looked up as Alex arrived. "Is the bike ready?" his grandfather asked.

"Dad's giving it a test ride. Uncle David's cleaning up," Alex replied.

"Good timing," Aunt Cathy said, glancing at her watch. "The Santuccis should be here any minute."

"They're coming?" Alex asked. *That would make my birthday complete,* he thought. That set of cousins only made it out to Monroe a couple of times a month.

"Wouldn't have missed it," Grandpa Sullivan said. Now re-tired after forty years as a corrections officer at the local penitentiary, he still went running or walking every day. He looked much younger than his eighty-two years.

"Your mother said you wanted hamburgers. Is that right?" Grandpa gestured toward the grill.

"Yeah!" Alex replied. His grandfather's charcoal-grilled burgers were so good, he felt hungry already.

Alex tossed the Frisbee with his cousins and Ben until they heard the rumbling of the Santuccis' big blue passenger van on Grandpa's gravel driveway. A moment later, the six oldest Santucci kids were streaming around the house to greet them. Uncle Paul and Aunt Theresa — who was carrying baby Agatha —

were close behind. Aunt Theresa was taller than his mother, and had darker hair that was always gathered neatly in a bun.

After greeting the Santuccis, Alex's mother immediately took the baby and made a fuss over how big she was getting. Alex marveled at how good his mom was with babies. They always seemed to fit perfectly into her arms, no matter what the baby's size or shape.

Mom hardly ever said anything about it, but Alex knew she wished they could have more kids. He wished he could have another little brother, too. Maybe even a little sister. But cousins were definitely the next best thing. He wondered if he'd ever meet the five cousins from his dad's side of the family, who lived all over the country.

Alex's dad emerged from the house, and warmly greeted Uncle Paul. He was fairly tall and thin, with short dark hair and wire-rim glasses. Alex knew his dad and Uncle Paul had been best friends since college. Soon after Alex's parents began dating, Alex's mom introduced Paul to her sister. Uncle Paul and Aunt Theresa ended up getting married even sooner than Alex's own parents did. Uncle Paul was now at a big law firm, and worked such crazy hours it was hard for their families to get together anytime but here at Grandpa's.

The backyard was soon a chaotic buzz of different conversations. Alex found it overwhelming. He stood back and just watched for a few minutes as everyone else talked.

Alex's cousin, Veronica, jogged over to wish him a happy birthday. "Ronnie," as everyone called her, was two years older than Alex, with dark hair tied back in a single long braid.

"I heard you put the keyboard to good use!" she smiled. "Mom told me about the bike movie. Sounds awesome."

"It's been fun. That keyboard's the best gift I ever got." *Except maybe my new bike,* he thought.

Alex chatted with Ronnie for a moment. Alex liked her because she could be so much of a tomboy — and, at the same time, so much like the big sister he'd never had.

The other cousins soon surrounded them and tried to join the conversation. The Santucci kids were all about two years apart: Joseph was his age, Anthony was roughly Ben's age, and then came Therese, Mary Claire, Vincent, and baby Agatha. Alex's mom was always saying how funny it was that he and Ben ended up looking so English and Irish, while his cousins were such a matched set of dark-haired Italians.

"Did you tell Alex the big news?" Joseph asked. Ronnie shook her head.

"What?" Alex asked.

"Ronnie got a lead in *Merchant of Venice!*"

Alex congratulated his cousin, and then Ronnie explained the details. "Our homeschooling group's performing at the community theater in Shoreline. Last week of July."

"Awesome! We'll have to go," Alex said. He marveled at how his cousin could love being up on stage. She seemed to come completely alive when the spotlight was on her. *No way am I ever performing for an audience,* Alex thought.

Joseph handed Alex a birthday card from the Santuccis. He thanked them, and placed it with the ones from Uncle David's family and his grandfather. He looked forward to opening them after dinner, because his cousins usually picked really funny cards. His grandfather always included a nice personal note.

He'd opened the card from his Peterson grandparents that morning, mostly to get it out of the way. It'd been dull, with generic wording and nothing but "Grandma and Grandpa" written underneath. Alex appreciated the $50 check, but it had all the affection of a rent payment. He doubted his grandparents would even call that evening. That was fine with him.

The cousins began a game of touch football, and Alex was grateful that Ronnie chose him first for her team. He wondered if she realized how much it meant, knowing someone thought Alex was worth choosing.

After they had played for a long time, Alex said he needed to take a break. His knee was starting to ache, but it was about more than that. As the four o'clock hour approached, something was increasingly on his mind. "I'll be back in a little bit," he told the others.

As his cousins and Ben continued their game, Alex went for a walk by himself in the woods. *I need to remember,* he thought, working his way down the trail. He passed an expanse of blackberry bushes, slipping deeper into a stand of towering maples and cedars. He took a deep breath, savoring the aroma of spring leaves and tree pitch.

Alex reached a familiar clearing. He gazed around to get his bearings. He found the large stump he'd been looking for, and then stood staring at it. "I'm alive," he said, kicking it. "You're dead."

Continuing his annual ritual, Alex sat down on the wooden stump. He closed his eyes, collected his thoughts, and treasured these long moments of solitude.

Finally, in the distance, Alex heard his grandfather's dinner bell. Finishing his ritual, he stood and kicked the stump one last time. "I'm alive," he repeated. "You're dead."

Alex ran as fast as he could, back to his grandfather's house and the grilled hamburgers that awaited him.

TEN

ALEX AND HIS FATHER WAVED AS THE LAST STP RIDERS rolled out of the Husky Stadium parking lot. "Seen enough?" his dad asked.

"I think so," Alex replied. The two of them began their long walk back to the station wagon.

Alex was overwhelmed by everything he'd seen. He and his father had arrived at the start line at 4:30am, long before dawn. Alex had never set his alarm so early. He'd definitely never seen so many people in one place at such a weird hour of the day. As they'd strolled through the parking lot, Alex had felt a buzz of energy everywhere. The sheer number of cyclists dazzled him, and they'd been so close he could touch them. The way the riders had spoken to each other, it'd had seemed like a real brotherhood.

At 4:45 sharp, someone from Cascade had started giving instructions over a loudspeaker. Then they'd sounded an air horn. All around him, Alex had heard cleats snapping into pedals and riders calling to each other. Then the sound of many hundreds of tires rolling on pavement.

At that moment, Alex had been certain he would do this ride someday. He didn't know when. He didn't know how. But he would do it. As soon as possible.

Wave after wave of cyclists had shown up and then departed this way. Alex noticed that as the morning had worn on, the types of bikes and riders had changed. The earlier waves had been filled with very serious-looking cyclists and very expensive-looking bikes. He knew these must be the one-day riders. The later waves had gotten more casual and more talkative, and many riders even had bizarre decorations on their bikes and helmets. Alex figured these were two-day riders.

I want to be a one-day rider, he decided. *I want to be as serious as I can possibly be.*

As the morning had progressed, Alex had also noticed more children on tandems with their parents. He assumed most were doing the two-day ride, but some looked like one-day riders. He wondered what it'd be like to ride a tandem to Portland. He envied those kids who were getting to do it today.

Alex and his father reached their car, and began driving toward Green Lake. "What'd you think of those riders you saw this morning?" Dad asked.

"Amazing! Totally better than the video," Alex replied.

"Why's that?"

"Because I could see everything close up. I could see all the details of their bikes. And their clothes and stuff."

Alex had been looking especially closely at the riders' shoes and pedals. After days of thinking, he'd put together a plan: today, when they picked up his bike, he'd buy the crank shortener. He would use an old set of pedals, with toe clips and straps, from his dad's parts bin. When he went riding, he would wear the standard left sneaker that matched his right shoe (which, after the prank at school, he'd made sure to keep), with a 12mm sole insert. With his left pedal in the shortener's 41mm hole, his leg lengths would be effectively equal. In the meantime, he would look for ways to earn enough money to buy some clipless pedals and cycling shoes with cleats.

His father had cautioned him not to over-commit to cycling before he was sure he really enjoyed it. Alex considered waiting before investing in a crank shortener. In the end, he decided he wouldn't really know if he enjoyed cycling unless his bike was set up the right way. He was just glad his father agreed to let him find out. His dad even phoned ahead and instructed the shop to install it for them. As Alex had counted out the money to pay his dad, he'd hoped he was making the right decision.

They got something to eat, and arrived at Gregg's just as the shop opened. The clerk soon found Alex's bike in the back. Alex was astonished at how much nicer it looked. He could hardly wait to take it for a test ride. His dad had even brought the Colnago, so they could ride together.

His father paid for the repairs, and then led Alex deeper into the shop. "Aren't we going to ride?" Alex asked.

"We need a few things for you first. And you're not going to look at price tags, okay?"

"Okay," Alex replied, with a sheepish grin.

His father found a sales clerk. The young man had short but spiky hair, and a nametag reading "Josh." After chatting for a moment, his dad started giving Josh instructions. "First, we need a good helmet."

Josh led them to a display of helmets, and helped find a blue one that fit Alex's head perfectly. It looked and felt a hundred times better than the dorky one he'd had.

"Now, gloves," his dad said, carrying the helmet.

"Why do I need gloves?" Alex asked.

"In case you fall," his dad explained.

"And to absorb road shock as you ride," Josh added, leading the way to another rack. The gloves were padded, and had the fingers cut out. Alex found some that fit.

"Anything else?" the clerk asked.

Before Alex could say, "That's plenty," his father spoke up. "We need shorts."

Alex tried to object. His father gave him a stern look, and shook his head. Reluctantly, Alex followed his dad and Josh to a rack with hundreds of pairs of shorts. Most were black, and some had mixed colors and different designs. All of them looked sleek and fast.

"Let's start with plain black," his dad said.

Josh picked out a few pairs, in different sizes. "I'm not sure which will fit you best, but I'll show you where the dressing room is."

Alex and his dad followed Josh across the store, and thanked him for his help. "Let me know if there's anything else you need," Josh told them. He then went off to help another customer.

Once Josh was out of earshot, Alex said, "I don't wear shorts out of the house."

"I know. But jeans will catch in your chain. Cycling tights are the only other option. That would be really uncomfortable in the summer."

Alex frowned and folded his arms. "You know my thighs are all scrawny and scarred. My kneecaps don't line up. It's all anybody looks at."

"The more you ride, the bigger your thigh muscles will get. And no one'll notice your kneecaps when you're riding."

"I suppose," Alex muttered. "But why do I have to wear shorts now?"

"Do you want to get serious about cycling or not? If you do, you need cycling shorts. And if you ride a lot with me, I bet your legs will look good enough to wear your uniform shorts when school starts."

Alex liked that idea, and allowed the faintest smile. "Okay," he agreed.

Once inside the dressing room, Alex removed his jeans and pulled on one pair of shorts. It was too big. He tried another, and it seemed just right. He liked the way it fit snuggly around his waist and thighs, and he imagined the padded crotch would feel good on long rides. The shorts were even long enough to hide the scar on his right thigh. He pulled the gloves onto his hands, put his shoes back on, and snapped the helmet onto his head.

Before opening the dressing room door, he caught sight of himself in the full-length mirror. Alex gasped in surprise. *Who's that boy?* he wondered. *Oh my goodness! It's me. Me. I'm a cyclist. A real cyclist. I'm an athlete!* His heart raced with excitement.

"What do you think?" he asked, beaming as he emerged from the dressing room.

"Perfect!" his dad replied. "How does it feel?"

Alex thought for a moment. "Like I can ride around Green Lake ten times in a row!"

His father paid for Alex's new clothes, and then they walked his bike out to the car. While Dad got his own bike set up, Alex swapped his elevator shoe for the standard sneaker. They then walked their bikes across Green Lake Way, to the park.

Alex's dad helped him mount the bike and tighten the toe straps on his pedals. Alex wondered how long it'd take to learn how to do that himself.

He balanced against a light pole as his dad mounted his own bike. Finally, the two of them pedaled past soccer and baseball fields toward the Green Lake bike path.

When they reached the lake, Alex and his father began riding counterclockwise on the outer portion of the path. Alex tested out all his gears, amazed at how perfectly silky everything functioned. They cleared the main parking lot and tennis courts, and followed the gentle curves that hugged the lake's amoeba-like shape. They eventually came to a straightaway, and were able to pick up some speed before getting stuck behind a rollerblader.

Once they passed the rollerblader, they accelerated to a comfortable cruising speed. They eventually passed the Bathhouse Theater, a really cool old brick building where they'd once seen Ronnie perform in *As You Like It*. Alex wondered if the Santuccis would be at Grandpa's tomorrow. He could hardly wait to tell his cousins all about his new bike.

As they continued working their way past Duck Island and then around the rest of Green Lake, Alex decided he liked riding with toe straps. They made him feel much more connected to the bike. He told his father the crank shortener worked perfectly. With the left pedal in the 41mm hole, both of his legs snapped the bottom of their stroke just right. "And my joints don't hurt, like when I'm running," he added.

The two of them rode along, side by side. Alex's face was one big smile. He wished the path would go on forever.

As they neared the end of their second trip around the lake, his dad got an interesting look on his face. "I've been thinking," his father said at last, and Alex listened more attentively.

"It'd be a shame to have a bike this nice, and just ride it around the block or to school. A bike like yours needs to be ridden on the open road. Or the Sammamish River Trail. Does that sound fun?"

Alex nodded, and tried not to look too eager.

"But your mother and I have been talking, and we think you're still a little too young to be riding like that on your own. You need experience riding in traffic. You need to learn to be aware of what's around you. Does that make sense?"

"Sure." They began their third trip around the lake.

"So, here's what I propose: if you want to ride this summer, I'll ride with you."

Alex studied his father's face for any signs of indecision or reservations. "You'll ride with me? Anywhere I want to go?"

"Anywhere. No matter how many miles you want to ride. If you can do it, I can do it. Assuming, of course, I'm not traveling. Like doing those focus groups in Boise this coming week."

"Right," Alex agreed, then focused on the trail ahead. He imagined himself riding his new bike along the Sammamish River, or Lake Washington. He imagined himself knowing which gears to use when, and when he should place his hands on which parts of the handlebars. He could already hear the music playing in his head, as he and his father soared along an open country road.

"That'd be awesome," he said at last. There was really no other word. *Awesome*. Still, Alex was curious about something. "How come you want to start riding again?"

"Because you do," his dad replied.

Alex thought for a moment. "Does this make us a team? A cycling team?"

His dad's eyes lit up. "Sure. We can be Team Peterson."

Team Peterson. Alex suddenly felt very important. He resolved to do everything he could to be a good cyclist and keep up with his dad.

Rob decided to let Alex keep circling the lake until the boy had enough. His son's smile, and the spark in his eyes, reminded Rob of the first time he'd taken his Peugeot for a ride. He'd been thirteen, and had finally finished piecing the thing together. Nothing matched. But it was a road bike, and it had ten speeds, and it was *his.* The world had opened, with the freedom to go anywhere. The only limits were his own curiosity and effort.

Now, watching his son, Rob felt the circle was complete. He'd connected with his son's passion. He'd even encouraged it. That in itself had been worth getting the Colnago out of mothballs. He kicked himself for having dragged his feet.

No one in Rob's family had even tried to understand his fascination with cycling, let alone connect with it. Only the other cyclists he'd met seemed to appreciate his obsession. He'd found himself increasingly spending time on the road, rather than with his family.

Rob's father, Jack, had run his own business piloting float planes out of Kenmore Air Harbor on Lake Washington. Most of his passengers were tourists taking sightseeing flights, or sportsmen traveling to remote lakes. He and Rob's mother, Fiona, would often fly off by themselves for weekend getaways. The kids would be left behind to squabble with each other and whichever older relative had been drafted to stay with them. The message Rob and his siblings had gotten was: the parents are a team, and the rest of you need to learn to fend for yourselves. His brother and sister, being twins, formed a natural team of their own. That left Rob as truly the odd one out.

"*Can you help me start peeling this banana?*" he asked his twelve-year-old sister, Jennifer, the time his parents had flown off to Lake Chelan.

"*You mean you're such an idiot, you can't even start a banana?*" she replied.

"*Jennifer and I could do that when we were your age, easy,*" Michael added.

"*I bet almost every seven-year-old can,*" Jennifer said.

Rob felt rage rising within him, but he knew better than to cry. "*I can only start peeling ripe bananas,*" he insisted. "*Not green bananas.*"

"*Aww. Wobbie can't stawt gween bananas,*" Jennifer said, mocking the way he'd pronounced the words.

"*Wobbie can only stawt wipe bananas,*" Michael taunted.

"*Stop! You know it's not my fault I can't say my Rs!*"

"*Or anybody else's Rs,*" Michael snickered, just before their grandmother burst into the kitchen.

"*No!*" Rob shouted, tears rolling down his cheeks.

"*Robert William Peterson, I am so sick and tired of your outbursts!*" Grandma scolded.

"*But—*" he tried to explain, as his twin siblings smiled at each other behind Grandma's back.

"*Silence! Go to your room until I say you can come out.*"

Rob let the bitterness fester inside him for the next two days. Then, when his parents finally returned from Lake Chelan, he tried to tell them what his siblings had done. Even if Grandma wouldn't listen, he figured Mom and Dad would have to.

Instead, his mother replied, "Robbie, nobody likes a tattletale."

"*And if you'd just work harder and learn to talk right, they wouldn't do it,*" his father added.

Rob couldn't help noticing the way his father had pronounced the word "right" with the slightest, almost-imperceptible hint of a "w" at the beginning. Rob then whirled and retreated to the privacy of his own room. Where he could sob and tell his stuffed animals how much he wished he could live anywhere but here.

What Rob had always found so attractive about Meg and her family was that they seemed "in it together." They *liked* seeing each other, and doing things as a family, even now. Rob thought of David Sullivan as more his brother than Michael ever had been. He thought of Cathy Sullivan and Theresa Santucci as more his sisters than Jennifer ever could be.

With Michael now in Denver, and Jennifer in Albuquerque, and his parents enjoying their retirement in Costa Rica, they seldom even saw each other. And, especially since he and Meg had moved back to Seattle, Rob didn't really care. Sunday afternoons at Pete Sullivan's in Monroe beat anything he could imagine doing with his own family. Following his own family on Facebook was plenty.

Sometime during their sixth loop around Green Lake, Alex spoke up. "This is awesome, Dad. Thanks for everything."

"I'm glad you like it."

"I really do like the stuff you got me," Alex continued. "But I just wanted to say that this is enough. You don't have to spend any more on me."

Rob had been wondering when that would be coming. "We won't spend too much. And I have another proposal: every hundred miles you log, we'll go on eBay and look for a good deal on something for you. Maybe shoes. Clipless pedals. A jersey. It's a way you could earn it, while making sure you're really interested in cycling."

Alex seemed to be turning this proposal over in his head. "I like being able to earn things, and I do want shoes and pedals. But you really shouldn't spend so much on me."

"We get baseball and soccer equipment for Ben," Rob pointed out. "Now we can finally get something for you."

"But you already pay for my organ lessons. And my shoes. That costs a lot more than Ben's sports."

Rob was puzzled, and the two of them rode in silence for a while. He wished he could get inside his son's head, and understand what was driving Alex's obsession with savings. He did appreciate Alex's frugality, and that his son wasn't constantly asking for things the way Ben was. His business had remained slower than in past years, and they were still depending on Meg's income to get the bills paid. There'd again been no question of a family vacation that summer. Or baseball camp for Ben. Or much of anything else. Even finding the money for today's shopping had been a real stretch. It wouldn't be long before they'd have to come up with $750 each month to cover the boys' tuition.

Alex finally said, "I'm ready to go home if you are."

"Sounds good to me."

As Gregg's came into sight, Rob thought back to the STP start line that morning. He'd gotten a tremendous charge of excitement, watching the riders depart. Part of him had wanted to throw everything to the wind, jump on a bike, and ride along to Portland with them. He'd even been stealing glances at his watch all day, thinking about where he'd now be on the route.

Rob knew he wasn't in shape to ride today, but a different question nagged at him: *What's keeping me from riding STP next summer? My work schedule is flexible. Training won't take me away from the family, if I ride with Alex.*

Rob decided he just honestly didn't want it badly enough. He knew firsthand how much it "cost" to prepare for a double century, and he was quite happy not paying that expense. He liked not having a training schedule. He liked staying up late. Riding STP would require an enormous amount of effort and training time — and a lot less staying up in front of a television. *As much fun as STP looked, it just isn't worth all that.*

ELEVEN

As MEG GOT THE BOYS READY FOR BED, ROB MADE HIMSELF comfortable on their front porch with a glass of wine. All around the neighborhood, sounds of children playing faded with the evening twilight. He figured the last of the one-day riders were streaming to the finish line in Portland. Rob almost wished he could be there to feel their triumph. But not their pain.

That morning, Rob had seen in Alex an eerie reflection of his own boyhood self. He still clearly remembered the first time he'd visited Gregg's. He'd been twelve, and he'd watched the Tour de France on *Wide World of Sports* several summers in a row. Whenever Rob had daydreamed, it'd been of Eddy Merckx. He longed for the day he could have a bike like Eddy's De Rosa — and start high school, so he could study French.

As the rest of his family had enjoyed a summer afternoon picnic at Green Lake, Rob had spotted his chance. He'd slipped across the street to Gregg's, to get a better look at "real" bicycles. Like Alex, Rob had drooled and dreamed as he'd browsed every display in the store. But Rob's excitement was to be shorter-lived than his son's.

"I just don't get it," his father said, as Rob rejoined their picnic. "Why does anybody need a bike with ten speeds?

"Ten speeds are so fast. And you can go so far. And you can climb any hill," Rob replied, his eyes still shining.

"That's what cars are for," his mother said.

"And planes," his father added.

Rob resolved to let nothing dampen his resolve to find or build his own road bike. "All I want for Christmas is help buying components," he said. "Or cycling clothes. Like you've always gotten softball stuff for Jennifer. Or football stuff for Michael."

"Sorry, Robbie," Michael cut in, putting down his fried chicken. *"Football's a real sport. Cycling's just a bunch of sissies pedaling around in tight black shorts."*

"Yeah," his sister added, between bites of watermelon, *"when the school starts a cycling team, with uniforms and a coach, we'll think about calling it a real sport."*

"And treating it like one," his father said, not even trying to hide his disdain. *"No son of mine will ride around in tight black shorts."*

The front door creaked open, and Meg stepped onto the porch. "I don't know what you did to work Alex so hard today. I've never seen him go to sleep so fast."

Meg joined him on the wicker loveseat, and Rob filled her glass with wine. "He'd have ridden the wheels off that bike if I'd let him," he told her.

"Will you be able to ride much this week?"

"Tomorrow and Monday," Rob replied, taking a sip of wine. "Then I'm in Boise and Helena, doing Decision Strategies groups for Frank. Home Thursday afternoon."

"You mean Frank didn't want to go to Boise or Helena?" Meg smiled.

"Believe it or not, some people actually like staying in Los Angeles," Rob chuckled.

Meg cuddled closer and gave Rob a quick kiss. "I'm glad I didn't marry any of those people."

Rob put his arm around Meg's shoulder and smiled. "I didn't say I don't like Los Angeles. I'd just take Seattle — or Boise, or Helena — over California any day of the week."

The two of them cuddled in silence for a long moment, watching the last of the twilight disappear.

"How'd it go at Women's Resources?" Rob asked at last.

"Had about a dozen people come in," Meg replied, with palpable reticence.

"Anything interesting happen?"

"I don't know," she said, frowning and rubbing the edge of her wine glass. "Three women in a row were giving babies up for adoption."

"All spoken for, I assume?"

"Long ago."

Meg took a sip of wine and thought for a moment before continuing. "I still wish we could pursue it, but I just don't see how. What with my needing to work…"

"And the crazy cost," Rob added.

"Not to mention the age gap we'd now have with Ben. Or that neither of us is exactly a spring chicken."

Rob cuddled her and murmured, "I guess our window's about closed."

"I just tell myself that this is the family God wants us to have," Meg said. "For whatever reason, we're not supposed to have the third kid that your folks or mine got to have."

After a long silence, Meg cuddled closer, kissed him, and whispered, "I wish I could have a dozen more babies who look just like you."

"Thanks," Rob smiled. Then he scooped her up and headed into the house to call it a night.

TWELVE

ALEX TREMBLED WITH EXCITEMENT AS HE PULLED ON THE yellow cycling shoes. Yes, they were badly scuffed. Alex couldn't have cared less. He'd paid the $20 for them himself, after his dad spotted the auction on eBay. They included cleats, which fit the pedals he'd earned two weeks ago. Alex hadn't been able to stop thinking about trying them out.

After some work, his father got the cleats adjusted just right. While leaning against his mom's car, Alex struggled to snap his feet into the new pedals. Eventually, his dad had to hold Alex's foot and guide the cleat at the proper angle. Even then, Alex had trouble making the cleat engage.

Both cleats finally snapped in place. Dad made him twist his ankles outward and unsnap from the pedals. Alex then had to practice the whole process again. And again. And again. "It's got to be automatic," his father explained.

Alex thought they'd never get on the road.

Once the two of them finally pedaled down the driveway and onto their street, Alex's frustrations vanished. He'd liked toe clips, but cleats felt ten times better. For starters, the annoying straps were gone. Then, as he made his first dozen or so powerful strokes, his feet felt much more securely connected to the pedals. "It's like the bike is part of me!" he exclaimed.

His father cautioned him to take it slowly, and insisted they circle the block several times before going anywhere else. "Why can't we ride the trail?" Alex asked.

"Too many stop signs between us and it."

"So?" Alex asked.

"So, why don't you come to a stop right up ahead?" his dad challenged him. "Then uncleat."

Alex slowed his bike, and tried to twist his left foot free. Despite all the practice, he couldn't unsnap it in time. The bike slowly toppled over, sending Alex sprawling on the pavement. Only when he landed did his feet pop out of the pedals.

His dad stopped to look at him. "Good thing we weren't at an intersection. You okay?"

Alex's left knee and calf were scraped, but his padded gloves had taken the worst of the fall. "Yeah," he muttered. His pride hurt more than any part of his body.

They spent the next 20 minutes or so practicing coming to a stop and uncleating. At last, Alex's father declared him ready to ride across town.

Although Alex had a couple of close calls at intersections, they eventually reached the trail and began cruising toward Woodinville. He savored the sun and a gentle breeze on his face. Alex wondered if they could begin extending the ten-mile rides they'd been taking so far. Pretty much the only days they hadn't ridden were when it'd rained, or when his father had been traveling. He'd managed to earn the pedals in no time, and was now within 25 miles of earning his first jersey. With cleats helping him, Alex felt there was no limit to how far he could go.

"How are the cleats?" Dad asked, as he pulled alongside.

"Definitely worth the investment."

The two of them cruised along, side by side. Alex wished the trail could go on forever. "How could you have ever stopped doing this?" he asked at last.

"I had good reasons." Then, after pedaling in silence for a moment, his father added, "I'm just glad I got an even better reason to come out of retirement."

Alex wanted to ask more about these "reasons," but his father seemed strangely far away. Whatever Dad's thoughts were, Alex decided it'd be best to leave him alone with them.

THIRTEEN

November 20, 1999

ROB SAT DOUBLED OVER ON THE SIDE OF JUBILEE PASS ROAD, northwest of Shoshone. Dirty sand, gravel, and scrub brush stretched as far as he could see, in every direction. After completing 130 miles of the Death Valley Double Century, stomach cramps had driven him off his bicycle again. *How can I climb Jubilee Pass, when I can't even stand straight?* He couldn't imagine summoning the energy to complete another seven miles, let alone the seventy miles to the finish.

He heard the sound of slowing bicycle tires, and then a woman's voice asking, "Are you okay?" Rob looked up. He recognized the speaker, who was seated on a tandem with her boyfriend. Rob had ridden with them earlier in the day.

Too ashamed to admit he was almost ready to flag down a support vehicle and beg for a ride, Rob forced a smile. "I'm sure I will be," he said, waving them on.

The tandem pulled away, and became a speck on the horizon. But Rob soon discovered how far sound can travel in clear desert air. As he continued squatting on the side of the road, praying his cramps would subside, Rob heard one of the tandem riders say, "You know, he really isn't a very good cyclist."

Indignation swept over him. If he'd been able, Rob would have jumped to his feet and shouted: *I am too a good cyclist! And I have a great bike! This is my nineteenth double! Hear that? Nineteen! How many have you done? I just can't ... manage ... these rides like I used to.*

Once Ben had arrived that April, and the family had moved to a location from which bicycle commuting was impossible, Rob had found he simply could not train. He couldn't ride during the week, before or after his long freeway commute to Decision Strategies. And as for extended rides on the weekends ... with two little boys under the age of two, and a wife recovering from an emergency C-section, he had to decide: time with a family that very much needed him, or time on a bike that he very much enjoyed. He knew he'd made the right choice by cutting his training to virtually zero.

Rob had known, weeks ago, that he never should have started the Death Valley ride. Even so, in Rob's mind, he was still the ultramarathoner he'd always been. That, and he hated seeing his nonrefundable entry fee and hotel deposit — sent in when he believed he could get into shape — go to waste. In Rob's mind, he could complete his twentieth double using will power alone.

Still smarting from the tandem team's insult, Rob summoned his reserves. Somehow, he managed to climb back on his Colnago. One at a time, he forced the pedals up and down. Eventually, he crested Jubilee Pass. Then, despite bone-jarring pavement and hands so numb he couldn't work the brakes, he survived the descent of the other side.

Sleek riders continued passing Rob with ease. Rob overtook almost no one. The sun began settling into the horizon, casting long shadows over the sparkling desert sands.

With miles of the world's loneliest pavement all to himself, Rob's thoughts danced and drifted. *How long to the rest stop at Ashford Mill, where I left my lights and warm clothes on the way out? If I drink a little more water now, and eat another apple slice, will I be able to make it there before it gets too dark? How cold is it going to get tonight? Will my lights last to the finish? I wonder if Meg has put the boys to bed back at home yet. Could I ever explain to them why I'm going through the motions of pretending I can still come out here and do this ride? Can I even explain it to myself?*

Rob realized he'd reached his own version of the alcoholic's "rock bottom." There was no denying he had a compulsion. He couldn't just ride "a little." But there was no way he could ride another double century, either. Not if he loved his family.

A complete break with *something* now seemed the only option. *Because this simply isn't working.* As pedal stroke followed pedal stroke, Rob's heart increasingly filled with love for his family — and disdain for the bicycle beneath him.

He did manage to roll across the finish line at Furnace Creek, in pitch darkness, more than sixteen hours after the start. Then, when Rob arrived home in Los Angeles the next day, he hung his Colnago on hooks in the garage. He swore he'd never ride it again.

FOURTEEN

August 30, 2008

EVERYWHERE THE BOYS LOOKED, ENORMOUS CLUSTERS OF blackberries practically begged to be picked. Alex, Ben and Connor sampled a few for themselves, savoring the sweet purple juice as it ran over their tongues and dribbled from the sides of their mouths. "This is a great spot," Connor said, stuffing another few berries in his mouth.

"My dad and I found it a few weeks ago, on one of our rides," Alex replied, spitting out tiny seeds. It was a vacant lot, overflowing with vines, on a lightly traveled road. One look at all the ripening fruit, and they'd known to keep an eye on it. "And we've scouted four more places, where we can pick next week."

"Awesome," Connor said.

The boys heard the thumping of plastic buckets approach. "Time to get to work," Alex's dad told them, setting out four large pails.

All three boys began eagerly filling buckets. Alex's dad paid five dollars for every five gallon bucket. The boys had few other ways to earn that kind of money. Alex and Ben had spent hours picking berries that Sunday with their cousins at their grandfather's place. Alex's father had already begun making his first batch of wine. They were hoping to get enough today to start a second batch.

"I wish my dad was around more, to go riding and do stuff like this," Connor said, grabbing a cluster of berries.

"He's working on a Saturday?" Alex asked. Connor's father was an electrician at a big printing plant outside Bothell, where he kept all the machinery running smoothly. He'd always had weekends off.

"They've cut so many people at his plant, they're making everyone else work crazy hours."

"That doesn't seem fair," Alex frowned. He reached for another bunch of blackberries.

"Dad's just happy his job didn't get cut," Connor shrugged.

The summer had gone by in a flash. None of the boys could believe the new school year was almost upon them. For Alex, August had been a blur of bike rides with his father. They'd continued going out several times a week, exploring back roads and traveling up and down the Sammamish River Trail. Even though most of their rides had been on flat and easy routes, Alex felt like he was becoming a real cyclist. Each time he snapped his cleats into the pedals, he grew more sure of it.

Just in the last few days, the jersey he'd earned for logging his 200th mile had arrived. He'd loved sitting down with his dad and finding a good deal on just the right one on eBay. He'd settled on a yellow and black jersey, with something printed in French across the front. He now proudly wore it on nearly every ride. Often, he carried an apple in one of the jersey's three back pockets, so he could practice eating as he rode. *Just like I'll have to do on STP*, he thought.

While browsing eBay, he and his father were surprised to see the prices some people were paying for vintage cycling components. They began digging Dad's old stuff out of boxes in the basement, and cashing in. Dad held these proceeds in a PayPal slush fund, to finance the rewards Alex earned every hundred miles.

When Alex wasn't cycling with his dad, or buried in a book, or watching the Mariners with Ben and Connor, he'd spent long hours playing the church organ or his keyboard. Mrs. Rossi had cut back his lessons to every other week for the summer. That gave Alex more time to play music just for fun. He was also glad to be saving his parents some money. He just wished Mrs. Rossi would stop asking him to think about playing in recitals. Or at the school's Christmas concert this winter.

Berry after berry plopped into Alex's bucket. He soon realized he'd filled it. "Ready for the next one," he told his dad.

Connor's bucket was also nearly full, so Alex's father hauled both of them to the station wagon. He returned with two empty buckets. "Nice work," he told them, then checked on Ben's progress. The younger boy looked like he'd been daydreaming, and had only filled half his pail.

Alex and Connor soon got back in the zone, dropping berries in their buckets as they chatted and joked. The longer the boys scoured bushes for berries, the more Alex reveled in how *free* he felt. He loved every moment of the time he got to do this. As they lugged their overflowing buckets back to the station wagon for the last time, Alex found himself whistling with joy.

He only wished he could take the final glorious week of vacation and freeze it, so he could hold onto it forever. This summer had been a thousand times better than being at school.

And a million times better than the summer three years back.

FIFTEEN

June 29, 2005

WITH ALL HIS COUSINS GATHERED AT HIS GRANDPARENTS' house, Alex's eighth birthday felt more like a Sunday than a Wednesday. That, in his mind, made the celebration even more special. His mother had left her part-time paralegal job for the summer. Alex loved having her around all day, and being able to do things like this on weekdays.

His grandmother was regaining strength after a recent round of chemotherapy. She greeted Alex with more enthusiasm than he'd seen in a long time. She made a big fuss over how tall he was getting. "You'll be passing me, soon!" she laughed, giving him a hug. The test results hadn't come back yet, and everyone was praying that her cancer had gone into remission.

His grandfather put together a big midday cookout, with grilled chicken and potato salad. As they talked and ate, Alex couldn't imagine a more perfect lunch.

The kids trooped off to the woods to play, and summer seemed to stretch ahead with endless possibilities. Ronnie was looking forward to her first speaking role in a play. Nicholas was getting ready for a week of soccer camp on Whidbey Island. Anthony was starting an art class. Ben and Alex talked about going to Disneyland in August. Their house was about to get a big makeover, with new windows and carpets and totally re-done kitchen appliances. Their folks had said maybe they'd even be moving to a bigger place.

Once they were deep in the woods, the kids decided to play hide and seek. This part of Grandma and Grandpa's property was the perfect place for it, and Alex found a hollow tree that allowed him to escape detection for several rounds in a row.

After one round ended with an especially intense run back to "base," all the cousins took some time to catch their breath. They panted and talked for a few minutes, and then Joseph seemed to remember something. "Guess what I did on Saturday?" he asked.

"What?" several cousins, including Alex and Ben, asked.

"I climbed a tree behind our house and broke the top off," he announced, his brown eyes sparkling. "It was kind of scary, and the tree was swaying. But it was really cool. I've never seen a view like that!"

Alex gazed up at the cedars surrounding them. "A tree this big?"

"Bigger," Ronnie said.

Alex's heart raced at the idea of being so high in the forest. He imagined showing off the tree top at school, like a trophy. All the other boys would look at him with awe. "Think I could do it?"

"You're lighter than I am," Joseph said. "If I can do it, you can do it."

"You'll get in trouble," Ben warned him. "Mom said no climbing trees."

"Only way she'll know is if somebody tells her," Alex replied, and all the cousins glared at Ben.

"Okay. I won't nark," Ben promised.

Alex knew he shouldn't be doing this. Still, he took a deep breath and strode to the nearest cedar. His cousins began cheering. Alex smiled.

Soon, Alex was higher than he'd ever been in a tree. Feeling a little nervous, he looked down to the clearing. Ronnie was smiling and giving him a thumbs-up. Alex swallowed hard and kept climbing.

Up, up, up, he went. He made sure he stepped at the base of each branch, where it was strongest. Before long, he was high in the forest. He was even above many of the other trees. The entire snow-capped Cascade mountain range spread out on the horizon, beyond the Skykomish river valley. *What an amazing view,* he thought. *I can see Grandma and Grandpa's whole property from here. I should do this again.*

As he approached the top, a breeze began rustling the branches. The tree swayed in the wind, and Alex trembled with fear. He clung to the trunk for dear life.

When the wind died, Alex slowly began climbing again. Ten feet to go. Eight. Six. Four. *Is the wind picking up again? I'd better hurry.* He reached as high as he could, bent the top, and felt it snap. *Yes! I did it!*

Alex tossed the top toward the clearing. It caught on a branch. He figured he'd try wiggling it loose on his way past.

Alex began descending, but the wind was soon gusting even harder than before. He stopped and waited. And waited. The treetop began swaying farther. And farther. He had a really bad sense that the tree had swayed too far to come back.

"Hellllllp!" Alex cried. An instant later, he heard and felt a sickening snap from deep inside the trunk.

Down, down, down he tumbled through the cedar canopy. He grasped wildly for something to break his fall, but he was moving too fast to get a grip on anything. Branch after branch whipped him in the face and hands. Alex continued slipping, and continued falling.

Finally, as the ground was rushing up to swallow him, Alex managed to hook his hands on one of the last large branches. He'd been falling horizontally. Now his legs swung downwards with the momentum. He felt them smash into another huge limb below, and his thighs exploded in pain. Losing his grip on the branch, Alex tumbled backwards. He hit the ground hard, flat on his back. Everything went dark.

Alex opened his eyes and stared up at the cedars. His legs were searing in more pain than he'd ever thought possible. He couldn't even begin to sit up without feeling like someone was jabbing a million hot needles into his thighs. He wanted to scream, but he couldn't draw a breath. His lungs seemed squeezed empty. He began to panic for air.

At last, he caught the breath that'd been knocked out. Alex let loose the most blood-curdling scream he'd ever made.

Ben was crying and yelling something about legs not supposed to be bending like that. Some cousins were running toward the house and hollering for parents. He wanted more than anything to get up and run far away from the pain. But one of his cousins (was it Ronnie? Nicholas?) told him not to move. His spine might be broken.

Everything after that was a blur. His mother crying and trying to comfort him ... sirens ... paramedics clamping a heavy plastic collar around his head and neck ... someone cutting his pants and moving and immobilizing his legs ... screaming in even more unbelievable pain ... strapped to a board ... the inside of an ambulance ... injections that finally made his legs hurt a little less ... sirens ... his mother trying to tell him everything would be okay ... a hospital ... a doctor ... more doctors ... poking ... the rest of his clothes being cut off ... x-rays ... rolling through hospital corridors, flat on his back, able to see nothing but his parents' worried faces and the ceilings ... a room with everyone bundled in paper masks and green gowns and caps, like Halloween costumes ... a plastic mask fitted over his mouth and nose ... a funny smell ... someone asking him to close his eyes and count backward from ten ... making it to 'seven' ...

And then, instantaneously, Alex was in a different room. He was flat on his back in some kind of hospital bed. There was a tube sticking out of his arm, and his legs didn't hurt. When he tried to look around, it felt like someone had smashed the back of his head with a baseball bat.

He groaned, and a moment later a nurse explained he was in "recovery." She said his legs were back together. His head was only hurting because of the anesthesia. They'd soon take him to his own room. His parents would be there.

Alex tried to nod. Even that small movement made his head feel like it was ripping open.

The next time he awakened, he was in a smaller room. In the darkness, he recognized his mother dozing in a chair next to his bed. A glowing digital clock read 2:48. He wondered if it was the middle of the night or the next afternoon. *Either way, it's not my birthday anymore. This was the worst birthday of my life.*

His head didn't hurt so badly now, but his legs were starting to. His right thigh was bandaged. His entire left leg was covered in a cast. He felt completely immobilized.

"Oh, Alex!" his mother whispered. A moment later, she was smoothing his sandy-blond hair. "Mommy's here, and will be here all night."

He wondered how she'd known he was awake. "I'm very sorry I climbed the tree," he whispered.

"Shhhh," she replied. "We're just glad you're okay."

"My legs are okay?"

"The doctor will explain it in the morning. All right?"

Alex nodded.

"Do your legs hurt?" she asked.

"Starting to. Maybe that's why I woke up."

Alex's mother showed him a small white cylinder with a button on the end of it. The cylinder had a wire that snaked out of sight under his bed. "This is called a P-C-A," she explained. "Press this button, and it releases morphine into your body. The morphine makes the pain go away. You just press the button again whenever it wears off. Okay?"

Alex nodded and pressed the button. "How long does it take to work?" he asked.

"A minute or two. If one click isn't enough, keep clicking every few minutes. It won't let you overdose."

"Thanks," he replied.

His mother kissed him and said, "We love you very much."

"I love you, too," Alex murmured, but he was already feeling himself floating away.

When he awakened, the room was full of sunshine. Alex felt an overwhelming urge to jump from bed and go outside.

Then, an instant later, he remembered where he was. His thigh was getting itchy, but he couldn't reach a finger far enough inside the cast to scratch it. His legs were aching again, so he clicked the PCA button. He found the controls for the bed, and adjusted it so he could sit up.

As he waited for the morphine to kick in, he got his first good look at himself. They'd dressed him in a skimpy gown that seemed to tie in the back. He wondered if his mom would bring him a normal shirt. The white plaster cast covered all of his left leg, from ankle to hip. He wondered how long he'd have to wear it, and why his right thigh was only bandaged.

The hospital room was clean and neat, with wood floors and lots of interesting equipment. An empty bed stood nearby, and a curtain could be pulled between them. He wondered if he'd be getting a roommate. Through the open door, he could hear the hospital staff bustling around and talking to each other.

Alex noticed they'd put a tray of food next to his bed, on a long-armed table. Suddenly, he realized how hungry he was. Alex realized he could swivel the table over his bed so he could eat. The tray had fruit, a bowl of raisin bran, a small carton of milk, and orange juice.

As Alex began eating, he noticed his legs didn't hurt so much. *Morphine must be working,* he thought. He spotted a television on the wall, and made a mental note to ask for a remote control later.

Alex smiled. *This isn't bad, really. My own room. My own TV. Meals on trays. A morphine clicker. Everyone's going to be making a fuss over me and bringing gifts. I wonder how long I get to stay...*

A young woman appeared at the door and smiled at him. She was very short, and looked Asian. From her green scrubs, Alex figured she must be a nurse. "Alex?" she said, and approached his bed. "It's so good to see you awake. My name is Christine Truong, and I'll be here all day today. You can call me Christine, okay?"

Something about the nurse's smile and manner put Alex completely at ease. He smiled back. Christine took Alex's temperature with a really cool electronic thermometer, picked up his wrist and timed his pulse, and measured his blood pressure with a cuff that made his arm hurt a little. "Everything looks good, considering what you've been through," she said, making notations in a file. "Dr. Silverman will be coming to talk to you once your parents come back."

Christine replaced his bag of IV fluid, and checked what must have been the amount of morphine in another reservoir. "Did someone show you how to use the PCA?"

"My mom. That thing's really great."

The nurse agreed. "We want to get you rested, so you can get home. If there's ever anything you need, you can press that button on the side of your bed. One of us will come. Okay?"

"Okay," he smiled.

Christine bustled back to the nurse's station. Alex decided he actually kind of liked being here. *Why would I want to go home?* he thought.

A moment later, his parents and brother were walking into the room. "Good morning, sleepy head!" his mother greeted him. "I see you found your breakfast. I told them what you'd probably like."

"It's perfect," Alex told her.

Alex said hi to Ben. His little brother just gaped at the enormous cast. "Great job. No wonder Mom and Dad said we can't go to Disneyland now."

Alex winced at the reminder of just how ruined his summer was. It looked like he'd ruined everybody else's summer, too.

"Benedict Michael Peterson," his mother said. "That was not necessary. Your brother is suffering enough. You will not say another word."

Ben sat down in a huff and folded his arms.

"I guess I broke it pretty good, huh?" Alex said.

"You never do anything halfway," his father said. "We saw Dr. Silverman in the hall. He'll be here in a minute to explain."

Alex chatted with his parents until an older, somewhat heavy-set man in a white coat poked his head through the door. "Good morning!" the doctor greeted them. "I understand someone tried to climb a tree yesterday!"

"Climbed up it fine. Coming down was what I messed up."

Dr. Silverman introduced himself to Alex, and then turned serious. "You're a very lucky boy," he said. "Your only injuries are two broken femurs. Thigh bones. You could've broken your back or neck."

Alex looked first at his mother, and then at his father. "I'm sorry again for doing something so stupid."

"What's done is done," his mother assured him.

Dr. Silverman placed a set of x-rays in a light box. "We'll start with your right femur," the doctor said, pointing at one image. "It was a relatively clean, mid-shaft fracture."

Even from where Alex was laying, he could easily see the bone was snapped. "How'd you put it back together without a cast?" he asked.

"We fixed the bone in place internally, with a plate and screws," Dr. Silverman explained, pointing to another x-ray image. "A cast isn't necessary. It should repair itself quickly, and then we'll surgically remove the plate."

Alex spotted the plate and screws on the x-ray. They looked painful. *No wonder they're giving me morphine.* "What about my left leg?"

"That is more serious," Dr. Silverman said. He replaced the x-rays with a new set.

Alex's parents glanced at each other. Alex figured that couldn't be good.

"You have what we call a distal femoral fracture. Meaning you broke your thigh bone near your knee," the doctor explained. "Unfortunately, yours is particularly nasty. We call it a Type Three fracture. Because, as you can see here, you separated part of the bone end from the shaft."

"Were you able to put it back?" Alex asked.

"Yes," Dr. Silverman replied. He put a new x-ray in the box. "In the surgery yesterday, we inserted pins to hold the bone together and ensure proper alignment. Because it's so near your knee, we need the cast to immobilize your leg until the bone heals."

"Will my left leg be okay?" Alex asked.

Dr. Silverman exchanged a long look with Alex's parents. "Go ahead and tell him now," his father said.

Dr. Silverman put the original x-ray back into the light box and pointed at the broken bone. "The problem is, the growth plate appears to be disrupted."

"What's that?" Alex asked.

"Growth plates are what allow your bones to grow as long as they need to. When you reach skeletal maturity, in adolescence, the growth plates close. But yours are still open."

Alex tried to absorb what the doctor was saying. "Does that mean my left thigh won't grow anymore?"

"We can't be sure how much more it will grow," Dr. Silverman said, "but it is likely that your left femur will end up shorter than your right. How much shorter, we can't yet say. Because there's another complication: your right femur may end up *longer* than it otherwise would."

"Why's that?" Alex asked.

"It's a phenomenon called 'overgrowth.' It often happens to children your age. With the surge of energy that repairs your femoral shaft, the bone could experience more growth than normal. Some children get a little. Some get a lot."

The room went silent. Alex looked at his legs. He pictured himself as some kind of circus freak, with his left foot reaching only as far as his right knee. Tears filled his eyes. He could feel his throat tightening. "But how will I run? Or play baseball? Or even walk?" he gurgled.

His mother put a hand on his shoulder. "We'll get you all the physical therapy you need, sweetheart." Then, using a tissue, she dried Alex's tears and helped him blow his nose. "Dr. Silverman told us you may eventually need a special shoe to elevate your left foot. You'll be fully mobile. You should think of it like having glasses."

Dr. Silverman said some other things about the course of treatment, and options for surgically equalizing his leg lengths as an adult. Alex tuned it all out. All he could think was, *It won't be like having glasses. My life is ruined. I'd trade every Christmas present I'll get for the next fifty years to go back. Please, just give me yesterday back so I can tell my cousins I won't climb the stupid tree.*

After Dr. Silverman left, Alex's parents and brother stayed and talked with him until after lunch. Once he had a full stomach, and he'd taken a couple clicks of morphine, he felt his eyes getting heavy. "We'll let you rest, sweetheart," his mother said. "We're taking Ben to Grandma and Grandpa's, and then we have a meeting with the hospital administration. We'll be back later this afternoon. Okay?"

Alex nodded. He was sound asleep before his family even left the room.

When he awakened, the light from the windows was dimmer. He noticed the curtain separating him from the other bed was pulled closed. Did Alex now have a roommate?

He heard hushed voices from the other side of the curtain. It was his parents, and it sounded like they were having an intense conversation while trying not to wake him. By remaining very quiet and listening carefully, Alex was able to hear almost everything they were saying.

"We were within two months of getting him on our insurance! Two months!" his father said.

"Are you positive he's asleep?" his mother whispered.

"Just checked," his father assured her. "Morphine has him out cold. And there's really nowhere else we can talk."

After a long pause, Alex heard his mother's whispered voice again. "I just can't believe it," his mother replied. "As much as thirty thousand, by the time they're through with therapy and removing the plates? It's completely outrageous."

Alex's heart raced in panic, as he realized they must be talking about his medical bills. *Thirty thousand dollars?* He didn't know how much his parents earned, but $30,000 was an unimaginable sum. Enough to pay his and Ben's tuition for years. His stupid leg was about to bankrupt his family! He wanted to cry out to his parents, to tell them how sorry he was, that he didn't mean it, that he didn't know … but his throat felt like it'd been tied shut with twine.

"I think we need to take their offer to split it into monthly payments," his father said. "No matter how many years it takes."

"We don't really have another choice," his mother replied. "And in the meantime, I think we need to cancel the renovations on the house."

"At least the vacation's already out," his father added. "That's a couple more thousand. Glad we didn't buy the plane tickets yet."

"I can call the firm, and see if they'll take me back for the summer," his mother said. "Would you be able to keep tabs on the boys during the day?"

Mom going back to work? Alex thought. *She was supposed to be home with us!*

"Sure, unless I'm traveling," his father replied.

I've totally ruined everything for everybody, Alex thought. *I wish I could get a job so I can pay the hospital. It's my fault. I should have to pay it. But what can a little kid do to earn money?*

Suddenly, Alex remembered something. *A penny saved is a penny earned. I can stop costing so much!* He decided to think of every way his parents had been spending money on him, and to find ways for them not to spend it. *Because I don't deserve a single thing. I've already blown everything they would've spent on me for the rest of my life. From now on, I will want nothing. I'll take cold showers. Eat plain bran flakes with no raisins. Never ask for pop or snacks. Never ask to go to the movies, or the fair, or a ball game. I don't deserve anything. I'm just a stupid kid who did a stupid thing.*

Alex realized his legs were starting to ache again. He tried to pick up the PCA device as quietly as he could, so his parents wouldn't know he'd awakened. Just as he was about to click the button, he realized something: *morphine must be expensive. The less I use, the less we have to pay for.* He set the PCA device down. He would wait until the pain was absolutely unbearable before clicking the button. *That'll be my penance,* he thought. *I'll save some money, and punish myself. I don't deserve morphine. I deserve to have my legs feel like they've been pounded through with spikes.*

The pain grew more intense by the minute. Soon, Alex could no longer stand it. He decided it was time to pretend he was waking up. He closed his eyes, and began moaning and rustling the sheets. Only when he heard the curtain being drawn back did he flutter his eyelids.

"How long did I sleep?" he yawned, using his "just awakened" voice.

"A few hours, Sweetie," his mother smiled.

"I'm glad you're here," Alex replied, reaching out and taking his mother's hand. He wished he could tell her how sorry he was about the money. He wished he could assure her that he'd cost them as little as possible from now on. But he didn't want them to know he knew. He figured that'd only make them feel worse. Plus, he knew they'd insist he not give anything up. *This has to be my special, secret gift to them.*

"How are your legs?" his mother asked. "Need morphine?"

"They're okay," Alex lied. He already had to struggle to avoid grimacing. He could feel beads of sweat forming on his forehead, and he hoped his mother didn't notice them. "I just want to go home." *Because we don't get charged for a bed at home.*

"Dr. Silverman says maybe tomorrow or the next day, depending on how you're feeling. I'll stay with you tonight."

"And I'll stay till dinner," his father said. "Then I have to get Ben and take him home."

Alex talked with his parents, and watched a Mariners game on TV. He managed to bear the pain in his legs for about twenty minutes before using the PCA. Even then, he limited himself to one click. *Just to take the edge off.* He glanced at the clock. *Let's see if I can go even longer next time.*

Alex convinced Dr. Silverman to discharge him after just three days in the hospital. On his second evening home, Alex was still in extreme pain. His parents had set up a TV in his room, but his legs hurt so much he could hardly pay attention. The codeine tablets they'd sent home with him worked so well, he figured they must be expensive. *And I don't deserve to have them spend that much on me. I can go five more minutes. That'll set a new record. I can do it.*

He heard a knock on his bedroom door, and then two surprise visitors appeared: his cousin Ronnie, and Uncle Paul. Alex smiled and greeted them, but was puzzled. Uncle Paul had never before shown up with only one child. He either came alone, or brought the whole family. He was wearing a suit, so Alex figured he hadn't even changed clothes after work.

Alex snapped off the TV, and the two visitors chatted with him for a moment from the doorway. Uncle Paul then said he was going out to Alex's dad's office.

Ronnie picked up a large box, which had apparently been leaning against the hallway wall. "Brought you something," his cousin said, dragging the box into Alex's room. "Sorry I didn't have time to wrap it."

Alex gasped as he realized what was in the box: a top-of-the-line electronic keyboard! "Oh, wow!" he exclaimed. For the briefest moment, he forgot how badly his legs were throbbing.

Ronnie tilted the box so Alex could read the description of the keyboard and all its features. It could emulate dozens of instruments, had a hard drive with hundreds of pre-recorded songs, and could interface with a computer. "Wow!" he repeated. "Thank you so much! But this is way too nice."

"I'll help you set it up. Hopefully this'll give you something fun to do while you're stuck inside."

"Definitely. But this is way too nice."

Ronnie shook her head, and then closed Alex's door. "I only wish I could get you one that's even nicer. I wanted to tell you how sorry I am for not stopping you from climbing that tree."

"It was my fault," Alex assured her. "It's not like you dared me."

"But I'm two years older, and I'm supposed to know better. I'm supposed to be setting a good example. And I'd thought about saying something, but decided not to. Thought it'd be fun watching you climb."

Alex considered his cousin's words for a moment. Ronnie had never confided in him like this before. "Did your mom and dad ask why you didn't try to stop me or something?"

"I told on myself to my parents," Ronnie said. "And I went to confession, too. Because, when I first saw you laying on the ground, I thought you were dead for sure. All because I didn't say something. And still, every time I close my eyes, I remember your legs all crumpled. And I'll never forget that scream you made."

Alex looked at his cast. He wasn't sure what to say. The throbbing pain in his legs grew more intense, and he redoubled his resolve to wait before taking any codeine.

"Anyways," Ronnie continued, "I'd been saving up for the last three years. Was going to buy a computer. But I told my dad I wanted to get you the nicest keyboard there was, 'cause I know how much you like music."

"You didn't have to do that. You didn't have to get me anything."

"Yes I did," Ronnie insisted, her voice breaking as she stared at Alex's cast. "My mom says you might be crippled for life. A keyboard's the very least I could get you."

Alex felt his throat tightening. He was afraid he might start crying in front of his cousin. "Hey," he said, putting out his arms. Ronnie leaned over the bed, and Alex hugged her as best he could. "I'll be okay," he whispered.

"I'm sorry again," Ronnie sniffled.

"I forgive you."

Ronnie straightened up, and the kids looked at each other awkwardly. "Want to sign my cast?" Alex asked. "You can be the very first one."

The keyboard turned out to be one of the few bright spots of that summer. Day after miserable day, Alex endured being laid up in a sweltering house, his leg immobilized in an itchy cast, and his mother gone at work all the time. Even worse, he had to watch as Ben and his friends rode their bikes up and down the street, shot baskets, and packed up to go swimming.

The friendship that Alex developed with Connor — the only kid from school who came to visit — was the summer's other consolation. They'd been good acquaintances before, but those months made them best friends.

Alex and Connor watched a lot of Mariners games that summer, and became experts in the whole squad. It was depressing, because 2005 was such a terrible season. In fact, the M's ended up finishing dead last in the AL West. The boys began making joking predictions about which player would blow each game.

When he wasn't watching baseball, or playing with the keyboard, Alex read. And read. And read. He'd always been a bookworm, and now had nearly unlimited time to devour printed pages. The problem was keeping enough books in the house. Connor solved that by lugging armloads of them to and from the local public library.

Apart from occasional doctor visits, Sundays were Alex's one chance to get out of the house. He'd never before looked forward to church, but he now saw it as liberation from the prison that home had become. After Mass, they would drive directly to his grandparents' house and spend the rest of the day there. Alex longed to be able to run and play with Ben and his cousins. Still, he enjoyed sitting on the porch in the sun and playing his keyboard.

Despite the chemotherapy, Grandma's cancer returned. The doctors gave her less than a year to live, which of course made Alex even more miserable. Once they'd gotten that news, the whole extended family began spending nearly all of every weekend in Monroe. He liked getting those extra chances to see his grandparents and cousins. Especially Ronnie. While the other kids romped in the woods, Ronnie went out of her way to keep Alex company. Alex often played his grandmother's favorite show tunes on his keyboard, and Ronnie sang along as their grandmother smiled and listened.

Alex finally got his cast and plates removed in August. He still faced months of physical therapy to get his legs back in shape, and still used crutches to get around, but he was glad to finally be on the upswing.

And for the only time in his life, Alex even looked forward to the starting of school.

SIXTEEN

September 10, 2008

ALEX STUDIED HIS LEGS IN THE MIRROR. FOR THE FIRST TIME in over three years, he'd put on a pair of navy uniform shorts and was considering wearing them to school the next day. Dad turned out to be right: all that cycling had helped his thighs get bigger. But both still sported ugly surgical scars. And an even more obvious problem remained: tan lines. His cycling shorts were longer than his uniform shorts. The difference meant a pasty white stripe across both thighs. Plus, his left kneecap was noticeably higher than his right. Without pants hiding his ankles, his elevator shoe screamed, "Look at me!" Alex slipped out of his uniform shorts. He decided they'd always make him look like too much of a dork.

His dad had told him he wouldn't be ready to ride for another hour. Alex figured he'd pass the time by playing his keyboard. He began with the second movement of Beethoven's Seventh. He soon immersed himself in the piece's angst and tension, harmonizing it with his own.

The first week or so of school had gone about as he'd expected. Alex enjoyed riding his new bike back and forth. He also liked having Mr. Jansson for math. His new homeroom teacher let him and Connor sit together. Other than that, school was as miserable as ever. Kids made the same old "Bigfoot" jokes about his elevator shoe. He still got picked last for every game at recess and gym class. Tim had even coined a new phrase: "The girls and Alex." As in, "Everyone else has been picked. Now we're down to the girls and Alex." Or, "Why don't we have all the boys go up against all the girls and Alex?" Brett

Zielinski even suggested — to howls of laughter — that the other sixth graders call him "Alexandra."

Alex had again started spending recess at the library. That at least got his homework out of the way. Once school was over, all he had to do was practice the organ for a half hour. Then he was free. *Free.* He and his dad could go riding. He could watch baseball. Or he could just dream about the kind of bike he might have someday.

A knock on the door interrupted Alex's concentration, and he stopped playing the keyboard. "Yeah?" he called.

"Ready to ride?" his dad asked, opening the door.

Alex was more than ready. He hurriedly changed into cycling clothes. A moment later, the two of them were cruising toward the Sammamish River Trail.

The late summer sunshine caressed Alex's face, and he wished this weather could last forever. He wondered how many more miles he and his dad would be able to log before the nasty fall rains set in.

"How's school going?" his dad asked.

"You know," Alex replied, frowning as he shifted to a new gear and studied the trail.

"I've been thinking about something," his father said. "You and I do all this riding, but you've never gone on an organized ride. With other cyclists."

"Like STP?"

Alex had been riding alongside his father, but now spotted another cyclist approaching them on the trail. He sped up and pulled in front of his dad.

"Same idea, except Cascade has a lot of smaller events. I thought maybe you'd like to start with one of those."

Alex was immediately interested. Once the other cyclist had passed, he pulled to the left and allowed his father to come alongside. "Like what?"

"There's something a few weeks from now. It's called the Kitsap Color Classic."

"Where?"

"Kitsap Peninsula. Around Poulsbo. North of Bremerton, across the Sound. We'd have a choice of several loops, depending on how far we want to go."

Alex thought for a moment, as they continued pedaling. "How big is the ride? I mean, how many people?"

"Several hundred, from what I've heard. But I know you're shy. If that's too big a crowd, we can start with something smaller."

"Oh, no," Alex assured him. "That'd be fun." *And I'll finally see if I can fit in with the whole cycling fraternity.*

He and his dad continued chatting, all the way to Woodinville and back. His father gave him some lessons in how to ride with groups of other cyclists. Alex hadn't realized there was a whole code of conduct and expected ways people would navigate their bikes and communicate with each other. "Car back" was what you shouted if you were the first to notice a vehicle approaching. "Riders left" was what you said if you were leading a group that was passing someone. "On your left" was what you said if it was just you passing. And there were hand signals for turning, and to warn people of railroad tracks, and to point out debris on the road, and ... and ...

Alex could hardly wait to start speaking that language, and to show he was part of the group that understood it. Most of all, he longed to spend a whole day with lots of other people who'd never, ever, call him "Alexandra."

SEVENTEEN

October 5, 2008

LEX PUT HIS HEAD DOWN AND STRUGGLED TO KEEP UP with his father. The hill they were climbing wasn't the steepest he'd ever done. It just seemed to stretch ahead forever. He didn't want to disappoint his dad, so Alex didn't dare admit he needed to get off the bike for another rest. He focused on cranking his pedals as hard as his father was cranking. Meanwhile, his lungs felt like they were turning inside out.

"You okay?" his dad asked.

Alex nodded. He was gasping too much to speak. It was all he could do to steer a straight line behind his father as yet another line of riders passed them. *How do they climb these hills with so little effort?* he wondered. Alex had been getting a lot of practice with "On Your Left" today, but it hadn't made him feel part of the cycling fraternity. It just made him feel like he couldn't keep up.

The Kitsap Color Classic had gotten off to an incredibly exciting start. Alex especially liked the idea of having an entire Sunday one-on-one with his father, particularly since his dad had just returned on Friday from a long series of focus groups in the Midwest. They'd enjoyed an early morning pancake breakfast in Edmonds with hundreds of other participants. Alex had even managed to strike up a conversation with some kids his age. Something about being dressed as a real cyclist, wearing his very own bib number, like the bib numbers in the coffee can in the basement that his father had shown him, had made him less shy about meeting new people who were dressed the same way and getting ready to do the same thing.

By far, the weirdest part of the pancake breakfast was spotting Mr. Jansson. His teacher looked shocked when he first recognized Alex, and then he'd cracked a big smile. Alex had been pretty surprised at seeing his teacher dressed in cycling clothes, too. Mr. Jansson chatted with him and his dad for a few minutes. "The new video, with your music, is going on the website this week. Turned out really nice. Look for it," he'd said. Alex had never before felt like he had something in common with a teacher.

Then there'd been the ferry ride. Alex had never seen a boat so completely taken over by bicycles and their riders. Everywhere he'd looked on the auto deck, bikes lined the railings. He and his dad had gone upstairs, and he'd marveled at how easy it was for him to chat with the other riders. Whether they were adults or kids, they'd talked to him like he was an equal.

Within minutes of rolling off the ferry, Alex had begun realizing he wasn't actually the equal of many other cyclists. Highway 104 climbed a long grade from the ferry terminal in Kingston, and at first Alex attacked it with gusto. He'd been so swept up in the excitement of actually doing the ride, he'd even pulled ahead of his dad. Only as Alex had struggled to reach the top, with a river of riders passing him, had reality sunk in.

The course had leveled out, and Alex had managed to enjoy himself a little. It'd rained overnight, but the roads were dry and no more rain was forecast. It was looking like a crisp and overcast 55 degrees, all day. Plus, the road was spectacular. It seemed carved out of a cedar forest. Trees towered above them on both sides, and the riders had the road pretty much to themselves. Cruising along with so many other people, his own bib number fluttering on his back, Alex had actually started feeling pretty good.

And then came this hill. Although the summit was finally inching into sight, Alex wondered how he'd manage to keep up with his dad now that he was so burned out.

They made a sharp left turn and pedaled into the historic town of Port Gamble. As they cruised past all its beautiful Victorian buildings, Alex was grateful his father suggested they pull into the post office parking lot for a quick breather.

"Have some water, and another fig bar," his dad suggested.

Alex took a long swig from his water bottle. The cool liquid felt good running down his throat. He'd been working so hard on the hill, he hadn't wanted to break his stride even to drink.

"I guess we need to do more practice on hills," his father said. "I honestly didn't know there'd be so many today."

They watched a steady stream of riders pass. "I just wish I wasn't such a burden to you," Alex said, continuing to catch his breath.

"You're not a burden. I'm doing this ride for you. At whatever pace you want to ride. Just try to have fun."

Alex couldn't imagine this ride getting fun. Especially if there were too many more hills like that last one.

They eased back onto the highway. Alex was thankful the terrain seemed to be remaining level. The road arced to the southwest, and he felt the salty breeze of Hood Canal in his face. They even started to pass some people who'd slowed to take pictures of the Hood Canal Bridge. Alex's heart filled with pride the first time he got to call out, "Riders left!"

The road began sloping downward as they pushed south on Highway 3 toward Poulsbo. Alex sat up more comfortably, and pulled alongside his father. "I know I'm not a burden. But I know you can ride faster than I ever could. I guess I just wish there was a way to even things out. So you could always ride as hard as you wanted, and I could always keep up."

"Don't worry about holding me back. It's not like I'm training for the Tour de France. Or even STP. I only got my bike out of the basement to have fun with you."

Alex still suspected that Dad wished he could smoke the course, like he could do before he had kids. *How could someone with that awesome of an Italian racing bike not want to ride fast? Or not want to train for STP?*

Alex liked that his dad seemed content to do easy rides, if Alex wanted to. But Alex didn't want to just spin his pedals up and down bike trails. He wanted to ride to more interesting places. Most of all, he wanted to keep up with the other riders on hilly courses like this one. He even wanted to start training for STP. Soon.

They cut off onto Big Valley Road, which had much less traffic. The road made a nice, easy descent through stands of cedars and past beautiful farms. One little boy, who was playing in a pasture with his dog, began waving at Alex. Alex waved back. He wished he could spend more time in places like this. He wondered if that boy knew how lucky he was.

A moment later, Alex wondered if the boy might be thinking the same thing about him. *I guess I am pretty lucky that I have a nice bike, and cycling stuff, and I get to do rides like these.*

Liberty Bay eventually came into view on their right, and it was obvious they were nearing the city of Poulsbo. "The food stop should be coming up soon," his dad said.

Alex heard someone shout, "Riders left!" A long line of cyclists blasted by them. There were three tandems leading the group, and two of them had kids on the back. Behind the tandems, there must've been twenty other riders keeping pace. Some looked not much older than Alex.

"Riding in a line like that helps you go a lot faster with less effort," his father explained, once they were alone again. "Too bad they surprised us, and we couldn't jump on the end of it."

The food stop was at a large city park. Cyclists were bustling everywhere, clunking around in special shoes. Alex felt like he belonged in this crowd, yet he was still a little shy. He used the toilet, refilled his water bottle, and loaded his jersey pockets with fruit and granola bars. Alex then hobbled back to where they'd left their bikes.

While still waiting for his father to return, Alex noticed another boy approaching him. He was about Alex's size, and dressed in a sharp-looking blue-and-red outfit. As the boy drew nearer, Alex realized he was black. He hadn't seen more than a handful of black cyclists all day.

"That's so cool you get your own bike," the boy said. "My dad says I have to ride the tandem for at least two more years."

"Were you in that group that came flying in here? It's cool you get to go so fast."

"I guess. My name's Jacob, by the way."

"I'm Alex," Alex replied, but had to suppress a smile. Their family knew so many boys named "Jacob," it was a running joke. There were two Jacobs on Ben's new soccer team, and there'd been two more Jacobs on Ben's baseball team that spring. Not counting the three Jacobs at their school.

"Did you get hurt? I saw you limping. My mom's a nurse and is riding the course as a medic."

"I'm okay," Alex replied, and explained about his legs. He was grateful that Jacob listened sympathetically, and that the boy thought the crank shortener setup was so interesting.

"We have crank shorteners on the tandem, too," Jacob said.

The boys chatted for another minute or two, and then a heavy-set man on a tandem coasted toward them. He was followed by a smaller woman on a single bike, who was wearing a red "MEDIC" jersey. Both were middle-aged, and both were white. Alex had to hide his surprise when Jacob said, "These are my parents," and then introduced Alex to them.

Alex assumed Jacob must be adopted, but he didn't want to ask. He figured Jacob must be as tired of answering those kinds of questions as Alex was about explaining why his school shoes didn't match. He wondered what it'd be like having parents who were a different color. *Would that be easier or harder than having legs of different lengths? Does Jacob get teased as much as I do?*

Jacob's parents made small talk with Alex about the beautiful route, and how their ride was going. Soon enough, Alex's dad joined them. Jacob's parents introduced themselves to him as Doug and Penny Lloyd.

"Your tandem came in here so fast," Alex said. "Did you get it for Jacob?"

"Penny and I've had it for years," Mr. Lloyd replied. "When Jacob was little, we pulled him in a trailer. When he got big enough to ride, we let him take over as stoker on the tandem. Penny moved to her own bike."

"He can work as hard or as easy as he likes," Mrs. Lloyd explained, as Alex studied the tandem. "And we don't have to worry about him swerving into traffic."

"But hopefully in the next couple years I'll get to trade with Mom."

Alex continued staring at the tandem. He thought the brand name, "Co-Motion," was very clever. Both riders had a set of cranks. Each set had an identically-sized chain ring on the left side, connected by a long chain. The person in the back had a regular set of chain rings and sprockets on the right side, like any other bike. Alex assumed the person up front shifted gears and worked the brakes.

Mr. Lloyd seemed to notice Alex's fascination with the tandem. "Are you in a hurry to finish?" he asked Alex's dad. "Think Alex might like to take a little spin?"

Alex's eyes lit up. "Can I?"

Alex's father gazed at the tandem's cranks. "We have a special configuration for Alex's pedals. Do you have wrenches to remove that right crank shortener, and move his pedals over?"

"I think so." Mr. Lloyd began rummaging through a bag on the tandem's rear rack.

As the two dads went to work, Alex could barely contain his excitement. Then he noticed the way Jacob was eying his own bike. "Would you like to try riding mine?"

Jacob looked at his mother, who nodded. "Awesome!" he exclaimed.

A few minutes later, the tandem was configured for Alex — and Jacob's pedals were on Alex's bike. Alex gave Jacob a quick lesson in how to shift gears, and then his new friend took off to explore the park.

Jacob's father straddled the front part of the tandem. The other adults helped Alex climb on the back. He snapped his cleats in the pedals, and then Mr. Lloyd shoved off. "Just hold the handlebars," he told Alex.

They pedaled slowly at first. "Don't try to steer. Trust me to do that, or you'll make us unbalanced."

"Okay," Alex replied. He felt nervous, because he didn't have any control over the bike. Every time Mr. Lloyd leaned into a curve, or even wiggled the frame back and forth, Alex was afraid the bike would topple over. He had to keep fighting the urge to lean the other direction, or to turn his handlebars.

"Now, a tandem lesson. I'm called the 'captain.' You're called the 'stoker.' Got it?"

"Got it," Alex smiled.

They cruised into a wide open stretch of the park, and Mr. Lloyd turned his head slightly. "Let's see how fast we can go!"

Alex grinned, and started working the pedals with all this strength. The wind raced past them, and the rest of the park became a blur. Alex watched as the speed display on the handlebar-mounted computer kept climbing. 25. 28. 30. 32.

Finally, Mr. Lloyd eased up. Alex followed his lead. They made a sweeping turn, and coasted back to where everyone else was waiting.

"This is so awesome!" Alex told his dad, once they arrived.

"So is your bike," Jacob said.

They returned the pedals to their original configurations, and soon everyone was pulling back onto the route. By the time they cleared the city limits, and were cruising north under a canopy of trees on a beautiful rural road, Alex was feeling good. He gazed up at the explosion of orange and yellow maple branches overhanging the road, and understood why this event was called the "Kitsap Color Classic."

It took about an hour to reach the final food stop, at Kitsap Bank. Alex enjoyed talking with Jacob, whenever the traffic was clear enough to ride alongside. Jacob said he and his parents had been doing rides like this since he was very young. Alex learned that Jacob was almost eleven, and in fifth grade at a public school north of Everett. He was an only child, and didn't even have much extended family in the area.

Alex was a little jealous that Jacob had been getting to ride so much, but Alex was glad to have a little brother. He also realized how lucky he was, that he got to see his cousins all the time. *I wouldn't trade my brother and cousins for all the rides in the world,* he thought. He wondered what they were all doing at Grandpa's that afternoon. He could hardly wait to tell them about this adventure.

At Kitsap Bank, they stopped to use the restroom before tackling the final few miles. "We shouldn't have trouble making the next ferry," Mr. Lloyd said.

Jacob said he wanted to see how fast they could ride the last stretch. Alex didn't want to hold them back. "See you on the ferry," he told them.

He and his father waved as the Lloyds said goodbye and accelerated down the road. The two of them then continued toward the finish at a more leisurely pace. "We've got plenty of time," his father assured him.

Alex enjoyed the long descent toward the Kingston ferry. Taking advantage of the generous shoulder, he pulled alongside his father. The two of them chatted as they rode.

"Did you like the tandem?" his dad asked.

"Oh, yeah! We were able to go so fast. I know Jacob wishes he had my bike. I kept wishing we could trade places."

The two of them coasted down the final slope toward the ferry terminal. They could see hundreds of bikes already aboard the waiting ship. "I wonder if we'll be able to find the Lloyds," Alex said. He liked Jacob, and wanted to talk more with him. Everett wasn't too far from where they lived. *Maybe we could do some training rides up there,* he thought.

Alex and his father secured their bikes along the railing of the auto deck. They then began clunking up the metal stairwell to the passenger compartment. "Do you think you'd like to have a tandem?" his dad asked.

Alex couldn't believe his father was even posing this question. He'd enjoyed his test ride, of course. But didn't tandems cost a fortune? The last thing he wanted was for his dad to blow a pile of money, when they still owed the hospital so much. "My bike works okay," he replied.

"That's not what I asked," his father said, pulling the stairwell door open. He allowed Alex to hobble onto the passenger deck. They found seats near the front of the boat.

The two of them got comfortable as they waited to depart. It felt good to finally sit on something that wasn't a bicycle seat. Alex savored the soreness in his legs that'd come from working so hard.

"I liked the tandem a lot. It'd be awesome riding one with you. But when we were at the bike shop, I saw how much they cost. Like four or five thousand."

Alex's father waved at someone. Alex turned to look, and he saw the Lloyds clunking toward them in their cycling shoes. "Thanks again for letting me try out your tandem," Alex said.

"I'm glad we got to ride together," Jacob replied.

Mr. Lloyd handed his son some money, and told him something privately. Jacob nodded and headed off toward the dining area of the ship. Mr. and Mrs. Lloyd sat down just as the ferry eased away from the dock.

They chatted about the ride for a few minutes, and then Jacob reappeared. He was carrying a cardboard tray with five cups in it. "Does everybody like hot chocolate?" he asked.

Alex suddenly realized that nothing sounded better. He took a long sip of the hot, creamy liquid. He felt himself glowing from the inside out. "Thanks," he smiled.

Everyone drank hot chocolate for a moment, and then Alex's dad spoke. "What does it cost to get a good tandem?"

"Brand new, entry level, good maker?" Mr. Lloyd replied. "About $3,500. For something nice? Easily twice that."

"That's quite an investment," Alex's dad observed.

"It becomes your family's 'thing,'" Mrs. Lloyd replied, taking a sip of hot chocolate. "Some families take expensive vacations. Some have cabins on the lake."

"Or an RV. Or a boat," Mr. Lloyd added.

"This is our recreational vehicle," Jacob smiled.

Alex's dad took a sip of hot chocolate. "How could someone find a good used tandem? Something solid, but not costing a fortune."

"Craigslist," Mr. Lloyd replied. "Or eBay."

"Cascade's website has classifieds," Mrs. Lloyd added.

"You can usually get something decent for around a thousand. Maybe less, since it's end of season." Mr. Lloyd told them.

Jacob's parents continued giving Alex's dad advice about shopping for a tandem, and where to learn about tandems online. They seemed passionate — almost evangelical — about sharing what they knew.

Although Alex's heart raced at the idea of having a tandem of his own, a thousand dollars was still an awful lot of money. *Almost a tenth of what we owe the hospital because of me.*

The next thing he knew, the ferry's engines were throttling down. The Edmonds terminal was coming up fast. The boys finished their hot chocolate, and their fathers exchanged email addresses. "I'll send you some links to websites," Mr. Lloyd told Alex's dad.

Alex liked the idea of his father staying in touch with the Lloyds. He hoped he'd get to see them again, and to get to know Jacob better.

All around them, cyclists were packing up and making their way down to the auto deck. The Petersons and Lloyds were soon in the middle of that crowd. They said their goodbyes at the bottom of the steps.

After all the auto traffic had driven off the ferry, Alex and his dad joined the flood of riders sweeping toward the parking lot. They found Mom's station wagon, and were soon cruising toward home. Alex was bone tired, yet still glowing from the excitement of the day.

"You really don't have to buy a tandem," he told his dad.

"Doesn't hurt to make some calls. We should definitely rent one first. But if we both like it and want one, I'm thinking I may have a way to get a thousand bucks."

"Are you sure?"

"I need to confirm one thing when we get home. But to get the money, it'll kill all my riding time this week. That okay?"

Alex nodded. As much as he'd miss riding with his dad, it seemed a small price to pay for a tandem. He was grateful his father was willing to do some extra work, to get something special. *Missing a week of riding is the least I can do to help.*

EIGHTEEN

October 6, 2008

ROB WAS READY TO BANG HIS HEAD ON THE DESK, BUT HE forced himself to settle down and begin again. He'd set the alarm for 5am that morning, two hours earlier than usual. He'd even been up before Meg. He knew if he had any chance of squeezing an extra $1,100 out of the focus groups he'd moderated last week, he needed to get started right away on transcribing the sessions himself. Emily Greer had estimated her charges at that amount, and he'd built it into the budget. The client was going to pay it, regardless of who did the transcription. He'd felt like a louse sending Emily an email the previous night, when they'd arrived home from the Kitsap ride, telling her he needed to cancel the transcription. He was just glad she hadn't started yet.

Now he was discovering why Emily charged what she did. The work was tedious, and he didn't have a foot pedal like hers to start and stop the audio on his computer. That meant taking his fingers off the keyboard, using the mouse to play the digital audio, stopping the recording, and typing the sentence he'd just heard. And then doing it again. And again. And again.

He promised himself a break, to surf tandem sites and classifieds, every two hours. That was pretty much all that was keeping him focused on his goal. He'd already started surfing the night before, and had sent a couple of emails about reasonably-priced tandems. *I need to stay on task,* he told himself. *I can't go look at any tandems until I've transcribed all five sessions.*

Rob would never admit it to Alex, but he wanted a tandem as much for himself as for his son. Having to keep to the boy's slow pace, especially on hills, really had been bugging him. He was just glad that Alex had come to the idea on his own, and that the Lloyds had been so helpful in making it happen.

Alex hurried to homeroom, and couldn't wait to tell Connor about the Kitsap Color Classic. There was so much to describe, he wasn't even sure where to begin. The ferry ride? Meeting Jacob Lloyd? Riding the Lloyds' tandem? Having an entire day with his dad?

"Hey!" he greeted Connor. "How'd things go this weekend?"

Connor's face fell. "Well, my dad's going to be around a lot more. They shut down his plant."

Alex looked at his friend with shock. "Oh, no. What's he going to do?"

"Don't know. Nobody's hiring. My mom's even had trouble finding something part-time."

The bell rang, and Mrs. O'Malley called homeroom to order. Alex tuned out the opening prayer and announcements, and tried to think. He could tell Connor was a lot more scared than he was trying to let on. Alex wished there were something he could do to comfort him. With all the terrible news lately about the economy, he knew any reassurances would sound empty. Alex looked at his friend and felt helpless.

After the announcements, they had about five minutes left. "How was your big bike ride?" Connor asked.

"It was good," Alex shrugged. "I had fun." He decided maybe the best way he could help his friend would be to say nothing more than that.

NINETEEN

October 16, 2008

ORANGE AND RED MAPLE LEAVES CRACKLED ACROSS THE roadway. Watching the tempo of his dad's legs cranking up and down on the captain's pedals, Alex redoubled his own efforts. He glanced behind at Ben. The younger boy's face was scrunched as he turned the pedals of his trail-a-bike. "Almost there," he told Ben, who nodded.

After spending an afternoon pedaling around Green Lake on a rented tandem, Alex and his father had been positive they wanted one. They'd had their own for nearly a week now, and Alex couldn't get enough of it. They could go faster and farther than on single bikes, because his dad didn't have to worry about Alex keeping up. If he got tired, he didn't have to crank as hard. If he was feeling energetic, he could pedal like crazy. Dad said he could always tell when Alex turned on the "afterburners." It felt like having a tailwind.

The Santana his dad found on Craigslist was solid, and ran pretty well for being so old. The frame's white paint was in fairly bad shape after 20 years, and the size wasn't perfect, but it worked for all three of them. Dad fit fine in the captain slot. Ben could reach the stoker's pedals with crank arm shorteners and the seat lowered all the way. When Alex rode as stoker, they raised the seat and removed the right crank arm shortener. For $800, it'd been a terrific deal. Especially since Dad assured him he'd been able to squeeze an extra $1,100 out of a project.

After trying the stoker seat just a couple of times, Ben said he wanted to start cycling more. That struck Alex as unfair. After all, Ben had plenty of other sports he could play. Dad assured Alex he wouldn't let Ben cut into Alex's riding time. He'd just do extra rides with Ben.

The trail-a-bike was a compromise for times when all three of them needed to go someplace. It was like a smaller version of Alex's road bike, and even had its own gears. Instead of a front wheel, it had an arched pivot arm that bolted to the stoker's seat post. It was easy to attach and detach, giving a temporary third seat to the tandem for Ben. The seller had thrown it in for an extra $100.

The three of them pulled into the parking lot of Canyon Park Junior High, and cut a sweeping path toward the field where Ben's soccer practice would be held. Alex smiled as people turned to gape at the "bicycle train."

Ben unsnapped his helmet, and then struggled to free his soccer shoes from the toe clips on the trail-a-bike pedals. Alex glanced down at his cycling cleats and thought, *For once, I'm the one who has exactly the right shoes for a sport.*

"We'll be back to get you at six, sharp," his father said. Ben waved, and then dashed off to join his teammates.

Alex and his father took a few minutes to disconnect the trail-a-bike. They locked it in a bike rack, and were soon cruising back toward downtown Bothell. Alex decided that as much as he enjoyed having Ben along, it was even more fun being alone on the tandem with his dad. He looked forward to their next hour and a half together.

"Where should we go today?" his father asked, turning his head to be heard in the wind. "Might be our last ride before the weather gets nasty for the next week."

Alex hadn't given it much thought. He didn't really care where they went, as long as he'd dressed warmly enough. So far, his gloves and tights and sweatshirt were keeping him comfortable. "Maybe pick up the Burke-Gilman Trail and ride toward Seattle until we have to turn around?"

"Sounds good!" Dad shifted gears as they crested the top of the hill. Alex joined him in hammering harder on the pedals. They picked up speed, and soon were descending quickly past the subdivisions lining the outskirts of town. Alex loved the way they could go down hills so much faster on a tandem than on single bikes. It more than made up for the extra effort it took to climb hills on a heavy tandem. As the wind filled his nostrils with crisp fall air, Alex decided there was no place in the world he'd rather be.

TWENTY

October 24, 2008

Alex and Connor helped themselves to more pizza, and then hurried to the basement to rejoin Ben and his friend, Jimmy Flynn. "You guys ready?" Ben asked, gesturing with the remote control as he chewed his own pizza.

"Press Play," Alex said. He and Connor settled into beanbag chairs around the TV. Yet another animated Pixar short film rolled, and all four boys were soon laughing. Before he knew it, Alex had completely forgotten his disappointment at not being able to ride that afternoon. With Dad on the road for a rare set of weekend focus groups, Alex was grateful to his mother for proposing a Saturday night sleepover.

The boys continued feasting, watching videos, and playing Monopoly until Alex's mother called for lights out at 10:30. Alex and Connor then set up sleeping bags in the basement, while Jimmy and Ben camped out in the living room.

Alex was happy his mom didn't seem to care how late he and Connor stayed awake talking, as long as they kept their voices low. The two boys laid on their backs for a long time, staring into the darkness and talking about teachers, other kids at school, the lousy season the Seahawks were having, Halloween, soccer … .

"I'm auditioning for a solo in the Christmas concert," Connor said. "Ever thought about accompanying us on the organ?"

"Mrs. Rossi keeps mentioning it, at my lessons. I just don't want to play in public."

"You should think about it, man. It'd be so cool. My folks streamed that STP video for me. That one with your music.

Your score was so awesome. Almost made me want to go do the ride."

Alex smiled with pride. *Maybe I am pretty good,* he thought. Then he tried to imagine himself playing the organ, with his classmates counting on him to get every single note right — all while 200 families were down in the church, listening. "Playing at the concert wouldn't be fun at all. I'd be way too scared."

An awkward silence hung between them. Alex looked for a way to change the subject. "Speaking of bikes, me and my dad, we've been out riding around on our tandem pretty much every afternoon it hasn't been raining. It's really awesome."

"I saw you guys go by our house the other day. Looked like you were having fun."

"It's *totally* fun. Maybe my dad can take you for a ride when he gets back next week. I bet my cleats'll fit you. Even if they don't, you could use Ben's pedals with toe clips."

Before Alex could think of anything else to add about the tandem, Connor said, "You're so lucky your dad has a good job he can do from home."

Alex immediately felt uncomfortable, and wasn't sure what to say. "Has your dad, you know, found anything yet?" he asked. That seemed safe enough.

"Nope. Been looking like crazy, but so's everybody else."

"What's he going to do?"

"Don't know. He's getting unemployment, but it won't last forever. My folks are really stressed about paying my tuition."

Alex suddenly got a sickening realization: Connor might have to leave St. Clement. He couldn't imagine anything worse. "Aren't there, like, scholarships?"

"Everybody's been applying this year. Not sure how much'll be left for us."

Alex wished there were something he could say or do for his friend. He felt powerless. He couldn't even pay his own hospital bills. How could he pay Connor's tuition?

After thinking for a long time, Alex said, "I know this is a dumb question. But is there anything I can do to help?"

Connor didn't answer at first. Alex wondered if his friend had heard his question.

Finally, Connor responded with a question of his own: "Do you ever pray?"

It wasn't at all what Alex had been expecting. He and Connor never talked about religious stuff, unless it was for religion class. "I guess. We go to Mass every Sunday, and at school on Tuesdays. Like you guys. And my mom has me say some prayers when I get up and go to bed."

"No. I mean, do you ever talk to God about stuff and ask him for stuff?"

"Not really very much," Alex admitted. "Unless I've got a big test or something."

"I never did, either. But now I've been praying all the time that my dad find a job. And offering up little sacrifices with my prayers, like they told us about in religion class. My dad getting a job is the only thing I can think about sometimes. Maybe if you prayed, too, God would hear us faster."

"I'm not very good at praying, but I'll make sure I start," Alex assured him.

Connor yawned, and Alex felt his own eyelids growing heavy. As his mind fogged over, just before he drifted into unconsciousness, he whispered a silent prayer for Mr. Crowley to find a job. *I'll do anything for Connor. He's the best friend ever. Please just give me a chance to help.*

TWENTY-ONE

October 28, 2008

ALEX WATCHED AS MRS. ROSSI DEMONSTRATED THE LAST OF the five new songs she was assigning for next week. "I've got it," Alex assured her. He thought the pieces were way too easy, but Mrs. Rossi insisted he do the lessons in order.

It was already 5:20. Alex was itching to get home. He heard his mother packing up her things, and he began snapping his music books shut. As an extra sacrifice, he'd gone without a snack that afternoon. He'd done it partly to save his folks money. He'd also offered it up, along with his prayers for Mr. Crowley to find a job faster. Now, his grumbling stomach was driving him crazy. He hoped Dad would have dinner on the table when they got home.

Before Alex could climb from the organ bench, Mrs. Rossi cleared her throat. "One last thing."

Alex set his books down and turned to face his teacher. Her thin build and graying hair reminded Alex of his late Grandma Sullivan. Mrs. Rossi gazed at him through her oversized glasses, with a look that was warm but firm. "We've discussed this before, but I would very much like you to play the organ for the school's Christmas program. I really think this is the year you should take over the accompaniment."

Alex stared at the organ's manuals, and tried to suppress his hunger enough to think. He liked Christmas music. He already knew how to play most Christmas carols by ear. But with a church full of parents hanging on every note? With a chorus of kids depending on him to get every note right? Kids who were salivating to find yet another thing to make fun of him for, if he screwed anything up? "I know I should. I just hate the idea of playing in public."

"You don't have to do it," his mother said, putting her hand on his shoulder. "But your father and I think it'd be very good if you can. Accompanying a group of singers, and playing for an audience, would be big for your development as a musician."

"If it makes any difference," Mrs. Rossi said, "preparing for the concert would take the place of organ lessons until January. The concert pieces would be your only pieces."

Alex immediately perked up. He liked the idea of practicing Christmas carols, instead of the silly organ course music. Doing some quick mental arithmetic, he figured he could save his parents about $200 in lessons.

"I'll think about it," he said, picking up his organ books.

"Good," Mrs. Rossi smiled. "And so you know: rehearsals have already started. Students have begun auditioning for solos. They'll need to know who they're working with. I'll need a decision by next week's lesson, okay?"

"Okay," Alex assured her. But he didn't know if he'd feel comfortable enough to say Yes after even a hundred weeks of thinking about it.

As they drove home, Alex's mother reminded him that she was just dropping him off. She was then immediately leaving for a Board meeting at Women's Resources. "Save me some dinner. I won't be home till late."

"What's going on?"

"Planning fundraising strategies. With the economy so bad, more women than ever need help. But donations are way down. We need to get creative."

Alex resolved to do more to save his parents money. He inched closer to playing in the Christmas concert for just that reason. Above all, Alex was grateful his mother didn't try to pressure him into doing it. He liked that she always seemed to know when to let him figure things out for himself.

That evening, after dinner, Alex sat down at his keyboard and tried playing some Christmas carols. He figured that might help him come to a decision for Mrs. Rossi.

He knew she believed in him. *You're the most naturally gifted student I've ever had,* she'd told him more than once. He knew his parents believed in him. They wouldn't be asking him to play if they didn't think he could do it. But did they really know Alex, and his world, as well as he knew it himself? Did they know how much of a miserable living hell the other kids were itching to turn his life into, if he screwed up?

Or, he wondered, *am I looking at this the wrong way? Should I be seeing it as a chance to finally show all the other kids that I can do something great, too?*

Alex knew he could perform the Christmas songs just fine. He knew he *should* play in the concert. He knew he owed it to Mrs. Rossi to play in the concert. And he did want Tim and Ritchie and Brett and all the others to finally see him do something they couldn't do.

He just couldn't quite make himself say Yes.

The next afternoon, after school let out and he'd finished practicing the organ, Alex was no closer to a decision. The overcast skies matched his mood perfectly. He didn't think he'd be able to smile or relax until the whole concert dilemma was resolved. He huddled more deeply in his jacket, and wondered when he'd have to start wearing his heavy winter coat.

Because the weather forecast called for rain, he and Connor and Ben had left their bikes at home that day. Now, as they began walking home together in the chilly autumn afternoon, Connor seemed to sense something was amiss. "What's on your mind, man?"

"Yeah, you've been even less talky than usual," Ben added.

Alex explained how Mrs. Rossi wanted him to play in the Christmas concert. "But I don't know. I just don't like having an audience."

"You should do it," Connor said. "It'd be so perfect if you were accompanying us."

"Yeah," Ben said. "And maybe all those other kids'll stop making fun of you when they see how good you are."

As they continued walking, Alex thought about what Ben said. It was almost exactly what he'd been thinking the night before. Alex pictured his classmates listening to him in stunned silence. They'd never again dare to call him "lame." *For once, I'd be the greatest. Everybody would think I'm awesome.*

After another block or so, Ben smiled and seemed to re-member something. "You know what I've always thought would be so cool? You playing the organ for Mariners games at Safeco Field."

Connor added, "Yeah, like that 'Charge!' tune!"

The boys all laughed, and waited at an intersection for traf-fic to pass.

"I could never play in front of that many people. I'm scared enough thinking about the Christmas concert."

"Wouldn't it be wild, hearing the crowd cheer while you were playing?" Connor asked.

Alex pictured himself playing a massive organ, deep in the bowels of Safeco Field. He could practically feel the whole sta-dium rocking with his music. "It would be pretty exciting," he admitted.

So why, he wondered, *would playing at the Christmas concert not be?*

TWENTY-TWO

ROB TOOK A GOOD LOOK AT THE BUICK'S HOOD, AND checked that he'd covered all of it with wax. As he picked up a chamois rag and began buffing the wax on the passenger side, he realized he was using the same technique he'd watched his father use.

Meg was always saying Rob was more like his father than he'd admit. He knew she was probably right. Much like his dad, Rob liked being his own boss, hated distractions and interruptions from kids when he was engrossed in a project, enjoyed solitude, and didn't have a lot of friends. With the exception of Paul Santucci, and the rest of Meg's family, Rob's "friends" consisted of a dozen or so college buddies and former colleagues — now scattered across the country — he kept up with on Facebook and through email. When he was traveling, he'd try to meet someone for breakfast or lunch. He was perfectly happy having no more direct human contact than that.

The long hours alone on open roads were what Rob had always found most attractive about long distance cycling. He figured his dad must've found the same blessed solitude in his Cessna 172 that Rob enjoyed on his Peugeot and Colnago.

His thoughts returning to the car, Rob remembered he had to call David Sullivan, and make sure he'd be in Monroe on Sunday. The Buick was due for spark plugs and an oil change. It was always nice having his brother-in-law's help.

Looking at the gathering rain clouds, Rob tried to finish the wax job more quickly. He shivered as the wind picked up. He wished he'd worn a jacket.

Alex and Ben appeared in the driveway, schoolbooks on their backs, and he greeted them. "Your mother just got home, and is taking you to soccer practice," he told Ben.

"Can I ride the tandem with you?" Alex asked.

Rob took another look at the sky. "Don't think we should try it. But I can show you how to wax the car."

Alex reluctantly agreed, and returned a few minutes later dressed in jeans and a Seahawks sweatshirt. Rob gave him a chamois rag, and got him started buffing the hood.

The two of them worked in silence for several minutes, and Rob marveled at how much Alex resembled his own sixth grade self. *I'm just glad he's getting the chance to work on the car with me, instead of watching from a distance,* he thought. Rob could even picture Alex, thirty years from now, waxing a car hood with a little blond-headed boy of his own.

As the silence continued, Rob sensed something was on Alex's mind. He also knew that, whatever it was, Alex wouldn't bring it up on his own. "Is there anything you want to talk about?"

Alex frowned and buffed the hood more intensely. "I know I should play at the Christmas concert. I just don't want to."

Rob pictured himself sitting in the darkened church with Meg and Ben, beaming with pride as Alex brought the house down with his music. He fantasized about announcing: *That's my boy!* And he could imagine everyone asking, "How did he get so good?"

If only Alex would actually do it.

"How come?" Rob asked, focusing on his own corner of the hood. He loved the way it was developing a beautiful, deep black shine.

"I never play in public."

"But you've never told me why."

Alex thought for a moment. "I guess I'm just scared," he admitted.

"Scared you'll mess up?"

"Sort of. I mean, I know I can play the songs when I'm alone. There's just something about knowing all those people are listening and watching me. Makes me scared even thinking about it."

"I understand. I was terrified the first time I moderated a focus group. And that was just eight people."

Alex stopped and looked him in the eye. "Do you still get scared?"

"Honestly? Sure. I get butterflies right before I walk into a focus room. But I tell myself I've done it before, and I can do it again. After a few minutes with a group, I'm not nervous at all."

Alex continued looking Rob in the eye. "Dad, is there anything really big that you know you *could* do, but seems scary or hard, and so you don't do it?"

His son's question caught him off guard. "How do you mean?"

"Don't know," Alex murmured. He stepped back to inspect the hood from a distance. "Maybe like … Seattle to Portland. You did that a bunch of times, right?"

"Yeah," Rob replied. He wasn't sure he liked where this was going.

"Think you could do it again? Like next year? If you really wanted to?"

The question surprised him. He sensed Alex was trying to turn the tables. "Sure. I guess I could. If I really wanted to."

"Then why don't you?"

Rob smiled. He'd seen Alex's question coming. "Because I don't really want to. I don't have anything to prove."

Alex frowned at his section of the hood, not making eye contact. He buffed more intensely. "Is STP just about proving something? I mean, I thought it was about doing something amazing. Something almost nobody else has ever done. Or do you only get that feeling the first time?"

"There's always a sense of accomplishment," Rob admitted, moving to finish one of the last spots. He didn't know what else to say, and hoped Alex wouldn't press him further.

Rob suspected his son wasn't satisfied with his answers. He knew Alex would be even less satisfied with the truth: *I really couldn't care less about senses of accomplishment anymore. Life's hard enough without training for a double century. Getting my work done, supporting the family, getting the boys to organ lessons and sports practice and games ... that's more than enough accomplishment for me. After getting all that done, I'm ready for a beer. Not a workout.*

The first rain drops began splattering heavily on the car. "I'll pull it into the garage and take care of the rest," Rob told Alex. As he climbed into the driver's seat, Alex ran for the house.

Once he was under cover, and could examine the car more carefully, Rob was pleased the wax was already helping the rainwater bead up so well. *It'll look terrific when I pick up Frank Hurwitz at the airport tomorrow, on the way to the focus groups,* he thought.

As he finished buffing the final corner of the fender, Rob thought more about Alex's questions. He was just grateful that Alex hadn't thrown down some kind of gauntlet like, "If I play at the concert, will you ride STP?" That's where Rob had feared Alex's questions were leading. As much as he wanted to encourage his son to play at the concert, and to bask in glow of his son's masterful performance, he really wasn't sure he wanted it badly enough to ride 200 miles.

Then he realized that, in Alex's typical avoid-all-conflict sort of way, STP was exactly the challenge his son had just laid down.

But why?

TWENTY-THREE

November 2, 2008

ALEX SPENT MOST OF THE WEEKEND STRUGGLING WITH whether he should play at the concert or not. He struggled even harder trying to understand why his father cared so little about riding STP. Alex couldn't imagine anything more exciting, even if it was scary at the same time. He knew his parents wouldn't let him ride STP by himself. Getting Dad on board, so they could go together, was his only shot at doing STP any time soon.

So, why couldn't his dad get excited about STP? *Do big adventures get less exciting when you've done them too many times? When you're too confident you'll finish, does that take the fun out of it? Is scariness and uncertainty what makes things so fun? Would scariness and uncertainty make playing at the concert sort of fun?*

Alex wondered why performing in public was so much easier for some people. His cousin, Ronnie, was always acting in community theater productions. She loved being on stage. She loved having the whole world watch her. Alex hoped she would be at Grandpa's that weekend, and that she might help him get over the fear. *I like being shy,* he thought. *I just wish I could turn the shyness off when I need to.*

When they got to his grandfather's on Sunday, both sets of Alex's cousins were already there. Alex was especially happy to see Ronnie, and tried to find a chance to talk with her in private. With four Sullivan kids and seven Santucci kids running around Grandpa's house, Alex wondered how he and Ronnie could ever find a quiet place of their own.

Alex spotted his opportunity as the clock ticked down to halftime of the Seahawks-Patriots game. He'd been watching in the basement with all the other kids. Alex turned to Ronnie and asked, as casually as he could, "Hey! You want to go outside and shoot baskets?"

He was grateful that Ronnie accepted the offer, and that the other cousins said they'd rather stay warm and watch the halftime show.

The two of them bundled up and made their way to Grandpa's detached garage. It had a basketball hoop mounted above the vehicle entrance, and a paved driveway in front.

Uncle David and his father were working on the Buick in the garage. "Whatcha doing?" Alex asked them.

Uncle David looked up from the engine and drank a swig of beer. "Making sure this car lasts long enough for you to get it someday."

Alex laughed. "Will you really teach me how to drive it?"

"When you're sixteen," his father replied, setting an old spark plug on the fender before drinking some of his own beer.

Ronnie found a basketball, and they closed the garage door. The two of them began shooting in no particular order. Whoever grabbed a rebound took the next shot. After several minutes, both kids hit a pretty good rhythm.

Finally, Alex spoke up. "I've been wanting to ask you something. When you're up on stage in a play, do you get nervous?"

"Not when I'm up there," she replied, her long braided hair bouncing as she lobbed a shot at the basket. "I get butterflies, but they go away as soon as the curtain opens."

"How do you do that?" Alex asked, scrambling for the ball. "Get rid of butterflies?"

"Yeah," Alex replied. His shot bounced off the rim.

"Don't know." Ronnie grabbed the rebound and quickly launched another shot. "Why do you ask?"

As they continued shooting baskets, Alex explained about the concert and his dilemma. "I know I can play," he concluded. "And I know I should play. I just don't know how to get over being scared."

Ronnie dribbled the ball, and seemed to be thinking. "I'm definitely more of an extrovert than you. But I was pretty scared my first time. Totally chickened out when I was supposed to go on stage. Almost had to put in a substitute."

"How'd you get over it?"

"My mom pulled me aside and told me something," Ronnie said, tossing up a shot that swished through the net. "Remember: nobody lights a lamp and puts it under a basket."

Alex retrieved the ball and dribbled as his cousin continued talking. "She said I had a lot of talent. I had to go out on stage and let it shine for everybody. Otherwise, I'd be like the guy who took the gold coin and buried it. And did I really want to be that person?"

Alex shot the ball, and it bounced on the rim before rolling into the net. "You *do* shine when you're acting in a play. I see you up there, and wonder how anybody can be so confident. Even with so many people watching."

Ronnie shrugged, and then grabbed the loose basketball. "Your music's better than my acting," she said, sinking an easy layup. "I watched that STP video, with the music you did. Totally amazing. Way better than the homeschoolers' recitals my brothers play at. If you play at the concert, I bet you'll hardly even have to practice first."

"Maybe." Alex dribbled the ball out to take a jump shot. He liked the way Ronnie always talked to him like he was an equal, even though she was a couple of years older.

He and Ronnie alternated shooting, but neither of them said anything for a few minutes. Alex had never thought of his musical ability as a lamp, or as a gold coin. *But that's really what it is, isn't it?* When he was playing little league, what if his folks had given him one of those fancy $250 composite bats — and then he'd left it on the bench, so he could hit with an old beater? What would he even say to his parents? "I was, uh, afraid I might damage the composite bat." *How stupid would that sound? But isn't that exactly what I'd be doing with my music if I didn't play at the concert? Covering it with a basket, or burying it in the ground, or leaving it on the bench? Because I'm afraid something bad might happen if I try to share it with everybody else?*

But then, as he and Ronnie continued shooting baskets, Alex tried to picture himself actually playing at the concert. He imagined hundreds of people in the church, expecting him to play perfectly. The very thought terrified him. *Maybe I've been given musical talent so I can compose scores for movies and TV programs,* he thought. *Leave the public performing to someone else. Maybe I've been given the gift of music, but not of courage.*

Just as Alex was about to decide not to play at the concert, his thoughts drifted deep into the surrounding woods. Back to the day he'd watched his grandfather cut down the tree he'd fallen from. And then to his ninth birthday, the very first time he'd kicked that tree's lifeless stump and declared, "I'm alive. You're dead."

What does it really mean to be alive? he asked himself now. *What's the point of even being alive, if you never try anything new or daring or scary? If you never see how far you can go, or what you can do? How's that really different from being dead?*

TWENTY-FOUR

November 19, 2008

A LEX AND CONNOR CROSSED THE PARKING LOT FROM
school to the church. Everywhere around them, children
were running, playing, and climbing into their parents'
cars to go home. The boys had another ten minutes before the
rehearsal began, so they walked slowly through the crowd of
other kids.

"Been meaning to tell you something," Connor said, leaning
closer so Alex could hear him above the din. His blue eyes lit
up, so Alex knew the news must be good. "My dad's had a
couple of really great job interviews."

"That's awesome," Alex said.

"No offers yet, but one plant wants him to come back for
another interview after Thanksgiving."

"I'll definitely keep praying."

"Thanks. I think it might be working."

Alex held the church door for his friend, and then the two of
them climbed the steps to the choir loft. It was already crowded
with more than two dozen students, of all ages, who seemed to
be carrying on at least ten different conversations. With the
building's acoustics, the church sounded like a beehive.

Mrs. Rossi clapped her hands, and the conversations ceased.
"Let's get started," she said. Next to her stood a young kindergarten teacher named Miss Ramona Perez. She had long black
hair and an olive complexion, and seemed to really enjoy helping out with music.

"The first order of business is the announcement of soloists," Miss Perez said, waving a piece of paper. She immediately
had the attention of every student.

Miss Perez began reading names. Alex scowled when he heard Tim Gilson got a solo in Angels We Have Heard on High. Tim didn't even have that great of a voice. He wondered if Tim had simply intimidated everyone else who'd thought about competing for that particular solo.

Miss Perez continued reading the names of different musical pieces, and the student or students who would have solos in them. Alex didn't pay much attention until she reached We Three Kings. Alex perked up, and he noticed several kids staring intently. "Joseph Cooper. Steve Florio. Connor Crowley."

Alex smiled at Connor and gave him a thumbs-up.

Once Miss Perez finished announcing the soloists, the choir loft became a buzz of discussions. Mrs. Rossi let these conversations continue for a moment. She then called the group to order, and described what they'd be doing for the rest of the afternoon's rehearsal. First, as they had in previous rehearsals, they would go through all the songs that the chorus would be singing together. Then, they would work on pieces that involved solo parts. Alex would work with each soloist in turn, so everyone could get comfortable with his or her assignment.

Miss Perez assembled the chorus in their positions, and Alex spent the next hour or so working through all of the pieces. This was his third rehearsal with the whole group, so he was getting a good feel for how to accompany his classmates. The trickiest part was giving them an effective lead-in, and then holding the final note so they'd know exactly when to start singing. They ended up spending more time practicing the beginnings of songs than anything else.

After finishing these hymns, the teachers allowed everyone to take a five minute break. Before Alex could even get up to stretch, a fourth grade girl named Sarah Schwartz approached him. She was short, wore glasses, and kept her brown hair in a long ponytail.

"Hey, Alex," she said. "I've been wanting to ask you something. How come the organ has two keyboards? And what are all those pedals for?"

"Yeah," a few other kids murmured, gathering around to gape at the enormous instrument.

"The keyboards are actually called 'manuals,'" Alex explained, feeling like an expert. "I can even play chords on one with my left hand, and melodies on the other with my right. The pedals are like a third keyboard, for my feet. That's why I always play with my shoes off. So I can feel them better."

"Why not do everything on one keyboard?" Sarah asked.

"Because I can customize each manual, and the pedals, to emulate different instruments or pitches." Alex flipped a few of the dozens of paddle switches lining the console. "It all depends on how I set these. They're called 'stops.'"

Alex demonstrated by playing a scale with his right hand, a chord progression with his left hand, and some additional chords with his feet. As his classmates murmured in wonder, Alex felt himself swelling with pride.

"How do you *do* that?" one of the other girls asked.

"I don't think about it," Alex shrugged, continuing to improvise. "It just sort of flows out of me."

"Like a golden stream," Tim snickered from behind.

Several kids laughed, and Alex's face flushed with embarrassment. He kicked himself for having said too much.

"Well I think it's pretty amazing," Sarah insisted.

"Sure," Ritchie said, moving toward the stairs, "Let's leave the organ to the girls and Alex."

Alex stared at the manuals, kept improvising, and pretended he hadn't heard. *Once the concert gets here,* he told himself, *they won't be able to pretend I'm not awesome.*

When his classmates had reassembled, Alex began working with one soloist after another. Most of them were quite good. The biggest issues involved the musical cues Alex would use to signal a soloist to begin. He also needed to adjust his volume when shifting from a chorus part to a soloist part, so as not to drown the soloist out.

Even Tim sang his solo reasonably well. Alex's problem with accompanying Tim was tempo. Alex tried playing the music at the correct speed, even though Tim kept singing a bit too slowly. Alex found it difficult to press ahead at the right tempo, when the soloist was lagging. Somewhere around the words "what the gladsome tidings be," Alex gave up and slowed to match Tim's pace.

When they finished Tim's verse, Mrs. Rossi shook her head. "You both hit the notes correctly, but you need to keep the tempo on track."

"Huh?" Tim asked.

Probably doesn't even know what "tempo" is, Alex thought.

Mrs. Rossi continued. "Alex, you had it exactly right. You should have maintained it. Tim, you need to speed up." She then began tapping out a beat with her hand to demonstrate the correct tempo. "Let's try it again."

Alex sensed Tim glaring daggers at him. He could already imagine the taunts he'd be hearing the next day. "Alex, you had it exactly right," Tim and his friends would tell him, using a high-pitched voice.

Alex ignored Tim's stares, and looked straight ahead at the sheet music. He resolved to keep the tempo steady no matter what.

When they finished, Mrs. Rossi again shook her head. "Alex, that was much better. Tim, you really need to sing less slowly. Follow Alex's lead."

Hell will freeze before Tim follows my lead, Alex thought. As Tim's glare intensified, Alex decided he'd definitely be spending tomorrow's recess in the library.

Mrs. Rossi finally gave up on Tim and turned her attention to the remaining song, We Three Kings. Alex was happier about that one, especially because he'd be accompanying Connor. It turned out his friend would be singing the third "king's" line, about myrrh. Alex liked that he'd be going straight from accompanying Connor into his final triumphant playing of the refrain. He could think of no better way to do it.

They went through the entire piece, including the refrains, several times. With this particular piece's three separate soloists, and all the different transitions from soloist to refrain, the rehearsal took longer than for the other songs. Mrs. Rossi often interrupted to correct a boy's technique, but everyone eventually got the hang of the transitions. By the fifth time through, Alex judged it to sound pretty good.

"Excellent!" Mrs. Rossi exclaimed, as the last notes faded. "I think that's enough for today. We will see you again next Monday." The students began talking and moving to find their school books.

With just a month to go now before the event, Alex was feeling increasingly confident — but still a little nervous about actually performing. He looked forward to waking up on December 20th, liberated from all these anxieties. He imagined having the entire Christmas break stretching ahead of him. He could hardly wait for the freedom of playing whatever music he wanted, just for fun.

TWENTY-FIVE

December 19, 2008

ALEX CLUTCHED HIS SHEET MUSIC AND PACED THE FRIGID driveway. He stared at the corner which Connor's parents' truck should have turned more than twenty minutes ago. Where could they be? Had they forgotten Mrs. Rossi's insistence that everyone arrive no later than 6:30?

Alex shivered and drew his hands as far back in his jacket sleeves as he could. He wished he'd remembered to wear gloves.

He squinted at his watch under the dim streetlight, and panicked as he realized it was already 6:35. With the concert starting in just 25 minutes, what were Mrs. Rossi and Miss Perez going to do if he was late? *Everything's going wrong already,* Alex thought.

Relying on Connor's folks had seemed like a good idea. It allowed Alex's family to pick up their two oldest Sullivan cousins, and come later to the church. That way, everyone wouldn't have to go early. That now looked like a colossal mistake.

Just as Alex was about to start walking toward the Crowleys' house, a familiar old crew cab pickup screeched onto his block and pulled to the curb. Alex jumped in the back seat. A moment later, they were speeding toward the church.

"So sorry we're late," Connor's mother told him.

"But there's good news," Connor said. Even in the darkness, Alex could see his friend's blue eyes flash. "My dad officially got a job!"

"I had to take the call, and couldn't cut it short," Connor's dad explained, pulling onto the main road. "They wanted to finalize everything for the contract."

Alex was still flustered and panicked about running late for the concert, but ecstatic at the news. "That is awesome!" he said. Both boys beamed as they exchanged a high-five.

"Thank you for your prayers," Connor's mother said. "The new job is a perfect fit for Connor's dad. He beat out a lot of other guys to get it."

"I am so happy for you. Where is it? What'll you be doing? When do you start?"

"It's at a plant that makes plastic pop bottles. We're going to take Connor down there tomorrow, and make a Saturday of it," Mr. Crowley explained. "We'll let him tell you about it after he sees everything."

"Awesome," Alex repeated, truly happy for his friend.

Then, glancing at his watch as they slowed for a stop sign, anxiety again swept him. *Fifteen minutes till the concert starts!* Alex felt so panicked, he wanted to jump out and run the final four blocks as fast as he could.

After a seeming-eternity, the Crowleys' truck arrived at the church and both boys sprinted toward the sanctuary. They then had to wade through a huge crowd of parents and kids in the church entryway. Finally, they reached the corner stairwell.

Connor dashed down to the basement, where most of the student participants would be assembling. Although everyone had been together in the choir loft for rehearsals, Alex and Mrs. Rossi would have it to themselves tonight. Everyone else would be performing in the church itself.

Alex spotted a familiar face in the crowd: his cousin, Ronnie. She smiled and waved as she hurried to greet him. "You'll do great, Alex! Our whole family is here and pulling for you!"

"Thanks," he replied, trying to force a smile. He wished he could stay for more of a pep talk. "I've gotta run, but I'll see you at the ice cream social after, okay?"

"Okay!" Ronnie gave him a quick hug.

Alex sprinted up the steps, three at a time, and burst into the choir loft out of breath. Mrs. Rossi looked up, concern etched in her face.

"So ... sorry ... late. Ride ... didn't ... come," Alex panted.

"Just get hold of yourself," Mrs. Rossi said, putting her hand on his shoulder. "You made it. You still have ten minutes."

Alex hurriedly laid out his sheet music on the table, and set the pages for the first song on the organ's music stand, while trying to catch his breath. The panicked adrenaline was still surging through him so hard, his fingers shook as he arranged the papers.

Mrs. Rossi glanced at her watch. "Warm-ups would be distracting at this point," she told him. "Fortunately, you've never needed much warming up."

Alex kicked off his shoes and slid onto the organ bench. He took a couple of deep breaths as he gazed at the manuals. *I know she's trying to reassure me, but I really don't play very well totally cold. I guess tonight I'm going to have to. I have to show everyone how great I can play.*

Alex glanced at the table with all his sheet music. Suddenly, he felt overwhelmed at the number of piles. *I have so many songs I need to play perfectly tonight. I wish I'd practiced more.*

He had practiced on his piano and electronic keyboard, at home. He knew all the notes. He knew all the melodies, backwards and forwards. But playing notes at home wasn't the same as playing on the real church organ. The real church organ had pedals, multiple manuals, and dozens of stops. All those little paddle switches had to be set correctly for each song. Some even had to be changed within a song. Like when he needed to hit the swells for the last refrain of We Three Kings, after Connor's solo.

All those days after school, when there hadn't been a formal rehearsal, he'd told himself he didn't really need to practice on the organ. With the sun going down so early, he hadn't wanted to miss the chance to go riding with his father. *I can handle stops just fine,* he'd told himself. *I'll just practice at home, when it's too dark to ride.*

A sudden hush fell over the packed crowd. Alex glanced down to the sanctuary. The lights were dimming, and Miss Perez was leading a long line of his classmates, all dressed in their Sunday best, down the center aisle. As if on cue, the whole audience began clapping. A moment later, the smiling students reached the risers that had been installed where the altar and tabernacle usually stood.

Just then, Alex grasped the enormity of the event. *I'm really here. Everyone's all dressed up. It's really happening. Look at all those parents! Everyone's counting on me.* Panicked adrenaline again surged through him, as he realized he'd have only one chance to get every stop and every note correct. *Why can't I just work in a recording studio?* he wondered.

A knot tightened in Alex's stomach. He was glad he hadn't eaten too much at dinner. He'd tried to get a full meal that evening, but hadn't managed to swallow more than a few mouthfuls. He was glad his mother had been so understanding.

"You look very nice," Mrs. Rossi added.

"Thank you," Alex replied, trying to calm himself. His mother had insisted he dress up, even though no one would be able to see him in the choir loft. "You'll want to look good at the ice cream social after the concert," she'd said.

After the concert. Less than 90 minutes from now, it would all be over. With the event looming so large in his imagination, Alex couldn't quite get his mind around "after the concert." He tried to picture everyone crowding around, telling him how amazing he'd played. He imagined being so mobbed, he'd barely even have time to get ice cream.

Alex's classmates finished assembling on the risers. Miss Perez thanked everyone for their hard work. She then thanked the parents for attending, and announced the first song.

Alex thought the butterflies swarming in his stomach would eat him alive. As Miss Perez turned to direct the student choir, Mrs. Rossi nodded. Alex took a deep breath, paused for a moment with his fingers above the keys, and then played the first chord of his lead-in for Hark the Herald Angels Sing.

Except what came blasting out of the pipes was completely wrong. It was way too high-pitched. Plus, the mix of stops sounded like a trumpet being choked by a flute.

Shocked and completely mortified, Alex jerked his hands from the keys. The organ went silent, and he frantically scanned the dozens of paddle switches. *Who messed up my stops?* he wondered. At last, he found and flipped the ones that'd been out of place. He hadn't realized anyone might touch the organ after last night's dress rehearsal. He couldn't believe he'd forgotten to make a final check before the concert.

With his heart still racing in panic, Alex again played the opening chord. This time, it sounded perfect. He worked his way through the lead-in, and then held the final chord just as he was supposed to. The student choir took the cue, and joined in as Alex began the song.

Alex knew that should've made him feel better. That should've restored his confidence. But his wrists and feet were still trembling from the panicked adrenaline rush. His muscle memory evaporated with it. The music wouldn't flow naturally. He had to consciously command his fingers to land on each set of keys, and his feet to land on each of the pedals. Terrified that he would get something wrong, he kept his eyes glued to the sheet music he thought he knew so well. He could feel every muscle in his thighs, arms, and upper back tense to the limit for a "prevent defense."

Somewhere around "peace on Earth and mercy mild," Alex's prevent defense cracked. His sweaty fingers slipped on the keys, producing not just a sour note but a whole sour *chord.* As he twitched in reaction, his stocking feet slipped on the pedals. That added two more dissonant notes to the ugliness.

He took his eyes off the sheet music, located the correct keys, and played them — but by then it was too late. The choir had been thrown off its timing, and struggled to match its words to his notes.

Alex tried to keep playing from memory, his eyes scanning the sheet music for where he'd left off. His fingers wouldn't cooperate. He played three more sour chords before finally hitting his stride again and finishing the piece.

Polite applause filled the church. Alex turned to his teacher with a shamed expression. "I'm sorry," he whispered.

"Shake it off," she replied, arranging Alex's next set of sheet music. "We both know how well you can play. Just do it."

Miss Perez announced that the third graders would be singing "Away in a Manger." Alex closed his eyes and took a deep breath. He tried telling himself his mistakes were over. *Everything will be fine from here. Mrs. Rossi believes in me.* Yet he couldn't shake a nagging feeling that something wasn't right.

The instant Alex began playing the song's intro, he realized what it was. His stops! He'd forgotten to change them! The organ was again emulating the wrong mix of instruments. *How could I have forgotten?*

"Just play," Mrs. Rossi said, firmly, before Alex could break off and throw any switches.

And so he did. But all the notes he played, though correct, struck him as unfamiliar. The song didn't sound the way he'd practiced. The third graders seemed to be adjusting all right, but Alex couldn't stop thinking about how "wrong" his accompaniment was. He again hunched up and glued his eyes to the music, terrified of playing the wrong chord. Which, of course, he soon slipped and did. And then did again.

As the audience again applauded politely, Mrs. Rossi set up his next pages. The first thing Alex did was set his stops correctly. Then he checked them, just to make sure.

Alex managed to survive the next six pieces, but not without several missed chords, muffed notes, and misplaced stops — each of which shook his confidence more deeply. *I never missed a single note in practice,* he kept thinking. *And now I can't play a single song without at least three mistakes. What's happened to me?*

As Miss Perez announced the next piece, Alex resolved to play it perfectly. *I know I can do it.* At the same time, he felt a new discomfort growing inside him. Not nerves. Those had been shot long before. He had to go to the bathroom. In all the frenzy of making up for being late, Alex hadn't relieved himself before the concert.

As he began playing "God Rest Ye Merry Gentlemen," Alex tried thinking of just how long it'd been since he'd gone to the bathroom. *Since before dinner?* His concentration broken, Alex played three wrong notes in a row.

They finally arrived at a ten minute break from music, as a group of students presented a Nativity skit. Alex got up from the organ and stretched, and was amazed at how sore his muscles felt.

"I've gotta run to the bathroom," he whispered to Mrs. Rossi. He was in such a hurry, he didn't even bother putting on his shoes before hobble-trotting toward the steps.

"Don't take long," she whispered, tapping her watch.

Alex snuck to the restroom, glad no one else was in the foyer. Especially not his parents, or any of the Santuccis. How could he explain to them how terribly he'd been playing?

With his mind churning a million miles an hour, Alex didn't pay much attention to what might be on the bathroom floor. His foot splashed into a puddle. It wasn't a big one, but big enough to soak his sock. It slapped on the floor as he hurried to a urinal.

Only when he'd finished, and was washing his hands, did Alex feel something else churning within him. All the crazy stress of running late, and straining to play perfectly, and knowing he was failing, and now knowing he had to hurry back and somehow play six more songs...all of it was tying his insides in knots. Deep in his gut, his bowels agitated like they wanted to expel every last bit of badness. Right now.

Alex hobble-sprinted to a stall, getting his socks even more wet. He managed to set himself on the toilet just in time.

The first wave seemed to flow out of him forever. When it'd passed, Alex figured he had finished just in time to get back upstairs. Then, Alex felt his whole gut twisting and wanting to empty itself again. He immediately sat back down and waited for it to happen.

And waited. And waited. He felt it there, trying to move. It just wouldn't. He heard two other people come in and use the urinals. That only made him feel more pressure to hurry up and finish. Except he couldn't. His stomach was so knotted, he could do nothing but sit doubled-over and wait.

Then he heard it: the rumbling of the organ coming to life upstairs. He glanced at his watch, and realized the skit must've ended. Mrs. Rossi was going to have to play the next song. *How mad is she going to be?* Alex wondered. Those thoughts only made his stomach twist even more.

Alex finally managed to finish, wash his hands, and dash back up to the choir loft. Mrs. Rossi was playing the final bars of Ye Watchers and Ye Holy Ones, in perfect harmony with the choir below. It struck Alex as spine-tinglingly beautiful. Perfect. *Why haven't I been able to play like that tonight?*

With his feet now soaking wet, Alex could feel his toes going numb. He pulled off his socks and stashed them in his shoes. He then picked up the sheet music he'd be needing for the next song.

"Sorry I'm late," he whispered, as Mrs. Rossi slipped from the organ bench. "I was —."

She waved her hand. "Just settle in and play."

Alex arranged his sheet music, and carefully set the stops for Silent Night. He was so focused on getting everything exactly right, he tuned out Miss Perez's introduction. Once she had finished talking, Alex closed his eyes, took a deep breath, and played the entire lead-in perfectly. *Yes! At last, I'm in the groove. I can do this!*

He opened his eyes as he held the final chord, and realized Mrs. Rossi was staring at him oddly. Puzzled, but resolved to keep going, Alex began playing the main part of the song. Except something was wrong. Only a few kids in the choir were actually singing, and the rest were murmuring in confusion.

"It's the wrong piece!" Mrs. Rossi half-whispered, shaking Alex's shoulder.

Alex abruptly stopped playing. A wave of horror swept over him. He'd been positive that Silent Night was next. How could he have been wrong?

Miss Perez came back to the microphone and made some jokes about "malfunctions." That bought enough time for Mrs. Rossi to put O Holy Night on the organ's music stand. To Alex's shame, Mrs. Rossi even set the stops for him. *I guess I'm not capable of doing anything for myself tonight,* he thought.

He was now completely rattled, and his bare wet toes were growing increasingly numb. Alex stumbled through all three verses of O Holy Night with about as many mistakes as he'd made earlier. Maybe more. He did the same for the next piece.

Mrs. Rossi arranged his music and set the stops for Angels We Have Heard on High. Alex gazed down to the sanctuary. Tim had already taken his place at one of the microphones, for his solo. Alex's mind flashed back to his final baseball game, when his incompetence had cost his team the championship. He thought about all the ways Tim had rubbed his face in it. *And now, here I am, incompetent as ever,* Alex thought. *About to choke for Tim's solo. And then for Connor's, in the song after that. And then for the grand finale of the night, after that.*

Alex gazed back at the sheet music, and down at the manuals. He couldn't imagine anything worse than continuing to choke. Tim would never let him forget it. Connor would be totally disappointed if Alex let him down — especially when his friend was so happy about his dad getting a job. He had to stop ruining everybody's night.

"I'm sorry," Alex whispered to Mrs. Rossi, then scooted off the organ bench. "I just can't do this. You need to finish."

He stood unsteadily on his mismatched legs, sandy-blond head bowed in shame, unable to make eye contact with his teacher. "Alex," she whispered, putting her hand on his shoulder, "I know you can do it. You have to do it. You can't just quit."

Alex shook his head, fighting back tears. They weren't tears of embarrassment at how he'd sounded for the audience. They were tears of shame at how far he'd fallen below his teacher's expectations.

"I'm sorry," Alex gurgled, refusing to let any of his welling tears actually fall. He hobbled to the corner of the choir loft, sat on the floor, and pulled his knees to his chin.

Alex went numb, wishing an earthquake would swallow him alive, as Mrs. Rossi played the final three songs perfectly. The choir and soloists sang perfectly. *Awesome job, Connor,* he thought, as his best friend finished. *I'm glad I didn't totally blow your big night.*

A few minutes later, the last notes of the evening faded into thunderous applause. Alex drew himself tighter into the fetal position and closed his eyes. He didn't dare even look at Mrs. Rossi when she stooped to comfort him. "Everyone has a bad night, Alex," she said, tousling his short hair. "Get yourself some ice cream, and get yourself some sleep. We'll talk after New Year's. Okay?"

"I'm sorry again. And I don't really want ice cream. I'm staying here."

Mrs. Rossi hesitated, but then turned and descended the choir loft steps.

Alex seethed for several long minutes, stewing in his anger and frustration. Then, footsteps approached the choir loft. Alex looked up, and saw his mother's worried face gazing at him from the doorway.

"We're all downstairs getting ice cream," she said. "Are you going to join us?"

Alex shook his head. Something inside him snapped. "I never should've let you talk me into playing this stupid concert. I never want to touch that stupid organ ever again."

His mother gazed at him for a long moment, not saying anything. Alex could see the hurt filling her eyes. He immediately felt bad about how he'd talked to her. But before he could apologize, she turned and hurried downstairs.

Alex returned to his "state of seethe," made even worse by the guilt of how he'd hurt his mother. Now he *really* didn't want to show his face downstairs. He wondered if he could just sleep in the choir loft tonight.

A moment later, Alex heard heavy and determined steps sounding on the stairs. He had a pretty good idea who was coming now.

Rob leaned against the doorjamb, arms folded, and gazed across the choir loft at his son. Just as Meg had described, Alex was curled up in the fetal position, barefoot. The boy stared back at him with an expression of anger and defeat.

Rob was at a loss as to where to start. He'd been dreaming about showing off Alex's talent, and basking in the boy's glory. He'd even imagined the awed congratulations from their friends. Then, as Alex's mistakes had multiplied, Rob had felt overcome with shame. Not at Alex. At himself, for setting the boy up and pushing him into something he may not have been ready for. More than anything, he was ashamed for even thinking about showing off his son. With every muffed note, and every sour chord, Rob had wanted to put his arm around the boy's shoulder and tell him everything would be all right. He'd wanted to tell Alex to just settle down, and play the way he knew he could. *Just play.*

Even now, Rob wanted to comfort his son. But first, he needed to take care of something else. "I know you had a rough night. But what you told your mother was completely unacceptable."

"I know. I'm very sorry. I'm just so mad about everything. All the words came out wrong."

"I'm not the one you need to apologize to. Your mother is very upset."

"I'll tell her I'm sorry," Alex promised.

Rob gazed at his son expectantly. "Are you coming any time soon? We're all down in the basement, saving you ice cream."

Alex shook his head. "Just come get me when you leave for home."

Rob thought for a moment, hoping he could reassure Alex enough to get him downstairs. "I know the concert was rough, but you really recovered at the end. Those last three songs were outstanding."

Alex stared back, exasperated. "Mrs. Rossi played those! All the bad ones — that was me."

"I thought you were playing all the songs."

"Was supposed to. But I didn't want to keep ruining the whole night."

"You mean, you quit?"

"Yeah, Dad. I quit. I'm a quitter. Not just a loser organist. And loser everything else."

Taken aback at his son's words, Rob needed a moment to think. "Alex," he said at last. "There's nothing you can do about tonight. It's done, and you need to put it behind you."

"Yeah," Alex muttered.

"And then, think about what's next. Set a goal. A big one, maybe with a lot of smaller ones in between that lead to it. Because your mother and I, and Mrs. Rossi, know you can get there."

"Yeah," Alex repeated.

Rob gave his son a long look before continuing. "Just promise me two things, okay?"

"What?"

"Number one, dream big. Number two, don't ever quit. Okay?"

Alex hugged his knees to his chin, and gazed at the carpet. "Okay. I promise. But I'm still not coming down for ice cream."

Alex knew his father was trying to be encouraging. And he knew his father was right about needing to put the concert behind him and set a new goal. He'd do that eventually. For now, he wanted nothing more than to be left alone and sort out his thoughts.

What went so wrong tonight? Why couldn't I just play the music? Why was I so worked up about what everybody would think of me? Was that my mistake? Wanting to show everybody I was better than them?

After several long minutes of blessed solitude, Alex heard a child's footsteps ascending. Hugging his knees more tightly to his chest, he glanced at the doorway. He hoped to see Ben, telling him they were leaving. Instead, to his surprise, it was Ronnie. She was carrying a plastic cup and spoon in each hand.

"Hey, Alex" she greeted him, with a nervous smile. "I brought you something."

A moment later, Ronnie was sitting cross-legged in front of him. She handed Alex one of the plastic cups and spoons.

"Ice cream!" Alex exclaimed. Ronnie had even added some fudge sauce and sprinkles to the vanilla soft serve. As he stirred the sundae, he couldn't help grinning at his cousin's thoughtfulness. At the same time, he couldn't help feeling the pent-up anger drain out of him. "Thanks," he added, taking his first bite.

The two of them ate in silence for a while before Ronnie spoke. "You never saw my first on-stage speaking performance, did you?"

Alex shook his head and savored the chocolaty mix of flavors. "I spent that whole summer at home with busted legs."

"Your folks tell you about it?"

Alex shook his head again, curious as to what'd happened.

"I had exactly three lines," Ronnie grinned, setting her empty cup down and fiddling with her long braid. "Totally forgot two of them. Had to be prompted by another actor. The other line I got right, but I delivered it at the wrong point in the play. Threw everybody off."

"You?" Alex had never imagined Ronnie making a mistake on stage. Certainly not a big one. "You've always been perfect."

"Not that time," Ronnie replied, still grinning. "I was so ashamed, I wanted to crawl in a hole and never come out."

"What'd you do?" Alex asked, taking another bite of ice cream.

"Went backstage and cried. Figured my acting career was over, at the ripe old age of ten. But then the director sat down with me, and said I'd just had a bad night. Said he knew I'd learn from the experience, and never mess up that way again. And he wanted me to perform the next night more than ever."

Alex stirred and ate the last bit of his sundae, thinking about what his cousin had said.

"Everybody has a bad night," Ronnie added. "What matters is what you do next."

"I suppose. But maybe I'm not like you. Maybe I'm just a lousy musician."

"You're not a bad musician," Ronnie insisted, putting her hand on his shoulder. "You're a very good musician who had one bad night."

Alex thought for a moment. "Tonight wasn't just a bad night. Tonight was 'Alexander and the terrible, horrible, no good, very bad concert'," he said, not even intending to make a joke. But Ronnie's eyes lit up, and she giggled.

Something inside Alex told him that the evening had been such a total disaster, there was nothing else to do but make fun of it. Without even thinking, chuckles began bubbling out of him. They felt so good, Alex began laughing. Really laughing. Soon Ronnie was laughing just as much. The two of them laughed so long and so hard, Alex wasn't sure it would ever end.

"Thanks," Alex said, when at last their laughter subsided to bemused smiles.

Ronnie looked at her empty cup, still grinning. "Think there's any more ice cream left downstairs?"

"Only one way to find out!" Alex replied.

TWENTY-SIX

December 20, 2008

WHILE CONNOR WAS VISITING MR. CROWLEY'S PLANT, Alex spent most of the day thinking about what Dad had told him after the concert. He should dream big, and pick a new goal. He knew he'd continue making music, and would somehow find a way to perform in public again. But the dream that really captured his imagination was Seattle to Portland. Alex couldn't stop thinking about it, or picturing himself riding it. He even streamed the video, with his musical score, several times in a row. *I will ride the one-day STP as soon as I possibly can,* he promised himself. *And I will not quit. No matter what.*

Mass that Sunday seemed to drag forever. Alex could see Connor and his parents from across the church, and he was dying to hear the details about Mr. Crowley's new job. All weekend, he'd been giving thanks that Connor wouldn't have to leave St. Clement school.

Connor went directly to the foyer after Mass, but Mr. and Mrs. Crowley straggled behind to chat with Alex's parents. Alex spotted his opportunity to talk with Connor. He hustled to the foyer to catch up with him.

They greeted each other, and then Alex asked, "Did you visit your dad's new plant yesterday?"

"Yes," Connor replied.

"What's it like?" The suspense was killing him.

Connor gave him a look that was almost cold. "I can't tell you yet."

Alex was puzzled. He and Connor never kept secrets from each other. He wanted to ask more questions, but the boys' parents were approaching. "Are you going to coffee and donuts?"

Connor glanced at his mother before answering. "My folks said we have a lot of … stuff we have to do today."

"Will you be done in time to come over and watch football this afternoon? The Seahawks are supposed to have a pretty good game against the Jets."

Alex's mother cut in. "Connor's mom was just telling me that they'll be busy all day. We need to let them get going."

The two families said their good-byes. The Petersons went down to the basement social hall, where Ben had already gone with several of his friends. The donuts tasted as good as ever, but Alex kept wondering why Connor had acted so strangely. Coffee and donuts wasn't nearly as much fun without the Crowleys. He was glad when his folks decided, despite Ben's objections, to head for home after just fifteen minutes.

Once they'd arrived, Alex and Ben changed into play clothes. Then, as they were tromping toward the basement to build a city of Lincoln Logs, their mother stopped them.

"Ben, you go downstairs and get started. Alex will be down in a minute. Okay?"

That was definitely strange. "What? Am I in trouble?" Alex asked.

"No. I wanted to talk to you privately about why Connor and his parents couldn't stay."

"I was wondering. What's going on?"

"Let's go to your room, okay?"

Alex thought that was even stranger, but he led his mother into his room. He sat, cross-legged, in the middle of his bed.

His mother closed the door before pulling up a chair to face him. The closed door made Alex especially uncomfortable.

"What has Connor already told you about his father's new job?" his mother asked.

"Not much."

"Did he tell you where it is?"

"Just that it's a plant making pop bottles," Alex shrugged.

Alex's mother looked like she was deciding where to start. "Mr. Crowley got an excellent long-term contract with a company that's very solid. But the plant is south of Tacoma. About 90 minutes from here. Or longer, if traffic is bad."

Tacoma. "Wow. That's a long commute. Dad's really lucky he can work from home."

His mother looked at Alex in silence. He sensed something bad was coming.

"Alex, suppose the only school you and Ben could attend were 90 minutes from here. And you *had* to go there. What would you want me and your father to do?"

"But that wouldn't happen. There are lots of good schools."

"I know. Let's just pretend."

"If Ben and I had no choice about going there, I suppose I'd want the whole family to—." Alex stopped himself. He knew the end of the sentence. In a flash, he understood what his mother had been getting at. *But if I don't say the words, it won't be real,* he told himself.

"I'm so sorry, sweetheart," she said, and put her arms out.

Alex pulled back. He didn't want his mother to comfort him. He refused to let her to hug him. If he allowed her to touch him, he'd only be letting her make everything okay. *And Connor moving to Tacoma could never be made okay. Not ever.*

"When?" he asked, struggling to control the rage he could feel boiling within him.

"Next week. The Crowleys thought it'd be best for Connor to start at his new school the first day back in January. They didn't even tell him until yesterday, because they didn't want him to be sad at the concert. They're moving some things to their new apartment today. They hope to have everything else moved a few days after Christmas."

Christmas. Christmas is totally ruined. No matter what I get, I refuse to be happy on Christmas. I would trade every single Christmas present for Connor getting to stay in Bothell. Alex felt everything in his world spinning out of control. *They have a new place. They're already moving things into it. It's already happening. When I told God I wanted to help, this is* not *what I meant.*

Alex crawled backward on his bed, all the way to the corner, as far from his mother as he could. He pulled his knees up and buried his face in them, just like he had after the concert.

"Sweetheart, I know this is terribly hard for you, but—."

"I'd rather break my legs again!"

"You don't mean that."

"I do mean that." Alex insisted. He could feel his throat tightening, and his eyes beginning to burn. He resolved not to let himself actually cry.

"I was trying to say that as hard as this is for you, and for Connor, don't you think it'd be much worse if his father were gone three extra hours every day? And was exhausted and stressed from a commute when he was home?"

Alex clutched his short hair and pressed his forehead harder against his knees. *I love being able to go to Dad's office, any time, and talk about stuff. It's awesome having Dad here when I come home from school. I love riding with Dad. Dad being gone all the time would be the worst thing in the world. But if I admit it out loud, I'll be admitting it's okay for Connor to move.*

"Please leave me alone," Alex said, covering his head with a pillow.

His mother stood up, then touched his shoulder for a moment. "I am very sorry, Sweetheart."

Alex somehow managed to last until his mother slipped out and closed the door before disintegrating into a raging mass of tears.

TWENTY-SEVEN

ROB WAS GETTING COMFORTABLE IN FRONT OF THE TV WHEN he spotted Meg emerging from Alex's room. From her pained expression, Rob assumed she'd just broken the news about Connor. Meg remained listening for a moment before coming to the living room and plopping down next to him.

"How'd he take it?" Rob asked, putting his arm around her.

"About as you'd expect," she sighed, cuddling close and resting her face against him. "Bawling his head off."

Meg looked emotionally drained, herself. "Should I go in there and say something?" Rob asked.

"No. He kept it together until I left, and he's muffling his sobs with his pillow. He doesn't want us to know he's crying. He'll especially crawl in a hole if you catch him doing it."

"You can tell that?"

"Trust me. I know Alex pretty well. He's done talking to me. He'll come to you when he's ready. But right now he's angry, and needs to get it all out of his little system before he can talk."

"He has every right to be upset."

"Absolutely. I just wish I could've explained it better."

"You probably did it better than I would have."

"Yeah," Meg said, sitting up and continuing in a deep voice: "Suck it up, kid! Be a man! Bad stuff happens! You just gotta deal with it!"

They both chuckled, and then Meg turned serious. "Please be understanding with him. I'm going to take Ben to the mall for some Christmas shopping, to give you two some time alone. I think you need to take the lead on this one."

"It'll be fine," Rob assured her.

Once Meg and Ben left, Rob tried to turn his attention to the Seahawks game. But Meg's words, *You need to take the lead,* echoed in Rob's mind. He liked that the two of them were such a team, and seemed to know instinctively when one or the other should be out front. And he knew Meg was right. Alex needed him today, more than he needed his mother.

Around the end of the first quarter, Rob heard a bedroom door opening. Alex hobbled slowly toward the living room.

Rob noticed the boy's bright-red eyes first. His face glistened with newly-dried tears. Alex's nose looked raw, and even his short blond hair was a mess. "Mom here?" he asked.

"She and Ben went to the mall. You want me to call her?"

Alex shook his head, then sat down on the couch next to his father. Rob put his arm around the boy and hugged him close. "I'm really sorry about Connor."

Alex nodded, and seemed to say, "Thanks," but the word didn't come out clearly.

"Want to watch the game?"

"Only if you do."

Rob clicked the TV off. "What would you rather do?"

"Is it too cold to go for a ride? I think I need to thrash on some pedals or something."

Rob glanced out the window and checked the thermometer. It was a gloomy thirty degrees. Trees were moving in a breeze, but the roads looked clear. "If you want to get bundled up, I'll do the same. And then I'll get the pedals and seat adjusted. I think Ben rode stoker last time."

Ten minutes later, father and son were pedaling through the quiet residential streets of their neighborhood. "Where do you want to go?" Rob asked.

"Woodinville?"

Rob turned the tandem toward downtown Bothell. "Road or trail?" he asked.

"Road, please."

They set out across town, working their way toward the 102nd Avenue bridge. Rob decided not to say anything until Alex was ready to talk.

Alex finally spoke up as they crossed high above the frigid Sammamish River. "Did you ever have your best friend move away?"

They made the sweeping curve onto Riverside Drive, and it felt like the wind was now behind them. Rob hoped the breeze wouldn't be too icy in their faces on the way back. In the meantime, he tried to think of a way he could redirect Alex's question. Like he would in a focus group.

"Not exactly," Rob said, turning so Alex could hear him in the wind. "But there've been some times when your mother and I were blindsided by something that seemed really hard. And then, and this is the big thing, something weird always seemed to happen later. We always seemed to end up better off than if we'd gotten exactly what we'd wanted at first. Does that make sense?"

"Maybe," Alex replied, leaning forward on the handlebars to hear better. "What's an example?"

Now Rob really had to think. "Ben. It took us a long time to get you, so your mother said we should start trying for another baby right away. We ended up getting Ben a lot faster than we'd expected. At first we felt overwhelmed by having two kids under the age of two. Now we can't imagine having waited any longer to get him. And isn't it great having a brother who's close to you in age?"

"I guess. We're able to do a lot together. If he were a lot younger, we wouldn't like the same stuff."

The two of them pedaled in silence for several minutes, and soon were approaching Woodinville. Rob was distracted by missing a couple of shifts with the gears. When he tried moving the chain to certain cogs in the rear cluster, it would rattle and not seat itself properly. He chalked this up to the cogs wearing out, and figured he should start shopping for a new freewheel.

Rob finally settled into the right gear. "How far do you want to go?" he asked.

"My fingers are getting cold. Maybe we can turn around at the stop sign."

At the intersection with 175th Street in Woodinville, Rob made a sweeping U-turn back toward Bothell. Just as he'd feared, the frigid breeze was now blowing straight into his face. He lowered his head and focused on cranking the pedals, all the while hoping Alex's fingers wouldn't grow any more numb. Rob made a mental note to buy some better cold weather gear for him before Christmas.

"There's something I still don't get," Alex said, once they'd pedaled back to their cruising speed. "What could ever be good about Connor and me being so far apart? Tacoma's way more than an hour from here. I'll hardly ever see him. He's my only friend. Who'll I eat lunch with? Who'll I ride home with? Who'll I talk to about homework and stuff?"

Rob concentrated on the road ahead, steering around a pothole before turning to answer Alex. "I don't know for sure. But I bet that six months or a year from now, you'll see some ways this has been good for both of you."

"I bet not."

The two of them pedaled in silence for a long time. "I just don't get why all the good kids like Connor have to go so far away," Alex said at last.

The two of them struggled to climb into downtown Bothell, and Rob considered Alex's question carefully. He was glad for the long climb, because it took him until they leveled out at Main Street to organize his thoughts. "Mr. and Mrs. Crowley like living here. But they like having time together as a family even more. It turns out they can only have one."

As the two of them pedaled through downtown residential streets, Alex didn't say anything for a full block. "Does that make sense?" Rob asked.

"I guess," Alex replied. "I just wish Mr. Crowley could work from home. Like you do."

"I have to travel overnight sometimes."

"Yeah, but still ... ."

They pulled onto their block, and began coasting toward home. "Dad," Alex asked, "can we keep riding for a little?"

"Your hands okay?"

"Getting numb. I'd just like to ride with you a little more."

Rob was starting to lose sensation in his fingers and toes, too, but he felt a warm glow that more than made up for it. "Where would you like to go?"

"I don't know. Just around."

The downtown streets were deserted, which made it easy to cruise up and down the blocks. "When do kids have to start making decisions like that?" Alex asked.

"Usually when they go to college. Or get their first job. Do they stay near their parents? Or go to a situation that's better for them, even if it's far away?"

"Was it hard for you, moving to L.A. after college?"

"My family wasn't very close-knit, so moving to L.A. was actually an escape. I'd gotten a great job offer from Frank Hurwitz. I knew Decision Strategies would be perfect for me. I didn't miss Seattle at all."

"What about Mom?"

"It was a lot harder for her, when we decided to get married a little after that. She had to leave her family to be with me in California. Just about killed her. But she knew it was right."

The two of them listened to the sound of rubber tires rolling on pavement for a minute or two, before Alex spoke up again. "Did *you* ever have to make a decision like that? Like Mom did? Or like the Crowleys? Something that was really hard, but was the right thing in some bigger way?"

Rob thought for a moment. "Remember all those bib numbers I showed you, before we did the Kitsap ride?"

"Yeah," Alex replied.

"Ever wonder why those ended in 1999? And why my bike had so much dust?"

"I guess I didn't think about it."

"What else happened in 1999?"

"Well, Ben was born."

"Exactly."

"You gave up cycling so you could spend more time with Ben?" Alex asked.

"And you. And your mother. I loved riding by myself. But I loved you guys more."

Alex seemed to be thinking about this. "I'm glad you can ride and spend time with us now. And hopefully Connor's dad will find a job in Bothell someday."

"Yes, hopefully."

They turned and rode up Main Street, past all the empty businesses. Rob caught their reflection in one of the plate glass windows. *We're a pretty good-looking team, if I say so myself,* he thought.

They pedaled several blocks in silence. "Dad?" Alex said at last. "I think I'm ready to go home now. Can we still watch some football?"

TWENTY-EIGHT

January 5, 2009

A LEX SAT STARING AT HIS HOMEROOM DESK. ALL AROUND him, kids buzzed with excitement. Everyone wanted to talk about what they'd done, where they'd gone, and what gifts they'd gotten.

Everyone except Alex. All he could think about was the empty desk next to his.

The days after Christmas, he'd helped the Crowleys load their moving truck. He'd been glad for the time with his friend. The hard work had been a welcome distraction, but it'd been over by the middle of last week. He couldn't stop thinking that this was the worst Christmas ever.

In the days since the Crowleys left, he'd spent a lot of time at the church, playing Beethoven symphonies by ear. He loved having the building to himself. He especially loved rocking the building's foundations during the finale fourth movement of Beethoven's Seventh. That was definitely his favorite piece of music, ever. He hadn't even cared when a group of people had stopped into the church and looked around while he was playing. He didn't really care what anybody thought of him, or his music, or what he played, or how loudly he played it.

Ben had been excited about staying up and watching the ball drop on New Year's Eve. All Alex could think about was how he and Connor used to stay up in sleeping bags on the living room floor that night every year. Connor's parents said they wished Alex could come to their new place, but it was too much of a mess with unpacking. And they were too busy to drive Connor to Bothell.

Maybe next year.

He wondered how he and Connor would stay in touch. Neither of them liked talking on the phone. His parents didn't let him have email or Facebook. Sitting down to write letters wasn't something Alex could imagine doing much. Their parents promised they'd find a way for the boys to get together, like for Connor's birthday next month. But that wasn't the same as being around a friend all the time. Alex figured Connor would have new friends pretty soon. They'd probably forget about each other.

Mrs. O'Malley called homeroom to order. Alex noticed a new boy standing next to her. The boy looked lost, and his blue sweater was definitely a uniform violation. With his olive skin and dark hair, he looked almost Mexican. Or half Asian. *I don't care who you are, or what your name is,* Alex thought. *You aren't Connor. And you never will be. They probably only let you in because Connor left and opened a sixth grade slot.*

Their teacher said the boy was Jacob Adams, and that his family moved here over Christmas break from Dallas. *Great. Another Jacob. That's original,* Alex thought. Mrs. O'Malley asked the other students to introduce themselves to Jacob sometime that day, and make him feel welcome.

Everyone stared at Jacob as he made his way to Connor's old desk. It reminded Alex of the first time he'd shown up to school with shoes that didn't match. *At least it's not me this time,* he thought.

As the prayer and announcements came over the PA speakers, Jacob looked around at the other students. Alex peered straight ahead and ignored him.

Once the announcements were over, Mrs. O'Malley came to Jacob's desk. "I forgot," she told him. "We need you to fill out this form."

As Mrs. O'Malley walked away, Jacob began fumbling through his brand new backpack. *Probably looking for a pen,* Alex thought. After searching in vain for a minute, Jacob looked toward the teacher and began raising his hand tentatively. Alex smirked as he watched from the corner of his eye. *That's it. Let the whole class know you didn't even remember a pen.*

As if reading Alex's thoughts, Jacob dropped his hand and rummaged harder in the backpack. Alex almost began taking cruel pleasure in Jacob's frantic search.

Suddenly, Alex caught himself. *What am I doing?* he wondered. *I'm not a bully. Why am I thinking like one?* His callousness sickened him, especially when another image came to his mind: Connor, in a classroom full of strange kids in Tacoma, unable even to find a pen. Alex could imagine Connor's exact facial expression. He felt even more overwhelmed with guilt.

Alex took a long look at the boy next to him. "Jacob?"

The new boy looked up from his backpack, and regarded Alex with a quizzical expression.

"Need a pen?" Alex asked, holding out one of his own.

Jacob looked visibly relieved. "Thanks."

"Sure. My name's Alex, by the way."

TWENTY-NINE

ROB STUDIED THE BACKGROUND MATERIALS THE CLIENT HAD sent. He wondered how he could transform this hundred-page mess into a coherent three-page discussion outline for next week's focus groups in Denver. The city was trying to impose a tax on soda pop, and a consortium of soft drink companies hired Rob to determine the most compelling messages against it. They'd produced this enormous document with facts and arguments, which was far too much to put in front of a focus group. Rob's challenge was to boil the document down to a dozen or so messages for testing.

He was glad the boys had returned to school, and that the whole world seemed to be getting back to work after the Christmas and New Year's holidays. Even with his own detached office, he always found it hard to get things done when the boys were home. Something about knowing he had the entire property to himself, and that no one would interrupt him with a "quick" question or request, helped Rob concentrate.

An audio tone alerted Rob to a new email. The Denver facility had sent an update on recruitment, so he opened the message immediately. He reviewed the "grids," showing how many respondents — and with which characteristics — had agreed to participate in each session. It looked like they'd had a good weekend. Rob was relieved everything was on track.

His concentration broken, Rob decided he didn't want to return to the discussion outline just yet. He'd awakened that morning with tandem bikes on his mind. He couldn't resist the temptation to surf a few different bicycle websites. He especially enjoyed checking out the different models Santana and Co-Motion were offering. Both companies were small enough to be specialized tandem experts, but large enough to have impressive websites.

Alex and Ben liked the tandem they had now, but Rob dreamed about what they could get if he managed to have a really good year. Not like this was shaping up to be one. After the Denver project, he had nothing in the pipeline.

That could always change, though. He'd recently submitted several strong proposals, and figured he had a real chance at winning more than one of them. Plus, Frank Hurwitz could always call with something. With a nice windfall, he could upgrade their tandem's drivetrain. Maybe he could treat himself and the boys to a new, lightweight tandem with modern components. Perhaps they could even find one of the three-seated "triplet" tandems, so both boys could ride with him.

Rob glanced at the clock. He knew he needed to quit daydreaming. Still, he wanted to browse just one more site: Cascade's page for STP. Doug Lloyd had posted something to Facebook about registration opening, and Rob couldn't help following the link. Cascade had already put up a lot of information about the event. The promotional video, with Alex's score, was featured front and center. He watched it three times in a row.

Rob's heart raced as he remembered the excitement of being part of something so big, and of being surrounded by so many people who were all doing the same challenge. He also remembered the start-line experience last summer, and how he'd almost wanted to follow the riders on their way. Alex's inspiring music made him want to chase those riders all the more.

He wondered if Doug and Penny Lloyd would be riding on their tandem. *What's holding me back from doing it this year?* he asked himself. *I've got more than six months to get in shape. I've been out riding so much, I'm not starting from zero. Training won't take me away from the boys. Training is the way the boys spend time with me. The Colnago is running sweet. It'll feel especially light after climbing all those hills on a tandem.*

Even after Rob closed the browser and tried going back to work, he couldn't stop thinking about STP. He knew he was running out of excuses for not doing it, especially after Alex had challenged him about tackling big adventures.

Wouldn't training for my first double century in ten years be a great challenge? he wondered. *Wouldn't that help me be more disciplined about getting to bed when I know I should? About drinking less? About getting up on time in the morning? How would any of those things be bad?*

In a flash, Rob wondered if "being more self-disciplined" was as daunting to him as "playing the organ in public" had been for Alex. Maybe that was just as important of a thing for him to confront. After all, he'd now wasted nearly an hour of good work time daydreaming about bikes. He couldn't even begin to count the hours he'd wasted because he couldn't get himself out of bed in the morning after a late night in front of the TV having "one last" beer or glass of blackberry wine.

Rob again looked at the clock, and forced himself to knuckle down on the discussion outline. He resolved not to break for anything but lunch until he'd produced an entire first draft. He wanted to make sure he was ready to ride as soon as the boys got home from school. It was Ben's turn to go with him that afternoon. Perhaps if they left early enough, there would be time later for Alex to go out, too.

THIRTY

ALEX GREETED JACOB, AND THE TWO BOYS SETTLED INTO their desks at homeroom for lunch. He wished Connor were here, so the three of them could eat together.

"Who've you met so far?" Alex asked, opening his brown bag.

"Not very many people," Jacob replied. He set a sandwich and orange on his desk. "I'm hoping recess will be different."

"Maybe I can introduce you to some kids."

As the boys enjoyed their lunches, Alex learned that Jacob's father worked for Boeing and had been transferred. He had four older sisters, the youngest of whom was named Maria. She was in the eighth grade at St. Clement. He also had a little brother in kindergarten. Jacob never did say what his family's ethnicity was, and Alex didn't think he should ask. He figured he'd find out soon enough. Alex was happy Jacob hadn't asked why his shoes didn't match.

"Did you go to Catholic school in Dallas?" Alex asked, offering some of the carrot sticks his mother had packed.

Jacob took one of the carrots and began munching on it. "Thanks. Actually, we were homeschooled. But things have been so crazy with moving, and we don't even have a house yet. We're probably going to be stuck in an apartment for a while. My folks thought it'd be best for us to go to school the rest of this year. Maybe homeschool again in the fall."

"Makes sense. Some of my cousins are homeschooled. Maybe you can meet them."

"That'd be cool," Jacob said, taking another of Alex's carrots. "My mom said going to school might help us meet new friends faster. She'll think it's funny if it helps us meet other homeschooled kids!"

Alex chuckled, and finished the last of the carrots.

Jacob started squinting at him, as if trying to remember something. "Hey, I've been thinking you look familiar. Were you the kid who was playing the organ at church?"

"You mean at the concert?"

Jacob shook his head. "We stopped to see the church one afternoon last week. We heard someone playing."

Alex remembered seeing a group downstairs at the church. There'd been several kids, none of whom he recognized. They'd all tried to move around and talk quietly. "That was me. They let me practice on it. I'm surprised you remembered."

"You were amazing. We were only going to look around real quick. We stayed fifteen minutes listening to you."

"Thanks," Alex said, feeling self-conscious.

"Do you play any other instruments?"

"Piano, and I have an electronic keyboard. Why?"

"Maria and I play violin. Maybe we could try playing a violin and organ sonata with you sometime after school."

Alex decided he was going to like Jacob a lot. As the bell rang to start recess, his only regret was not knowing more kids he could introduce the new boy to.

THIRTY-ONE

January 11, 2009

ROB BROUGHT THE SPLITTING MAUL DOWN ON A CEDAR LOG. It separated neatly into two fireplace-sized pieces. "Nice one," Paul Santucci commented. Paul then smashed his own maul into another log.

They'd been working their way through this mountain of cedar for the last hour, and the two of them were hitting a good rhythm. Despite the chilly, thirty-degree day, Rob and Paul were so warm from exertion, they'd had to remove their jackets.

As Rob set up another large piece and prepared to split it, he spotted movement out of the corner of his eye. Turning, he saw Alex jogging across his grandfather's frozen lawn. His son was bundled up and pushing a large wheelbarrow.

"Hey, helper boy!" Paul greeted him.

"Hey, Uncle Paul," Alex replied. He began tossing freshly-split firewood into the wheelbarrow.

"Aren't Ronnie and Joseph going to help?" Paul asked.

"They're getting dressed. I'm going to take wood from here to the pile by the house. They're going to stack it for Grandpa."

"Make sure you stack at the far end of what's already there. This wood should age for next winter," Rob reminded him.

Pete Sullivan had broken his wrist a couple of weeks ago, and he'd been really heartened by how enthusiastically all the grandkids had pitched in to take care of chores like these. Rob knew it had to be killing the old man, not being able to help.

Rob and Paul split wood in silence for a few minutes, and then Alex returned for another load. "Hey, Uncle Paul," he said, as he began loading split logs. "Guess what? I've been meaning to tell you something. There's a new boy at my school. His family just moved here from Dallas, and they've got six kids. And they've been homeschooled."

Paul put one foot on a log and leaned against his splitting maul. "Did you tell him about us?"

"Yeah. I said hopefully you can meet them. His name's Jacob. We're good friends already. And he and his sister are going to play a sonata with me after school tomorrow."

Rob and Paul exchanged a quick grin. "Make sure you tell your Aunt Theresa. Then you should give Jacob our number so his mom can call."

"Okay. And I almost forgot. His mom's from Mexico. I told him your kids study Spanish, and are always wanting to meet native speakers."

"Have you told Ronnie and Joseph?"

"I will!" Alex promised. He began pushing the wheelbarrow away. He'd loaded it too heavily, and strained to make it move.

"Nice to see he's making friends," Paul commented, once Alex was out of earshot.

"He's always been so shy," Rob said, splitting another piece of wood. "I was worried the concert fiasco would make it worse. He seems to have recovered."

Paul smashed another log of his own, and kicked the pieces aside. "Too bad about the concert. Ronnie says she feels really bad for pushing him to do it."

"Meg and I pushed him, too. He does need to learn how to perform in public, and handle the pressure. Maybe we should've started with something smaller."

Paul thought for a moment, as he set up another log. "Our kids play piano and violin recitals every few months, with a couple dozen other homeschoolers. Theresa helps organize it. If Alex is interested, I'm sure he could join them."

"Interesting idea," Rob said, tossing his split pieces aside. "I'll have Meg talk to her."

The two of them worked in silence until Alex returned with the wheelbarrow. "Try a smaller load this time," Rob advised.

"I know," Alex said, with a sheepish grin.

"Ronnie and Joseph working hard?" Paul asked, as Alex filled the wheelbarrow.

"Yeah. Anthony's helping, too." A moment later, Alex was jogging back across the lawn.

Once his son disappeared, Rob saw the chance to talk to Paul about what'd been on his mind for the last week. "I realize this sounds weird. But when we were pushing Alex to play in the concert, I got thinking about something I honestly never thought I'd think about again."

Paul split his log, and began setting up another. "What's that?"

"STP," Rob said.

Paul dropped the maul and began laughing. "Now *that's* a non-sequitur! Unless the organ made you think about Oregon."

Rob couldn't help chuckling at the pun. "Organ/Oregon never even crossed my mind."

Then, resting his own maul on the frozen ground, Rob told the story about waxing the car with Alex. How he'd challenged the boy to do something big. How Alex had turned the tables and challenged *him* to do the same thing.

"Talked to Meg yet?"

"Yeah. Long talk. She said she's okay with it, as long as the boys want to train with me. Doesn't want me ditching them to be alone on the road. But before I pull the trigger, I guess I want to make sure I'm not crazy."

"I personally think anyone who does that ride is crazy," Paul said. He picked the maul back up. "Of course, maybe if I'd trained more, I would've had a better time keeping up with you. Whatever year that was you talked me into it."

Alex returned for another load. The two of them split several logs before he was again out of earshot.

"You never did tell me why you stopped riding. I just remember you sort of stopped talking about cycling or going to do any doubles."

"We had two little kids, and Meg needed me around. Once I stopped, inertia took over. Even when the kids got older, I couldn't get motivated to ride again."

"Until now," Paul said, with a bemused grin.

"The tandem's a lot of fun."

"So Ronnie and Joseph and Anthony tell me Alex told them. They want me to buy one."

"Now *that* would be interesting," Rob chuckled.

As they continued working, Rob explained more about what had been on his mind. "Everything in my head tells me this is something I should do. It'd be a great excuse to spend more time with the boys. Training would be really good for all of us. The self-discipline sure wouldn't hurt me. But it's just … I don't know."

The two of them split several more logs, and Paul seemed to be thinking. In the meantime, Alex returned for another load and then headed back toward the others.

"Would the boys ride with you to Portland?"

"Not this year. The tandem's a good way for me to rack up miles, while still spending time with them. They're just not old enough for STP. Maybe Meg could drive them to the finish line. We could make it a family vacation."

"Think they'll want to do that much training? I remember you used to be gone riding all day on Saturdays, when we were at the U-Dub."

Rob split another log, and kicked the pieces aside. "I think that's the big issue. But if the boys are willing to do it, I'm inclined to take the plunge."

"For the record, I think you're insane. But it might be the kind of insanity the world can use more of."

Rob laughed, and set up another log. They'd made a serious dent on their father-in-law's woodpile, and were pulling into the final stretch.

"I still do like to get out on a bike, by the way," Paul added. "My office is just a couple blocks off the Burke-Gilman trail. Any time you want to swing down for an easy lunchtime ride, I'd be happy to join you."

"Might just take you up on that."

As they worked to split the last several pieces, Rob found himself increasingly wanting to be alone with his thoughts.

More than that, he wanted to be alone on the open road, cruising on his Colnago.

Part of him agreed with Paul: preparing to ride STP again was insane. There was no reason for it. He had nothing to prove.

Yet, at the same time, Rob couldn't shake his excitement about the enormity of the adventure. He couldn't resist the thrill of once again doing — what was it that rider in the video had said? Something that "not a whole lot of other people in the world have ever done."

Rob decided that was some insanity the world could definitely use more of.

THIRTY-TWO

February 3, 2009

ROB IMMEDIATELY RECOGNIZED THE COMMOTION OUTSIDE his office. Alex and Ben had rolled up the garage door and were talking excitedly as they parked their bikes. A moment later, right on schedule, both boys burst through the office door. They were still wearing their school uniforms and backpacks.

"Who gets to ride first today?" Ben asked.

"You rode first yesterday. And you rode three days last week. I only rode two. And one of those was rainy."

"But you'll get to ride a lot more than me when baseball starts next month," Ben objected.

Rob held up a hand for silence, and then finished typing the sentence he'd been working on. He'd made good progress in writing up the report from the Denver soda pop focus groups, and this stopping point was as logical as any. He saved the document, then looked up and greeted the boys.

"If we get moving, there should be enough daylight for both of you to ride for a half hour today. Or we could do one long ride, if Ben wants to go on the trail-a-bike."

Ben shook his head. "I'd rather be a real stoker."

"Okay. Alex, go get dressed. Ben, we'll be back by 4:45. Be ready when we pull up."

The boys hurried off to the house, and Rob changed into the warm cycling clothes he'd stashed in the office closet. By the time he'd pulled on his thermal underwear, tights, turtleneck, jersey, and windproof jacket, he could hear the distinctive sound of Alex's cycling shoes hobbling across the driveway.

Alex arrived, dressed in the same warm outfit as Rob. He was glad he'd found good deals at Christmas for so much quality gear for both boys. His stokers stayed in much better spirits when they weren't frozen.

He and Alex pulled insulated shoe covers over their feet, wool balaclavas over their heads, and then snapped their helmets in place before putting on gloves. A moment later, they were gliding through their neighborhood on the Santana.

"Too bad it takes almost as much time to get dressed as it does to ride," Rob joked.

"But it's worth it."

"Glad to hear you think so." He then steered toward downtown Bothell.

The two of them chatted about Alex's day at school, and his organ practice, as they navigated the quiet streets of town. Soon they reached the bike trail, and were cruising south toward Kenmore. With overcast skies and temperatures hovering in the upper thirties, they had the trail almost entirely to themselves.

"I've been wanting to ask you something," Rob said, sitting up in the saddle. He rested his hands comfortably on the tops of the handlebars.

"Yeah?" Alex replied, assuming the same posture.

Rob steered around an elderly woman walking her dog, and waited until they were well past her before continuing. "I want you to be completely and totally honest with me, okay?"

"Okay."

"Is riding on the tandem something you really, truly love? Or is it something that's kind of fun, but only one fun thing among many?"

"I'd ride with you every single day if I could."

"Are you sure? It won't offend me at all if you're not that crazy about it. If you'd rather have more time for music."

"Positive. But why are you even asking? Isn't it obvious?"

Rob steered around another pedestrian, and waited a moment before responding. "Because I want to ride the one-day STP this year, but I can't commit to training if it means being away from the family too much. Before I buy the registration, and jump in with both feet, I need to be absolutely positive that my training partners are in it with me for the long haul."

"I am totally all in! Count me as your one hundred percent partner."

Rob grinned at Alex's enthusiasm. He'd intended to continue explaining why it was so important to have the boys along, so the extensive training wouldn't be something that took Rob away from them. Alex clearly already got that. If anything, his son's reaction struck Rob as a little *too* enthusiastic. Yet the last thing Rob wanted was to dampen Alex's commitment to a sport. He simply said, "I figured, but I wanted to make sure."

"Ben know yet?"

"Not yet. I'm going to tell him when he goes riding later."

Rob decided the upcoming intersection was the best place to turn around. He slowed and made a sweeping arc. The two of them were then riding back the way they'd come.

All the way home, Alex peppered Rob with questions about STP. Some of his son's questions were extremely detailed, and seemed better suited for someone who'd actually be participating in the event ("How early do you want to start?" "How much time do you want to spend at each rest stop?" "What kind of food do they have?"). Rob happily answered all of them.

The rest of Alex's questions were about the number of training miles they'd be logging. The boy seemed excited about how much they'd be together on the road. Rob wondered how his son would be feeling in mid-May.

Ben was dressed and waiting in the garage as they pulled up. Alex dismounted, and then helped Rob reconfigure the pedals and seat height for his brother. A moment later, Rob was back on the road with his new little stoker.

As they worked their way across town, the two of them made small talk about schoolwork and the new baseball team Ben would be on. Once they reached the trail and were riding north toward Woodinville, Rob sat up and began a more serious conversation.

"I have a question for you. And I want you to be completely and totally honest with me, okay?"

"Okay," Ben replied.

"Is riding on the tandem something you really, truly love? Or is it something that's kind of fun, but only one fun thing among many?"

"This is fun. Good way to stay in shape. And I'm glad you've gotten me cycling cleats and warm tights, like Alex's. But I like soccer and baseball better. I can hardly wait for little league to start next month."

The answer was no surprise. Ben had talked of little else but baseball, ever since getting the call a few weeks ago from his new coach. The coach had been impressed with Ben's performance in January tryouts. He was one of the first players the coach had selected for his Minors level team, the Dodgers.

Ben had been ecstatic about moving up from Triple-A. He was already thinking about playing in Majors next year. Ben's only disappointment was that he hadn't been able to skip straight to Majors this year. Rob had had to remind him that few kids his age got to do that. Especially not kids who'd been getting over the flu at the time of tryouts, like Ben had been.

"I thought so, and that's perfectly all right. You can ride as much or as little as you want. I'll never be disappointed if you don't want to go." He glanced back briefly, to make eye contact with his son. "Okay?"

"Okay," Ben smiled. "Why are you asking me this?"

"Trying to figure out how I'm going to train for STP. I'm going to need a lot of training miles, and I want to make sure you guys are interested."

"Cool. What do you need from me?"

Rob waited until they'd passed a rollerblader before answering. "It's more a question of what *you* want. Alex said he'll train every single mile with me."

"Big surprise," Ben said. Rob glanced back and could see him grinning.

"I know. And because this is his only sport, I want to let him."

Ben was quiet for a moment. "Is Alex kicking me off the team?" he asked.

"No way. But what would you think if Alex and I were gone for five or six hours on some Saturdays? And an hour or more on most weekdays?"

Ben cranked the pedals and thought. "That's not fair," he said at last. "It's way more time than I'm at little league. Alex would have all the time with you. I'd hardly ever get to ride unless it's on the trail-a-bike. Which is totally not as fun."

Rob spotted the turnaround point, and slowed to make a sweeping turn back toward Bothell. Once they'd regained their cruising speed, he told Ben, "That's what I figured, but I wanted to make sure."

"So, how are you going to make it fair?"

"I need to think about it."

Rob was grateful that Ben left him in silence to sort through his thoughts. He'd been unable to shake the memory of Alex's enthusiastic response about STP, and didn't want to dampen his older son's commitment. This was Alex's sport. If Alex wanted to do the maximum training, Rob wanted to oblige.

But Ben was right: it wasn't fair for Alex to monopolize the stoker's seat, or their father's attention. And the trail-a-bike just wasn't the same. "What would you think if we made a deal?" Rob asked. "You get to come along whenever you like, and we bump Alex to the trail-a-bike at least half the time?"

Alex shut his bedroom door and danced with joy. *I'm riding to Portland! I'm riding to Portland!* he sang, over and over, quietly enough so his mother wouldn't hear him and think he was a fool. He'd been floating on a cloud since hearing his father's words: "I need to be absolutely positive that my training partners are in it with me for the long haul."

The long haul meant only one thing: Portland. He knew the training would be grueling and intense, but — like he'd told his dad — he was all in. Whatever it took, he was coming along.

He realized what an interesting twist this was. Last summer, when they'd taken their first ride at Green Lake, his father had told him, "No matter how many miles you want to ride, if you can do it, I can do it." Now it was Alex who was getting to tell his father the same thing. And, as he'd resolved after the Christmas concert fiasco, he absolutely would not quit. Not in training. Not on the route. *Not ever, no matter what.* He only hoped his dad could work out a way for him to do all the training he needed, and to keep Ben happy with enough chances to ride.

As Alex changed his clothes and waited for the others to return, he had no doubt they'd figure all those things out. He was positive that nothing would keep him from Portland.

THIRTY-THREE

February 21, 2009

A LEX STUDIED THE DIRECTIONS CONNOR'S PARENTS HAD sent. He wished he could be of more help to his mom. "It says the mall should be the first thing on the left, but I don't see it," he said, trying to hide his exasperation.

"Let's circle one more time. Maybe we missed something."

Alex tapped his foot on the floor of the station wagon, and watched as block after block of dreary Tacoma scenery rolled past. Connor's birthday party was supposed to have started fifteen minutes ago. He knew the Crowleys couldn't wait forever. They were meeting at a Chuck-E-Cheese near the Tacoma Mall, and Alex could find no sign of it. Making matters worse, his mother had been late getting home from volunteering at Women's Resources. That'd meant leaving late for Connor's party. He wondered if he'd get to see his friend at all today.

Alex's mother turned back onto Tacoma Mall Boulevard and scanned the road ahead. "I think that's it, up there. We must've taken the wrong exit from the freeway."

Alex spotted the restaurant, and finally relaxed. He *would* get to see Connor. This was the first time they'd gotten together since the Crowleys moved. For the last week, Alex had thought of little else. He had dozens of different things he wanted to tell Connor about, and just as many things he wanted to ask his friend about. He knew Connor had to go to public school for the rest of this year, and he was curious to hear what that was like. And if he'd found a new baseball team. And how they liked their new parish. And if his dad was any closer to maybe finding a new job back in Bothell. And … and … and … .

Alex lugged the gift he'd picked out, a nice aluminum bat, as they searched the noisy restaurant for the Crowleys. He knew Connor's old bat was really dinged up. He'd even heard some kids on Connor's team making fun of it last year.

Finally, in a large booth toward the back, Alex noticed Mr. and Mrs. Crowley waving at them. Alex and his mother waved in return.

To Alex's surprise, the booth was crowded with several other sixth-grade boys. All of them were laughing and carrying on an intense conversation. Alex had to look hard even to find Connor. Connor was so intent on talking to one boy, he barely seemed to acknowledge Alex.

Alex felt as if the whole table were surrounded by a force field, pushing him back. *Where did all these other boys come from?* he wondered. *I thought it was going to be just me and Connor. I thought it was going to be the day together we haven't had in months.*

"Hey everybody!" Connor announced at last. "This is Alex, from Bothell."

Alex tried to smile and say hello.

"Hi, Alex From Bothell!" one especially tall boy blurted out. Everyone else laughed.

"Have a seat, Alex From Bothell," another boy cracked.

Alex felt his throat tightening. He reflexively clutched Connor's gift as he backed away from the table. He wanted to draw himself into a tiny bundle that could hide unnoticed from all these other people.

His mother rested her hand on his shoulder. Alex froze. Her touch reminded him that he wasn't alone, and assured him that somehow everything would be okay. He thought ahead to the music recital that his cousins had invited him to, and that he'd agreed to play in, next month. He thought ahead to STP. *If I'm going to survive either of those, I need to start by surviving this.*

"Was there a power outage in Bothell this morning?" a short boy with curly brown hair asked. He was sitting at the end of the table, and had the best view of Alex's feet.

"No, we just took the wrong exit from the freeway," Alex's mother replied. She then greeted Connor's parents.

Alex wondered if his mom even realized the curly-headed boy had been making fun of his mismatched shoes. Alex had heard variations on this joke more times than he could count.

Alex had been feeling especially self-conscious about his shoes lately, because his right leg had been getting noticeably longer and making him limp. He'd tried to even things out with shoe inserts. He was still adjusting his gait to the new feel of his shoes.

Another boy craned his neck to see what the first boy was looking at. "I thought for sure he picked his shoes out in the dark," the first boy snickered to the second one.

There was an awkward silence. Alex looked at Connor. His friend must have heard this, but wasn't saying anything to either of the boys.

"Alex, these are my friends from school," Connor said at last. Then, going around the table, he gave all their names: Dylan, Hunter, Austin, Jacob, Jordan, and Cody.

Alex barely heard the names. He knew he wouldn't remember them. He didn't *want* to remember them. All he could think was that Connor had heard these two boys joke about his shoes, and Connor wasn't coming to his defense.

Just hearing the name, "Jacob," Alex wished he could go home and spend the afternoon playing music with his new friend from St. Clement. Or go cycling with the boy he'd met on the Kitsap ride. His knew his father stayed in touch with Mr. Lloyd on Facebook, and he hoped they could connect for some training rides soon.

Alex put his gift on the pile of other gifts, and sat down with his mother at the table. She began talking with Mrs. Crowley. The boys resumed their own conversation, but no one asked Alex any questions. Everything they discussed seemed alien to him: pop music stars and actors, teachers he'd never heard of, movies and television shows his parents never let him watch, and books he'd never wanted to read. Alex felt himself shriveling up and wanting to be very, very small.

Mr. Crowley did try to talk to Alex. All of his questions were the vague things adults ask when they don't know what else to say to a kid: "How are things at school? How's your dad doing? Are you looking forward to spring?"

Alex mumbled some responses. Finally, he thought of something the other boys might like to talk about. "Hopefully the Mariners'll do better this year. I heard they picked up a few good players."

"The Mariners suck," one of the boys declared.

"Totally, one hundred percent, suck," another agreed. "Always have, always will."

Alex was taken aback by the intensity of what they'd said. He was especially angry hearing it said about his favorite team. He wanted more badly than ever to run for the door.

A moment later, three people dressed in crazy animal costumes arrived with pizzas. The characters sang some silly songs, and then the boys scrambled for food. Alex was glad to have pizza to keep him busy, so he wouldn't have to talk.

Once they'd finished, each of the boys got a handful of tokens and ran off to play video games. Alex thought he'd finally have a chance to talk with Connor, but the other boys quickly got him started with some multiplayer shoot-out game.

Alex hung back, and began looking for a game. As he dropped his first token into a classic Pac-Man machine, he felt oddly liberated. *I can finally get away from all those other kids.*

As much as he enjoyed the game, all he could think about was how much he wanted to be home. And how jealous he was that Ben was getting to ride with Dad this afternoon. Alex would've traded every token in his pocket to be out hammering on the open road. He could practically feel the wind in his face as he took all his frustrations out on cranking the pedals. He wondered if he'd get back in time to ride, and if the weather would still be clear.

Alex played Pac-Man four times in a row. He knew Dad had played it a lot in the eighties, and would enjoy hearing that it's still around and still fun. As he was digging the fifth token out of his pocket, someone touched his arm and said his name.

Startled, Alex turned toward the touch. "Hey, man," Connor said. "Just wanted to say I'm sorry this is so lousy. And I'm really sorry Dylan said that stuff about your shoes."

"It's okay," Alex lied.

"It isn't okay. I just explained to Dylan about your legs. He said he'll apologize. Let me know if he doesn't, okay?"

"Thanks," Alex said, feeling the slightest bit better.

"I told my mom I only wanted one thing for my birthday. To have you come spend the weekend with us."

"That would've been great."

"I know. But Mom said our apartment is still too much of a wreck. She's the one who said I should have this party, and invite everyone from school. So I can make friends."

Something about Connor's explanation, and his apologetic tone, made Alex feel less lonely. "Are these guys your friends?"

Connor looked around, and then shook his head. "I miss Bothell."

Alex searched for something to say. "Maybe you can come stay with us for a few days over Spring Break?"

Connor smiled. "That'd be awesome. And maybe we'll finally have enough stuff unpacked, so you can come here for part of Spring Break, too."

While the boys were playing a round of Pac-Man together, Mr. Crowley told them it was almost time for Connor to open gifts. "After that, you can stay and play games for as long as you want."

Once they finished the game they were on, Alex and Connor began walking slowly back to their booth. "Would you mind if I went home right after you open presents?" Alex asked his friend.

Connor shook his head. "I just wish I could go with you."

THIRTY-FOUR

March 3, 2009

ROB SLAMMED THE DELETE BUTTON, SENDING THE EMAIL TO the trash. It was another "thank you for your proposal, but we've decided … ." They'd been arriving all week. He was thankful he'd managed to win one of the six projects he'd bid on, because it was just enough to keep the bills paid. *Good thing I haven't made offers on any new tandems.*

Pacing his office, Rob felt like a caged animal. He didn't really have any work today. He didn't have anywhere else to go, either. No errands to run. The breakfast dishes had been washed. Laundry had been folded. Today's only commitment was a noontime bike ride with Paul Santucci, and he didn't need to leave for another hour.

What the heck. I'm leaving now. Might as well log some extra miles before I have to meet Paul. He bundled up in winter clothes and hit the road.

It took a good fifteen minutes for Rob to warm up and settle into a comfortable pace. Paul's office was on Sand Point Way in north Seattle, a few blocks off the Burke-Gilman trail, so he cruised in that general direction. He decided to take the trail all the way into Seattle. He'd time his turn-around to meet Paul at noon on the way back north.

Cruising south on the Burke-Gilman, a nicely-paved former rail bed that hugged the shores of Lake Washington, Rob relished the solitude and opportunity to clear his head. Except for a few intrepid dog-walkers, and young mothers jogging behind well-bundled strollers, he had the chilly trail to himself.

Rob's mind began churning through thought after unrelated thought. An upcoming project, and how he could tighten the discussion guide. Ben's baseball season that was about to start. The wonderful piece Alex had practiced that morning on the piano. All the bankruptcy cases Meg was helping the attorneys at her firm prepare. Meg's worries about finances at Women's Resources. His calculations about their own finances. The tuition check he'd just written. And how much extra he might be able to pay the hospital this month. If anything.

Before he knew it, Rob was nearing the University of Washington campus. The trail here seemed carved out of a forest. He thought of the times he and Meg had strolled this same path, 20 years earlier, holding hands as they made their way to a football or basketball game. Gazing across Montlake Boulevard, at the Husky Stadium parking lot, he imagined the excitement of riding STP this coming July. He could hardly wait to be part of that river of cyclists he and Alex had watched depart last summer.

A ringing cell phone interrupted Rob's thoughts. He pulled over to fish it from his jersey pocket. Seeing Paul's number, he answered with a simple, "Hey!"

"Hey," Paul replied. "I'm tied up on a conference call that's going late. Would 12:30 work for you? Hour from now."

"Sure," Rob replied, trying to mask his frustration at having more time to kill.

"Thanks. Sorry for the last-minute change."

Rob had been considering turning around. Instead, he continued riding south. The trail was filling with more UW students, unmistakable with their backpacks and beater commuter bikes. Rob slowed to the pace of traffic. *No rush. Nowhere to be.*

The trail terminated a few miles up, at Gas Works Park. Rob thought of the times he and Meg had taken the boys here, and the fun they'd had playing Frisbee on the huge grassy expanse. He remembered the adventure of hiking to the top of the hill with the enormous sundial. He loved the spectacular view of the Space Needle and city skyline across the water.

Rob checked the time and began riding back. Once he cleared the University District, he picked up the pace. He arrived at their agreed meeting place — the 70th Street trail crossing — two minutes early. That turned out to be just in time to take another call, with Paul's apologies that he'd be another ten minutes late.

Trying not to get annoyed, Rob pedaled up and down the trail again. He arrived back at 70th just as his brother-in-law did.

"Sorry I'm late," Paul greeted him, pulling up on a silver Giant mountain bike. He was dressed in black tights, an old UW sweatshirt, and white helmet. "Work's been crazy busy. I've got to be back in the office at 1:15. Should we ride north a little?"

The two of them pedaled side-by-side up the empty trail. Rob was disappointed they'd have so little time, but was glad Paul hadn't canceled altogether. Which, he figured, Paul probably had been tempted to do, given how short this ride was going to have to be. "Meg says her firm's been busy with bankruptcies. Same for you?"

"Foreclosures, for banks," Paul replied, shifting into a higher gear. "We don't really handle personal bankruptcies."

"Tough times," Rob muttered.

After an awkward silence, Paul said, "Speaking of which, I guess Meg was talking with Theresa about the troubles at Women's Resources."

"Yeah?"

"Tell Meg that Theresa and I talked. We'll be sending a check this week."

As another cyclist approached, Rob pulled ahead to ride single file. Once the trail was again clear, Paul swung out to Rob's left.

"I know she'll appreciate it," Rob replied.

"Glad we can help out some way. Theresa just doesn't have time to volunteer anymore. Between Ronnie's plays, Joseph and Anthony doing sports and piano and violin, and then the younger kids..."

They approached a dog-walker, and rode single file until they'd passed her. "Speaking of music," Rob said, pulling back alongside, "Tell Theresa and the boys thanks again for inviting Alex to play at the recital. He's been practicing up a storm. Pretty nice piece he picked, too."

"Bouncing back from the concert?"

"Pretty much. I know he worries. But he worries about everything. I'm just glad he's not giving up."

They rode in silence for a moment, then slowed to approach a road crossing. "Should probably turn around here," Paul said.

They again pedaled up to speed, heading south. "Hey — we had Alex's friend from school over for dinner last week," Paul said. "Jacob. Whole family came. Great bunch of kids."

Jacob had been over to the Petersons' house a few times after school, mostly to play music. He'd brought an older sister once, too. "Definitely, from what I've seen. Glad you guys connected with them."

"Theresa told them about the recital. I guess Jacob and a couple of others are going to play. Wish I could remember all their names."

Paul glanced at his watch, and increased his speed a bit. Rob shifted into a higher gear to keep up. The two of them continued chatting about kids and activities. After a few minutes, they arrived back at 70th Street.

"Sorry again it was so short," Paul said, as the two of them came to a stop. "Maybe next time we can do a full hour."

"Glad you could get away and join me at all."

"Really appreciate the break. I needed it."

Riding home, Rob again enjoyed clearing his head and letting his thoughts range free. *Why does Paul have so crazy much work, while I landed only one of those six projects? What I wouldn't give to be more busy. To have no time to kill. To not be worrying so much about money. Being able to write checks for Meg's charities.*

But then, he had to ask himself, *what if I had gotten all six projects? I'd be so swamped, and traveling so much, I'd never get free. I'd never get to ride. I'd never get to put my feet up and enjoy Alex's piano, or Ben's baseball games.* He decided there was no point getting jealous of Paul. *We've got our problems. They've got theirs.*

Rob continued speeding northward, all the while looking forward to being able to greet Alex and Ben when they got home from school that afternoon.

THIRTY-FIVE

March 20, 2009

THE ENORMOUS STAINED GLASS WINDOWS OF BLESSED SAC-
rament church lit up in yellow and blue as the late afternoon sun slipped behind them. Alex gasped as he took in
the sanctuary's beauty. He stood in the rear of the empty church
and gazed toward the main altar. The building's vertical lines,
arches, and pitched ceiling all drew his eyes and heart upward.
He completely forgot his anxieties about the impending music
recital. "Wow!" he whispered.

"No kidding," Ben agreed, resting his hand on the lid of an
ornate marble baptismal font.

"It's really something, isn't it?" their mother smiled. "This is
where I went every week when I was in college."

His mother led the boys down the church's center aisle, and
then to a side chapel on the right that held the tabernacle. They
genuflected, then knelt in a pew for a moment. In the silence of
the beautiful church, Alex felt his heart spontaneously open in
prayer. *Please help me play my very best tonight. Not to show off.
Just so I can show You and everybody else what I've done with the
gold coin You gave me.*

Ben got up to wander around the church. Alex was anxious
to get started with the organ. He was grateful his mother had
agreed to bring him so ridiculously early, so there'd be no
chance of repeating the Christmas concert disaster. His dad
would be coming straight from a meeting downtown. Hopefully he'd arrive before the 7pm start.

The organ, with its square case of 900 pipes, was easy to
spot in a chapel on the other side of the altar. It was just past the
grand piano that most kids would be using. Alex hurried to-

ward the organ, clutching his sheet music. He'd completely memorized his four-minute Bach organ concerto, and had practiced it for hours on the organ at St. Clement. Still, he wanted the notes in front of him in case he blanked.

Alex reached the organ, folded the keydesk cover open, and got a huge surprise.

"Oh, no!" he exclaimed.

"What?" his mother asked, hustling to join him.

"Nobody told me this is a real, classic pipe organ."

"St. Clement's organ has pipes."

"But all the stops and controls are electronic. This one's totally different. All the stops are manual sliding knobs. Probably over 100 years old. Really primitive. I've never played one of these. Don't even know how to turn on the air pump, or whatever makes it go. And the parish office is closed. And—"

"Slow down," his mother said, putting a hand on his arm. "Let me make a few calls."

While his mother found a cell phone in her purse, Alex wandered around the sanctuary. Other children and their parents were now arriving. That reminded him time was getting short. *So much for getting here early. Now I'm going to be rushed, and blow it again.*

Finally, his mother waved him back. "Here," she said, handing him the phone.

"You must be Alex," a teenage boy's voice greeted him. He sounded friendly, and immediately put Alex at ease.

"Yeah."

"I'm John Paul. The other organist. I'm on my way, and can show you how it works."

"Thanks. For now can you tell me how to get it started? I'd like to get warmed up."

John Paul gave Alex instructions for turning on the air pump, and explained how the stops functioned. Alex flipped the switch marked MOTOR, and heard the pump rumble to life. "I think I've got it," Alex said, watching the console's air pressure gauge climb. "Thanks very much. I'll see you soon."

Alex kicked off his shoes, sat down, and tapped some keys. To his great relief, tones resonated from the pipes. He began experimenting with the fifteen stops.

As his mother wandered off to chat with the other moms, Alex immersed himself in the organ. He slid stop after stop, playing a couple of scales on each manual and the pedalboard each time. Within a few minutes, he had a pretty good idea how they worked. He decided on a combination that would sound best for his recital piece.

His stops in place, Alex began playing his favorite warm-up. It was basically a set of slow chord progressions. He wasn't even sure it had a name. With one hand on each manual, and his feet working the pedals, he closed his eyes and was soon floating on waves of harmony. The organ definitely felt different from St. Clement's. He liked it. The rich tones emanating from the pipes were heavenly, and comforted his anxieties away. All the other kids and parents, and their buzzing conversations, and their warm-ups on piano and violin, disappeared as the chords enveloped him for many long minutes. How many minutes, he neither knew nor cared.

A hand touched his shoulder, making him start. "Hey, Alex," a familiar voice spoke. Alex stopped playing, turned, and recognized Jacob. "You sound terrific," his friend smiled.

Alex realized that Joseph and Anthony Santucci were right behind Jacob. And, flanking *them*, another dozen or so kids of all sizes. Apparently, they'd all been watching and listening to him.

Other kids from the crowd began speaking. "Your playing sounds awesome," one short boy with glasses said.

"It's so cool we finally have another organist," a young, red-haired girl added.

"Great to see new people here," an older girl said.

Alex thanked them, and already felt at home. Then, he spotted a high school-aged boy with short brown hair making his way toward the front. "Sorry I'm late," the boy said, extending his hand to Alex. "I'm John Paul."

Alex greeted the older boy, who added, "From what I can hear, it sounds like you don't need any more instructions."

Alex shrugged modestly. "Thanks for getting me started. It was pretty easy figuring out the stops. Do you need to get warmed up?"

The boys noted Alex's stop settings, and then John Paul took over the organ. The crowd of other kids began flowing toward the main part of the church, sweeping Alex and Jacob with them. So many kids wanted to talk with him, Alex didn't have time to get anxious about the recital. He didn't even feel shy.

As one of the only kids there who'd never been home-schooled, Alex felt self-conscious at first. Fortunately, none of the others seemed to care. They were music nuts, and he was a music nut. That's all that seemed to matter. *At last,* he thought, *I can talk about Brahms versus Bach and nobody thinks I'm weird.*

Eventually, Aunt Theresa Santucci nodded toward John Paul. The boy gave three sharp blasts on the organ. The parents and kids grew quiet, and everyone began taking seats toward the front of the church. Alex knew that only 25 or so kids would be performing, but there were well over 100 kids in the crowd. It looked like there were only 20 parents. *There must be some seriously big families here,* he thought. He decided it might be fun having a lot of brothers and sisters, and doing school at home — as long as he still had a quiet place to be alone with his books and music.

As one of the moms began thanking everyone for coming, Alex browsed the printed program and found his name toward the end. He settled comfortably into the pew, and looked forward to a night of music. Especially the part where he would get to share his favorite Bach concerto with everyone else.

THIRTY-SIX

April 14, 2009

ROB GLANCED UP FROM HIS LAPTOP, TRYING TO KEEP AN EYE on Ben's baseball practice, as he finalized a focus group discussion guide. He'd found a shady section of bleachers, where he could view the computer screen well enough to work. One of Ben's teammates stepped to the plate for batting practice. The coach announced he would be the last.

Ben served up pitch after pitch, and Rob scanned the field. One of Ben's good friends, Jimmy Flynn, seemed to be missing. That was unusual, because Jimmy was the Dodgers' star pitcher and typically tossed batting practices. He wondered if Jimmy would be well and able to play the next game. *Or does this mean Ben will be starting on the mound?*

As batting practice continued, Rob wondered what Alex and Conner were doing down in Tacoma. Alex had told him Connor had baseball practice this afternoon, too. The Crowleys would be taking the boys out for pizza later. Rob was supposed to drive down sometime tomorrow to get both boys, and then Connor would be staying with them for the next couple of days. He made a mental note to confirm the time when he spoke with Alex tonight. In the meantime, Rob began shutting down the laptop. He then stashed it in the padded bag that fit on their tandem's rack.

Rob was just glad everyone was having such a great Spring Break. He'd sure enjoyed having one-on-one time with Ben. And it seemed Alex and Connor were having the time of their lives. The excitement in Alex's voice last night had been palpable, even over the phone. It sounded like they had a long list of things they wanted to do together in Bothell the rest of this week — including getting together with Alex's new friend from school, Jacob. Alex had said something about Jacob having a video camera, and the three of them making a little movie. Rob's only question was whether Alex would do the whole score himself, or if Jacob would accompany him on the violin.

The practice began breaking up. Rob climbed down the bleachers to meet his son. "Nice pitching out there," Rob told him. "Looks like your hitting's more consistent, too."

"Thanks. We're looking good for Thursday's game. Coach says I might get to start on the mound. But I hope I get a few innings at shortstop, too." Ben secured his baseball shoes and glove to the tandem's rack, and then put his cycling cleats and helmet back on.

"That bike is so cool," Tommy Gilson commented. A few others murmured their agreement. A couple of boys peered intently at the tandem's drivetrain, trying to figure out how it worked.

"It's fun riding to practice," Ben told all of them. He snapped his cleats into the pedals. "But my big brother's the real cyclist. He's an awesome athlete."

Tommy looked surprised, but didn't say anything. For his part, Rob was happy to see his boys sticking up for each other, even when the other wasn't around.

A moment later, the two of them were pedaling home along the Sammamish River Trail. Ben having all his practices this year, and most of his games, at the Northshore Athletic Fields had turned out to be excellent. The facility, which everyone called "The Complex," was located literally just off the bike trail. It was a fairly easy five-mile ride from their house. If the weather was clear enough for baseball, it was clear enough for cycling. Rob and both boys would typically ride with the trail-a-bike to both of Ben's weekly practices and at least one of his two games. For games, everyone would stay. During practices, Rob and Alex would ditch the trial-a-bike and ride as long and hard as they could.

"Hey, I noticed Jimmy wasn't at practice today. Is he okay?" Rob asked.

"Got called up to Majors," Ben said, not even trying to hide his envy. "A slot opened on the Marlins."

"Good for him." He wasn't sure what else to say. As much as he knew Ben was dreaming about getting The Call himself, he didn't want to get the boy's hopes up. "You guys going to be okay without his pitching? And his bat?"

"We'll make up for it. And I might get to pitch more now," Ben replied, but Rob could tell he wasn't happy. "You get your work done?"

"Pretty much."

Rob steered the tandem around a traffic control post designed to keep cars off the trail. He hated those things, and would almost rather deal with the occasional rogue automobile than have to look for posts.

"How long'll you be gone doing groups?"

"A few days next week. Milwaukee on Tuesday and Phoenix on Wednesday. I'll be back Thursday when you get home from school."

"That means Mom'll have to drive me to the game next Wednesday. I like riding the bike, because I'm already warmed up when I get there."

They pedaled in silence for a few minutes. Rob thought ahead to Saturday's ride, and how they'd structure it. He was aiming to do 45 or 50 miles, which was too much for Ben. He figured the best plan was to take both boys on a flat 25-mile round trip to Marymoor Park, using the trail-a-bike. Then, he and Alex could take the tandem by themselves on a hilly course for another 20 or 25 miles. Alex had been asking to try the nasty Maltby Road hill, and that seemed about the right distance. He'd just need to make sure they packed enough fruit and fig bars in their pockets.

They'd been gradually increasing their Saturday mileage. Rob had been impressed with Alex's commitment. If anything, his son had been pushing to do more miles, and harder routes, than Rob suggested. On weekdays when they didn't have as much time to ride, Alex would ask to maximize their workouts by going up and down the big 108th Avenue hill that cut off from Riverside Drive. With all this training on the heavy tandem, Rob figured a solo STP would be a snap.

Alex had even asked if he could ride alone when Rob was traveling — but that was where he had to draw the line. Meg really did not want Alex out by himself on the open road. Rob didn't necessarily agree, but he decided it was important to back his wife up. No solo rides, other than to school and back.

"Do you like doing focus groups?" Ben asked.

"It's fun. I like getting to talk to so many different people. Finding out what they think. Then seeing my clients communicate a message better."

"I hope I can be a baseball player. I think it'd be cool to go all over the country, except getting to play baseball instead of just sitting around talking. Is traveling fun?"

Rob concentrated on steering around an older pair of walkers, and considered his reply carefully. He did enjoy seeing the country at someone else's expense. And there was nothing like the solitude of his own hotel room, with no interruptions. But he didn't want the boys to think he took pleasure in ditching them. "It's gotten less fun, now that it means I can't ride with you guys," he said. That was true enough.

"Yeah," Ben agreed.

"You've been working really hard at practices. Making some great plays in games. Keep it up, and maybe you can be a baseball player when you get older."

"Hope so. Coach said I'll make Majors easy next year."

As they pedaled the last few miles of trail, Rob realized how much he treasured this one-on-one time with Ben. He got plenty of it with Alex, but he hadn't had many chances to do things with just his younger son. "What would you think," he asked, glancing back at his stoker, "if once a week I took you to practice without Alex? Maybe when he has organ lessons?"

"That'd be cool," Ben smiled. "And I like it when you stay and watch my practices."

"I'll make sure I'm home in time from the airport next Thursday," Rob assured him.

THIRTY-SEVEN

April 22, 2009

ALEX FINISHED PRACTICING THE LAST OF HIS LESSON PIECES, and then spent a few minutes playing the church organ just for fun. With his father on the road in Phoenix, and Ben at a baseball game, he was in no rush to get back to an empty house. *An empty church, on the other hand...* Alex loved the building's acoustics. He especially loved how the mighty organ sent melodies resonating to his core.

He eventually pulled on his jacket, packed his music in his backpack, and made his way down from the choir loft. Alex unchained the Trek, snapped his helmet in place, and secured his pants leg so it wouldn't snag in the chain. He then shoved off and began enjoying an easy twelve-block ride home. He wished his parents would allow him to take longer rides on his own. *A few degrees warmer, and this would be the perfect day for it,* he thought. He savored the sunlight filtering through the budding tree limbs above.

Alex's thoughts drifted to the past week. He'd had a great time visiting with Connor, and getting to introduce him to Jacob. They'd taken turns riding the tandem with him and his dad. Then, they'd used Jacob's video camera to make a short movie about bike racing. He and Connor had stayed up late, talking, both nights he'd stayed over. Both of them were disappointed Connor's dad didn't seem any closer to finding a job around here. At least their parents promised to help the boys get together more often.

Turning onto a long straightaway, Alex shifted into a higher gear and thought about the tandem. He and Dad had taken a 30-mile ride on Monday after dropping Ben at baseball practice.

He could still remember the way his brother's teammates gathered around them at the end. The other boys were especially amazed that Alex and his dad had gone so far.

Alex spotted three kids on bicycles, riding toward him on the other side of the street. As they drew closer, he recognized Tim Gilson, Ritchie Quinn, and Brett Zielinski. *Great,* he thought, putting his head down and pretending not to notice.

Alex heard the scrunching of fat tires on pavement. He looked back, and saw all three boys making a U-turn to swing behind him. Alex shifted into a higher gear, and tried to pedal faster — but not so fast as to seem like he was running away.

"Look at the big-time biker!" Brett taunted.

"Training for the Tour de France!" Ritchie added.

Tim pulled alongside on a really nice mountain bike. Alex gave him little more than a glance. "Must be hard," Tim said, "Not having any little kids like my brother around, thinking you're an athlete just 'cause you wear girly black shorts while Daddy gives you rides."

All three boys burst into laughter. Alex flushed with rage, and something inside him snapped. "You think I get ridden around? Out on the tandem, I work as hard as my dad. Sometimes even harder."

"Sure," Richie smirked.

In a flash, with just half a block separating him from home, Alex realized what he needed to do. *No matter how much trouble I might get in, it'd be worth it,* he thought.

"Okay," Alex told them, slowing to turn into his driveway. "Wait here a second. I'll be right back."

"With your daddy?" Brett asked, coming to a stop.

"Nah," Tim said. "With his baby brother."

Ignoring the boys' laughter, Alex rode around to the back door and dug the key from his pocket. Once in his room, it took him less than three minutes to strip off his school uniform, pull on his favorite cycling outfit, and find his cleated shoes. Finally, after fastening his helmet in place, he hustled outside. He wheeled his Trek to where the other boys were waiting.

"It's a little cold for girly black shorts, so I thought you'd like to see my girly black tights and girly French jersey," Alex announced. The words were so audacious, and the other boys looked so taken aback, even Alex couldn't believe he'd actually said them.

Once the others overcame their shock, Alex added, "But unless you're good enough athletes to catch me, this is the last you'll see of the front of them." In one fluid motion, he locked his cleats in his pedals and accelerated down the road.

As he turned onto the next street, Alex glanced over his shoulder. The three boys had gotten over their surprise, and were now pedaling hard after him. Alex pulled himself into a tuck, and sped toward downtown Bothell. He knew the stop signs would slow him down. If he could just reach Riverside Drive, he assumed he'd be home free.

Main Street was the last big intersection standing between him and his goal. As he balanced on his wheels, waiting for his turn at the four-way stop, he again glanced over his shoulder. The bullies were now closing fast. When he turned back to the intersection, one of the drivers was waving for him to go next. Alex sped across Main Street, giving the driver a quick wave.

As he descended across the Sammamish River, Alex stomped on the pedals and threw the bike into high gear. *Just one more stop sign,* he thought.

At the bottom of the hill, there were several cars at the intersection. Alex slowed, and again glanced over his shoulder. He could see Richie leading the other two in a makeshift paceline. Alex steered around the waiting cars. He followed the first car as it made the sweeping left turn onto Riverside Drive.

Yes! No more stops!

Alex eased up, and took a good look over his shoulder. The three boys were about fifty yards back and pedaling hard on their mountain bikes. He decided this would be a good chance to catch his breath. Alex kept glancing over his shoulder, and watched as they closed to within forty yards. Then twenty-five. The nearer they drew, the more intent their expressions became.

Alex moved his hands to the bottom of his drop bars, and went into a tuck. As he accelerated away, he shifted into a higher gear and cranked all the harder. He wished the three of them could see the smile on his face.

Alex wanted to simply stay on Riverside Drive for miles, until the other boys gave up. He knew he could do it. The only problem was, his mother wouldn't be gone forever. Ben's game would be over soon. Alex had to get home before she and Ben did, or he'd be in really big trouble.

As he approached the turnoff for 108th Avenue, Alex saw a solution. He and his father had gone up 108th several times on the tandem in training. It was a huge hill. He couldn't imagine many kids being able to handle it alone. Should he try it now, even without his dad's help?

Alex figured that even if he couldn't scale hills like an adult, he was still a better climber than the average boy on a fat-tire mountain bike. He leaned into the turn, and downshifted the way his dad always did.

Alex climbed with all his might for the first several hundred feet. As the road arced to the left, he glanced back. The elevation gave him a clear view of everything below. Tim and Richie were comfortably behind, and there was no sign at all of Brett. Both bullies were struggling. Alex knew there was no way they'd be able to catch him.

"Come on!" Alex called to them, sitting up and pedaling easily. "I'm so lame!"

Richie gave up first. He pulled his bike to the shoulder and doubled over the handlebars like he was about to vomit. Tim followed suit a moment later.

Alex continued climbing. The road curved to the right, and he followed it all the way to the summit. Finally, he whipped around and hauled back down.

He spotted Tim and Ritchie, and slowed to get a better look. As his squeaking brakes approached, both boys looked up. Alex slowed to a crawl, stood on his pedals, and stared at the boys for a moment. Then, with a few decisive strokes, he was again racing down the hill.

Alex sat up in the saddle and steered triumphantly onto Riverside Drive toward Bothell. As he pedaled home, he knew without a doubt he'd be ready for STP in July. *If I was that strong on my single bike, just imagine what I can do with Dad.*

Suddenly, Alex had to pedal harder to maintain his speed. Something was making the bike sluggish. A moment later, the noise from his rear wheel confirmed Alex's suspicion: the tire was losing air fast.

Alex pulled off the road and dismounted. The tire was completely flat. It couldn't be ridden home without seriously damaging the rim. He knew how to fix it — but he had no tools, no spare tube, and no pump. They carried all those things on the tandem, and on his dad's single bike. Alex was never supposed to be alone far enough from home to need them.

Alex realized he had a single option: hoof it. His only hope was that by some miracle, Ben's game stretched an hour longer than scheduled. He'd probably ruin his cleats. He'd probably look like a fool, limping without an elevator shoe to correct his gait. Still, it was his only chance to get home before his mother.

Alex began hobbling toward town, staying well off the road as he pushed his wounded Trek. He looked over his shoulder frequently, scanning for traffic. Every time a car approached, he moved even farther into the weeds, just to be safe.

After several minutes of hobble-trotting, Alex spotted a couple of cyclists approaching from behind. As they drew near, Alex summoned all his courage and flagged them down.

To his relief, both riders pulled off the road. One was much taller than the other, and both rode exotic-looking carbon bikes. "Need help?" the taller one asked.

"Flat tire. Do you have any patches? I totally forgot to take a repair kit."

"Sure," the shorter rider said, unzipping a small pack under his seat.

Alex removed his rear wheel, and the taller rider took it from him. "Looks like you're riding 650s," he observed. "Too bad. Mike and I both've got spare tubes for 700s."

Before Alex could ask to borrow any tools, the tall rider was already pulling the tire from the rim.

"I can do that," Alex offered.

"Dylan worked in a bike shop for ten years," Mike explained. "He'll have you back on the road in no time."

Alex sure hoped that was true. He figured his mother must be well on her way home by now. "I really appreciate this. Any way I can pay you back?"

Mike laughed, and handed Dylan the patch kit. "If you ever see someone who needs help, make sure you stop."

"Pay it forward," Dylan murmured, smearing liquid cement on the punctured tube.

As Alex continued watching Dylan work, he at last felt like a full member of the cycling fraternity. Two guys he'd never met stopped to help, just because he was one of them. All they asked was that he do the same, for another rider. It was an odd way to get initiated. He was just glad to know he was in.

Alex spotted a pair of mountain bikes approaching from the direction he'd come. They drew nearer, and he winced as he recognized Tim and Ritchie. He turned away from the road, hoping they wouldn't recognize him.

Alex heard their tires slowing to a stop. He braced himself for a fresh round of insults. Instead, Tim's voice announced, "Hey! It's Peterson!"

"Flat tire?" Ritchie asked, pulling off the pavement.

"Need any help?" Tim added.

"We've got it covered, boys," Mike replied. "But thanks for stopping to check."

Tim and Ritchie watched for a moment, and then steered back toward the road.

"Good luck!" Tim called.

"See you in homeroom!" Ritchie added. Both boys began pedaling toward town.

"Friends of yours?" Mike asked.

"Kids from school," Alex shrugged, surprised that Tim and Ritchie were now treating him like a normal human being.

"You look kind of young to be out here. Been riding long?"

Alex explained about usually riding with his father on a tandem. He and Mike continued making small talk, mostly about the crank shortener and Alex's mismatched legs, while Dylan finished patching the tube.

Eventually, Dylan connected a small hand pump to the tube's valve and gave a few strokes. "Looks like she's holding air," he announced, then deflated the tube. Before reassembling the wheel, he ran a finger along the inside of the tire. Stopping, he began working a particular spot. "Here's your culprit," he said, and pulled a tiny thorn from the tread.

Alex was amazed at how quickly Dylan got the bike ready to go after that. He was even more amazed when the two other cyclists asked if he'd like to ride with them. "Sure!" he replied, not even trying to hide his excitement.

As they cruised along, Dylan seemed to be studying Alex's pedaling motion. "Your fit on the bike isn't bad," he said at last. "One thing you might try, though, is moving your left cleat farther back on the sole. Should give you a more efficient downstroke with that shorter leg."

"Thanks. I'll try that," Alex said. He wanted to ask Dylan more about what it was like working in a bike shop, but it took all his effort — and breath — just to match the other riders' pace.

Finally, their little group stormed into town. "This is my turn," Alex told the other two. "Thanks again for everything!"

Alex pedaled harder than ever before in his life, all his adrenaline surging, as he wove through the residential streets of downtown Bothell. *Maybe, just maybe, I can make it home before Mom*, he thought.

Nearly breathless, Alex turned onto his own street and then into his own driveway.

And spotted his mother's Taurus in the garage.

Alex's heart continued racing. Now it was pure fear. He put his bike away, limped to the door, and tried to sneak in.

He could hear his mother on the phone, in the kitchen. Though he could catch only certain words, the tone in her voice was unmistakable: anxious concern. He felt really bad for making her so worried, and he sensed he was going to get in all the more trouble.

Before Alex could slip into his room and change out of his incriminating bicycle outfit, Ben emerged from the kitchen. "Mom!" he exclaimed. "Alex's back!"

His mother hurriedly finished her conversation, then dashed to the living room. Her eyes were red, and Alex could see the anxiety in her face. "Alexander Robert Peterson! I have spent the last 30 minutes calling all over town trying to find you! And you've been out CYCLING?"

Alex had never seen his mom so angry at him, so worried about him, or so disappointed in him. As he tried stammering a reply, something in his brain short-circuited. All the words came out in a jumble. "Everything's okay ... really sorry ... had to do something ... these boys from school ... really an athlete ... had to show them ... flat tire ... didn't mean ..."

"I don't care WHAT you thought you were doing, young man," his mother interrupted, her frustrations rushing out in a torrent. "You KNOW you don't have permission to ride alone. I had no IDEA what happened to you. For all I knew you'd been taken, or been hurt, or, or ... How can we ever TRUST you in anything if we can't TRUST you to obey a simple..."

Something inside Alex shut down. He stopped processing the words. He stared past his mother in silence, as she continued showering him with wrath.

Ben only made things worse. From behind their mother, visible only to Alex, his smirk clearly said, *For once, you're in trouble. Not me.*

Finally, his mother grabbed Alex's shoulder. "Don't you have anything to say for yourself?"

Alex shook his head, his eyes filling with tears. Not because he'd disobeyed. Because he'd done it in a way that had frightened his mother so much. "I'm sorry," he managed to say. "I deserve any punishment you give me."

His mother sent him to his room, of course. But first she took his keyboard, and the computer's power cord.

Once Alex was alone, he changed clothes and did his homework. He then immersed himself in a novel, until hours later a knock on the door interrupted him.

"It's Dad," Ben said, opening the door and handing him the phone. "Mom's told him what you did."

Alex closed the door, and took a deep breath before saying "Hey, Dad."

"Want to tell me what this is about?"

Alex curled up on the bed, grateful that Dad wanted to hear his side of the story. He poured everything out. The years of pranks and taunts. Trying to ignore them, but things only getting worse. Seeing a way to finally put the bullies in their place. And it worked. *It worked.*

His father was silent for a moment. "Alex? Man to man?" he said at last. "I understand. Maybe better than you think. Okay?"

The words surprised him. Alex felt a ray of hope. "Yeah?"

"Your idea, to race them? Brilliant. If I'd been home, or if you'd even called, and you'd asked permission? I'd have given it in a heartbeat. I'd have run interference with your mom tonight, and taken all the flack."

His father paused, and Alex knew something else was coming. "But you didn't, did you?"

"I didn't have time," Alex protested.

"You should've *made* the time. Or, at the very least, left a note saying where you'd gone. Right?"

"Yeah," Alex admitted.

"Look, we have to punish you. For the next ten days, your bike is gone. Period. You can ride the tandem with me, but you're walking to school. Okay?"

"Okay," Alex sighed. Walking to school was lousy. Still, he knew the punishment was a lot lighter than it could've been. Certainly lighter than what his mom would've given him.

"And Alex, just between you and me?" his father added. "I'm proud of you. Not for disobeying. For standing up and showing them who you are and what you can do."

"Thanks, Dad," Alex smiled, then wished him a good night.

As bedtime approached, Alex began laying out his uniform for the next morning. Suddenly, he had an inspiration. He returned his slacks to their hanger. He then rummaged in the dresser until he found a pair of navy uniform shorts. He slipped them on, and was pleased they still fit.

Alex hobbled to the closet, and took a long look at himself in the mirror. Yes, he had tan lines showing. Yes, his kneecaps were still badly misaligned. But both of his scarred thighs, and both of his calves, were as muscular as they'd ever been. He flexed up and down on his knees, watching the quadriceps ripple.

Alex smiled. He carefully laid the shorts out with his polo shirt and sweater. He was wearing them, no matter how cold it was tomorrow.

THIRTY-EIGHT

April 24, 2009

ALEX CRUISED TOWARD HOME WITH DAD ON THE TANDEM, with Ben in tow on the trail-a-bike. There'd been only a half day at school. The boys had been thrilled at the prospect of a long Friday afternoon ride — especially given the spectacular sunshine, and that Dad was finally home from his trip. The blackberry brambles along Riverside Drive were all in bloom. Spring seemed to be exploding all around them.

Last night, he'd taken Dylan's advice and moved his left cleat back. With his calf now more vertical, Alex's pedal stroke felt better already.

Roughly two miles from home, the boys' father sat up comfortably. "Thanks for the strong ride today, guys."

"Sure. It was fun," Alex smiled.

"And for all the miles you've helped me log. I'm positive I'll have a fast STP in July."

Alex wondered why Dad had said "I'll," rather than "we'll."

"The tandem's been really been helpful, I think," Dad continued. "It's so heavy, especially with the trail-a-bike. Once I switch to the single bike for STP, it'll be much easier."

"Like warming up swinging a bat with weights," Ben said.

"Exactly."

Alex felt himself going numb. *What?!* he thought. *Dad and I were supposed to be riding STP together. We're a team! Why's he dumping me now? Am I nothing but dead weight? Just here to help him get ready?*

Alex's feet continued to rotate on the pedals, but he couldn't put any power into the strokes. He'd never felt so deflated. So misled. So betrayed. He settled into a sullen hush.

Back at home, the boys' father steered the bicycle train into the garage and dismounted. Ben clunked off toward the house to change his clothes. Alex stood staring at the floor in seething silence. He was glad to be wearing sunglasses, so his dad couldn't see his eyes.

"Is everything all right?" his father asked.

Alex wasn't sure what he should say, or if he should say anything at all. Finally, he couldn't keep the words and emotions bottled up. "I thought we were riding STP *together!*" he exclaimed, his voice breaking.

His father looked at him, puzzled. "Whoa, Alex. I had no idea. When did I tell you that?"

"You said we were training for it together!" Alex insisted, struggling to keep his voice from breaking again. "The day you asked me and Ben if we were really, truly, committed to training hard with you for the long haul. For STP."

His father thought for a moment. "I wanted to make sure training wouldn't be taking me away from you and Ben, like when we lived in California. If you got the impression that meant you'd actually be riding STP, I am truly sorry. That wasn't the impression I tried to give. Ben certainly didn't get that impression."

"But Dad," Alex objected, folding his arms, "Who studies for a test unless they're taking the test? And besides, remember the very first day we rode at Green Lake last summer? You told me that no matter how far I wanted to ride, you'd ride with me. If I was in, you were in. Well, I'm in for STP."

Alex's father looked blindsided, as if he'd forgotten that conversation. "That wasn't what I meant," he stammered. "I was talking about riding to Marymoor Park, not Portland."

"Then you should've said that."

"Didn't think I needed to. But if you want me to spell it out, fine. You can't ride to Los Angeles, either. Or Boston. I mean, how did you even get it in your head that you could ride to Portland?"

Alex stopped and thought for a moment, and tried to calm down enough so he didn't say anything that'd get him in trouble. "Remember when I bailed out at the Christmas concert? You told me I should set my sights on something big and scary and hard — and not ever quit. Well, the one-day STP is big and scary and hard. And I want more than anything to do it."

"Wait a minute, wait a minute, wait a minute. You can't just go do anything you want, simply because it's scary and hard. You might as well climb Mt. Rainier, while you're at it."

Alex felt rage rising within him. This was a complete betrayal of everything he'd thought was true. Everything he'd been believing had been yanked out from under him — by the very person who'd given him everything he'd been believing in. *I was supposed to dream big. You were supposed to be dreaming with me.*

As much as Alex wanted to slam his helmet to the ground, he knew he had to talk to his father like the young man he wanted to be treated as. If he melted down and started stomping or pounding a wall, his father would see him as an out-of-control little kid. Little kids didn't get to go on STP.

Alex closed his eyes, took a deep breath, and gathered himself like he had at the music recital last month.

"I'm not talking about climbing Mt. Rainier, Dad. I'm talking about doing a ride with you in July that I've been training for along with you. You know that video I helped Mr. Jansson with? It's what I think about when I'm going to sleep at night. It's what I think about when I wake up in the morning. I tell myself to work really hard, because I'm getting ready to ride the one-day STP with my dad."

His father removed his helmet and sunglasses, and took a long look at him. "I don't know, Alex. I'm going to need to think about it, okay? You should go in the house."

"Okay," he replied, trying his hardest to sound like a grown man who was negotiating a serious contract. But as much as he wanted to get his hopes up, he suspected this was going to end as badly as every other sport he'd dreamed about playing.

THIRTY-NINE

A S ROB WATCHED ALEX LIMP ACROSS THE DRIVEWAY, HE shook his head in wonder. *How could he have been thinking, all this time, he was getting to ride STP?* Rob retreated to his office, changed clothes, and sat down to sort out his thoughts. *And how could I have missed it? Have I really been that oblivious to what was in his head?*

What struck Rob most was the way Alex had stood up to him and talked back to him. In Rob's mind, that was a good thing. A year ago, Alex would've heard 'No,' and then slunk away with his tail between his legs. *Come to think of it, a year ago, Alex wouldn't have even asked to do something special. He would've kept his head down, played his keyboard, and made sure no one spent money or went out of their way for him.* Rob was elated at seeing his son now passionate enough to take a stand.

But still, Rob thought, *riding from Seattle to Portland? In one day? Absolutely crazy. He's going to be twelve. Twelve. Can a twelve-year-old boy ride STP in one day? There were some kids at the start last year, but I think they were two-day riders. I remember seeing young teens on tandems at the Davis Double. STP isn't as hard as Davis. But it's still 200 miles! Am I in good enough shape to pull both of us the last 50 miles if he runs out of gas?*

Besides, every time Rob visualized the upcoming STP, he imagined himself hammering in a paceline on his Colnago, head tucked, smoking the course. It was going to be his own special day, doing his own special thing. This would be his chance to get back in the saddle and make sure *he* could do it himself. Having Alex along would introduce several layers of complexity. He'd have to worry about the boy training enough. Then eating enough. Drinking enough. And that heavy tandem would be really slow on the climbs. *Maybe next year. This is my year.*

Still, he wasn't sure. This was such a big decision, he knew he really shouldn't make it on his own, anyway. He called the house and asked Meg if she could come out.

A few minutes later, she'd joined him. "I know what this is about," Meg said, before even sitting down. "Alex told me about your little misunderstanding."

"What's he doing now?"

"What he always does when he's frustrated. Closed himself in his room, put on his headphones, and started playing his keyboard," Meg replied, settling into one of Rob's chairs.

"Why the headphones?"

"He doesn't want me to know he's playing the second movement of Beethoven's Seventh. It's what he always plays when he's upset about something."

Rob wondered how Meg could be so sure. He decided it was better not to probe. If he did, he'd only be admitting he didn't know Alex as well as she did.

"Do you think he's crazy for wanting to go?"

"Of course. But I think *you're* crazy for wanting to go, too."

They both chuckled, and Rob said, "There's a reason the one-day STP is so overwhelmingly male."

"Women have more sense than to do something that stupid," she smiled. Then, turning serious, she continued, "But, like it or not, Alex is one-hundred-percent boy. And he's more like you than you'd like to admit."

"I know. But why does he think he has to ride *this* year?"

Meg shrugged. "You tell me. You're the one who's been spending the most time with him."

His wife's answer caught Rob off guard. He *had* been spending the most time with Alex. Despite all that time, he didn't really know what was going on inside his son's head. Maybe that was because, all these months, he'd been so wrapped up with his own thoughts and his own dreams. He felt ashamed, and wasn't sure how to respond. "You know Alex," he managed to say. "He doesn't talk a lot."

"Maybe you need to ask more questions. Haven't you noticed what's been going on with him?"

"What do you mean, exactly?" he asked, feeling defensive.

"All the ways he's changed! Look at him compared to a year ago. Does he even seem like the same boy?"

Like he'd been thinking earlier, Rob realized Alex did seem to have a different outlook on just about everything. It'd happened so gradually, Rob hadn't really noticed. Not until Alex had stood up and talked back to him. Rob was embarrassed to admit he hadn't noticed the change unfolding.

"When was the last time you saw him sulk about how much money we spend on him?" Meg continued, not waiting for Rob's response. "Were you as surprised as I was when he asked to play in that recital last month, even after blowing the concert? That he dealt with Connor's moving away as well as he did? That he's making new friends? A few minutes ago, he even told me he'd get pledges and ride STP as a fundraiser for Women's Resources, like the Fun Run is for St. Clement, if that would change our minds. I would never set that as a condition of riding, but did you think he'd ever offer to do something he hates as much as fundraising?"

"Of course not. But what do you think has changed him?"

"The time he's spent with you. And that you've told him there's nothing he can't do. He really believes that now."

"He told you that?"

"He doesn't need to. Alex did confide in me a while ago that he wants to do STP someday. I thought he meant the two-day ride. Five years from now."

"Think he'll crawl back in his shell if he doesn't get to ride STP this year?"

Meg thought for a moment. "I hope not. But I do know this: he sleeps in his Kitsap Color Classic t-shirt every night. He told me once that he loves cycling because it lets him go everywhere, and fly, the way he used to think only other kids could."

"Which is great. But why does it have to be STP? And why this year?"

Meg looked at him, as if surprised he couldn't answer his own question. "You're going, Rob! He wants to go with you!"

Rob felt a twinge of conscience at the prospect of letting his son down. He quickly talked himself out of it. *This year is my year. Alex can wait. Next year can be his year.*

"I just think he's a little too young," Rob said.

"And I agree," Meg said. "Especially for the one-day ride. I personally think he should wait at least one more year. But I will completely support whatever decision you make."

FORTY

BEN'S PRACTICE PITCH SMOKED INTO ALEX'S GLOVE WITH A tremendous thud. "That is so *bogus*," the younger boy declared.

"Great pitch," Alex said. He stood and tossed the ball back.

"I was talking about STP." Ben took his stance on the makeshift mound they'd built in the backyard. "It's totally unfair Dad isn't letting you ride this year."

Alex squatted to receive the pitch, and his little brother again delivered a thunderbolt. "Better save something for the game," Alex advised, before returning the ball.

Ben fiddled with his cap, and then experimented with his grip on the ball. "I mean, you've proved you can work hard. Kids your age've done STP. What's the big deal?"

As Ben continued pitching, Alex recounted everything their father had told him the night before. How impressed Dad was with Alex's dedication. That he'd noticed their average speeds improving. That their long-ride mileage was on track just fine. That Dad couldn't ask for more.

"Let me guess," Ben interrupted. "BUT..."

"Yeah, basically," Alex replied, tossing the ball to Ben. "He and Mom just don't think I'm old enough. This year's too soon. I should get a little more experience."

"Bogus!" Ben repeated, then threw his hardest pitch of the morning. "If you can do the miles, you can do the miles."

"That's what I told him."

Alex stood and juggled the ball a couple of times before returning it to Ben. "He said he was sorry, but his mind was made up. And if I keep pestering, and ask again to ride STP, I definitely lose next year's too."

Ben experimented with a two-finger grip, and shifted his stance slightly. "Did he say you definitely get to ride next year otherwise?" he asked, and then delivered the pitch.

Alex caught the ball, and dug it from his mitt. "Yes, if I keep working hard this year and next."

"What does he mean by 'working hard'?"

Alex tossed the ball to him and returned to a squatting position. "Basically, just not slack off from what I've been doing so far. And we've got to do four century rides. At least one ride of 125 miles. We have to do the big Flying Wheels Century, which is about a month before STP, in no more than six hours. Then, we'll have a performance review right before this year's STP. He'll tell me what I need to improve next year if I'm actually going to ride."

Ben turned the ball over and over in his pitching hand. "You know what you should do?" he said at last. "Pretend it's baseball, and you didn't make Majors a year early like you wanted. You should work extra-hard, like you're trying to get the Agent's attention. So they realize they made a mistake. And maybe even call you up."

Ben delivered a slider, but so far off the plate that Alex couldn't catch it. "Sorry!" Ben called.

As Alex jogged to retrieve the errant pitch, he considered his little brother's advice. It actually made pretty good sense. If he couldn't ride STP this year, the next best thing might be meeting his father at the finish and hearing him say, "Alex, I had fun, but I really wish I'd taken you."

As for actually getting The Call, like Ben's friend had, and like Ben was still hoping to get? Having his father actually change his mind about Alex riding this year? Alex wasn't sure he should get his hopes up that high.

"Any sign you might get called up?" Alex asked, throwing the ball to his brother.

Ben pulled his cap off, ran his fingers through his sweaty blond hair, and shook his head. "Last week, Coach told me he's surprised I didn't make Majors this year. If anybody else from our team gets called up, it'll probably be me. Until the Player Agent calls, nobody ever knows."

Alex returned to a squatting position. "Try another slider," he called. "That'll be a killer pitch once you get it down."

As the boys continued playing catch, Alex let his thoughts drift back to STP. He decided he'd never quit trying to make his father regret the decision to leave him home.

FORTY-ONE

May 12, 2009

A LEX HIT THE SNOOZE BUTTON AGAIN, AND WAS READY TO pay any amount of money to skip school today. He wasn't sick. He wasn't sore. He wasn't even sleepy. He just could not will his body to crawl out of bed.

For the next ten minutes, he stared at the ceiling as his mind drifted aimlessly. The last two-and-a-half weeks, cycling had been his obsession. He'd insisted he and his dad ride farther, and often asked if they could explore just one more new road. And then another. He'd asked to go up and down the 108th Avenue hill the whole time Ben was at little league practice. He'd strained with all his might, whenever he could, to show his dad what a strong stoker and equal partner he could be.

They'd done 90 miles this last Saturday. The first thirty had been fairly easy, and Ben had joined them on the trail-a-bike. He and his father then rode a hilly 60 miles up past Snohomish and back while Mom drove Ben to his baseball game. They'd been so far north, they'd even seen Jacob Lloyd and his parents and ridden with them for about ten miles that day. Then they'd gone to early Mass on Sunday, and ridden 40 miles to Grandpa's in Monroe. They were supposed to be extending both routes by ten miles this coming weekend.

Except Alex couldn't get out of bed. He hated the very idea of bikes. He almost wished he'd never heard of STP. He was even almost glad his father had told him he couldn't go to Portland this year.

Alex heard someone knocking. "Yeah?" he half-groaned.

The door opened, and his father poked his head through. "You okay? You need to hustle to get ready."

"Don't want to go to school."

His father put a hand on Alex's forehead. "Are you sick? You don't feel warm."

"Just don't want to get up. Feels like there's a hundred-pound blanket pinning me."

His father thought for a moment, and then pulled the covers back. "You *are* going to get ready for school." He grabbed Alex by the wrists and pulled him to a sitting position. "I'm driving you. In fact, I'm driving you all week. Both ways."

"Huh?" Alex asked, rubbing his eyes.

"I'm ordering you not to touch a bike, look at a bike, or think about a bike until Friday afternoon. And to drink lots of water and take it easy between now and then."

"Why?"

"You're overtraining. You need a clean break. I thought we might be doing too much. This is my fault for not making you go easier."

Alex felt bad about getting "benched," but deep down he was relieved at the break. "Sorry I did too much."

"I'm just glad you're not sick. We'll take an easy ride Friday afternoon, and decide then what you're up for on Saturday. Okay?"

"Okay," Alex repeated, and swung his legs out of bed. He still didn't want to go to school, but he knew his dad was right: he couldn't call in sick today. He said his morning prayers, then hurried to get dressed and eat. His dad managed to get him and Ben to school just ahead of the warning bell.

At homeroom, Jacob greeted him. "You look tired," his friend observed.

Alex explained about pushing too hard on the bike, and that his dad was making him stop riding until Friday. "Right now, I'm so burned out I don't care," he concluded.

After the announcements, the boys had a few more minutes to talk. "If you can't ride this week, does that mean you'll have more time for playing the organ?"

"I guess so. I still have to practice my lessons, but there's no law saying I've gotta go home at 3:30."

"Maria found a new organ-and-violin concerto," Jacob told him. "Maybe she and I could play with you right after school tomorrow? And if my mom picked us up at 3:30, could you practice your lesson after we go? Like you did those other times?"

Alex had played music after school with Jacob and his sister several times earlier in the year, but they hadn't done it lately. He'd been in too much of a hurry to get out on the bike.

"Sounds fun. We really should do that more."

FORTY-TWO

E VEN FROM HIS SEAT IN THE BLEACHERS, ROB COULD READ the stress on Ben's face. The boy had walked two batters, with only one man out, to start the third inning. He'd now thrown two balls in a row to the next batter. Clinging to just a one-run lead, and with the opponents' best hitters coming up, Rob knew this situation could get really ugly really quickly.

Ben worked the ball in his hand and gazed intently at the batter. *You can do it*, Rob thought.

"Come on, Ben!" Alex shouted.

Ben settled into his stance, and then delivered a fastball in the dirt. That left him one bad pitch from walking the bases loaded.

Ben glanced at his coach, who was studying a clipboard. *No doubt wondering who he can move to the mound in Ben's place*, Rob thought.

"Get him, Ben!" Alex called, clapping his hands as the younger boy again settled into his stance.

Finally, Ben wound up and threw a slider low across the heart of the plate. The batter swung, connected, and lined a "worm burner" ground ball directly to Tommy Gilson at second base. Tommy stepped on the bag, then threw to first base to complete the double play.

As Ben and his teammates high-fived and jogged from the field, all the Dodgers' fans jumped to their feet and cheered.

"That was close!" Alex said.

Ben said something to his coach, who nodded. As the others took their seats on the bench, Ben hustled toward the restrooms.

Rob's cell phone vibrated with an email alert, which turned out to be from Frank Hurwitz. The subject line, "New Project," immediately got Rob's attention. He quickly read through the message. Frank said he could use Rob's help moderating a pair of groups in Spokane two days from now. A nearly-complete discussion outline would be coming over this evening. Sorry for the short notice, but would he be able to make edits tonight? And go to Spokane for the sessions?

Absolutely. His only commitment before then was a lunchtime ride tomorrow with Paul Santucci.

"What's up?" Meg asked.

"Good news. Quick little project from Frank. Thursday in Spokane. Home Friday morning."

Rob sent a brief affirmative reply, then put the phone away and scanned the area for Ben. He hadn't yet rejoined his teammates on the bench, so Rob looked toward the restrooms. A moment later, Ben emerged. The boy was immediately approached by a thirty-something man in a blue jacket.

Blue Jacket began talking with Ben. Rob felt a twinge of anxiety. Turning to Meg, and gesturing toward Ben, he asked, "Do you know who that guy is?"

Meg looked intently. "No," she replied.

"I don't recognize him, either," Alex said. "But Ben doesn't look scared or anything."

Indeed, Ben looked to be his usual outgoing self. He smiled and talked freely with the mystery man. Rob decided to keep an eye on them, but not to go down to investigate yet.

Ben now appeared to be listening, and nodded his head a few times as the man spoke. Blue Jacket gave him a slip of paper, and shook Ben's hand. The boy then jogged back to the bench with his teammates. Blue Jacket strolled toward a different playing field at The Complex.

All of Ben's teammates, and the coach, looked focused on the game. None seemed to have noticed Ben's conversation. For his part, Ben appeared to have grown serious. He watched the action without joking around the way he usually did.

"I wonder what that was about?" Rob asked.

"No idea," Meg replied.

Ben's team scored three insurance runs in the bottom of the third, and Ben retired all three batters in the fourth. Although he enjoyed pitching, Ben looked happy when Coach rotated him to shortstop for the remainder of the game. Two innings later, Ben and his teammates whooped and celebrated their victory.

Rob noticed that Ben seemed oddly detached from the celebration. It looked almost like he was simply going through the motions. He gathered his glove and bat, and then joined the family without staying for the usual conversations with coaches and friends.

"You guys ready?" Ben asked.

"Yeah," Alex replied. "Who was that guy in the blue jacket you were talking to?"

"Nobody," Ben muttered. Then, turning to his mother, he added, "Can we get home? I'm hungry."

Rob and Meg exchanged a look, which told him they were both thinking the same thing: *Whoever that guy was, he wasn't 'nobody.' But let's wait for Ben to talk about it when he's ready.*

In a strange role reversal, Alex spent more of the drive home talking about the game than Ben did. As his older brother recounted the highlights, and how much he'd enjoyed them, Ben did little more than grin. Or agree, "Yeah, that was great."

Ben's silence continued through dinner. While the rest of the family dug into Meg's roast chicken with gusto, Ben took a significantly smaller portion than usual. Even then, he left a fair amount of it on his plate.

"What's wrong?" Alex asked his little brother. "Thought you were hungry?"

Ben looked ready to say something, but caught himself. "I don't know," he replied. "Maybe I'm just tired." With that, Ben excused himself from the table.

"Hey!" Alex exclaimed, as Ben carried his plate to the kitchen. "He's not allowed to just get up like that."

"It's okay this time," Meg told Alex, before exchanging an *I'll figure out what's going on, and then fill you in* look with Rob.

Rob finished eating, and retreated to his office to get going on Frank's project. After printing the discussion guide, he stretched out on his office couch to mark it up. Rob could never do this kind of thing at a desk, or on a computer monitor. It had to be a hard copy, and he had to have his feet up. Otherwise, he couldn't immerse himself in the material, or think of the best way to improve the flow of discussion.

The sessions were sponsored by a credit union, and designed to test potential communications with members. Rob was quickly deep in the guide and marking it up. He soon lost all track of time.

As Rob was jotting down a transitional statement, bridging one discussion section to another, a knock on the door interrupted his concentration. "Yeah?" he called.

Meg led their younger son into the office. "Ben would like to talk with both of us, away from Alex. Do you have a minute?"

The boy looked more anxious than Rob had ever seen him. "Of course," he replied, putting his papers aside. "What's up?"

Meg made herself comfortable on the couch with Rob. Ben turned a chair around backwards, and sat straddling it. "That guy who talked to me at the game?" he said, looking glum. "That was Mr. Matt Jacobson. He's the league's player agent. The go-between, when a team needs a new player."

"Who needs a new player?" Meg asked.

"The Tigers. They're a Majors team. One of their guys broke his arm yesterday, and they need someone to fill in the last three games. I guess I've been on the top of everybody's list to move up from Minors."

"Wonderful!" Rob exclaimed, curious as to why Ben wasn't celebrating. "Isn't this The Call you've been waiting for?"

"Yeah. And the Tigers are only one game behind the leaders. Mr. Jacobson said I can help them win the division."

Ben's demeanor remained entirely wrong. Rob was stumped as to why.

"When's the first game?" Meg asked.

"Tomorrow. I have to call tonight with a decision, 'cause otherwise he needs to find someone else."

"Why didn't you just say Yes?" Rob asked, incredulous that there was even anything to think about.

"I was going to, but he reminded me I can only be on one team. Once I move, that's it. So he said I should talk with you."

Ben looked even more glum, and now Rob understood why. His current team was tied with the Rays atop their division, and they had a huge match-up next Tuesday. In fact, all three of their remaining games were critical. Everyone was counting on Ben's bat — and his skills in the field — to get them over the line.

"Does your coach know?" Meg asked.

Ben shook his head. "That's why Mr. Jacobson talked to me in private."

Something Meg had mentioned earlier continued to puzzle Rob. "Why do you not want to talk with Alex?"

"Because if I don't take the offer, I don't want him to know I even got called," Ben shot back.

"Why's that, Sweetheart?" Meg asked, looking surprised.

Ben looked surprised that his mother looked surprised. "Cause I don't want him to feel bad. I'm always getting the honors and championships, even though he's a way better athlete in lots of ways."

"Let's not worry about Alex," Rob said. "He's very proud of you. And he's happy playing a sport that unfortunately the rest of the world doesn't care much about. There's no 'Call to the Majors' he's missing. He won't be jealous."

Ben started to say something, but stopped.

"What?" Rob asked.

"Nothing," Ben muttered.

After an awkward silence, Rob realized he needed to play focus group moderator and get the discussion back on track. "What position would you play on the new team?"

"Mr. Jacobson doesn't know. Said it depends on what the new coach needs. The Tigers don't have much depth at pitcher, so I might even get to pitch. And it would be *Majors*. But … I might be getting in over my head. And flop."

Rob thought for a moment. "This is a real pickle, isn't it?"

"You could say that," Ben replied.

"If you want my opinion," Rob said, putting his arm around Meg, "this is a tremendous opportunity. Don't be afraid of moving up. Or playing with bigger boys, even if they knock your pitches out of the park. You should go up against the best other players, to stretch your skills."

"Absolutely," Meg agreed.

"I know. If this'd happened a month ago, I'd have jumped at it. Like Jimmy did. And I was going to jump at it today."

"So, why not?" Meg asked.

Ben rested his chin on the back of the chair and thought. "I guess it's not really 'cause I'm scared of Majors or anything," he admitted. "I guess it's because the guys on my team are counting on me. I'm supposed to be the starting pitcher next Tuesday against the Rays. How can I leave now, just like that, and forget about the guys on my team? The guys on the Dodgers are my friends. We're supposed to be in it together. These guys on the Tigers, they're not my *team*. You know?"

"But they'll *become* your team," Meg pointed out.

"And I'm sure the boys on the Dodgers will understand," Rob added. "If they're your friends, they'll be happy for you."

Ben looked skeptical, and no less glum. "But I don't think *I* would be."

Then, standing and thanking his parents for listening, Ben hurried back to the house.

FORTY-THREE

May 13, 2009

ROB KEPT HIS PACE STEADY AS PAUL SANTUCCI PULLED alongside. The two of them cruised north on the Burke-Gilman trail, enjoying a sunny lunchtime hiatus from work.

"You're kidding, right?" Paul asked.

"I wish. But no, Ben really did turn it down. Called the player agent last night before bed, and told him he wanted to stick with the Dodgers. Meg said she wouldn't have believed it if she hadn't watched it happen."

Paul pedaled in silence for a moment. "Why do you say, 'I wish'? I mean, I'm as surprised as you and Meg. But do you think he was wrong?"

"Given how hard he's worked? How much he's wanted it? I think he passed up a great opportunity."

"I guess. But it's only three games, right?"

"Correct."

The two of them approached a woman pushing a baby stroller the other direction on the trail. Paul pulled ahead to ride single file. Once the horizon was clear, he moved left and slowed slightly. "Maybe he's already learned something more than he would have by playing at a higher level," Paul said.

"Such as?"

"Thinking about other people before you think about yourself," Paul continued. "I mean, that's something Theresa and I tell our kids to do. It's not very often you see a boy Ben's age actually give something up for his friends."

"Fair enough."

"Kind of interesting, when you think about it. A year ago, I remember Ben talking my ear off one Sunday about his baseball stats. How sure he was about skipping straight to Majors the next year. How much money he'd raised for the Fun Run. How fast he'd finished it."

"No kidding. Just imagine what he was like the rest of the week," Rob grinned.

"Probably no worse than my kids. Like Ronnie walking around, reciting pages of Shakespearean dialogue." Paul shifted into a higher gear and picked up speed. "But Ben's changed. A year of baseball with this team seems to have done something for his attitude."

"Being on the bike with Alex has probably helped, too," Rob said, cranking harder to keep up with Paul's new pace. "He's never seen his brother as a real athlete before. It's been interesting watching their camaraderie develop."

"Probably been good for Ben to see he's not the only one who's good at sports," Paul added. "Probably helps him keep other things in perspective, too."

Rob thought about Ben's not wanting Alex to know about The Call, and had to agree.

They reached their turn-around point, and began riding back toward Paul's office. With significant trail traffic surrounding them, they rode single file for several minutes.

As Rob pedaled along behind Paul's mountain bike, he thought about what his brother-in-law had said. Last night, quite honestly, Rob had been disappointed in Ben's decision. Part of it was seeing Ben miss out on an opportunity. But, though he'd never admit it aloud, part of the disappointment was missing out on "bragging rights" of his own. Now he wouldn't be able to say, "That's my boy — the one who moved up early." He knew he should be proud that Ben had done the work and earned the promotion, whether he'd actually taken that promotion or not. Still, it didn't have quite the same ring as "My kid moved up to Majors."

He hadn't really thought about it the way Paul did: *be proud that your son showed some real maturity. He's grown up a lot this year.* The more he turned it over in his mind, the more he realized his brother-in-law was right. Ben *had* shown real maturity. He *had* done a lot of growing up. Rob decided he should say something to his son that afternoon, about how proud he was of his choice.

Out of Alex's earshot, of course.

FORTY-FOUR

May 23, 2009

RAIN POURED DOWN ALEX'S BEDROOM WINDOW IN WAVES. As he slowly awakened, all his groggy mind could think about was how much he loved the sound of rain on the roof — especially on Saturday mornings, when he didn't have to get up. He smiled, felt cozy, and burrowed more deeply under the covers. Alex decided he'd just lie here listening to the rain all morning.

His father had let him back in the saddle last Saturday. They'd stuck to a fairly easy route for another 90-mile ride. They took Ben for the first 35 miles or so, and then did 55 more flat miles on their own. Dad had told him to focus on spinning the pedals, eating lots of food, and drinking lots of water. He also encouraged Alex to enjoy the scenery, without worrying about their pace. They could pick up their pace at the Flying Wheels Century, when there'd be lots of other good riders to work with.

Ben was supposed to have a game today. Alex figured it'd be postponed for sure. He figured he and his father would put off their century ride until tomorrow, too. He wondered if they might try a more hilly route this time, or simply extend last week's flat route by 10 miles.

A knock interrupted Alex's thoughts. The door opened, and his father leaned in. "Aren't you getting up? If we're doing 100 miles today, we need to be on the road by 8am."

"I thought it was supposed to rain all day," Alex replied, burrowing deeper into the covers.

"It is. Which is why we have good rain gear."

Alex suddenly realized his father wasn't joking. "Can't we just do it Sunday?" he asked. "Go to Mass tonight? End our century ride at Grandpa's tomorrow?"

"You don't have to go."

At first, Alex felt relieved. Then, a moment later, he wondered if this might be a sort of test as to how committed he was. Even if his father didn't intend it as a test, Alex decided he would treat it as one.

"Yes I do," Alex replied, rolling off his bed and into a kneeling position on the floor. "I'll be out in a minute."

Alex said his morning prayers, and added a very emphatic request for the rain to stop. And for the roads to dry very fast.

A half hour later, Ben was still sound asleep. Alex found himself standing in the garage and gazing out on a steady rain. He wore a set of yellow rain pants and jacket over his cycling outfit. The hood fit under his helmet. His jersey pockets were stocked with apple slices and fig bars, but he wondered how he'd reach them under the jacket. He was just thankful the tandem had good fenders, so he wouldn't be in a stream of spray from the rear wheel.

Alex's dad emerged from his office a moment later, dressed the same way. "Ready?" he asked.

No. But I'm going to ride anyway. The sooner we start, the sooner we'll finish, Alex thought. "Sure," he shrugged.

Despite the fenders and rain gear, Alex's face and hands were soaking wet by the time they reached the Sammamish River Trail. He seemed to be constantly wiping water from the bike computer's display, and from his eyebrows. Alex eventually gave up on the computer display. He realized that getting fixated on the number of miles they'd gone only made the ride seem longer. It was kind of like watching the clock during a really boring class at school.

They passed The Complex, where Ben had most of his little league games and practices. All four fields were completely deserted, except for a few seagulls and Canada geese. Even the parking lot was empty. *Baseball players have the sense to come in from the rain,* Alex thought. His gloves and socks were now completely waterlogged. He could feel and hear his shoes squishing with every revolution of the pedals.

Alex and his dad passed a couple of intrepid people carrying umbrellas as they walked their dogs. Other than that, the trail was empty from Woodinville to Redmond City Hall. *I guess most cyclists have the sense to come in from the rain, too.*

As mile after mile of empty pavement rolled under their wheels, Alex began strangely enjoying the quiet and solitude. Even his dad was silent, except for the occasional reminder to eat and drink. Alex gazed at the steady stream of raindrops dancing on the green surface of the Sammamish River, listened to the soft drumming of raindrops on his helmet, and decided this wasn't all that bad. Once you got used to it. The miserable part had been going from cozy and dry to soaking and wet. Now that all of him that could get wet was indeed wet, it wasn't such a big deal.

They turned around at Marymoor Park and headed back toward home. "How you holding up?" his dad asked. "You've been kind of quiet back there."

"Pretty good," Alex replied, as they pedaled up to their cruising speed. "Rain gear's working. Fender's working. Kind of nice having the trail to ourselves. Just wish my fingers and toes would dry out."

His father turned to glance at him, and gave a quick grin before refocusing on the trail ahead. He noticed his father's face was as wet as and mud-splattered as his own. "Still up for a century today?" his dad asked.

"We're already as wet as we're going to be."

His father chuckled, and didn't say anything else. They eventually arrived back home, and Alex wiped the computer display. "Twenty-six miles," he announced.

The two of them dismounted, left their wet rain gear in the garage, and walked toward the house. "I figure we can ride up to Arlington after we eat," his dad said. "Go until the display says 63 or 64 miles, and then turn around."

"Works for me," Alex replied.

"Oh, and before I forget, Mr. Lloyd sent me a note on Facebook. He and Jacob are planning to ride in that general area today. I told him maybe we'll see them."

Alex brightened at the prospect of seeing Jacob Lloyd again. "Hopefully they're braving the rain, too," he said.

Once inside the house, Ben glanced up and shook his head. "Glad it's you and not me," he muttered.

"It's really not that bad," Alex replied, trying to smile.

Ben glanced at the rivers of rain washing down the windows, and said something about taking Alex's word for it.

Alex and his dad heated up some boiled potatoes, and ate them with butter and salt. Alex loved the way the potatoes warmed him from the inside out. The carbohydrates made him feel totally satisfied.

"We shouldn't let ourselves cool down too much," his dad cautioned, glancing at the clock.

Alex stood up. *Too late,* he thought. His thighs were already tightening and urging him to call it a day. He made himself put on some clean socks, and he took his father's advice to put a plastic bag over each foot before inserting it into the shoe. He hoped that would keep him a little more dry.

For the first ten miles or so back on the tandem, everything inside him was urging Alex to turn around and go home. Then, just like before, he found himself in a nice rhythm. He again started actually enjoying the peace of being alone with his thoughts in the rain.

All that changed once they reached the four-lane Highway 522 toward Maltby. The traffic interrupted Alex's thoughts, and drowned out his imagined musical accompaniment. Despite the wide shoulder, every whizzing car pelted them with a muddy wall of spray.

He was glad his father knew a lot of quiet, tree-lined country roads between Maltby and Snohomish, and then from Snohomish to Arlington. Alex liked that these roads had enough rolling hills to be interesting, but were still flat enough to keep him from getting burned out.

As they started down a particularly steep hill, Alex realized the gear wasn't right at all. It was way too easy. They were spinning their pedals too fast. If he'd been on his single bike, he would've upshifted several seconds earlier. For whatever reason, his father hadn't done the same.

His father suddenly recognized the problem. He shifted up to the largest chainring, but the chain kept right on going. The next thing Alex knew, his pedals were jammed and wouldn't turn at all. Glancing down, he could see what was wrong: the chain was tangled up in his right crank arm.

"Chain's stuck!" Alex called.

He and his father tried working the pedals back and forth, while his father worked the shift lever. The chain only got more hopelessly twisted.

They coasted to a stop at the bottom of the hill, and dismounted. Alex held the tandem steady, trying to ignore the drizzling rain. His dad struggled to untangle the chain.

"Any worse, and we could've ruined it," his father said. He carefully repositioned the chain. "Better adjust that front derailleur when we get home."

The two of them resumed their northward trek. Every fiber of Alex's body now screamed in protest. The ten minutes of standing around in the rain had cooled him off and re-tightened his calves and thighs. As Alex forced the pedals up and down, he realized he was losing sensation in his toes. Soon, the numbness was creeping further into his feet. His fingers were so numbed, he could barely grip the handlebars. He tried to blow on them, but it didn't help much.

Alex stole a peek at the computer. Seven miles to the turnaround point. *Tell Dad we've gone far enough,* he thought. *My toes and fingers can't take any more. Eighty-six miles is plenty, especially in this weather.*

"How you holding up back there?" his father asked, his voice trembling a bit.

"F-f-f-fine," Alex lied. *If I tell him we need to turn around early, that'll be quitting,* he told himself. *Just like having Mrs. Rossi finish the concert for me. Even if I can't feel my feet, I can't quit.*

"You sure?"

"I can make it." *That much is true.*

They eventually rolled into Arlington. Alex told his dad once they'd reached the right mileage. When they turned around and began heading south, Alex's heart skipped a beat. *I made it all the way out. Now it's just the homestretch. Every pedal stroke gets me closer to finishing my first century ride.* He began cranking harder, and had to consciously hold himself back from working too hard.

Although the rain still drizzled around them, Alex could see the skies clearing on the horizon. He felt a little disappointed that they'd been riding away from the clearing, rather than toward it. He did like this peaceful route, with its cathedral ceiling of gnarled oak branches arching overhead. He especially liked the tailwind, and that the sensation was finally returning to his fingers and toes. Alex decided he'd a hundred times rather have a tailwind on this quiet route in the rain than a headwind on a dry but busy road.

Rob's favorite part about riding in the rain had always been the super-clean air when the rain finished falling. Cruising toward home with Alex, he savored deep breath after deep breath. *It's almost worth getting soaked to the skin and losing sensation in my extremities,* he thought. *Almost.*

A short distance ahead, a tandem bike pulled onto their road. Rob could make out a large captain, with a stoker about Alex's size.

"Think that's the Lloyds?" Alex asked.

"Could be. Surprised Penny isn't with them. Let's catch them and find out."

Rob shifted into a higher gear, and the two of them easily overtook the other tandem. The captain and stoker glanced back as the Petersons drew near.

Alex exclaimed, "Hey! It's Jacob!"

Jacob and his father both smiled and greeted the Petersons. "I wondered if we'd see you out here, what with all the rain," Doug Lloyd said.

"So glad it's finally clearing up. I'm soaked," Jacob said.

"No kidding!" Alex replied.

They continued riding along, side by side, chatting. "Where's Penny?" Rob asked.

"Mom got called in to work at the hospital," Jacob said. "Dad said he still really wanted to ride."

"Only ride in good weather, and we'll never get ready for STP," Doug said.

"Got that right," Rob agreed. "Only reason I'm out here."

"Hey, Jacob. Are *you* riding STP?" Alex asked. Rob could practically feel the envy dripping from the boy's words.

"Maybe. Depends."

"Penny and I are definitely going," Doug explained. "She's volunteering as a ride medic. If she's needed on the one-day, and we're in good enough shape, we'll go on the tandem and leave Jacob with his grandparents."

"But if they do the two-day, and I've trained really hard, I get to ride stoker," Jacob announced.

"We'll see," Mr. Lloyd cautioned. "Penny and I'll have a better idea next month, after Flying Wheels."

"If you do the two-day, where are you staying?" Alex asked. "A motel or something?"

"A park just outside Chehalis. Every motel's been sold out for months, but we like camping anyway. Camped in that park the last two years. Not far past the midpoint."

Traffic approached, so Rob pulled in behind. He was glad the Lloyds' tandem had a good set of fenders, so the road spray was minimal.

They rode single file for several minutes. Rob enjoyed the quiet, and the chance to think. *I bet Alex could do the two-day ride on a tandem. This year. Not that I'd want to do the two-day. Just in theory. If I were to take him, I'm sure Alex could handle it.*

As they continued pedaling, Rob glanced back at his son. The boy's wistful expression made something inside him melt. *He's really worked his heart out. I know he wants more than anything to ride with me to Portland this year. I wish there were a way he could do it, but the one-day is just too much. Could I maybe think about switching to the two-day?*

A moment later, Rob caught himself. *There's no way I'm pitching a tent in Chehalis, and then getting up and riding another hundred miles. Maybe next year we can book a motel early. Or maybe Alex'll even be big enough for the one-day. But this year is my year. Next year it can be all about him.*

Mr. Lloyd pulled to the left, and waved for Rob to come up alongside. "Jacob and I were streaming the STP promotional video the other night, and had a question," he said.

"It said *Music by Alex Peterson* at the end. That you?" Jacob asked. "Or a different Alex Peterson?"

"Yeah," Alex smiled. "My math teacher, he's with Cascade. Asked me to compose some stuff. It was a lot of fun. Someone else mixed it in with the video, though."

"That's so cool! Didn't know you were so musical. I can't carry a tune in a bucket."

The two fathers and sons continued chatting, as the next several miles rolled past, until the Lloyds reached their turn-off.

Alex waved good-bye to Jacob. He'd really enjoyed riding with another kid his age. He hoped he and his dad could connect with the Lloyds again. Maybe if Dad saw Alex was an even stronger rider than Jacob, and Jacob were going on STP, Dad would change his mind and let Alex come along, too.

"Would you like to start with the two-day STP next year?" Alex's father asked.

I want to ride this year, Alex thought, but knew better than to say so. Instead, he replied, "The two-day ride is for wimps."

His father jerked his head around in surprise. "What makes you say that?"

"On the video, the two-day looked like a big party," Alex explained. "Almost too easy. I mean, I'd do it if it was the only way you'd let me go. I'd just rather do the one-day."

Dad glanced back and smiled, like he knew a secret.

"What?" Alex asked.

"Tomorrow morning, when you wake up in your nice comfortable bed, every muscle in your body will be aching. I want you to imagine how you'd feel if you'd slept in a tent. Or even on a gym floor. And then I want to hear about how much you're looking forward to doing another century ride. Like those 'wimps' on the two-day STP."

Alex considered his father's words. "Okay," he admitted. "I guess the two-day ride's a challenge, too. But I want to start with the one-day ride."

"Good. Because I'd personally rather pull through to Portland on Day One than have to wake up on Day Two and slog another hundred miles."

The two of them rode in silence for a long time, enjoying the empty rural roads. Alex dreamed about someday following roads like these on the way to Portland.

Finally, just when Alex began thinking the ride would never end, he and his father reached the familiar streets of their neighborhood. "How'd we do?" his dad asked, sitting up and pedaling easily.

Alex wiped the computer screen and began cycling through the various displays. "A hundred point seven miles." He savored the extra digit lit up on the trip odometer. "Six hours, thirty seven minutes on the bike."

"Your first century!" his father exclaimed. They pulled into the garage. "Congratulations! And we made pretty good time."

Alex glowed with pride. He'd really done a hundred miles! He'd even done it in the rain, when riding had been the very last thing he'd wanted to do. He removed his helmet and rain gear, and shook them out.

Just as Alex was about to begin limping to the house, his father put a hand on his shoulder.

"Hey," his dad said. Alex turned to face him.

Looking him in the eye, his father continued, "I have a confession to make. Standing in the garage this morning, I didn't want to ride today. If you hadn't come out, I probably wouldn't have gone."

"Really?"

"Really. Thanks for pushing me."

"Sure," Alex smiled.

Once in the house, Alex made a beeline for the shower. He leaned against the wall, and adjusted the nozzle to wash all over him with wonderfully hot water. He closed his eyes as the grime rolled off his face. The steamy liquid worked wonders for his aching muscles.

Alex smiled and whispered, "I did it. I didn't quit. No matter how cold and wet I got. I did it."

He'd been pretty sure he could conquer a hundred miles. Now, he realized he'd done much more than that. From the coziest imaginable bed, he'd gone out in the rain and conquered *himself*. He'd gone when even his dad had been ready to bail.

Since he'd been able to do that, he wondered how hard it could be to ride to Portland in nice July weather, with thousands of other cyclists to work with. And what it would take to convince his parents to let him try it.

FORTY-FIVE

June 12, 2009

A LEX AND BEN HELPED THEIR FATHER LIFT THE TANDEM TO the roof rack of Mom's station wagon. They needed to leave so early the next morning for the Flying Wheels Century, Dad had suggested getting as much as possible packed the night before. Alex liked the idea of just getting up in the morning, grabbing something to eat in the car, and going.

Once the tandem itself was secure, they loaded their shoes, helmets, and the trail-a-bike in the wagon's cargo area. Ben would be accompanying them roughly halfway, to the big lunch stop in Monroe. The plan was for Mom to meet them there using Dad's car. She would take Ben and the trail-a-bike to Grandpa's place up the road. Dad and Alex would finish Flying Wheels. Mom and Ben would meet them at home.

"Looks good," their father said. He gave the Taurus a final once-over. "You should both get your riding clothes ready tonight, before doing anything else. And Ben should pack something to wear at Grandpa's."

Alex retreated to his room. He began laying out his favorite cycling outfit, just like he would lay out his school uniform. It was supposed to be chilly and overcast, so he made sure he had tights. He also laid out warm gloves, and an extra layer for under his jersey. Thinking back to his first century ride, he figured it couldn't hurt to throw in some rain gear as well. The tandem had a cargo rack, and rain gear didn't weigh much.

My first century ride ... Alex could hardly believe he'd done two more century rides since then. One even stretched to 110 miles. His dad kept saying he was pleased with their speed. Between all that riding, and preparing for another music recital, the weeks had flown past.

He had gotten together a few times with Jacob Adams, and his sister Maria, to play music after school. During one of these sessions, Jacob made an intriguing proposal: "Instead of each person doing a separate recital piece, why don't we perform an organ-and-violin ensemble?"

They all enjoyed the Mozart concerto they'd been practicing. This would give the perfect excuse to keep playing it. Alex ran the proposal past his Aunt Theresa, who said, "Why not?"

The recital itself had gone smoothly last week, but with an amusing twist. The time had been moved up, which meant Alex and his friends would need to come straight from school. The three of them had shown up still wearing their St. Clement uniforms. "Hey!" one of the homeschoolers announced, "The Catholic school kids are here!"

Especially after performing together as a trio, the label stuck. At recitals, Alex, Jacob, and Maria would now be known as "The Catholic School Kids." Jacob even joked that they should start a band with that name.

Alex arranged the last of his cycling clothes. He imagined what it would be like laying things out for STP. How much thought and care he would give to every last detail, knowing it was for the event of a lifetime! Not that his father had said a single word about letting him ride this year, but Alex supposed he could still dream.

Or should I do more than just dream? he wondered. *Should I go all-out tomorrow? Pretend it's next year, and this is my last qualifier for STP? Try to break six hours? Maybe even hint to Dad that I sure wish he'd give me a chance this year?*

Overcome by a sudden inspiration, Alex closed his eyes and lifted his heart in prayer. *Please, God. Please help me change my Dad's mind. Please help him see how much I want to go with him.*

Later that evening, just before he fell asleep, Alex hit on a plan. It was so audacious, he figured it might just work.

FORTY-SIX

June 13, 2009

ROB STEERED ONTO OLD SNOHOMISH-MONROE ROAD, AND felt the wind shift into his face. He was glad he'd insisted everyone wear warm clothes. Despite being just a week from the first day of summer, the skies were overcast as far as they could see. The temperature wasn't supposed to reach 55 degrees. This wind made it feel even colder. He was glad Alex had packed rain gear, just in case.

Their bicycle train cleared the Snohomish city limits, and soon they were rolling past open farm fields. Rob spotted six strong-looking riders ahead. "Let's catch that group," he told Alex. While he had his head turned, he noticed at least eight single bikes drafting them.

All three Petersons dropped to the lower portion of their handlebars. Rob upshifted, and after a couple of intense minutes they managed to connect with the other group. "Great job!" someone shouted from behind.

Rob glanced back. Ben was waving in acknowledgment to another rider. They'd now assembled a long paceline, and were hauling at a fast clip. The remaining five miles of country roads between them and Monroe went by in a blur.

Cruising through the streets of Monroe, Rob had to chuckle at the number of people who gawked at the Petersons' setup. He figured Ben must be keeping busy waving back at everyone.

Finally, the United Methodist Church, with its mile-55 food stop, came into view on the far edge of town. Rob could see dozens of bikes entering and exiting its parking lot. He sat up and coasted. "Nice job, boys," he called over his shoulder.

"Thanks, Dad!" Alex replied.

"Glad my ride is over," Ben said. "It was fun, but I'm looking forward to playing at Grandpa's."

As they continued coasting, they spotted a couple of tandems leaving the food stop. "Are the Lloyds riding today?" Alex asked.

"Mr. Lloyd has been posting on Facebook that they're doing the 65-mile loop. So, we might see them later, when our loop overlaps with theirs."

"Cool," Alex said.

They pulled into the food stop. Rob scanned the parking lot for Meg. Instead, he spotted Paul Santucci waving. He had his four oldest kids along, and they ran to greet their cousins.

"Wasn't expecting to see you here," Rob smiled. He leaned the tandem against the Santuccis' large passenger van.

"Weren't expecting you so early," Paul replied. "You made good time."

As Ronnie looked on, Alex began punching through the computer displays. "Two hours, 53 minutes on the bike, 18.8 MPH," he announced. "We're smoking."

"We were out at Grandpa's today with Meg," Paul explained. "When she told us she was leaving to get Ben, our kids wanted to go along. I offered to drive, so she could stay and hang out with Theresa and their dad."

"I'm sure she appreciated that," Rob said.

Alex and Ben ran off to use the toilets. Rob filled his jersey pockets with fruit and granola bars, and continued chatting with Paul.

The boys returned and loaded up with food. Rob made his own trip to the toilet. When he returned, Paul was disconnecting the trail-a-bike.

All the kids were standing apart, crowded around a large piece of sketch paper. "This is awesome!" Ben laughed.

"Perfect!" Alex agreed. He had a big smile on his face as he munched a granola bar.

While the kids continued talking and laughing, Rob helped Paul with the trail-a-bike. "What's so funny?" he asked.

"Anthony made a drawing of you guys and the tandem. He's taking an art class. Getting pretty good."

Before Rob could look at the drawing, the boys were stashing it in the van. "Make sure this gets home," Alex told Ben. "I want to hang it next to my bed."

Once the trail-a-bike was stowed, Rob and Alex said their goodbyes to the others. They were soon back on the road.

Rob was glad they'd only spent 20 minutes at the rest stop. His chief concern wasn't so much total elapsed time. He was more worried Alex would cool off, and have a tough time hitting his stride again.

Once they turned onto High Bridge Road and began pedaling toward Duvall, the wind shifted in their favor. Rob very much enjoyed this stretch of rolling hills. It had terrific scenery, and virtually no traffic. Each little roller gave a wonderful view of the Snoqualmie River and thousands of acres of pasture. In high school, this had been one of his favorite places to train.

As the miles flashed by, they caught a couple of small groups of other cyclists. They were in turn caught by some other groups. Before Rob knew it, they were in a paceline of at least two dozen riders. Well less than an hour after leaving Monroe, Rob spotted the next food stop ahead. Seventy-one miles down. Less than thirty to go.

"Want to stop, or keep going?" Rob asked, sitting up and turning his head so Alex could hear him.

"Just need to use the bathroom real quick."

"Good. That means you've been drinking."

"Yeah. Guess I should refill my bottle, too."

They coasted into Camp Korey and rolled toward the toilets. A black kid about Alex's size started waving at them. The boy was standing by himself, with a tandem and a single bike, as if waiting for someone.

"Hey! It's Jacob!" Alex exclaimed, waving back.

Rob and Alex dismounted. They chatted with Jacob as they waited for the younger boy's parents to return. "We're having a great ride," Jacob said. "It's my first metric century — 100 kilometers. Just wish it was warmer out."

"No kidding. I've had this jacket on all day," Alex replied.

"My folks say the weather should be a lot nicer for STP next month."

"Are *you* going?" Alex asked.

"Yeah!" Jacob replied. "Dad says since I did every training ride, even in the rain, I can go too."

Glancing at Alex, Rob saw unmistakable envy and resentment flash in his son's eyes. "Is your mom riding as a medic on the two-day?" Rob asked Jacob.

"That's why I get to come along. I could never do the one-day. You ever done STP?"

"A few times. Two-day and one-day, different years," Rob told him.

"Wow," Jacob replied.

"I'm doing the one-day ride this year, and Alex might even do it with me next year."

"That's amazing! One day seems *impossible!*"

Rob was expecting Alex to join the conversation, or at least say something about next year's STP. Instead, the boy's sullen expression intensified. He hurried off toward the toilet.

Jacob's parents joined them a moment later. They greeted Rob, and chatted with him until Alex returned.

"So good to see you guys out on a tandem," Penny said.

"Yeah," Alex replied, forcing a smile. "Not sure I ever said 'thank you' for helping us get started."

"Well, you're quite welcome," Doug said. "Staying long? We just got here, and this'll be our main stop."

Rob was about to say they were in no hurry. "We were going to get right back on the road," Alex cut in. The boy avoided eye contact by acting like he was studying the route guide.

"Don't want to hold you up," Penny told them.

The two families said their goodbyes. Soon Rob and Alex were on the road, and hit their cruising speed.

Rob turned his head and told Alex, "We really didn't have to rush out of there."

"I know. But remember those goals you gave me for riding STP next year? One of them was doing Flying Wheels in a certain time. Want to see how close we can get."

Rob thought for a moment, and then added, "Another thing. You didn't have to make it quite so obvious that you're jealous about Jacob doing STP. Or that you didn't want to hear them talk about it."

"Sorry," Alex muttered. Rob could barely hear him above the wind. "Guess I'm just not very good at pretending I'm all happy when I'm not. Guess I'll try harder next time."

Rob thought about saying something, but didn't want to start a fight. He focused instead on the group of cyclists they were overtaking.

They spent the next ten miles enjoying a moderate pace on flat country roads, chatting with groups of other riders as they cruised along. When they reached the busy Redmond-Fall City Road, however, everyone lined up single file. Traffic whizzed past, and they began a three-mile climb into the wind. No one seemed in the mood to talk.

After just a few hundred yards of climbing, the wind seemed to shift. The ascent became noticeably easier. Rob up-shifted into higher gears twice. As they pulled to within sight of the top, they even passed two riders on single bikes.

The wind seemed to catapult them over the crest. Rob began upshifting like crazy as they began their descent. Their big tandem was soon flying down the other side of the hill, passing every single-bike rider. Rob smiled as Alex kept trumpeting, "On your left! On your left!"

They continued at this speedy clip to within a few blocks of the Sunny Hill Elementary stop. Pedaling through quiet residential streets, Rob slowed and was finally able to chat with other riders.

"Quite a climb back there!" one older gentleman said.

"Thought it'd never end," a heavy-set woman on a mountain bike added.

"Monster tailwind sure helped, though," Rob told them.

The others looked at him, puzzled. "What tailwind?" the woman asked.

"I saw two flagpoles on Redmond-Fall City Road. Wasn't much wind," the older man agreed. "If anything, a headwind."

"Huh," Rob replied. "Guess I read it wrong."

They cruised into Sunny Hill Elementary a moment later. The riders went their separate ways. As the Petersons coasted toward a set of portable toilets, Rob turned and said to Alex, "That was you, wasn't it?"

"Yeah," he smiled. "Wanted to see how fast we could go."

"Just don't burn yourself out," Rob cautioned. They parked, and then hurried to restock their food and water. A moment later, they were back on the road toward Redmond.

The remaining miles were quiet or had wide shoulders. The Petersons were able to talk with and enjoy the company of other riders as they cruised at a good clip. Rob enjoyed listening to Alex talk about the tandem and describe his favorite training routes.

Eventually, they blasted triumphantly into Marymoor Park. Rob could hear Alex beeping through the computer displays. "Five-forty-seven on riding time," the boy said. "But our total time was six-thirty-five with stops. Drat."

Rob glanced back as they approached the finish line. "What do you mean, 'drat'?" We made awesome time."

"Not the 6:35," Alex explained. "You said we have to break six hours for me to qualify for STP next year."

Now Rob understood Alex's hurry at the rest stops. "The six hour goal was *riding* time. You did great back there today."

Alex's face lit up in a smile.

The parking lot was a sea of bicycles and colorfully-dressed riders. Everywhere they looked, cyclists were cruising into the park, standing around talking, or packing up cars. Celebratory music, and the smell of grilled chicken, drifted toward them from the finish line festival and beer garden.

Rob steered toward where they'd left Meg's car, and dismounted. As Alex began his post-ride stretches, Rob searched through their pack for the keys. He looked in every compartment. Nothing. Frantically, he checked his pockets. Again, nothing. "Do you have the keys?" he asked Alex. "I thought I gave them to you this morning."

Alex shook his head. He peered through the passenger window. "In the ignition," he announced.

Rob kicked himself for not paying more attention that morning. He could've sworn he'd given the keys to Alex. "Shoot. Locksmith would take forever. I'll call your mother and have her bring the other set," he said, digging the cell phone out of his jersey pocket. "We could get something to eat at the festival while we wait."

Alex frowned and looked at the tandem. "Or we could just ride home. It's only twelve or thirteen miles. We've done it a million times."

Rob stopped dialing and looked up. "You sure?" he asked. With all the effort Alex had put into the day's ride, volunteering to tack on more miles was the last thing he'd been expecting. Riding home was the last thing Rob himself wanted to do.

"Why not? We'd get home faster. We could ride back and get the car tomorrow after church. That'll be our recovery ride."

Rob still wanted to call Meg. For him, it was more psychological than physical. When you think a long, hard ride is finally over, it's tough to adjust your mind enough to get back on the bike for another 45 minutes. But Alex's offer was so generous, he didn't want to turn the boy down. "Let's use the toilet real quick and get going before we cool off."

It took Rob several miles to get his head back into riding. Cruising the ultra-familiar Sammamish River Trail did help the time fly more quickly. They pedaled mostly in silence.

Finally, a few miles from town, Alex spoke up.

"Dad, I have a question," he said, sounding very serious. He seemed to have been gathering himself for something.

"Yeah?" Rob asked.

"I know you told me I can't ride STP before next year. And I promise I'm not asking to ride this year. But let's pretend you'd told me I could do the two-day ride, like Jacob. Would you say I've trained enough?" Alex's words sounded rushed. His nervousness was obvious.

"Absolutely," Rob replied, trying to put his son at ease. "You've done awesome."

"Good enough for the one-day ride?"

Rob thought for a moment. "Even with your training, that might be a reach for you this year. If you were a little bigger and older, I'd be more comfortable."

They pedaled in silence for another long while. Then, Alex spoke again. "Is there anything, this whole spring, you think I should've done better? Anything more I should've done? Besides get older?"

Rob thought for a moment, amused at the boy's earnestness. "Nothing," he assured him. "And your volunteering to ride home today? Big plus. Just do it all again next year."

"So," Alex said slowly, "You're saying I've trained hard enough for STP. There's nothing I could've done better. How come I can't at least try this year? See if maybe I am big enough?"

"Alex," he said, resenting that the boy had laid such a good trap. "We've been over this. Don't. Push. It."

Alex didn't say another word the rest of the way home.

FORTY-SEVEN

ROB SPRAWLED ON HIS OFFICE COUCH IN FRONT OF THE TV, enjoying some blackberry wine. Everyone had gotten a good shower, and plenty of pasta. The boys were headed toward bed. He looked forward to decompressing a little before doing the same. Alex had really worked him hard today. Muscles from his ankles to his neck were letting him know it. He'd forgotten he even *had* some of those muscles.

After a brief warning knock, Alex let himself in to the office. Clad in shorts and a new red Flying Wheels t-shirt, he looked almost ready for bed. "Do you have a minute to talk?" he asked.

"Sure," Rob replied, clicking the TV off. "What's going on?"

Alex pulled up a chair. Rob couldn't help noticing how the boy's quadriceps and calves rippled as he sat himself down. His head held high, and his back ramrod straight, Alex looked his father directly in the eye for a long moment.

"I need to apologize for something," Alex said at last. "I locked the keys in the car this morning on purpose. So I could offer to ride all the way home."

"What?" Rob asked, pulling himself upright on the couch. He felt angry that Alex had deceived him and played such a dirty trick. At the same time, he was puzzled and curious as to why he'd done it. *And why is he apologizing? He clearly had gotten away with it.*

"I know it sounds stupid, but it was the only way I could think of to get your attention. To show you that even after we'd ridden a ton of miles, and we were both really tired, I'd be happy to keep riding more and not give up. So maybe you'd think about that, and how hard I worked all the other times, and maybe think I'd be a good teammate for STP. And let me come with you this year."

"Alex …" Rob started. The boy was so earnest, and so utterly without guile, it was impossible to be mad at him. Besides, Rob figured it must've taken a huge amount of courage to come out here for what was obviously not an apology, but a last-ditch plea to be taken along. He needed to let Alex down gently.

"Thank you for being honest, and for being brave in coming to me. I do think you'll be a great partner on STP. You don't have to play tricks to prove it," Rob told him. "But it's just too late this year. As strong as you are, I'm not sure you're ready for the one-day ride. And even if I wanted to switch to the two-day ride, all the Saturday night lodging at the midpoint is sold out. I barely even got a room in Portland near the finish line. And our family doesn't go camping."

"I know, Dad," Alex said, continuing to look him in the eye. "It's just that I want this more than anything else in the world. I promise I won't quit, no matter what. Are you sure there isn't a way to take me?"

"Even if there were, you'd need your own rider number. Registration's been sold out for months."

Alex's face fell. Rob realized he'd played the ultimate trump card. Seeing how deeply crushed his son looked, he even felt a twinge of guilt. *But this is my year,* he reminded himself. *Alex needs to learn that sometimes you don't get everything you want.*

"Okay," Alex said, standing to leave. "Sorry again about the keys. I hope you have a good STP."

Once Alex departed, Rob tried to return his attention to the TV. He couldn't focus on the program. As he sipped blackberry wine, his thoughts kept drifting back to the extreme dedication Alex had shown. *He's come so far since the Christmas concert. The way he looked at me tonight, it was like a grown man negotiating a contract. Not a little kid pleading for a treat.* As much as Rob wanted to ride STP by himself, he couldn't stop feeling guilty about leaving Alex behind.

A knock sounded, and Meg let herself in to the office. "Sorry to interrupt, but can we talk about something?" she asked. Concern was etched clearly in her face.

"Of course," he replied, clicking the TV back off.

Meg made herself comfortable in a chair. She looked uncertain about where to begin. "It's Alex," she said at last. "You saw how he moped through dinner. Then he closed himself up with his keyboard after dinner. I knew something was really bothering him. He wouldn't tell me what it was. Just said it was between you and him."

"He did come out here a little bit ago. We talked about it. He's disappointed he can't ride STP."

"I suspected as much."

"Yeah. Even made a strong pitch for why I should take him. But it's just not his year."

Meg thought for a moment. "Driving home today, Ben asked me something: 'Why can't Alex get called up to STP a year early, like I got called up to Majors?'" Meg paused, and gave Rob an uncomfortably long look before continuing. "I had to say, I didn't know. That it was up to your father."

"Alex has Ben lobbying for him?" Rob smiled.

"I don't think Alex put him up to it. I can usually spot that a mile away. And besides, Alex isn't that kind of kid."

"What, then?"

"Ben's got the youngest child's gift for sniffing out when things aren't fair. And, hate to say it, this time he may have a point."

"How do you mean?"

"I've never seen anyone train as much for an event as Alex has," Meg replied. "I can't even remember a single long weekend ride where he didn't go along. You're always talking about how hard he works."

"And?"

"If it were next year, would he be going?"

"Sure. But it's not next year."

"*That's* your reason? I mean, I'm not pushing you to change your mind. I'm just trying to understand. If he's ready, what difference does a year make?"

Rob took a sip of wine and swished the glass a bit. "He's definitely ready for the two-day ride. I'd even be comfortable letting him ride 150 miles in one day and 50 the next. I want him to get bigger before he tries a whole double century."

"Fair enough. Is there any way you'd consider switching to the two-day ride?"

"Even if I did, it's too late. Everything along the way is sold out. I barely even got a room in Portland for Saturday night, and that was months ago. We'd have to pitch a tent somewhere, which isn't happening. And besides, Alex would need his own rider number. Registration closed a long time ago."

Satisfied that he'd again played the trump card, Rob topped off his wine glass.

"But people buy and sell those registration packets, right?" she asked. "I remember you sold one that year we had to cancel our trip up from L.A."

"I'm not sure Cascade allows that anymore."

"You could check," Meg suggested. "And even if they don't, maybe you could talk to Alex's teacher. Mr. Jansson. He might know a way they could make an exception. Alex sure spent a lot of time helping them with that music."

Rob frowned and swished his wine glass. "There's still the problem of lodging. I don't do tents. Neither does Alex. Even if we crashed in a gym or church basement, a second hundred miles is a long way to go after sleeping on a floor."

Meg thought for a moment. "What if you rode 150 miles, and then Ben and I drove you to the motel in Portland? Then, after church the next morning, back to where you left off?"

"Logistical nightmare," Rob muttered, not daring to admit the genius of her solution.

"Rob...," Meg said, after a long silence. "I can always tell when there's something you're holding back."

Rob stared past her, not making eye contact.

"Do you want to talk about it?"

Rob set his wine glass down, folded his arms, and tried to decide where to start. "You want the whole, honest truth?"

Meg nodded.

Somewhere inside, Rob felt an emotional levy breaching. He sensed he could tell her everything, and she'd understand, and not call him a selfish pig or try to change his mind.

"This is my year. The year I come out of retirement. The year I see what STP is now all about. The year I ride, and worry about nothing but having a good time and getting to Portland on an Italian racing bike. In one day, not two. Not making extra stops because Alex is sore. Not worrying about whether he's eating or drinking enough. Not figuring out what to do when he's exhausted and has to be talked back onto the bike. Not carrying extra clothes and rain gear and food. And not struggling to pedal a 45-pound beast over all those hills."

Meg looked relieved. "Thank you for your honesty. I figured it had to be something like that."

"Next year can be Alex's year," Rob added, picking his glass back up. "I'm totally fine with that. I just need him not to get all ugly because this year happens to be my year."

The two of them looked at each other in silence. Rob nursed what was left of his wine.

"He'll get over it. He's pretty resilient," Meg said at last.

Rob sensed there was more on Meg's mind, but he didn't want to probe. He knew the longer they talked, the more he'd have to defend himself. He felt guilty enough already.

"Coming to bed?" Meg asked.

"Sure," he muttered.

Rob finished his wine, secured the office, and followed Meg back to the house. As he locked doors and turned off lights, Meg checked on the boys.

"Rob!" she whispered, waving for him to come to Alex's room. "Look at this!"

Alex was sprawled across his still-made bed, arms and legs bent at impossible angles, still wearing shorts and his Flying Wheels t-shirt. "Looks comfortable," Rob smiled. Meg contorted her limbs in an exaggerated impersonation of their son.

"You lift him, and I'll pull the covers back," Meg whispered.

Rob slipped one arm under Alex's thighs, the other arm behind Alex's back, and picked him up. Meg pulled the covers back. She then tried to arrange Alex's arms more comfortably. The boy began to stir, and his eyes briefly fluttered open.

"I'll take it from here," Rob whispered. Meg slipped out.

Rob knew he could simply lay Alex down and tell him to go back to sleep, but Rob didn't want to. Instead, he set himself on Alex's bed, his back to the wall. He arranged the boy's exhausted body more comfortably in his arms, and gently rocked him. "Everything's okay," Rob whispered.

As Rob continued cradling his son, he was struck by how huge the boy's thighs and calves had become. He couldn't believe how much his arms and chest and everything else had filled out, too. *He's not a little kid anymore,* Rob thought. *He's grown up so much, in so many ways, I can't believe he's the same boy.*

Alex stirred again. Rob clutched the boy closer, and rocked him until his breathing slowed.

For a long moment, Rob savored the peace and innocence of Alex's face. *He may have grown up, but have I? Is cycling still all about me? About me going out and having a great time, just like it was before he was born? Have I been treating Alex like he's just along for the ride?*

Rob's gaze fell on a large piece of sketch paper hanging next to Alex's bed. He realized it must be what Anthony Santucci had given them at the Monroe rest stop. The title, in colorful block letters, announced, "MEET THE AMAZING TEAM FLYING WHEELS!" Under it was a strikingly well-done illustration of their tandem and trail-a-bike. The bicycle train looked like it was cruising at high speed. Anthony had given each of the helmeted riders a block-letter title, and a smaller cartoon "speech bubble." At the front was CAPTAIN DAD, his head turned, saying, "Great job, boys! Keep up the good work!" In the middle was THE LITTLE STOKER WHO COULD, head down, declaring, "I think I can, I think I can." Finally, perched on the trail-a-bike was THE TAIL GUNNER, sitting up and waving as he said, "Hi! I'm Ben! What's your name?"

Rob smiled. He couldn't stop looking at the sketch, or thinking about how well Anthony had captured their team. *Team Flying Wheels. I like it.* Although Alex had insisted they not spend money on event jerseys, Rob decided he needed to find some on a clearance rack. It would be their team uniform.

Rob's gaze turned to some of the photographs with which his son had festooned the walls. He and Alex, pedaling up Grandpa Sullivan's driveway on a Sunday morning. He and Alex, inspecting the tandem's drivetrain. He and Alex, bundled up for a Christmas afternoon ride.

Rob closed his eyes. His mind drifted to all the other images that hadn't been captured on camera. He and Alex, cruising along the Sammamish River as the boy related what'd happened at school that day. He and Alex, soaked to the skin, but with no regrets about riding in the rain. He and Alex, whooping as they crested the mammoth Maltby Road hill. He and Alex. He and Alex. He and Alex.

Suddenly, in his mind's eye, Rob was in Death Valley. Alone in the shadow of Jubilee Pass, he watched a tandem disappear on the horizon. *I guess I've come full circle,* he thought. *Or "full cycle," as it were. A tandem team helped me understand I needed to hang my bike up. And now* being *a tandem team has gotten me back on the road.*

Team. With that, Rob's mind jumped to the evening he and Meg and Ben had talked so intensely in his office. *We're supposed to be in it together,* his younger son was saying. *How can I leave now, just like that, and forget about the guys on my team?*

And Rob realized he couldn't, either. He laid The Little Stoker Who Could gently in bed and tucked him in. "I'm so proud I get to have you on my team," he whispered, resting his hand on Alex's sandy-blond head. "We'll always be a team. Really a team. I can't imagine getting to Portland any other way."

Rob gave his son a goodnight kiss, and slipped quietly from the room.

FORTY-EIGHT

June 29, 2009

A LEX LAID IN BED, SAVORING THE MORNING SUNLIGHT. *I love having a summer birthday,* he thought. *Perfect weather, and no school to get up for.* Connor was even coming tonight, for dinner and a sleepover.

Eventually he made his way to the dining room. Ben and his father were already eating breakfast. They greeted him with a hearty "Happy birthday!" Alex smiled and thanked them.

"Mom's already left for work, but she wishes you a happy birthday, too," Ben told him.

Alex noticed a large manila envelope propped against a cereal box, at his seat. "What's that?"

"We're starting a new tradition," his father said, exchanging a grin with Ben. "You'll still open most of your gifts after dinner, but we have one for you to open right now."

Ben gestured toward the cereal box and announced, "The envelope...please!"

"Okay, okay," Alex smiled. "Are you sure it can't wait?" He usually liked to save all his gifts for late in the day, savoring the anticipation.

"Nope," his dad insisted.

Alex took the envelope in his hands and felt it carefully. He couldn't figure out what might be inside. Finally, with the suspense killing him, he unhooked the metal clasp and gently tore it open.

He could now see it held several sheets of paper, of varying sizes. Alex carefully slid them out. To his shock, the papers were a route map and rider guide for Seattle to Portland. And, on top, was a large rectangular bib number!

Alex remained stunned. Did this mean what he thought it meant? "I ... I ..." he stammered, still staring at the paper and reading its numbers over and over. Two. Four. Five. Six. *Am I really now an official rider? Number 2456?* "I thought I had to wait for next year," Alex managed to say.

His father grinned and shook his head.

Alex stood speechless. This was the absolute last thing he'd been expecting. He felt like dancing and whooping and hollering, *I'm riding STP! I'm riding STP!* But he didn't want to look like a little kid. He was going to be his dad's riding partner. He needed to act the part.

"One day or two?" he asked.

"One and a half," his father smiled. "We're going 150 miles, to the Columbia River, on Day One. There's no place left to stay there, so Mom will drive us to Portland. We'll drive back and finish on Sunday after church."

It wasn't quite the one-day ride Alex had dreamed about. Still, it was more miles than he'd ever done. And it was *STP.* He was going! "Thank you! Thank you so much!"

"Thank your brother," his father said, to Alex's surprise.

"Huh?"

"He's the one who reminded me that boys who work especially hard can get called up to Majors a year early." Then, after a meaningful pause, he looked Ben in the eye and added, "Even if they might have reasons for not actually going."

Ben smiled self-consciously. Alex tried to process what Dad had said. "Ben got called up? And didn't take it? How come nobody told me?" he asked.

"Something opened up a month ago," Ben explained. "I decided I should stay with my team for the stretch. Didn't want you thinking I was a better athlete than you or something, just 'cause I got called up. So I didn't say anything."

"You didn't have to do that," Alex said.

"Well, I wanted to. Anyways, after Flying Wheels, I told Mom that you deserved to get called up even more than I did. That it wasn't fair you didn't get to ride STP. She told Dad. I just wish I was good enough to come, too."

Alex couldn't believe what he was hearing. He was so grateful, he wanted to give his little brother a hug. Instead, he turned to his father and asked, "Could he? Maybe for part of it, on the trail-a-bike? Then Mom could pick him up? She has to drive anyway." As much as it would complicate things and slow them down, it didn't seem right to leave his little brother at home.

"That'd be so much fun!" Ben exclaimed.

"I'll think about it," their dad said. "Support vehicles aren't allowed on the route. Just at the major stops. But if your mother's willing to meet us at one of them, and if Ben were committed to going, I could try scrounging up a registration packet."

"Speaking of which, how'd you get me a packet? I thought registration was all sold out."

His father smiled. "Talked with Mr. Jansson. Cascade had an extra packet they'd been holding for volunteers. He said the music you did on the promotional video more than earned it."

Alex thought for a moment. "I guess that makes me a professional musician!" he beamed.

As they ate breakfast, Alex and Ben and their father discussed different ways they could do the trip. If Mom were driving and meeting them at the major stops, she could pick up Connor as she drove through Tacoma. "Let's ask him and his parents tonight, when they drop him off," their dad said.

Then Ben grinned and changed the subject. "I *knew* you were good enough for Majors," he said.

"Thanks," Alex replied.

Then Alex realized something. *Dad was going to do the one-day ride. To call me up to Majors, he had to come down a level.* He felt guilty about making his dad miss the one-day ride, and was all the more grateful about going.

"Something on your mind?" Dad asked.

Alex shook his head. "Just thanks again for taking me."

After breakfast, Alex triumphantly carried his rider packet to his room. As he listened to one of his favorite Mozart concertos, he couldn't stop staring at his bib number. He studied the logos of all the event's sponsors.

The longer he studied his number, the more he felt a troubling unease. *Now it's real,* he thought. *Now I actually have to do it. A hundred and fifty miles. Then fifty more, when I'm sore and exhausted the next morning.*

He realized that all these months, he'd been thinking about STP the same way he used to think about the high dive at the Northshore Pool: *That looks so exciting. I wish I could take a turn. I'd give anything for that to be me.* Now, as he held and studied the actual rider number he'd be wearing in the actual STP in less than two weeks, he felt the same fright as the first time he'd stood at the end of the high dive. *Now I have to jump. I can't climb back down. What on earth have I gotten myself into?*

FORTY-NINE

July 10, 2009

ROB DISHED HIMSELF ANOTHER HELPING OF SPAGHETTI, AND looked across the table at the boys. "There's plenty left, if you'd like more," he told them.

"So stuffed," Ben groaned. He pushed his plate back.

"I'm totally carbo-loaded, too," Alex agreed, staring at his own plate. "Don't think I could swallow another bite."

Rob smiled as he dug into the last of his dinner. After ravioli on Wednesday, lasagna on Thursday, and now spaghetti on Friday, the boys had started telling friends about their "Pre-Portland Pasta Pig-out."

"Why don't you both go pack your bags for tomorrow and lay out your riding clothes," Meg suggested. "Then you'll be ready to help your father load the car when he finishes."

Alex nodded like that was a good idea, but looked too full to get up from the table. "We're wearing our Flying Wheels jerseys tomorrow, right?"

"Yes," Rob replied, between bites. "Also, tights over your shorts. Turtleneck under your jersey. Sun won't be up until 5:23, and I want you warm at the start. We can remove layers later." He thought for a moment, and then added, "Put rain gear in the car. We won't need it tomorrow, but Sunday's looking iffy."

Alex and Ben asked a few more questions about things they should pack, and they confirmed various details about the next morning. They'd been over these things dozens of times, but Rob didn't mind a final review.

At last, both boys cleared the table and scampered off to their rooms to pack. "Think Alex is ready?" Meg asked, once they were out of earshot.

"Nobody ever is, the first time," Rob shrugged, and continued eating. "We'll get to Portland one way or the other. Alex isn't a quitter, no matter how much pain he's in." He almost added, "barring an accident," but caught himself. Getting Meg worried was the last thing he needed.

Rob couldn't think of much he'd have done differently over the month since Flying Wheels. He and Alex had managed a 120-mile ride on Saturday the 26th. Their pace had been fairly slow, and Alex hadn't known yet he was going on STP. Still, it'd been a good final test of the boy's endurance and technique.

Since Alex's birthday, he'd taken both boys for several easy rides down the Burke-Gilman Trail to the University of Washington. From there, they'd explored the first dozen or so miles of the STP route. He wanted everyone to be completely familiar with these roads and how the bicycle train handled, especially on the twisty portions. Rob knew they'd be surrounded by fast-moving bikes the morning of STP. It would be dark. He didn't want any surprises.

The one thing he hadn't been able to do was get the tandem in for a good tune-up. By the time he decided to let Alex ride, all the local shops were jammed with pre-STP service. But apart from the front derailleur, which still occasionally overshifted, the tandem had been running fairly well.

If anything, Rob worried their preparations had gone *too* smoothly. They'd smoked Flying Wheels. They hadn't even had any flat tires. Alex had continued working hard, without overtraining. Ben seemed eager and ready to join them for the first 50 miles, and perhaps for some of the second day. Rob had kept waiting for a shoe to drop, and it hadn't happened. Even the weather forecast for Saturday was looking nearly perfect.

Maybe, just maybe, they'd catch a break and cruise easily all the way to Portland. But he doubted it.

FIFTY

July 11, 2009

A S THEIR BICYCLE TRAIN CRUISED SOUTH ON LAKE WASH-
ington Boulevard, Ben pointed and called out, "Alex,
look at that!"

Alex glanced up. He locked his gaze on a spectacular sight:
Mount Rainier looming on the horizon above Mercer Island,
illuminated in the soft tones of summer daybreak. *Yes!* he
thought. *Yes! We are really, actually, truly here and doing it!*

Now roughly five miles into STP, Alex was still running on
pure adrenaline. His father had cautioned both boys not to get
sucked into the "blaze of glory" at the ride's opening. Alex
couldn't help himself. Neither, it seemed, could Ben. Both of
them were working the pedals as hard as in any training ride.
Their father had to continue upshifting to match them. The blue
expanse of Lake Washington became a blur.

As far as Alex could see ahead, and as far as he could see
behind, was an ocean of bicycles riding two or three abreast.
Never had he imagined riding in such a massive group. From
the frenzied look on his little brother's face, neither had Ben.
Alex had been particularly amazed at all the police officers sta-
tioned at various intersections, waving this sea of cyclists
through stop signs and red lights. Never had he felt part of
something so important.

Alex wasn't sure exactly how much sleep he'd gotten the
night before. It hadn't been much. He'd been so wired, he'd
ended up staring at the darkened ceiling of his bedroom for an
eternity. When he hadn't stared at the ceiling, he'd watched the
minutes tick away on his digital clock, like the slow drip of a
water torture. Sometime after 1am, he'd eventually lost con-

sciousness. When his alarm had sounded at 3:15, he'd leapt from bed as if propelled by a thunderbolt.

Thanks to Ben being so disorganized, they'd left the house later than planned. Ben hadn't even laid out his riding clothes, and had to rummage in a closet for tights! Alex had wanted to scream in frustration at the delay. Their car ended up getting caught in a swollen river of traffic near the start. They missed being able to leave at 4:45 with the very first group. *It's already going wrong,* he'd thought.

The only good thing about leaving late was running into Mr. Jansson. He said he'd be looking forward to seeing Alex in Portland, which oddly made the whole thing seem even more real. *I'm actually going to be in Portland tonight, even if that last part of it will be by car,* Alex thought. *In a whole different state. The first time in my life that I'll remember crossing a state line.*

Alex had explained to Mr. Jansson about their plan to stay in Portland, and drive back to finish the next morning. "But I really want to watch the one-day riders come in, so we'll come to the festival for a while."

"I'll be at the finish line festival all evening, because I need to be available for the media," Mr. Jansson had told them, as they'd waited for the air horn to signal their departure. "If you don't see me at first, just keep looking."

They'd soon lost sight of Mr. Jansson. Alex assumed he was now several miles ahead. He'd said he was aiming to finish in less than 12 hours of total time. Alex's dad said their own goal was to reach the 150-mile point in Longview by 4pm.

Alex wished this frenzied stretch could last forever, but he soon saw cyclists slowing and making a sharp right turn ahead. This was as far as he and his father had gone in their preparatory rides, because the right turn was followed immediately by a steep hill. Alex turned his head, and told his little brother, "Here we go."

His dad began downshifting even before they made the turn. By the time they came out of it, they were already in a nice low gear.

Suddenly, they had to dodge another cyclist who almost cut them off. *That was close. I guess there's a downside to having so many other riders with us.* Once his father straightened the bicycle train out, all three of them began cranking hard.

Dozens of cyclists on single bikes began passing them easily. "Don't worry," their father said, about halfway up the hill, between heavy breaths. "We'll pass them on the way down."

That made Alex smile, and helped make the climb more bearable. The first block was most intense. Once they made a left turn, the climb became more moderate. As they continued spinning their pedals and watching other riders pass, Alex turned his attention to the houses lining the residential street. He was amazed at the number of people sitting on their porches, sipping coffee. Lots of these spectators waved at them. Ben stayed busy waving back.

They eventually crested the hill, and began picking up speed coming down the other side. Alex barely had time to catch his breath before his father started hammering again. They were still in a small gear, and their feet spun very fast.

Alex looked down, and tried to figure out what gear they were in. Dad shifted the front derailleur toward the largest chainring. The shift was too forceful, pushing the chain all the way past the largest ring.

"Stop pedaling!" Alex shouted, just before the chain became tangled in the crank arm. "Derailleur over-shifted again."

As they coasted down the hill, Dad fiddled with the shift lever. Alex backpedaled to return the chain to its track.

"Good catch. We really need to get that thing adjusted right." Dad said.

"Yeah," Alex replied. He smiled as they found their biggest gear, and hammered down the rest of the hill.

They kept riding hard for the next dozen or so miles. Then, before they knew it, their father was sitting up comfortably in the saddle and coasting.

"What's going on?" Alex asked.

Dad gestured ahead. Alex spotted several young people in green REI t-shirts jumping up and down on the sidewalk and waving. REI was a local outdoor sports chain, and the sponsor of the first rest stop.

"Have we gone 24 miles already?" Alex asked. He began punching through the computer displays. He was astounded they'd only been on the road for an hour and a quarter. He'd never in his life covered 24 miles so quickly.

"Cool bike!" two of the REI volunteers called out, as their father maneuvered into the large parking lot.

"They're so young!" another volunteer remarked. Alex and Ben smiled and waved as they went by.

There were almost as many volunteers manning the food tables as there were cyclists, and so many portable toilets there was no waiting. *I'm glad we started early, before the big crowds.* Alex hustled to fill his pockets with fruit and granola bars.

On his way back to the tandem, he spotted a young man in a red "MEDIC" jersey. It was just like Mrs. Penny Lloyd's jersey. He wondered where the Lloyds were on the course, and if they'd see them tomorrow.

Within ten minutes, the Petersons were again cruising south. Alex enjoyed the early morning quiet. The still-sleepy towns of Auburn and Sumner melted past them.

The next thing he knew, they were crossing into Puyallup and going past block after block of tidy 1950s ranch houses like the ones surrounding his school. Alex wondered if they'd go anywhere near the Puyallup Fairgrounds. The Fair was his absolute favorite field trip in September of each year.

They soon made the turn onto 5th Avenue, and pedaled easily toward the Grayland Park mini-stop. Mini-stops were much smaller than the main food stops. They had portable toilets and water, but the food at them was for sale rather than free. "Anyone need to stop?" their father called out.

"Nope!" both boys replied.

They cruised through the remaining two miles or so of Puyallup streets. Alex peppered his dad with questions about The Hill that was coming up. Everyone said it was the biggest on the course. A mile long. A 7% grade. He'd seen it in the video, but video is different from real life.

Then it was there. The Santana swung left onto 72nd Street, and Alex's dad began downshifting. Even as they knuckled down and focused on climbing in earnest, Alex kept stealing glances ahead. *This hill isn't that big*, he thought. *Maltby Road's way harder*. As they continued spinning their pedals and moving upward, Alex actually started to enjoy the change of pace.

Until, that is, he heard the distinctive sound of an unsnapping cleat. "Ugh!" Ben exclaimed. Their bicycle train slowed to a crawl, just a quarter of the way up the hill.

"What's wrong?" their father called.

"Shoe came out!" Ben replied. With each revolution of the pedals, Alex could hear his little brother trying — and failing — to get the cleat snapped back in.

Finally, their father pulled to the side of the road. Everyone unsnapped from the pedals.

"Sorry," Ben said, between heavy breaths, "Was working so hard, I must've twisted my foot too much."

All three Petersons cleated back in and resumed the climb. With their momentum shot, they had to spin in their very smallest gear just to get underway. Alex was soon cranking so fast, he could feel his inner thighs burning. Despite all that effort, their heavy bicycle train was still getting passed by lots of sleek riders on single bikes.

By the time they reached the summit, Alex's little brother was panting hard enough to cough up a lung. *Reminds me of me, on the Kitsap ride*, Alex thought.

They steered onto Canyon Road, at the crest of the hill. Their dad took a long look back at the boys. "Ben, you okay back there?" he called.

Ben nodded, but was too breathless to speak.

"That's the last big hill you'll have to do today," their father told them. "The bridge is tomorrow."

Alex knew the Lewis and Clark bridge, across the Columbia River at Longview, was the second-biggest hill on the course. He was glad they wouldn't have to make another big climb today. He was still struggling to catch his own breath, and his inner thighs and calves continued to burn. *I was doing so great, until Ben screwed everything up*, he thought.

Their dad stayed in a relatively easy gear for the next several miles. Before long, Alex was feeling ready to pick up the pace again — but he knew Ben wasn't. This, he decided, was the most frustrating part of being on a team. He wondered if this was how his little league teammates had felt, every time they'd seen Alex hobble to the plate.

The big 53-mile food stop at Spanaway Junior High eventually came into view. Alex began checking the computer screens as his father coasted through the crowded parking lot. "We got here in two hours and fifty-eight minutes of riding time!" Alex announced. "That's 18.1 MPH!"

"Excellent. Let's try to get in and out of here in 15 minutes," his father replied.

"I'm definitely done for the day," Ben told them. "It was fun, but I'm wiped out. Don't know how you guys are going to do three times that many miles today."

They parked the bicycle train. A moment later, Alex saw Connor waving and jogging toward them. "You guys are hauling. Your mom and I just got here. Thought we'd be waiting a while for you."

Alex gave his friend a high-five. "I'm feeling great!"

"I'm just glad I'm done," Ben said.

Connor stuck with them and chatted as they walked back and forth across a sports field to the bank of portable toilets. The Peterson boys then explored the food being offered at long tables. Connor went off to refill Alex's water bottles.

Everything looked delicious, especially the wrap-style sandwiches and chocolate chip cookies. And Alex made sure he picked up an apple and a few energy bars for his pockets. The best part of the Spanaway stop were the enthusiastic local kids staffing it. They were all smiles as they collected the food that Alex and Ben and the other riders requested. They seemed to be having the time of their lives.

"You're the youngest riders we've seen so far," said an Asian boy. He couldn't have been much older than Alex.

"I'm ten," Ben told them. "But I'm riding in the car from here. Alex is twelve, and he's going to Longview tonight."

As the Spanaway kids expressed their awe, Alex tried to be modest. "We're on a tandem with our dad. I couldn't do it on my own bike."

At the same time, Alex couldn't help thinking, *I just wish we were riding all the way to Portland. I can hardly wait for next year.*

A flash of understanding crossed the Asian boy's face. "Were you on that three-seater contraption?"

"The one and only," Ben smiled.

"That is so cool," both of the other boys said.

Alex wished he could talk more, but other riders began crowding in for food. He thanked the volunteers. They in turn wished the Peterson boys good luck.

Alex and Ben wolfed down their sandwiches as they looked for their father. They found him in the parking lot, chatting with their mom and Connor. He'd already detached the trail-a-bike and packed it in the back of the station wagon. "Get enough to eat?" he asked the boys.

"Yeah," they replied. Then they excitedly filled their mother in on the ride's details.

Alex's dad took his shoes off and removed his tights. "You getting warm?" he asked.

Alex realized it *was* getting a little warm for tights, especially now that the morning sun was well up in the sky. He followed his father's lead, and stashed his tights in the car.

"We should get moving before we cool off," their dad said. He stood and straddled the tandem.

As they pedaled toward the main road, Alex realized how much he'd cooled off and begun cramping up. *Maybe it's okay we're only going to Longview tonight,* he thought.

Once they reached their cruising speed, and Alex's legs loosened up, he began looking around at the dozens of other cyclists surrounding them. *I know almost all of them are one-day riders,* he thought. *But they don't look like Greek gods. Their bikes don't look like something from the Tour de France. They look as totally normal as anybody we'd see on Riverside Drive at home.*

From somewhere deep in Alex's mind, the smallest voice began to ask: *Is there really anything keeping you and your dad from following them all the way to Portland?*

FIFTY-ONE

ROB WAS LOSING TRACK OF THE NUMBER OF TIMES HE thought, *Wow. This sure has changed.* The rest stop in Spanaway was much bigger than he remembered. There were a lot more volunteers cruising the course on Gold Wing motorcycles, ready to give assistance. Above all, he couldn't get over the sheer number of other cyclists. They'd been in long pacelines pretty much all day — even now, on the lonely stretch of Highway 507 that connected Spanaway with Roy and Yelm. In past years, this was where the pacelines had broken up and he'd had to slog ahead pretty much alone. Now, they were whizzing along with yet another big group of riders.

The lively conversations they'd been having had made the time fly especially fast. It also helped that they'd ditched Ben and the trail-a-bike. After so many miles of captaining a bicycle train, their Santana now felt almost like a sports car. Almost.

"How's our speed?" he called to Alex.

"Steady at 19.1," the boy replied.

Because of how early they'd started, Rob knew that nearly everyone they'd seen was a one-day rider. That made him more than a little wistful. He quickly shook the feeling. *I'd a hundred times rather share these two days with Alex, than blast triumphantly into Portland alone tonight,* he thought.

They cruised through a large stand of cedars, and past the east gate of Fort Lewis. It was then one sunny horse pasture after another as they approached and passed the town of Roy.

They next passed through McKenna and the outskirts of Yelm. Rob was blown away by how much the place had grown up. Strip malls and shopping centers had sprouted everywhere.

When did this happen? he wondered. On his last STP, Yelm had seemed almost as rural as Roy.

They approached a mini-stop. Rob asked Alex if he needed to take a break.

"Doing fine," the boy assured him.

The route cut onto a quiet, 15-mile stretch of bike trail which hadn't even existed the last time Rob rode STP. The trail followed an old rail bed that seemed cut out of an alder forest. He loved the way the tree branches arched overhead, with sunlight filtering through the canopy. The pavement was smooth and clean. They flew along without worries about cars.

"This is nice," Alex said. Rob agreed, and glanced over his shoulder. Alex seemed to be thoroughly enjoying the scenery.

Toward the end of the trail, Rob realized he was nearly out of water. "Don't think I've got enough in my bottle to make it to Centralia. When's the next mini-stop?"

He heard Alex rustling pages in the route guide. The boy announced, "About two miles up. There's a park where the trail rejoins the road."

They made a quick stop for water, and used the toilets. The two of them then regrouped at the tandem. "How're you holding up?" he asked Alex.

"Getting kind of sore, but I'm okay."

Rob dug around in his pocket for a bottle of ibuprofen. He gave a tablet to Alex, and swallowed one himself. "This should help," he said.

Back on the road and navigating the streets of Tenino, the Petersons were soon riding with another large group. They chatted about their tandem, and how everyone's day was going.

Once they'd cleared Tenino, the route headed into the country. The group of cyclists surrounding them had grown to about two dozen. Rob figured they'd be able to haul at a fast clip on these open roads.

What happened next seemed to develop in slow motion, but with a sickening certainty that Rob was unable to avoid. A speeding cyclist wearing a blue jersey began passing their group on the left. He cut back in just ahead of a woman who'd been riding in front of their tandem — except Blue Jersey misjudged his arc. Rob watched in horror as the young man's rear wheel got closer and closer to the front wheel of the woman they'd been following. He knew Blue Jersey was going to cut her clean off.

Before Rob could even grab his brakes, the bikes ahead collided. The woman's front wheel slammed 90 degrees to the right, and she pitched over the handlebars. Trying to avoid her sprawling body, Rob steered toward the frame of her bike. As the Santana hit, it listed hard to the left and sent him airborne. Rob put his arms out and prayed that he and Alex wouldn't break their collarbones on impact. And that the riders behind could somehow avoid plowing into them.

FIFTY-TWO

ALEX NEVER SAW IT COMING. ONE INSTANT HE WAS WORKING his way through the computer displays, trying to figure the distance to Centralia. The next instant, a heavy jolt was heaving him through the air. He landed hard, but broke the worst of the fall with his hands. His first thought was, *I guess this is why we wear padded gloves.*

Before Alex could pick himself up, another bike swerved and narrowly avoided his head. He saw the tires pass just inches away. The rider crashed into a mailbox.

Alex's left leg felt like it was on fire from the knee down, but not nearly as bad as when he'd broken it. His dad was already sitting up, and didn't seem seriously hurt. "I'm okay," Alex assured him. "We should see if the other people need help."

His father's cell phone seemed to have survived the crash, because he pulled it out and began making a call. The woman whose bike they'd slammed into also looked all right.

Alex hobble-trotted as fast as he could to check on the guy who'd hit the mailbox. Alex's leg stung with each step, and he struggled to ignore the searing pain. The other guy looked like he'd taken a much worse spill. All to avoid Alex.

"You okay?" Alex asked. A crowd of other cyclists encircled the fallen rider.

"Think so," he moaned. He'd been thrown clear by the impact, and seemed to have landed safely in a grassy ditch. He looked to be in his mid-twenties, with a short and fairly lean build. He slowly stood up and brushed himself off. His white "Hammer Nutrition" jersey was stained with grass and blood, but he wasn't acting seriously hurt. In fact, he seemed more interested in checking his pale-green Bianchi bicycle than checking his body for injuries. "Can probably straighten out the fork enough to get to Portland, but my wheel's toast," he observed.

"I'm the one you swerved to miss. I'm really sorry your bike got wrecked."

"Not your fault," the rider said, wincing as he walked. "Better my bike than your neck. Anybody get the number of the idiot who caused this?"

Before anyone could answer, a rider with a red "MEDIC" jersey swooped in and asked who was injured. Alex wondered how the medic had gotten there so quickly.

"Me," the rider said, taking off his helmet to reveal a head of sweaty brown hair, "but look at the kid first. He's got some pretty bad road rash." The rider then sat down and began looking something up on a smartphone.

"My leg's just scraped," Alex said, removing his helmet. But once he took his first good look at the injury, he realized there was a lot more blood and gravel than he'd first thought.

The medic dug in his rack bag, produced gauze and antiseptic, and began cleaning the wound. As he went to work, Alex winced and added, "I know my legs aren't the same length. That's from a different accident."

"Must've been some accident," the medic muttered.

"Long story," Alex replied.

Meanwhile, the crowd kept growing. Lots of ordinary riders stopped to see if anyone needed help. Then, two guys on Gold Wing motorcycles parked their machines and began directing automobile traffic around the crash. Finally, his mother's Taurus wagon screeched to the side of the road.

"Alex!" she cried, running to him. "I got your father's call. Are you all right?"

"I'm okay," he called, hoping to avoid a big embarrassing scene. She reached him about the same time his dad and Ben did. Connor was close behind. His father was limping slightly as he pushed the tandem. Dad's arms and legs were scraped, but not as badly as Alex's.

"How's the tandem?" Alex asked his father.

"Battered but functional. We need to make sure you are, too."

"I'm fine," Alex insisted. His mother looked skeptical.

The medic continued working, digging gravel out of Alex's knee and thigh. Alex clenched his teeth and tried not to say "ouch," even one time. *I can't let Mom think I'm hurt,* he thought. *She'll make me quit for sure. And if I quit, Dad'll have to quit, too. Ben's too wiped out to take my place.*

Once his wounds were cleaned, Alex thanked the medic. The red-shirted man then went to work on the other rider.

"I really don't know about this," his mother said, with a concerned look on her face. "It's awfully close to the knee. It ought to be checked by a doctor. Maybe x-rayed. You could've opened the old fracture up."

Alex's heart sank. He shot his father a pleading look.

"Just road rash. I've ridden on worse," Dad said.

"Yeah," Alex added, trying not to wince. "It's just scraped. I know what 'fractured' feels like."

His mother folded her arms on her chest and looked conflicted. Finally, she asked, "Alex, are you *sure* your leg is okay?"

"Positive," he insisted.

"Moms always worry," the other rider joked, even as he himself winced at the medic's cleaning of his wounds.

Alex's mother thought for another long moment. "Okay," she said at last, to Alex's great relief. "But I want you off the bike the minute it feels any different."

"I promise," he assured her.

Alex's dad looked at the other rider's crumpled wheel. "Need a ride?" he asked. "My wife's meeting us at the major stops. She could get you as far as Longview."

The other rider looked relieved. "That would be a huge help. Just need to get to this bike shop in Chehalis," he said, waving his smartphone. "They say they have a wheel. And my name's Scott, by the way. Scott Roberts."

Alex's dad shook Scott's hand. He introduced everyone from their group.

"Chehalis isn't too far past the lunch stop," Alex's mother said. "If we hurry, we could drop you there and still get back to Centralia before Rob and Alex."

The medic finished cleaning Scott's scraped leg. Scott thanked him, and then Alex's dad helped load Scott's Bianchi into the Taurus.

Dad straightened out the tandem's handlebars and seats. Other than that, it did appear undamaged.

"This thing's a tank," Connor joked.

"No kidding," Alex's dad replied. He threw his leg over the frame and straddled it. "I wish it weighed less, but at least it's indestructible."

"Steel is real!" Scott smiled.

Alex climbed aboard. He settled painfully into his seat. The several minutes they'd spent off the bike, combined with all his scrapes and bruises, had made him especially sore. At that moment, Alex decided *STP isn't fun anymore.*

His father took it easy for the first few miles, letting other riders pass them, as their muscles loosened up. By the time they crossed the Centralia city limits, Alex was starting to feel halfway decent. Three miles of residential streets later, they were closing in on the midpoint stop at Centralia College.

Thank God it's half over, he thought, as they turned down the college's driveway, *and that we're only going to Longview.* As much as Alex hated to admit it, part of him wished he could call it quits right here. He'd definitely worked too hard in all the frenzied excitement of the opening miles, especially given how little sleep he was running on. His muscles were now loose, but still aching. His shoulders and upper back were getting particularly sore. His leg had stopped bleeding, but it continued to sting. And, though he'd dutifully eaten as instructed, his body was craving "real" food. He simply had to have something other than fig bars, fruit, and granola.

Alex considered telling his parents he was worried about his leg. That way, he could end the ride with dignity.

Then, an instant later, Alex realized that would not only be a lie — it would also leave his father alone on the tandem. There'd be no way Ben could help his dad finish. *I need to suck it up and keep going.*

"Hey, look at this!" his father exclaimed.

Alex glanced up. On the pavement, someone had written with chalk: "GO ALEX!" Alex smiled and felt his spirits rise.

Further ahead, about a hundred yards from the college itself, Alex noticed three kids jumping up and down. They were waving homemade signs and ringing cowbells. One sign read, "GREAT JOB ALEX!" Another said, "GO UNCLE ROB!" He immediately recognized Ronnie, Joseph, and Anthony Santucci. "All right! Way to go!" they hollered, as the tandem approached.

Alex smiled and waved at his cousins. "Thanks!" he told them. All the annoyances and discomforts he'd been obsessing over began fading into background noise. He never imagined something as simple as chalk, poster board, and cowbells could make him feel so much better.

"You guys are awesome!" Alex high-fived all three cousins as the tandem rolled past.

Once at the rest stop, Alex filled his water bottles and then used the toilet. He bypassed the free food, because it was officially for one-day riders only. *Next year*, he thought. He wished he'd taken an extra sandwich from Spanaway.

He and his father found Mom's car, where Uncle Paul and his cousins had already gathered. Everyone greeted them, and then Uncle Paul gestured to Alex's leg. "Your mom told me about the spill. Doing okay?"

"It's just scrapes. I've had worse," Alex said, with a wry smile. His uncle laughed, but his mother clearly didn't think it was funny.

"I'm really glad you guys came," Alex said, trying to change the subject. "I had no idea you'd be here."

"Wanted to surprise you," Joseph said.

"We never would've missed seeing you do STP," Anthony told them.

"Since this is the longest stop, we thought it made most sense to meet you here," Ronnie said.

The late-morning sun was starting to feel quite warm. Alex pulled off his jersey, and the turtleneck he'd been wearing underneath. He put his jersey back on, and started doing stretches to keep his arms and legs loose.

"Make sure you get something to eat," his mother said. She opened a cooler with hot dogs and boiled potatoes.

Alex picked two boiled potatoes, and sprinkled them with the salt his mom had also packed. He bit into one, savoring the pure carbohydrates. "This is *exactly* what I needed."

"When I rode support on doubles in California, before you were born, salted potatoes were always your dad's favorite," she explained. "That, and hot dogs."

Alex sat on the open back of the station wagon, all smiles. He relished his potatoes and hot dogs, and chatted with his brother and cousins and Connor about their adventures. Suddenly, Portland didn't seem nearly so far away. *Not really that much farther than Longview. If I can do 150,* he wondered, *why not 200?*

FIFTY-THREE

L EWIS COUNTY HAD ALWAYS BEEN ROB'S LEAST-FAVORITE stretch of the STP course. Coming out of a half-hour break in Centralia, with cold muscles and a full stomach, he was more often in the mood for a nap than for climbing back on a bike. What's more, riders were usually spread far out. That meant battling headwinds alone.

Rob was pleasantly surprised when he and Alex came charging out of Centralia so intensely. His stoker was noticeably stronger and in better spirits than before. It seemed to have helped that Alex had gotten a good meal and another ibuprofen tablet. No doubt the nice conversation with his cousins and Connor had helped, too.

Although Rob was getting tired and sore — especially around his shoulders — he still felt generally good. As the ibuprofen worked its way into his system, he hoped the soreness would fade.

Rob's biggest surprise was the number of other riders. When Rob had first done STP, fewer than 1,800 people participated. Now that STP had grown to more than five times that size, it meant no problem connecting with others. He and Alex were now hauling south at a comfortable clip in a large paceline.

Their group wound its way through the streets of Chehalis, stopping a few times for red lights. Then, the road opened and they were again headed out into the country. Rob shifted into a higher gear, and accelerated to keep up with the group's brisk pace. He settled comfortably into the saddle, thinking, *I could cruise like this all day.*

After several long minutes of spinning their pedals and listening to the whirr of tires on pavement, Alex spoke up. "Dad?" he asked.

The seriousness of the boy's tone made Rob smile. "Yeah?"

"Most of these guys we've been riding with, they're one-day riders. Right?"

"Probably. Why do you ask?"

"Well, you were going to do the one-day ride. Right?"

"Probably," he repeated. He hoped Alex wasn't feeling guilty about holding him back.

Alex was silent for a moment. Suddenly, his words flooded out in a torrent. "Do you think maybe we could just go for it this year?" he asked. "Go all out? See if we can do it? I'm feeling strong. I promise I won't quit. And the weather's not supposed to be very good tomorrow. And my scraped-up leg's good and loose now, but'll probably be really hurting in the morning. I bet we can make it."

Rob eased off the back of the paceline, which was now going a little faster than he thought prudent. He turned to give Alex a quick glance. He smiled at the boy's earnestness. It was especially amusing the way he'd run all his arguments together, over-making his case. "Tell you what. I'll think about it."

"Okay," Alex replied, again a little too quickly. "Thanks. That's all I'm asking."

They were alone now, pedaling their way further into the countryside. *Alex really has been a trooper,* Rob thought. *Not just today. All spring. I know he'd ride himself into the ground before he'd quit. But can he really make it to Portland tonight without riding himself into the ground? I know I can. I'd sure rather do those 50 miles today than tomorrow. I just don't want to be dragging an exhausted, burned-out boy with me.*

Before Rob could make up his mind, a group of about a dozen cyclists glided past them at a perfect cruising pace.

"Let's jump on their tail!" Alex called. The boy immediately began cranking harder on his pedals.

Rob mashed his own pedals, and realized he was spinning too small of a gear. Desperate not to let the paceline get away, he flipped the front shifter firmly toward the large chainring and tried to crank even harder.

An instant later, their pedals jammed to a halt. Rob nearly catapulted over the handlebars.

"Dad! The chain!" Alex exclaimed. "Totally tangled up!"

Rob tried backpedaling, but the cranks wouldn't move. "Guess we need to stop," he said. He carefully steered the tandem onto the shoulder.

"You okay?" another rider called, turning to look at them as he cruised past.

"Fine!" Rob waved.

After he and Alex dismounted, and got their first good look at the chain, Rob wasn't so sure. Alex held the bike steady, while Rob tried unwrapping the chain from the crank. It wouldn't budge. He tried jiggling the cranks forward and backward while tugging on the chain. No success. Every move only jammed the chain more severely.

Cyclist after cyclist zipped past. "What're we going to do?" Alex asked.

Rob had no idea, and was kicking himself for having shifted so carelessly. He'd have given anything to trade places with the riders cruising by on perfect bikes.

"Let's give it one more try," he told Alex. "This time, push the rear derailleur forward, to give the chain more slack."

With the additional slack, Rob was able to get the chain to move a little. Then, jiggling the pedals, he eventually managed to get the chain untwisted from the crank arm.

"Thank God," Alex muttered.

Rob made a quick inspection. He immediately spotted three links that were crushed beyond repair. "Chain may be free, but it's ruined," he said, shaking his head.

"What'll we do now?"

"We have no choice but to call your mother," he replied, fishing the cell phone from his jersey pocket. "And hope she remembers how to find that bike shop."

Meg had just gotten onto the freeway back in Centralia. Rob explained the situation, and that they would be needing some new parts. He studied the map, and found a road just off the course where Meg could meet them without interfering with other riders.

"I'll get there as quick as I can," she assured him.

Rob and Alex walked the tandem to the spot where Meg could meet them. Time seemed to slow to eternity. Rob began tapping his cleats in frustration. He felt like he was in a dream where he had to hurry and catch a plane, but was rebuffed and restrained at each turn by some invisible force.

"Could we still make it to Portland before sunset?" Alex asked.

"Don't know," Rob replied. He folded his arms on his chest, and gazed down the road Meg would be arriving on. "Depends on how fast the shop can get us in."

Once Meg and the boys arrived, Alex helped Rob load the tandem on the roof rack. Then they both climbed in.

"I took Scott to a place called Chehalis Bicycle," Meg explained. "On St. Helens Avenue. I'm not sure exactly where that is, but it is on the route. I saw a lot of STPers going past."

"Let's just drive backwards on the route. That won't interfere with any riders," Rob said.

As Meg began heading toward Chehalis, Alex scanned the route guide. "I found a St. Helens Avenue," he said. "Looks like about four or five miles."

They eventually reached the shop, and unloaded the tandem. "You should stick around until we know for sure they can fix it," Rob told Meg. Then, with Alex's help, he wheeled the wounded Santana inside.

The place looked like a grand old house that'd been opened up and converted into a bike shop. Rob immediately liked it. "Another STP breakdown!" one of the employees greeted them.

"I imagine we're keeping you busy," Rob joked.

"Not as busy as we'll be tonight and tomorrow, with the two-dayers," the young man replied. He had short blond hair, and wore a green smock. "Looks like you took a tumble," he added, gesturing to Alex's badly-scraped leg.

Rob explained that they needed a new chain, and an adjustment to the front derailleur.

"We can do that, easy," the mechanic assured him. "But you've got some people ahead of you. Should be about thirty minutes."

As incredibly frustrating as it was to lose so much time, Rob knew they had no choice. "Sure," he replied, and helped roll the tandem to the service department. He and Alex then went outside to rejoin the others.

Somehow, they managed to kill a half hour. By far, the most difficult part was watching all the perfect bikes stream by as they waited.

He and Alex strolled back inside, but the service manager said they still needed another ten minutes. Rob summoned every ounce of self-control to keep from venting his frustrations aloud. He smiled, and then browsed some displays with Alex.

Eventually, another green-smocked employee did bring the Santana out. "Brand new chain, and the derailleur should never throw it off again," he said.

Rob gave the repairs a quick inspection, thanked the service guys, and paid. He and Alex rolled the Santana out the front door as quickly as they could.

"Now we have to figure out a way for your mom to get us back to where we left off," Rob said.

"Why not just ride?" Alex asked. "My legs are screaming to be back on the bike. It's only a few extra miles."

Rob thought for a moment. "Good idea. And by the time we load the bike, drive off the route, and unload the bike…driving probably won't save much time."

He filled Meg in on their plan, and she agreed it made sense. "See you at the Lexington stop!" she said.

As they pedaled up to speed, and joined a group of other cyclists, Rob was glad Alex had suggested they "just ride." It felt good to crank on the pedals, working off frustrations. Above all, he liked feeling they were *getting* somewhere under their own power.

They eventually cleared Chehalis, and the place where they'd broken down. Finally, as they cruised down Newaukum Valley Road, Rob tried to relax and take in the scenery. He especially enjoyed the warm sunshine, and their panoramic view of the river below.

Rob looked ahead to the right, and spotted a family setting up a table in their driveway. A couple of kids were lugging coolers toward the table, and a woman was putting up a sign reading "Ice Cold Water. $1."

"They'll probably make a fortune today," Alex said.

"Or tomorrow, when the serious traffic comes through. How you holding up?"

"Fine on water, if that's what you mean," the boy assured him. "Need to use the toilet in Napavine, but feeling okay. And I know you're still thinking about it, but I'd still like to shoot for Portland if you do."

Napavine was the next town. A long climb up Rush Road stood between them and it. This was their first real hill after Centralia, and they struggled to ascend it. Bike after bike passed them. Rob could tell that, all enthusiasm aside, Alex was getting tired. *I should've done more to make him and Ben take it easy back at the start.*

He still had no doubt Alex could make it 150 miles today. A double century was looking like more of a stretch, especially given all the unexpected delays. *Should I tell Alex we'll do the one-day ride next year?* he wondered. *Or let him stretch, and see just how far he can go?*

FIFTY-FOUR

ALEX KNUCKLED DOWN AND WORKED TO ASCEND A LITTLE hill coming out of Winlock. He couldn't stop thinking about the name of the road they were on, and the small town to which it led. He hadn't quite believed it when he'd seen it in the route guide. Now they were really on it: the Winlock-Vader Road.

As soon as they reached the crest of the hill, he asked his father, "Is there really a town called *Vader?*"

"That's our next mini-stop."

"Is it named after *Darth* Vader?"

For some reason, his father thought that was really funny. But Alex was being totally serious.

"I was always curious, so I finally looked it up," his dad told him. "The town's been named that for almost a hundred years. I guess there was a German guy named Vader who lived there."

His curiosity satisfied, Alex went into a tuck. He hammered on the pedals as they began descending the other side of the hill. A beautiful valley opened up ahead, and Alex savored the view of trees and open pasture. He whispered a silent prayer of thanksgiving that his name was "Peterson" and not "Vader."

A quick break back in Winlock, for hamburgers cooked by a community group, had really hit the spot. He was glad his father had stopped, despite his own insistence that they hurry and make up for lost time.

Feeling good, Alex looked over his shoulder. He discovered a long line of other bikes had assembled in their slipstream. There were so many, he couldn't even count them.

"Great job up there, tandem," the rider immediately behind him called, as they continued speeding toward Vader. "You guys are awesome!"

"Thanks!" Alex replied. He felt especially proud that someone from outside his family believed he was a good cyclist.

"I've been thinking," his father said, turning slightly to be heard above the wind. "We should have just enough daylight to make Portland tonight. I called your mother back in Winlock, and told her what we're thinking about doing. She says she's willing to change things up. And I know I can go all the way. Question is, do you still want to try it?"

"Absolutely!" Alex replied. His heart raced in excitement.

"Before you commit, here's the deal," his father told him. "If you decide to do this, I'm finishing tonight. Period. If you have to quit, there's no falling back to the two-day ride. Your STP will be over. Ben takes your seat. He crosses the line tonight in your place. I've already asked, and he says he'll be ready."

Alex cranked the pedals and closed his eyes. He tried to picture his little brother getting all the glory yet again. *Is a shot at the one-day ride worth the risk of maybe not finishing at all?* he wondered. *Maybe it'd be better to stop at Longview, get a good rest, and cruise to the finish tomorrow. It might be rainy, and I might be sore, but I'd be an official finisher. Nobody could take that away from me.*

His father swung the tandem to the left, and eased up a bit to allow the long line of riders to pass them.

"Great pull," the first cyclist told them. Alex smiled and nodded in return.

"You're the youngest one-day rider I've ever seen," the next cyclist remarked, as he cruised past on a carbon fiber bike.

As the other dozen or so members of the paceline added their words of thanks and encouragement, Alex's heart swelled. Not so much with pride, but with the joy of being a full member of this special fraternity-within-a-fraternity. *They think I'm one of them,* he marveled, beaming from ear to ear. *I am one of them. A one-day rider! A real one-day rider!*

As they pulled behind the last person in the paceline, Alex had no doubts. "I'm all in! Portland tonight. No quitting."

Dad turned to shoot him a quick smile. "Portland it is!" Alex's spirits soared still higher.

They made good time into Vader. Both he and his dad needed a quick break at the mini-stop. Five of the riders in their paceline joined them.

Alex was starting to feel tired again, especially as the excitement of committing to the one-day ride faded. This was farther than he'd ever before ridden in a single day. He secretly wished he could take a little nap. Still, he acted chipper as he chatted with his father and the other riders at the mini-stop. His biggest problems now were his aching shoulders and back. The ibuprofen was wearing off. Alex knew that taking too much more might upset his stomach.

He and his father regrouped around the bike. Alex's dad studied the route guide. "Seventeen miles to the big Lexington food stop," he announced. "I'm ready for that. Hopefully just another hour."

"Just another hour" sounded like "forever" right now. Of course, Alex knew better than to say so.

Back on the road, they were immediately confronted by a nasty little hill taking them out of Vader. It wasn't long. It was just very steep. They and all the riders around them had to stop talking and focus on the climb. It seemed to Alex that his dad was reaching for their very lowest gear. Even the riders on single bikes were gearing way down and struggling with the climb. That made Alex feel better.

Alex's legs and lungs were burning when they finally got to the summit. He was relieved as they made the turn onto Westside Highway toward Castle Rock.

It took Alex a long time to catch his breath, and for his legs to stop burning. He now felt much more generally tired than he had going into Vader. He also felt much less talkative. He was glad none of the riders around them felt like chatting.

They struggled up a series of rolling hills, and enjoyed the fast descents on the other side of each. Alex tried to remember to eat and drink. He was still sucking down water at a pretty good clip, but it was tasting less and less good. He'd never imagined it could take so much effort to swallow water.

Or eat food. None of the stuff in his pockets seemed appetizing. He forced himself to chew yet another fig bar. The way it sat in his mouth almost gagged him. He had to will himself to swallow it. He decided to wait for the food stop in Lexington, and see if they had something more appetizing. He hoped his mom had some potatoes or hotdogs left. *Maybe the one-day ride wasn't such a great idea after all*, he thought.

As they came off the last rolling hill and into Castle Rock, Alex looked at the route guide. He was really starting to feel weak. His body craved carbohydrates badly. Worse, his crotch was now getting as sore as his shoulders. He thought about asking his father to stop at the Castle Rock mini-stop. But since they were only six miles from Lexington, he figured his dad would want to pull through. Alex decided he could wait another 20 minutes or so for food.

A few local kids, a little younger than Alex, stood at the main intersection in Castle Rock. All of them were shaking cowbells and waving at passing riders. Alex waved back. One of them smiled and gave a thumbs-up. Alex felt his spirits lifting, and he almost forgot his hunger.

When they finally wound their way into the huge Riverside Park in Lexington, Alex felt conflicted. The shady grass seemed to be begging him to lay down and take a long rest, but he knew they needed to make up for lost time if they were going to finish by sunset. *I can rest tonight in Portland*, he decided.

Alex spotted Ben and Connor waving in their direction. He pointed them out to his dad. Alex was relieved when he was finally able to dismount. He stretched his legs, popped some ibuprofen, and rubbed his aching shoulders. Then he limped straight for the food tables and got in line.

The wrap-style sandwiches looked excellent, as did the chocolate chip cookies. The volunteers made a big fuss over him for being so young, and for continuing despite the nasty road rash on his leg. Alex felt self-conscious, but did secretly relish the attention.

His whole family, and Connor, sat down at a shady picnic table Alex's mom had staked out. It felt wonderful to put his bottom on something other than a narrow saddle, and to be out of the blazing afternoon sun.

"I can't believe you're going the whole way to Portland tonight!" Connor exclaimed. "That is so amazing!"

"Yeah," Alex replied, smiling weakly as he bit into a sandwich. *What've I gotten myself into?* he wondered. *I know it's only sixty miles from here, but it seems like a million.*

"Are you sure about the one-day ride?" his mother asked.

"Absolutely!" Alex shot back.

His parents glanced at each other. Neither said anything. Alex hoped his reply hadn't sounded suspiciously over-eager.

Alex returned his attention to the food. As hungry as he was, and as good as the sandwich and cookies looked, he still had trouble making himself swallow more than a few mouthfuls. *What do you do when nothing tastes good anymore?* he wondered. He wanted to put his head down on the picnic table, but instead forced himself to eat the rest of his sandwich.

"Four-thirty already. We should get a move on," Alex's dad said. He climbed to his feet and stretched. "Next stop is St. Helens. Oregon. Thirty miles."

Oregon! The very word rekindled Alex's enthusiasm. *Thirty miles isn't that far. Basically home to Marymoor Park and back.* He just wished his body could be as enthusiastic as his mind.

"I checked, and I do have the official vehicle directions to the St. Helens stop. We'll meet you there," his mother said.

"I think I'm going to take a nap in the car," Ben yawned.

Alex didn't want to admit it, but that sounded like the best idea he'd heard all day.

FIFTY-FIVE

ROB TURNED THE TANDEM BACK ONTO WEST SIDE HIGHWAY toward Longview. Between getting warmed back up, battling head-and-cross-winds, and steering around potholes, it took the two of them several miles to reach a comfortable cruising speed. Even then, they were getting passed by far more riders than they were passing.

"Wind's a killer!" Alex called out.

"Just hope we're not fighting it all the way down Highway 30," Rob shouted back.

They struggled along in silence for several minutes, drawing nearer and nearer to the Columbia River. They eventually caught up to a couple of other riders, and tried to get a little paceline started. Even that didn't make much difference.

Just then, a young man's voice called out, "Hey! Petersons!"

Rob looked to the left. He immediately recognized Scott Roberts overtaking them. The young man's new wheel appeared to be working perfectly.

Rob and Alex greeted him. They all chatted about the day's events, while navigating the rest of Longview. Scott told them to thank Meg again for the lift. Rob described their own emergency visit to Chehalis Cycle.

"Look at the flags," Scott said, gesturing toward a pole in the distance. "Are they blowing south?"

"Don't get your hopes up. It's usually a nasty headwind all the way in Oregon."

They worked their way through downtown Longview and onto Industrial Way. Rob began looking at flags, himself. They did seem to be pointing generally south, but it was hard to be certain. He wouldn't believe it until he felt the wind at his back.

"Sounds like you've done STP before," Scott remarked.

As they continued pedaling, Rob explained about having ridden STP — and other doubles — several times in the 1980s and 1990s before hanging up his bike. And the way Alex had gotten him out of retirement.

"That's awesome," Scott replied. "This is my third STP in a row, but I've only been seriously riding for the last five years."

They continued chatting about STP and how much the event had changed. Rob welcomed the distraction from his aching shoulders and the nagging headwind.

Their conversation eventually fell silent, and Rob was again alone with his thoughts. *Out of retirement,* he mused. *I'm so glad Alex got me off the couch and back on the bike. I can't imagine being home in front of the TV this afternoon. Or on any of those other long afternoons he and I spent out on the road.* His only regret was not having found his way back to the sport sooner.

A moment later, they turned left onto SR-433. The steel cantilever Lewis & Clark Bridge loomed straight ahead. "Whoa!" Alex exclaimed. "I've never seen a bridge like that. That's like, huge! It's so tall!"

Rob was already downshifting. The bridge deck was much higher than he'd remembered, and his legs were in no mood for this kind of a climb. The bridge almost seemed to be taunting them: *I'm the gatekeeper! I'll never let you into Oregon!*

The higher they climbed, the stronger the crosswinds grew. Making matters worse, the shoulder was narrow. Traffic whizzed by just a couple of feet away. Even though the winds appeared to be blowing up the river toward Portland, Rob still wouldn't let himself believe they'd get that lucky.

As they approached the center of the bridge span, Alex was astounded by the enormity of the Columbia River. He'd definitely never seen a river this wide, or one that seemed to stretch away so far. What's more, they seemed impossibly high above it. *If I get blown over the railing, I'll die for sure.*

Alex looked up, and spotted an "Entering Oregon" sign mounted on the bridge's steel girders. His legs were burning from the climb, and the passing cars were scaring him to death, but a huge rush of adrenaline shot through him as they closed in on the sign. At last they passed directly under it. "Yes!" he exclaimed, pumping a fist in the air.

Alex's joy soon evaporated into fright. He'd been hoping they could fly down the bridge at 40 MPH, but there was a problem: expansion joints. He knew from science class that these allow the bridge deck to expand and contract with temperature changes. He hadn't been expecting the tandem's front wheel to hit each one with such a sickening *thud*. He imagined the tire would blow or the wheel would crumple, sending them sprawling into the path of these whizzing cars. He was glad his father pumped the brakes, and kept their speed fairly low.

Finally, near the bottom, his dad stopped braking and shifted into high gear. They picked up speed, and made the sweeping curve onto Highway 30 toward Portland.

Scott pulled alongside, taking advantage of the wide shoulder. "Ever been to Oregon?" he asked Alex.

"Not that I remember. Drove through it when I was little, when our family moved from California."

"Well, welcome back to my state," Scott smiled. "I live in Portland. It's great to be in the final stretch."

I'm in Oregon, Alex told himself, as they settled into a comfortable pace on the highway shoulder. *Oregon.* It looked exactly like Washington, but with one difference: the road signs. Here, they said "SPEED" with just a huge "55," instead of including the word "LIMIT." Every time he saw one, it was a striking reminder as to how far he was from home.

The novelty of being in Oregon quickly wore off. The highway appeared to slope upwards forever. The wind did seem to be at their backs, but the climb was so unrelenting it didn't make much difference. With traffic blowing past them on the four-lane highway, no one was in a mood to chat. Riders, Alex included, all set their faces in grim determination. The St. Helens rest stop was only 20 miles ahead, but Alex figured it might as well be 120.

After several miles of more or less steady ascent, broken up only briefly by level stretches or downhill runs, Alex was drained. It felt like several steak knives had been plunged into his shoulders and upper back. His crotch was getting so sore, he could barely keep it on the saddle.

As they approached the tiny town of Goble, even remaining upright was taking a conscious effort. Alex began leaning forward, as if to lay his head on his father's back for a nap. He felt the pedals moving his legs around in circles, but he knew his muscles weren't contributing anything.

The tandem began moving more slowly. Several riders passed them. Alex didn't care. He just wanted to sleep.

"Hey, Alex!" Scott called out. "You okay?"

Alex shook his head. He no longer even cared about appearing strong.

"Rob!" Scott said, more loudly. "Alex might be bonking."

His father shot a concerned glance backward. "You're bonking?" he asked.

"What's 'bonking'?" Alex asked, barely able to focus on his dad's question. He'd never heard the term before. It sure didn't sound good.

"Hitting the wall," Scott told him. "When your liver and muscles run out of glycogen."

"Extreme fatigue. Like you've got no energy at all. Maybe even dizzy," his father added.

"I'm not dizzy. Just totally out of gas."

A moment later, Alex's father pulled into a mini-stop at the Goble Tavern's gravel parking lot. Scott followed them, and everyone dismounted.

"We need to call Mom and swap stokers," Alex's father said.

Alex's heart sank, but at this point he almost didn't care. He clutched the tandem's saddle, hung his head, and felt the sweat trickle down his face.

"Just curious, but what've you been drinking?" Scott asked.

"Plain water. Like Dad."

"You guys allergic to sports drinks?" Scott asked.

"No. I just didn't like the ones they had in the nineties," Alex's father replied. "Gave me bad cramps. Ended up sticking with water. Put extra salt on my food. Worked for me."

"Even if he's done for the day, we need to get some carbs and electrolytes in him," Scott said. He handed Alex his own bottle, adding, "I've got a sports drink that's loaded with both. Start with this. And take a couple of these electrolyte tablets."

"Don't you need them?" Alex asked.

"I brought plenty. Drink!" Scott insisted.

Alex limped to a straw bale in the shade, and sat down heavily. He removed his helmet, popped the tablets in his mouth, and took several long swings from Scott's bottle. The stuff had a sweet orange flavor. It felt wonderful as it ran down his throat. "This is perfect. Thank you."

"Keep drinking. Slowly," Scott instructed. Then he removed both of Alex's bottles from the tandem's cages and dumped them out. "I'll mix these up for you to take. Even if you don't ride, it'll help with recovery."

"That is so thoughtful. Thanks very much," Dad said.

Once Scott had left for the water station, Dad sat down. He put his arm around Alex and leaned close. "You gave it your very best shot," he said quietly. "There's nothing to be ashamed of. You made it to Mile 161. That's 166 miles, counting the extra we did at Chehalis. You did awesome. More than any other ride of your life. I am so proud of you."

Alex nodded. Despite his father's consoling words, he could already feel hot tears trickling down his cheeks and mixing with sweat. Sniffling, he clutched Scott's bottle more tightly. He resolved not to look up.

His father found his cell phone. A moment later, he was explaining the situation to Mom. *I guess I'm done,* Alex thought. He took another swig of sports drink. He scuffed his feet in the dusty gravel, and tried to ignore the prickly straw poking his bare calves.

His father listened for a moment, and then his tone changed to incredulity. "You're kidding, right?" Silence. "All the way *where?* Really?" Silence. "Okay. We'll wait."

Alex's father snapped the phone closed and exclaimed, "I don't believe it."

"What?"

"I thought your mother was right behind us. But, apparently, the official support vehicle instructions say not to cross the Columbia River with the bikes in Longview. And to drive all the way down to Portland on I-5, cross the river there, and drive all the way back up to St. Helens on Highway 30. So, she and the boys stopped in Portland and checked us into the motel. She's still at least 45 minutes away."

Scott returned as Alex's dad finished speaking. "That's quite a wait," the young man observed. He exchanged the two fresh bottles for the one he'd given Alex earlier.

Alex's father thanked Scott again for the sports drink. "At least I'll have a good rest until Meg gets here with Ben. But there's no need for you to stick around."

"Yeah, I need to hit the road," Scott agreed. Then, addressing Alex, he added, "Don't feel bad. Everyone bonks sometime, if they're in the sport long enough. I bonked really bad, two years ago, around Castle Rock. Managed to rest and get enough calories back in me to finish, but it was tough."

That made Alex feel strangely better. It seemed almost like he was passing an initiation rite. Especially when his dad said, "I almost had to drop out of the last double century I did, at 130 miles. Death Valley. Still remember it like yesterday."

Alex looked up and half-smiled. "Thanks. And I do think the sports drink is helping. Definitely feel some energy coming back." He could even sense his appetite returning. He reached for the granola bar and Fig Newtons he'd stashed in his jersey pocket. As he began eating, he decided to take some ibuprofen for good measure.

"Drinks have gotten a lot better," Scott told Alex's dad. "You really should take another look. I can't imagine getting enough carbs or electrolytes without a good sports drink."

"It's now definitely on my list. Learning a lot, getting back into this sport after so long," Dad replied.

The Petersons said their good-byes to Scott, and then watched as the young man pedaled off toward Portland.

Alex's dad put his arm back around him. "Maybe you should try to sleep," he suggested.

As miserable as Alex was feeling, and as much as he wanted to curl up for a nap, something inside him revolted at the suggestion. *I can't come this far, and not do the whole thing. I just can't. I can't go home a quitter. No matter how bad it gets today, the broken legs were worse. I made it through that, even with all those long stretches without pain meds. I can make it through this.* He shook his head and replied, "I'm not ready to give up."

"Alex, it's pretty clear you're done for the day. We don't want to kill you."

"Did you think you were done for the day in Death Valley?" Alex retorted. His father's only response was awkward silence.

"I know you want to protect me, but I've had a good rest." Alex paused to savor another swig of orange sports drink. "I'm getting some energy back. I really think I can do this."

Despite his bravado, Alex wasn't actually all that sure of himself. He *wanted* to be sure. He figured that was as good a place to start as any.

His father looked at him skeptically. Alex's mind raced for a way to close the deal. "If you wait for Mom, you'll never make it the 40 more miles to Portland by sundown. Especially not with Ben. He's never done close to 90 miles in one day."

Alex looked his father in the eye and said, "I can stay on the bike. No matter what."

His father thought for a moment, seeming to weigh the genuineness of Alex's determination. "Okay," he replied at last. He flipped open his phone. "You're on probation for the 13 miles to St. Helens. I'll call Mom and tell her to meet us there. If you're dead weight, Ben takes over. Deal?"

"Deal!" Alex pulled on his helmet for emphasis.

A moment later, Alex hobbled to the tandem and climbed aboard with his father. Despite the padded shorts, he still had to ease his aching crotch gingerly onto the saddle. His upper back and shoulders still felt like they'd been pounded with a baseball bat. But as the tandem began rolling back down the highway, Alex resolved to let nothing stop him. He soon slipped into a simple and steady cadence with the pedals, broken up only by a near-religious fidelity to eating or drinking at least one mouthful every five minutes.

"Look over there," Alex's dad said, pointing high to the left. Alex studied the trees across the highway, but nothing looked especially notable. "What?" he asked.

"Mount St. Helens. That white stubby thing on the horizon." Alex looked more closely, and spotted the mountain his father was pointing at. "Why does it look so funny?"

"It's the one that blew up in 1980, when I was a kid. Sent ash around the world."

"Cool," Alex smiled. He tried imagining his father as a boy his own size. He couldn't get his mind around it.

As Alex's body eventually limbered up, his mind drifted into a foggy zone that allowed him to block out the dull roar of passing cars. And the number of cyclists who kept passing them with ease. And thoughts about the number of miles remaining.

After a seeming-eternity, his father steered into the St. Helens High School parking lot. Ben and Connor were tossing a football around under some shade trees. Both boys came running once they spotted the tandem.

Instead of stopping near the food tables, Alex's dad rode to where someone had set up hose misters. They both dismounted. Alex removed his helmet, and tottered into the spray. As cold water soaked his hair and face and clothes, he felt deeply refreshed from the inside out. He hadn't realized how much of a toll the afternoon of 80-degree sunshine had taken on him. He asked Connor to please pack as much ice as possible into his water bottles.

Before he could do anything else, Alex's parents pulled him aside. "Are you sure you're feeling up to continuing?" his mother asked.

"Absolutely. I mean, I'm really sore and tired. But I'm still okay to ride."

"Ben said he can do those last 30 miles if you need to call it a day," Mom told him.

"And we both want you to know that nobody would think any less of you," his father added. "You wouldn't be a quitter."

"I know. And I promise to stop if I just can't finish. But I really think I can do it. And I really want to do it. More than anything." *I've gone way too far to finish in the car.*

His parents looked at each other, and at him. *Please don't make me quit now,* he thought.

"Then let's get something to eat, so we can finish before sunset," his dad said.

"I'm off probation?" Alex asked, with great relief.

"You're off probation," his father smiled.

Alex used the toilet and took an ibuprofen tablet. He then sat in the shade with Connor and Ben to enjoy his sandwich, macadamia nut cookies, and watermelon. Lots of watermelon. Nothing had ever tasted so good.

After about fifteen minutes, Alex's father approached. He figured that meant it was time to get on the road. It was almost 7pm, and sunset was at nine.

Instead, Dad walked Alex to a shady area with padded tables and a sign reading "Massages."

"I'm getting a massage?" Alex asked. He'd never had a massage in his life. He'd always figured they were for sissies or luxury-lovers.

His father paid the young Hispanic masseuse, and then helped Alex pull off his jersey and lay down on his stomach.

The masseuse went to work. Alex soon felt all the tension and soreness draining out of his shoulders and neck. "I think you're the youngest one I've had all day," the masseuse told him.

Alex tried to say something, but his mouth was no longer responding. Neither were his eyelids. As he drifted off to sleep, his last conscious thought was *massages definitely aren't for sissies. Or luxury-lovers. They're for boys who've bitten off way more miles than they can otherwise chew.*

FIFTY-SIX

ALEX DIDN'T KNOW IF HE SHOULD CALL IT A "SECOND wind." It was more like the day's fifth or sixth wind. Blasting down Highway 30, with a breeze at his back and a ten-minute catnap under his belt, Alex felt good. Really good. At least for now.

He glanced back, and could see at least fifteen bikes drafting them. After the long climb they'd made to St. Helens, Alex savored every moment of this long descent toward Portland. His heart skipped a beat when they rounded a curve, and he spotted an enormous green suspension bridge framed in the evening twilight. He knew it was the St. John's Bridge. That meant they were getting close to the city.

A moment later, Dad exclaimed, "Look at that!"

Alex glanced up. His father was pointing at a huge "Entering Portland" road sign. Alex pumped his fist as they passed it, and he heard a whoop from the riders behind them.

Alex's father turned and told him, "No matter what happens now, you can say you rode your bike to Portland."

Alex smiled and settled in to work all the harder. "Just don't throw the chain, Dad!"

They crossed under the St. John's Bridge. A few miles later, they angled off Highway 30 into a grungy industrial area. Dad sat up and pedaled more comfortably, allowing the line of other bikes to pass them.

"Aw, I was hoping you'd pull us all the way to the end," the first rider joked as he went by.

"Great pull," the next rider said.

"Cool bike," said another.

Alex smiled and greeted each person. He also tried to focus on the route guide, and figure out where they were. "Looks like four or five miles of city streets to the finish," he announced. With daylight fading, and streetlamps coming on all around them, Alex was glad to be nearly done.

The last bike to pull alongside was a tandem, pedaled by an older-looking husband and wife. "Nice job, young man," the captain said.

Alex greeted them, and his dad did the same. Alex couldn't help noticing that their bike was called a Burley Duet. He liked the musical connection.

"Wish we would've thought about taking our daughters along this way when they were younger," the woman riding stoker told them.

The two teams rode side by side, chatting as they navigated the last few miles of the route. It was mostly small talk, and Alex was glad for the distraction. Block after block of darkening city streets went by in a blur. Alex almost forgot how tired his legs were, and how much his bottom ached.

The other team got caught at a red light that the Petersons barely made it through. Alex's father looked back, wondering if he should wait for them. The other captain waved for them to keep going. "We'll find them later," Dad said. He and Alex powered into the final stretch.

Alex glanced back at the Duet, with the older husband and wife who looked so happy together, and something occurred to him. Just like the times he'd played concertos with Jacob and Maria Adams, working together in harmony on a bike with his father — playing a duet, as it were — was more fun than what each of them could've done alone today as individuals. If he hadn't been so exhausted, he even would've started humming "Heart and Soul."

Heart and Soul. Was it really just last summer that Mom and I were playing that duet? And I was moping about wanting to be a cyclist? Seems like that happened a million years ago. To a different person. I can't believe I used to be such a pathetic little kid, who didn't think he could do anything. And was even afraid to ask for a new pair of shoes. Now, the world seemed as wide open as the 200 miles he and his father had just conquered. *I can take on absolutely anything*, he thought.

As the finish came into view a block ahead, their tandem got stopped at a red light. *An entire day of riding, and now we're down to a single block.* He could already hear the festival music, and a woman's voice on a loudspeaker congratulating each finisher.

Whenever he'd fantasized about finishing the one-day STP, Alex had always pictured himself as exhilarated. Triumphant. Ecstatic. Practically with tears of joy filling his eyes. With the finale of an orchestral score swelling in his ears. But now that he was actually here, and had actually done it, all he felt was … empty. Strangely empty. Not sad or disappointed. Just *spent.* He couldn't feel much of anything in the place of that emptiness. He couldn't hear any music in his head.

The light changed to green, and they snapped back into their pedals. As they crossed that final block, and passed under the FINISH banner at the entrance to Holladay Park, Alex was more numb than anything else. Even as the announcer read his number, and made a big deal about "this boy, so young, rolling in here in just one day!" Alex couldn't make himself feel much of anything about her words.

On top of it, Alex couldn't have cared less about their ride statistics or what the computer said. He noticed the clock read 9:12pm. Even that didn't matter to him. He was done. It was over. That was that.

They rolled past a smiling young woman, who handed "One Day Rider" patches to Alex and his dad. They thanked her, and hung the patches around their necks.

Connor ran to them, and gave Alex a high-five. But as he told Connor how happy he was, and how great he felt about what he'd done, Alex knew he was just saying the words he was supposed to say. They were simply the words he'd always imagined saying. They weren't exactly the things he was actually feeling right now, but Alex decided it was too complicated to explain. He wasn't even sure he understood it, himself.

Connor took the tandem and led it off through throngs of riders, and their families, to a parking spot. As he and Ben waited for Connor to return, Alex gazed around and marveled at how completely the huge park had been taken over. The wonderful aroma of grilled chicken, steaks and burgers overwhelmed Alex's nostrils. He would've danced to the festive music if his legs hadn't been so sore. *I did it,* he kept telling himself. *I'm an athlete. I belong here. This is my brotherhood. No one else at my school has ever done anything like this.*

Once Connor returned, they all talked about the ride. Alex was soon having so much fun, filling in Connor and Ben and his mom on the different things he'd seen and done, he even forgot how hungry he was.

A few minutes later, Alex spotted a familiar figure working his way across the park. "Mr. Jansson!" he called, waving with a huge smile. "I finished! Today!"

Mr. Jansson greeted them all, congratulated Alex and his dad, and then excused himself for a moment. He returned leading a middle-aged man and woman through the crowd. The man had a laptop slung over his shoulder. The woman had a professional-looking camera around her neck.

"These are Terry Parker and Rachael Stein, from the *Oregonian*," he told Alex. "They were about to file a story. I told them they might want to include something about you."

Alex smiled self-consciously, and greeted the pair.

"We heard you came in on a tandem," Rachael said. "Could we get some pictures of you with it?"

"Sure," Alex replied.

Alex's mom stayed to talk with Mr. Jansson, while everyone else followed Connor to where he'd parked the Santana. Rachael Stein then snapped a half-dozen shots of Alex and his father posing with it under the lights.

Terry Parker said he had a few questions for Alex. Connor and Ben wandered back to where his mom had stayed. The reporter then asked him all about the ride, how he'd decided to do it, and what he liked best about it.

Alex answered everything as best he could. Mr. Parker took a lot of notes on his laptop. Alex's mother drifted over to join them, but simply listened without saying anything.

Finally, Mr. Parker scanned through his notes and asked, "What I find especially interesting is that your teacher said you're disabled? I saw the way you've been limping. Is that it?"

Alex cringed as he heard the D-word. "I'm not disabled! Please don't say that in your story."

Mr. Parker looked confused and taken aback. Alex realized the reporter might think he was accusing Mr. Jansson of lying. "I mean, my legs *are* different lengths," he added. "It's from an accident four years ago. But we correct for it on the bike."

Alex explained about the crank shortener. The reporter took a long look at it, and his legs. "Fascinating," Mr. Parker said.

"It's really no different from wearing glasses," Alex said. He gave his mom a quick smile.

Alex was glad when the interview ended, and he could set himself down on a park bench with Connor and Ben. Their father took a moment to buy STP shirts at the concession stand. When he returned, he and Alex re-mounted the tandem for a six-block trip to their motel. His mother drove with the other boys and met them there.

Once they arrived, Alex made a beeline for the shower. He undressed, and was startled at the starkness of the tan lines he'd developed today in the hot sun. Then, like the day he'd ridden a century in the rain, he simply leaned against the shower wall and let the wonderful warm spray work its way into his skin, washing away the grime. He felt like he could go to sleep right there in the shower, if only he weren't so famished.

The others were already watching TV and enjoying pizza when Alex emerged, dressed in clean shorts and his new STP t-shirt. He made himself comfortable on the bed, and then ate five slices in a row. He decided nothing had ever tasted better, except maybe the watermelon at St. Helens.

Soon after filling their stomachs with pizza, all the boys' eyelids grew heavy. Alex crawled into bed with Ben, closed his eyes, and could think of nothing but whizzing roadway as he evaporated into unconsciousness.

FIFTY-SEVEN

July 12, 2009

ALEX AWAKENED FEELING CERTAIN THAT HE'D BEEN RUN over by a Mack truck. And that his bladder was about to explode. On top of it, he couldn't figure out why a strange, scratchy bedspread was tickling his face.

A moment later, he remembered. Adrenaline shot through him. *I made it. I'm in Portland. And I must've drank a lot more down the stretch yesterday than I'd thought.*

Alex slipped out of bed, trying not to awaken Ben. His parents were sound asleep on the other bed. Connor was sprawled on the couch. He made sure he didn't turn on the bathroom light until he'd closed the door behind him. He didn't dare flush the toilet. As he crept back through the darkened motel room, he noticed the clock read 5:48. He crawled under the sheets, but was too wide awake to sleep.

Alex stared at the ceiling, and wondered what he would do until everyone else woke up. He wished he'd thought to bring a book and flashlight. In planning for the trip, this was the absolute last situation he'd imagined.

Fortunately, Ben awakened about a half hour later. He wasn't nearly as quiet getting to or using the bathroom. By the time he returned to bed, everyone else was also rubbing their eyes and yawning.

"How's everybody feeling this morning?" their dad asked.

"Sore!" Ben replied.

"Like I've been hit by a truck. But it feels great, because I know what it's from," Alex said.

"I'll take your word for it," Connor smiled.

Their mother looked at the clock. "I asked about churches last night. Holy Rosary is right around the corner. We can make the 7am Mass, easy."

"You mean we have to go to *church?*" Ben groaned.

"Did you think we were going to skip it, just because we're in Portland?" their father asked.

"Just wish I could sleep all day," Ben muttered.

Alex got dressed in slow motion, trying not to bend his aching joints. He was just glad his mother let him wear comfortable jeans, and the "One Day Rider" shirt his father had bought last night. She usually insisted they wear dress clothes to church.

Everyone was ready to go by 6:45. "I know it's the last thing you want to do right now, but we really should walk rather than drive," Dad said. "The more you start using your muscles, the faster your recovery. And we should take an easy ride later before we drive home."

"A *very* easy ride," Alex said.

The walk to Holy Rosary was torture. The cold, damp air that'd moved in overnight only made it worse. *At least I don't have to ride 50 miles in this today,* Alex thought. *Maybe the one-day ride actually is easier than the two-day ride.*

The old brick church, with its gorgeous stained glass windows, was among the most beautiful Alex had seen. The organ music touched him to the depths of his soul. He just wished his aching body could've let him enjoy all that beauty. He was so sore, he barely managed to pull himself into a standing position at the gospel reading and creed. He had to ease himself very slowly back to a sitting position each time.

Fortunately, breakfast at a Denny's restaurant was only a couple of blocks from the church. Although every step was a challenge, he found himself strangely savoring each aching reminder that he'd ridden all the way from Seattle in just one day.

The restaurant was bustling when they arrived. As the hostess led them to a booth, Alex noticed several other people wearing STP shirts and hats. He smiled and nodded as he passed them, now even more glad that his mother had let him wear his own STP shirt. The other riders caught his eye and smiled back. Alex had never felt so much a part of a fraternity.

The padded booth felt wonderful. Alex wished he could melt into it. He quickly looked over the menu and decided on something, and then savored the chance to relax while everyone else talked.

Alex noticed a woman at the next table. She glanced at the Petersons, and then back at her newspaper. Then she did it again. Finally, she made eye contact with Alex's dad. "Is this you?" she asked, holding up her paper.

To Alex's shock, there was a picture of him and his father, standing with the Santana in Holladay Park. Their expressions looked exhausted but triumphant. "Yeah!" Alex told her.

The woman passed her paper to Alex's dad, and told him they could keep it. Alex and Ben crowded around their father to get a better look. The caption under the photo read, "Rob Peterson with his son, Alex (12), after completing the one-day STP on their tandem bicycle."

"And they mention us in the story," their father said. He pointed to a paragraph toward the end. The rest of the story seemed to be about the event in general and other individual riders.

The boys immediately skipped to where their father indicated. Ben read the passage aloud:

> Among the youngest single-day participants was Alex Peterson (12), of Bothell, Wash., who rode with his father on a tandem. "It was really tiring," said Alex, "but there's also the excitement and satisfaction of knowing you've done something not a whole lot of other people in the world have ever done."

"Awesome!" Connor exclaimed. "You know what you need to do? Highlight that paragraph. And the caption under the picture. Then have Mr. Jansson put it on the bulletin board outside the office. Every kid in school will read it."

"Connor is totally right. Nobody'll ever call you lame again," Ben agreed.

"I like it," Alex grinned.

The waitress arrived with their food. As she set the plates down, she looked at Alex's shirt. "Are you the boy in the paper?" she smiled, gesturing toward the photo.

Alex nodded, and the waitress congratulated him. He felt self-conscious, but decided he needed to get used to it.

Everyone turned to their breakfasts. Ben said, "I hope I can do the whole 200 miles next year."

"Maybe, but you'll have to work as hard as Alex did," their father replied.

"If Ben rides stoker, maybe I could ride my single bike all the way," Alex said.

"Maybe," his father replied, with a thoughtful look.

They ate in silence for a moment, and then Ben spoke up. "What *are* we going to do to top this?" he asked, addressing no one in particular.

Alex savored his pancakes, sausage, and hot chocolate. He decided that no matter what they might try next, he and his dad and his little brother would be able to do it.

ACKNOWLEDGMENTS

Patricia Dupuis professionally edited the manuscript. I am also grateful to Kevin Aldrich, Cyprian Blunt, Mary Grace Blunt, Ellen Gable Hrkach, James Hrkach, Julie Meierdirks, and Lisa Wanta, who reviewed earlier versions of the manuscript. All provided invaluable editorial advice. I am particularly indebted to Mrs. Meierdirks' sixth grade class, for their suggestions about challenges Alex could face from his peers.

Kyle Netterfield, a Seattle-area little league coach, provided very helpful background information about Northshore youth baseball. Any of the novel's departures from actual NSLL practices are purely for dramatic purposes.

Dr. John Cosgrove directed me to innumerable resources regarding the story's medical issues.

Raphael Kronenberg, a professional bicycle fitter, consulted about the challenges of properly setting up a bike for a rider such as Alex.

Mark Johnson's website, Precision Tandems, is an outstanding resource for ideas and products to fit children of all sizes and abilities more comfortably on a tandem.

I am particularly grateful to my parents, Charles and Nancy Blunt, for supporting my own early interest in cycling, including allowing me to ride my first STP (unaccompanied) at the age of fifteen. I am also indebted to my kids, whose love of riding stoker on a tandem helped revive that interest.

ABOUT THE AUTHOR

Christopher Blunt's writing has appeared in *Ultracycling, Columbia, Our Sunday Visitor, MercatorNet,* and a host of professional publications. His debut novel, *Passport,* won a bronze medal for best religious fiction in the Independent Publisher Book Awards. He currently manages his own public opinion research consulting practice, Overbrook Research.

An accomplished cyclist, he has completed over thirty double century rides, multiple triple centuries, 12-hour, and 24-hour races. He is a four-time winner of the California Triple Crown, and a sixteen-time finisher of the Seattle to Portland Bicycle Classic.

A native of the Seattle area, he and his family currently reside in rural mid-Michigan. He welcomes reader comments, which should be emailed to CCBlunt@aol.com.